"Danie Ware's first novel is not so much assured as explosive. This is science fiction with the safety catch off. I hope she never runs out of ammunition." ADAM NEVILL, AUTHOR OF *APARTMENT 16*

"*Ecko Rising* explodes onto the page with the manic energy of Richard Morgan's cyberpunk novels before taking a surprise turn into Thomas Convenant territory. It is strange, surprising, haunting and exceedingly well written. Not to be missed." LAVIE TIDHAR, AUTHOR OF *OSAMA* AND *THE BOOKMAN HISTORIES*

"This may be Ware's first novel, but she's been intimately tied to the science fiction, fantasy and horror genres for years through her publicity work. That exposure and experience come to the fore with *Ecko Rising*, a novel that blends fantasy and science fiction together into an epic story about the titular anti-hero who aims to do nothing less than save the entire world from extinction." KIRKUS REVIEWS

"A curious genre-bender that thrusts its anti-hero from a dystopian future into a traditional, Tolkienesque fantasy world... marks Ware as one to watch." INDEPENDENT ON SUNDAY

"Ware writes fearlessly and with great self-assurance, and Ecko is a magnificent creation." FINANCIAL TIMES

"An admirably ambitious genre-bending novel, bringing us a memorable character...and world(s) we can't wait to see more of. Ware's writing style is a joy to read... brilliant filth with heart... A genuinely impressive exercise in world-building... [A] very memorable piece of work, long may Ecko rise." STARBURST MAGAZINE

"*Ecko Rising* is grimy and crazy, and so action-centric, it should have an explosion on every page. It's crammed with sci-fi cuss words, real cuss words, monsters, and violence. In other words: *Buy me.*" REVOLUTION SF

"Ware has successfully blended elements of science fiction and epic fantasy to create a unique story in a landscape that has just enough of a modern, dark edge to elevate it from a traditional fantasy journey to something new and compelling. Ware writes with an eloquence that is not often encountered in genre fiction... with a language almost of his own, and a witty inner monologue to match, Ecko is a captivating hero... A successfully fresh 'something for everyone' approach to genre fiction."
THE BRITISH FANTASY SOCIETY

"*Ecko Rising* is an incredible read, with completely unexpected twists and turns... The worlds described within the book are complete and understandable, and you might want to live in at least one of them. The author's diverse knowledge of subcultures within our society is evident and well used. The cliff-hanger at the end has left this reader aching for more." GEEK SYNDICATE

"Ingenious... The story itself is engaging and totally unique, a plot that pushes the boundaries not for the sake of it but clearly to offer something different." SFBOOK

"Danie Ware effortlessly juggles a dystopian hard sci-fi environment with a fantasy world with its own very specific set of rules, and comes up with a story that keeps you gripped... This is a strong debut; I suspect Ware will be a name to watch out for in future." SCI-FI BULLETIN

"*Ecko Rising* mixes science fiction à la early years Michael Marshall with the comedic fantasy of Terry Pratchett and the sprawling authenticity of J. R. R. Tolkien's Middle-earth... staggeringly impressive in both its richness and detail... A hugely enjoyable genre mash-up that promises great things to come from first-time author Danie Ware."
ALTERNATIVE MAGAZINE ONLINE

ECKO RISING

ECKO RISING

DANIE WARE

TITAN BOOKS

Ecko Rising
Print edition ISBN: 9780857687623
E-book ISBN: 9781781162835

Published by
Titan Books
A division of Titan Publishing Group Ltd
144 Southwark Street, London SE1 0UP

First US edition: June 2013
10 9 8 7 6 5 4 3 2 1

A CIP catalogue record for this title is available from the British Library.

Printed and bound in the United States.

What did you think of this book?
We love to hear from our readers. Please email us at:
readerfeedback@titanemail.com, or write to us at the above address.

To receive advance information, news, competitions, and exclusive offers online, please sign up for the Titan newsletter on our website.

www.titanbooks.com

FOR BONES
F.T.W.

CONTENTS

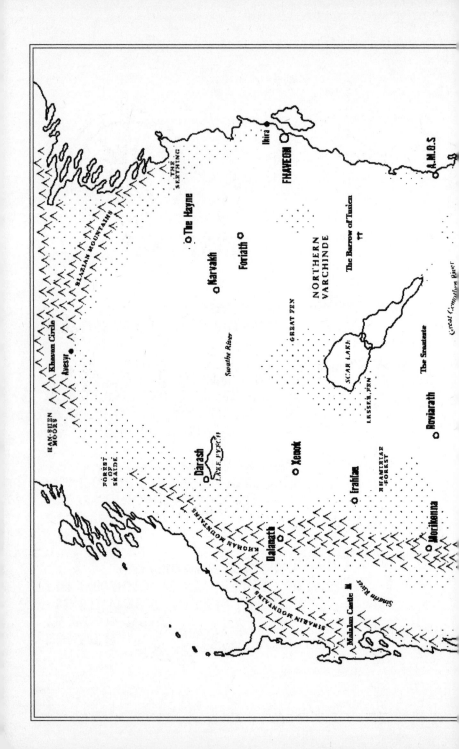

PROLOGUE LONDON

"We're bein' stalked."

It was evening. The press of people was close, huddled and submissive to the public monotone that accompanied them home.

Overhead, the streetlights were halogen brilliant, obscuring the heavy, belly-down sky. The drizzle sparkled like shrapnel.

Fuller, tarnished aplomb in suit and overcoat, gave Lugan a nervous look. "You're sure – ?"

"Shut up an' keep moving." One of the cell commander's massive, oil-stained hands grabbed Fuller's elbow and propelled him swiftly through the crowd. A gang of kids, laughing at their own defiance, barged into them and were gone.

Reflexively, Lugan checked his pockets.

Get Collator. Subvocalised, his voice was transmitted from the back of his throat directly into Fuller's ear. *I want CCTV access – like, now. Drones if we can get 'em.*

Fuller gave a brief nod.

Tense now, Lugan checked the street. The light pools were bright but the shadows were hard edged and darker than oil. Everywhere he looked, unseen eyes looked back, teeth were bared in unseen grins. He shivered, bristled.

What're you looking for? Fuller asked him.

Dunno. Trouble.

Half a head taller than the blindly ambling workers, Lugan picked out the police-blue glow of the hoverdrone, watched it swing about and head back towards them.

Fuller was rebroadcasting Collator's info-stream. *Data input commencing 18:42:06... 07... Camera locations accessed. Drone ID: 23-987b accessed. Download commencing one minute and forty-five seconds...*

Lugan reached for a dog-end. "This stinks." Watching the drone, he headed for the shelter of the buildingside. As he moved, the crowd stirred and parted.

A shred of silent darkness flickered in his wake.

What was...? Further back, Fuller's voice came over the aural link. *Lugan!*

"What?" Without thinking, Lugan spun, back to the wall and crouching, hand going for the ten-mil that wasn't there. Breathing tightly, he kicked in his ocular heatseeker, but the ambivalent temperature of the blankly trudging people defeated him.

There was nothing there.

Telling himself he'd imagined it, pillock, he watched a moment longer.

There was nothing there.

A burst of distant shouting made him start; the hoverdrone swung about to investigate.

Then a voice in his ear said softly...

"Boom."

"Shit...!" Lugan spun sideways and back, fists balling. "Fuller!" Two paces ahead, Fuller dropped into cover behind a heap of dustbin bags shining with rainwater.

You get it? Lugan snapped.

No, I...

Did the drone get it?

A moment later, he heard Fuller's voice reply, *No screen. It's gone.*

What? Lugan slammed his back to the brickwork, searched his pockets. *My smartcard, my headset, my fucking lighter.* One black boot kicked the wall, rubbish scattered. *What are we – fucking amateur night? We catch this joker, I'm going to wring its neck. Update Collator!*

Spitting out the dog-end, Lugan sought the drone. Above his head, the light show had started: bright lasers played on the clouds as if to cut them open. In the wealth of the City and the West End, London still pulsed with life. Here, the shadows were –

Eyes. Some two metres above his head – the shadows were eyes.

A frisson shivered up his spine – whatever this character was, it was playing with them.

Fuller's rebroadcast was telling him about the building. *Human Resource Container standard design 12a, security level eight... Purchased by Mortimer, Hiner and Thompson Finance in 2018... Population: fifty single units...*

Lugan watched the eyes. They were red. Just as he figured they were LEDs, they winked at him and were gone.

The frisson became a shudder; he found he was holding his breath.

Under the public monotone, a breath of laughter reached him – dark, malicious, cynical. It stroked his ear like a cold hand.

They were being *watched*.

The sound had come from the heart of the homeward-walking workers, as if the drugged-up drudges themselves mocked his efforts.

Swallowing hard, Lugan forced himself to move normally. What the hell was this character? Security level eight – and it just... hung on the wall like a gargoyle? Laughed as they tried to track it? Picked their pockets without getting –

Oh wait a fucking minute...

Snarling through his beard, Lugan went back through the pockets of his old leather. He chucked a handful of washers onto the pavement and held up the piece of paper that remained.

"All right, smart-arse," he said, "you got my attention. Now what the *hell* are you?"

The laugh came again. "I'm caught. Red-handed." The voice was a rasp, savage, gleeful and absolutely fearless; a faint hint of an American accent. It came from behind them, but this time neither Fuller nor Lugan turned. "You gonna try an' shoot me, biker-boy, or are you gonna turn me in?"

"I'll turn you into fuckin' chop suey, mate, if you don't give me back my stuff."

Still scanning the wall, Fuller said, *Rebroadcast kicked, Collator's with us. Report's uploading.*

"So, the mighty Lugan loses his kit like a rookie. Y'know what they say, the bigger they are –"

"The harder they kick your arse. Whatever you are, you better get out where I can see you –"

"Yeah? Why don'tcha make me?"

Incredible. The rebroadcast was dumping info so fast that Lugan could barely keep pace. *The voice was male, adult, lacking a formal education, Chicago-born but living in London for ten years or more; there was a cruel, childlike quality that could indicate psychological damage and/or cybernetic overload...*

The eyes were back, closer. "Y'ever heard of the Bogeyman?"

Through Fuller's aural link, Collator's smoothly androgynous tone said, *ID confirmed, 98.83% probability...*

"Yeah," Lugan said. "He's the bloke you don't boogie with."

The laughter became a cackle. "That 'One Percent' tattoo your sense of humour?"

"I know the 'Bogeyman'," Fuller said. Tall and wiry, Fuller's quiet presence and calm voice cut the laughter with a sharp, informative edge. "He worked towards a better world, a liberated world – a world free from pharmaceutical control.

He was a crusader, fought for the people. The graphic novel was banned –"

Comic books? Lugan raised an eyebrow. *You're pullin' my chain...*

Fuller ignored him. "It was you last night, wasn't it? You took out Pilgrim's new facility, the Serena Installation."

The rasp twisted into a humourless cackle. "I'll take any op to fuck with Pilgrim – 'til some grunt gets lucky an' raises the alarm." The eyes blinked once and were gone. "Didja see the bang?"

Lugan swore. "That bleedin' buildin' did a double backflip an' swallow dive. You ain't tellin' me that was you?"

The shrug was audible. "Hey, it's traditional to blow up a major London landmark on Fawkes' Night. Besides, I jus' laid the charges. Ol' Bobby Pilgrim set it off."

Lugan stared at Fuller. "Our stalker trashed..." He glanced at the drones, but they paid him no attention. The crowd was thinning, now. "Our stalker jus' trashed Robert Pilgrim?"

Fuller snorted. "World'll be a better place if you ask me." He nodded at the last of the walking workers. "Look at these poor bastards –"

"Not the fuckin' point!" Over their aural link, Lugan went on, *This nutter must be wanted by every security agency in – !*

A cloaked figure dropped into the light.

He was small, slight, as strong as coiled steel wire. His skin and cloak were dappled a shadowy, shifting blue-grey. As he put back his cowl with one thin hand, Fuller gasped, Lugan swore softly. Neither man was a stranger to cybernetic enhancement, but they had never seen anything like this.

This couldn't be human.

The little man's face was savage, sharp cheeked and gleeful. His skin was the same dark mottle – it seemed to be actually part of his flesh. Across it slashed a nightmare sneer – a black-lipped, black-toothed grin. But his *eyes*...

Black, blacker than pits, featureless and soulless, too large for his thin face. They were inhuman, alien – reminiscent of too many horror movies. Somewhere in their depths, there was the cold, blue glitter of an optical scan.

Even as the men stared, the skin-mottle was changing. Seeping, spreading. In a moment, it had flowed to the greys and reds of the surrounding buildings, the blue flicker of the distant laser show. Camouflaged perfectly against his background, the little man was almost impossible to see. Belatedly, Lugan tried his ocular heatseeker, tried to see weaponry and cybernetics; somehow he was not surprised when the man had no visible body temperature.

"You're the 'Ecko'," Fuller said.

"The 'G' is silent." The sprite grin was pure malice. He was a flicker, a fragment of nightmare; his empty black eyes as cold as blades. There was no mercy in his smile. "Last night... was a little 'illustration' –"

"You lookin' for attention?" Lugan said. "Or you lookin' for bidders?"

The face turned from Lugan to Fuller and back.

"Maybe I'm lookin' for asylum."

"No shit," Lugan said.

"You're killin' me. Look, you're kinda infamous round here – most bad guys know to stay outta your face. Take me in – turn me in. I'm the fuckin' phantom fireworker and y'got me cold – whatcha gonna do?"

Fuller? Profile? Lugan said.

Tamarlaine Benjamin Gabriel, aka the 'Ecko'. Age: 32. Address: no fixed abode; suspected tunnel rat, Southwark area. No smartcard on record, no PIN. Criminal record: street-kid stuff; nothing after age 17. Collator says that, as of 19:00 hours, no one is yet wanted in connection with last night's explosion.

But Bob fuckin' Pilgrim, for gawdsakes! Lugan said.

Tell the Boss we've got Pilgrim's nemesis – it's a major blow to them, Lugan, big kudos.

Big risk, y'mean. If 'e gets found...

He's just the 'Echo'. He's got no criminal record to speak of – he doesn't get found!

Unless he wants to be?

Self-evident. Fuller glanced at his commander and shrugged.

Lugan pulled out a dog-end. He stuck it between his lips, paused for a moment and spat it out again. From somewhere across the river, the laser show danced on the glowering clouds.

It began to rain, drops of fat, filthy water.

"All right, all right, I'll speak to the Boss," Lugan said. "You, us, here, same time, tomorrow. And gimme back my lighter!"

Ecko tilted his head, his attention flicked from one man to the other and his black grin remained. "Do your research, guys. Then here. Tomorrow."

"Aren't you going to tell us to come alone? No tricks?" Fuller asked.

With a snort, Ecko slid his hood back into place. "You try whatever you like." He took a pace away, two; the chrome glint of Lugan's lighter held in his hand. "But I'm keepin' your kit – you get it back if you play nice." He flicked a flame, like a farewell.

As Lugan blinked to clear the rain from his eyes, the little man was gone – faded into the London night until only the fire remained.

Just an echo.

PART 1: IMPACT

1: TO BE A PILGRIM

THE BIKE LODGE AND THE BOSS'S OFFICE, LONDON

Through the single grubby window in the Bike Lodge office, the sky was a thunderous black. It was still early spring, but the London weather was close and stifling, and it was making Lugan tetchy.

On the old couch, Fuller had long since fallen asleep. Still in his habitual battered suit, he was curled round his laptop as if he couldn't bear to let it go. He was snoring, gently and sweetly, as if he didn't have a care in the world.

Both men had been working through the night, systematically digging for obscure information, but for all their spade work, they were no closer to realising a decision. Ecko had been with them for three months, his probation was nearing its end, and Lugan still didn't know which way he was going to jump. The little bugger was invaluable, had skills that surpassed the Boss herself, but he was about as reliable as a... Oh for fuck's sake, Lugan was getting too tired for creativity.

Wincing, the cell commander took his glasses off, laid them on the desktop and then tipped his chair back to stretch the kinks from his shoulders. Tendons crunched, and he swore.

Bloody Pilgrim, Lugan thought, *all the tricks they've pulled in the last ten years, all the bullshit they've promised, the new fuckin' world they've built, they could at least have done something about my vision, about the old road wounds that still gimme gyp in the cold.*

Nah. Fuckers. We know what their priorities've been...

Searching his pockets for a dog-end, he slammed the chair back onto all fours and Fuller started awake, blinking.

"What? What? What's the time?"

"Half one?" Lugan patted another pocket. "An' I ain't no closer, mate. If I'm gonna make the Boss listen, I need more than old-school biker loyalty and all that bollocks – I need *facts*." He patted the pocket again. Stood up. Patted the pockets in his jeans. Turned to his battered leather, hung on the back of the chair, and patted the pockets in that, too.

He'd been working sixteen hours, and he was *not* in the mood for this.

"On the other 'and, I could just let her shoot the little bastard." Sending the old desk scraping backwards with a hefty shove, Lugan slammed the office door open and bellowed, "Ecko? Ecko! Bring me back my fucking lighter or I'll wring your fucking *neck*!"

Fuller groaned and sat up.

Outside the office door, the big, open floor of the Bike Lodge was silent, the roller door shut and locked down. Metal shelving and skeletal frames made odd shadows on the oil stains, the current chop-job watched them from its one lidless and lightless eye.

Half expecting Ecko's characteristic cackle to come from somewhere in the ceiling, or from down among the bikes themselves, Lugan was disconcerted to find the shop as quiet as the proverbial grave. Over his shoulder, he said, "Get the kettle on, willya?"

And the now-familiar voice in his ear said, "Boo."

In no mood for it, Lugan spun, scowling.

"*Will* you fucking stop doing that?"

Ecko was standing directly behind him, his skin and cloak reacting to the overspill of light from the office. Lugan had no idea how he'd got there or where he'd come from, and his sense of humour was struggling. He'd been all night trying to find a concrete reason to keep this little bugger, to add him to the Boss's tightly run cell network, and right now, Ecko's pranks were a temptation to just tie a bike frame to his ankles and chuck him in the Thames.

Lugan said, "Gimme my lighter back."

"Don't have it."

"It's too early for this. Give me my lighter."

"Don't have it. Not this time. This time you lost it all on your ownsome."

The commander drew a breath. "I'm warnin' you –"

"I *said*, I don't have it. An' if you keep bein' an asshole, you don't get dinner."

Motion pulled Lugan's attention downwards. In Ecko's hand, swathed in his stealth-cloak, was a crumpled brown bag. From it came the faint, curling scent of takeaway.

The smell made Lugan's belly grumble, loud in the stillness. Shaking his head, he said, "I don't s'pose you paid for that?"

"Don't be stupid." Ecko grinned like a fiend.

Unable to help himself, the cell commander chuckled, half in relief, half in exasperation. Ecko might be off-the-fucking-wall annoying, but what they'd do without him... Lugan didn't want to finish the thought. Instead, he cuffed Ecko's shoulder, made the smaller man wince. Ecko's ability to get in and out of local businesses was frankly astonishing – hoverdrones, cameras, recorders – the little man might as well have been invisible.

One way and another, it was sodding handy.

And not just for free food.

"Well, what the fuck have I done with it, then?" His dog-end still between his lips, Lugan made one last search of his pockets and then shrugged and reached for the arc welder, behind him on a shelf.

He shielded the cigarette with his opposite hand and then swore round the thing as the arc nearly torched his beard.

Ecko cackled. "Addict."

"Freak."

The welder went back on the shelf with a bang.

"Serious for a minute?" Fuller's voice came from the office. "My newsfeed's just gone batshit. I think –"

From outside, there came the first wail of sirens.

Half two.

The lights in the Bike Lodge were off. Outside, it was quiet; the last yowl of siren was finally fading. Inside, the curry was roiling uncomfortably in Lugan's belly, and he still hadn't found his lighter.

Agitated, the cell commander was pacing.

In this new age of Pilgrim's social tranquillity, sirens were rare and disturbing things. Sirens for almost an hour could well mean the fucking apocalypse.

Bollocks.

Lugan spun on his boot heel and paced the other way. The various oil-stained papers tacked to the wall – ID numbers, serial markings, notes, addresses – fluttered in his wake as though trying to escape.

On the couch, Fuller had discarded the older laptop and was glued to his tiny, secure flatscreen, trying to track and identify the night's events. Ecko was sat next to him like some sort of urban grotesque, hunched up with his knees almost into his chest.

Lugan had never seen him look this pensive.

And it made him angry.

"What the fuck did you do? I thought you went out after dinner! Tell me you got out clean and they didn't follow your arse back 'ere?" The commander paced back, jabbing a stained and callused finger at Ecko as he did so. A dog-end was still clamped in the corner of his mouth and reflexively his hands kept going for the lighter that wasn't there. "I got your future to fight for, mate, an' you better not be takin' the piss."

Ecko snarled back at him, "I'm doin' your job, for chrissakes. I went out after leads, on Pilgrim, on how to take them down. Better than sittin' on my ass in here."

"What I don't want is the Met on my doorstep…"

"Please." Ecko snorted. "They couldn't find me with Sherlock Holmes and a bloodhound."

That much was probably true. One advantage to the little fucker being so reckless – Ecko wasn't afraid of much, and that made him honest.

Lugan spun again. "I 'ope you're right, you little bastard, because if they do, I'll slit your throat myself."

"You wouldn't dare."

"Watch me."

"Chrissakes, I can't watch my own throat."

Fuller chuckled at their double act, smothered it.

For a moment, Lugan stopped pacing and glared at the pair of them as if he was the only sane man left in the city. Then he flung himself back in his chair, swore venomously, and picked up the now-cold mug of tea.

"What says Collator?" he said to Fuller. "You trackin'?"

"Still on radio silence," Fuller answered. "For the moment, I got nothing."

"Fuck."

"Easy, Luge," Fuller said. "If the Met knew anything, they'd be here with the tear gas by now. The chaos is calming down." He glanced round at Ecko, the light from the little screen making his eyes glitter. "Luck is on your side, it seems. Again."

"Luck, for chrissakes." Ecko grinned back, like the Cheshire Cat's evil twin. "Skill."

"I swear, one of these days you'll give me a fucking 'eart attack." Lugan eyed the tea and thought better of it. He smacked the mug back on the table. "Now. Quit dodging the subject. If I'm gonna defend your arse to the Boss, I need to know what you did. And 'ow much of a mess you made."

Ecko shrugged. "I went after the pharmacist, Grey."

As Lugan opened his mouth to answer back, Ecko cut him off.

"C'mon, Lugan, we've done fuck all for months. D'you wanna do this, or what?"

"Grey's the cook, not –"

"In fact," Fuller commented, "Grey's another major shareholder. When Pilgrim bought out the NHS in the early tweens, he was the orchestrator. It's *his* utopia we're living in."

Ecko said, "See? Major bad guy. I found his Secret Lair." He grinned. "So now we can go bust his ass."

Lugan said nothing. On the desk in front of him was an old pub ashtray, half full of roll-up remnants. Carefully, he began to shred them and collect the remaining tobacco. It was a habit he'd picked up a decade or more before, while waiting on His Majesty, and he'd never quite given it up.

Ecko was bristling with anticipation, his obsidian-black eyes flickering with a faint, red light. His impatience was infectious, and Lugan could almost hear his thoughts, *C'mon, let's go let's go let's go let's...*

"We can get Grey? You serious?" As the realisation sank home, Lugan was beginning to think that, aggravating or not, Ecko needed to stay on his team.

Like, big time.

Ecko's grin spread. "You wanted leads. I know where's he's at. An' we can fuckin' *get* him." He was almost bouncing on the seat. "Well, *I* can."

Fuller said, "It's tempting, Luge. Pilgrim's utopian society is largely attributable to Doctor Grey. You know the story –

every GP, every researcher, every psychologist, was given a choice by their new employer: you prescribe the drug we give you, or you lose your job. Suddenly every dissenter, student, protester, everyone who's unemployed – they all have ADHD, or depression, or anxiety, or maybe they just can't sleep... A decade later, we've got almost complete servitude. No unrest, no remonstration, no riots, no freedom. The internet's full of happy cats, and everyone loves their job. Whatever it is. It was bloody *genius*."

Lugan glanced up – Fuller rarely swore, and his flash of rancour was unusual.

The commander shot back, "We're not all fucking brain-dead. Pilgrim 'asn't won yet."

"The pockets of resistance get smaller with every year," Fuller said. "You're an anachronism, Luge, a relic, and they know it. They'll get bored with you one of these days, and then they'll send the boys round. I fear our time is borrowed."

So we'd better make the most of it.

He didn't actually say it, but Lugan heard him anyway.

Ecko said, his rasp soft and sinister, "So let's gettem, for chrissakes, before they get us, huh?"

Lugan rolled the shreds of collected tobacco into a new cigarette that was almost pure tar.

"All right," he said, shoving himself to his feet. "I trust my team. You included. I dunno what kind of mess you just made, mate, but if you've just given us Grey, I'll back any fucking play you make."

"That was well timed," Fuller said suddenly. "Collator's back online – and we're wanted in the office."

"Bollocks," Lugan said cheerfully. He leaned back in the big black chair and thumped his size fourteens on the conference table. He'd picked up a disposable lighter, and a tail of greasy smoke curled from the dog-end that was glued to his lip.

Beside him, Fuller fidgeted like a child expecting a scolding.

Around them, the Boss's office was silent, soulless and dark. It was steel and glass and cold, VIP perfection; long black windows were silvered with skitters of rain. Outside, the harsh, halogen lights of the city were smeared to a watery blur.

The room's only illumination came from the big flatscreen at the far end of the table – and from its image, reflected in the tabletop's gleam.

Lugan took another drag from the dog-end.

The screen showed a familiar figure, a phantom of gleeful darkness, his skin and garments shifting with shadows, his movements framed in blood and smoke. He was terrifying, more extreme than Lugan at his worst, and utterly unhampered by conscience. He was swift as a thought and just as fucking careless. He carried no firearm, no blade, but the goons fell like a street kid's tin cans.

Ecko.

His skill and savagery were horrifying.

Lugan blew brown smoke, and kept watching.

From impossible stealth positions, Ecko taunted his targets – they coiled in fear long before they coiled in pain. While they were still looking for him, his fists and feet broke bones, and when they fell, he burned them and they died screaming.

Lugan took another lungful of smoke.

Jesus 'Arry Christ on a fuckin' scramble bike...

Then, with a silent snap, the screen went black.

And the Boss's soft, Scandinavian voice said, "Well, gentlemen? Would either of you care to explain?"

Lugan and Fuller exchanged a glance, their faces now almost in darkness. Tobacco wreathed in the air. Neither of them spoke.

Instead, Lugan blew out an irritated tail of tar that made the smoke curls dance. He'd no fucking clue how the Boss had got Ecko on camera, but the devastation only made his resolve stronger – he was going to keep Ecko on his crew.

And then, they were going after Grey.

The voice said, "I'm waiting."

Biting back his initial, blistering response, Lugan answered, "'E did the job, didn't 'e?"

The light on the screen came up, brightening the room and returning the shine to the table. It showed a woman, blonde and in profile. She was beautiful, flawless and pale skinned, and apparently naked right down to the part of her shoulder that Lugan could see. She didn't turn to face them – her attention was on something else, a screen within the screen, a light source that decorated her porcelain flesh in a shifting, fractal pattern of illumination.

"He left a *crater.*" Even speaking, the Boss didn't turn. She gestured with one pale hand.

Lugan said, "They didn't track 'im –"

"That really isn't the point." The lights teased her skin, danced over the tabletop. "If we're to tackle Pilgrim effectively, then strategy is crucial, discipline is crucial, orders are crucial. I'm not taking chances on a loose cannon."

Lugan's dog-end was coming unstuck. Wetting a tarred and callused fingertip, he made an industrious effort to dampen and reroll it. Choosing his words, he said, "Just because 'e ain't good with orders doesn't mean 'e can't do the job. 'E's got 'is own ways of doing stuff." He examined the dog-end, frowning. "An' they work."

The Boss ignored him. "I've no tolerance for chaos. I've dedicated my life and this organisation to taking Pilgrim down – and I *don't* like surprises."

Down by her bare shoulder, the Pilgrim logo folded onto the corner of the screen – the image of the strongly travailing worker, bent under his load. Beside it unrolled the strapline that now bound the heart and mind of every man, woman and child, the words that framed their lives, the flag that had become their only compass and motivation, and the banner against which the Boss's organisation had pitched itself.

Valiant Be.

"Valium Be", more like. Lugan relit the repaired dog-end and coughed tar. *There's a Fifth 'Orseman an' his name's "Apathy".* He flicked the little flame on the lighter, glanced at Fuller.

But Fuller shrugged, and pointedly turned his attention back to the screen.

The Boss said, cool and clear, "Quite apart from the collateral damage, Ecko killed fourteen people, one of them an approved Pilgrim medic –"

"An armed-to-the-teeth combat medic with an 'ypo fetish –"

"A *trail* of bodies, and a media *circus*. I don't appreciate having to tidy that sort of a mess." Her profile was perfect, pure and cold. "Unless you two have anything to add, this hearing has one conclusion."

Fuck.

Thinking hard now, Lugan chewed stray tobacco.

Bloody Ecko. The little man was a genius – an erratic, irritating, indispensable fucking genius. He'd got a smart mouth and a ready wit, and a thing for practical jokes – in the three months he'd been with Lugan, he'd grown on the cell team like a particularly virulent form of mould.

Shit!

He wasn't going to let her do this.

Aloud, Lugan said, "Without Ecko, we'd have fuck all. No info, no lead on Grey, a boot up our collective arse-crack."

The Boss's flawless face gave the faintest hint of a smile.

"Without Collator's clean-up," she said, "your collective arse-crack would be sitting on a cold metal bench. And that would be the fun just beginning. Ecko has a peculiar charisma, certainly, and I know you're fond of him –"

"'E did the *job*." Lugan gripped the dog-end between yellow-stained thumb and forefinger and blew a long, dirty plume of smoke. "You know I need 'im – 'e's deniable, 'e can do the shit I can't. My 'ands stay clean."

"Unless they're covered in bits of *medic.*" The lights on her flawless face changed, shadows flickered and cycled.

Her skin was shifting with mottle like Ecko's. With a grin like a rusty knife, Lugan flicked the lighter's wheel with a tiny, metallic *chink. Nothin' like takin' a trip down Irony Lane...*

"I need 'im." Lugan blew the flame out and dropped the lighter back in the pocket of his old denim cut-down. "I want 'im on my team."

"Do your team want him?"

"'E needs family," Lugan said. "We –"

"He *has* family." The Boss cut him short. "His mother still lives in London. The charity she founded isn't large, but it operates. His siblings have lives and families that are easily traceable. He had a solid and loving –"

"*Four* bleedin' half-sisters, an' a storybook wicked stepdad. It's enough to make anyone retreat into a world of comic-book 'eroics."

"Yes, but I question his ability to come *out.*" Her voice hinted at a steel edge. "He's critically damaged, socially certifiable and an unnecessary risk to my security and yours. You're a radical."

"I'm a businessman –"

"But Ecko's *insane.*"

"Yeah." Lugan leaned forward, he wasn't backing down from this. "'E's also a fuckin' *gem.*" He coughed smoke, inhaled harder. "'E got a *lead* on Doc Grey – got a location! We can get that bastard, kick Pilgrim where it *'urts.*" In an "up yours" gesture, he tapped his ash into the glass carafe on the table.

There was a tiny, defiant hiss.

"Lugan." Almost regretfully, the Boss said, "I know why you've taken to Ecko so strongly. He's the part of you that you miss, the part that Pilgrim's new society has taken from you. You've learned to conform – at least as far as you have to.

Ecko..." She trailed off into a pale, perfect shrug. "...Hasn't."

Conform, my arse. Goaded now, Lugan marshalled his assault.

"Yeah, maybe I was like that once – no fuckin' brakes." His tone revved like a gunned engine. "It's why I understand 'im – I get it. But think – just *think* what 'e could bring down!"

"Us?" Her tinkling laugh was ice-cold; she almost turned to face them. Lugan held himself still, lungs full of oily smoke. Her chin was lifted, the lights tinged with colours, tantalising hints of shapes that teased her perfect, ageless skin.

She said, "Your faith in him is touching." Light and laughter pulsed again. "But I think his presence affects your decisions. If he won't follow orders, then I can't use him. And neither can you."

Lugan glowered. "We got the location of Grey's lair. You know Ecko's gotta do this..."

The Boss inhaled, mustering patience. "Don't be ridiculous. If the data you've given me clears, then this may be one of the single most important penetrations we've ever attempted. Ecko's Tech was one of the doctors that went renegade when Pilgrim took over. What she did to him has damaged his mental stability beyond repair. We can't let him handle something like this – we send in a full team."

"Bollocks," Lugan said again. He dumped the dog-end in the carafe and exhaled a double lungful of oily smoke. "That'll just be a mess. 'E can do this. In an' out. Quick an' clean. Recon first – full stealth. No muss, no fuss."

The lights on the Boss's face were moving more swiftly. "Your loyalty is impressive, but –"

"But I've never quit on a mate an' I never will. That's why I've got this." From beneath his t-shirt, he produced the half-black, half-white symbol that marked him as a ranking member of the Boss's organisation. "It says you trust me to run my ops, my way."

"Of course I trust you. But…" She gave a tight sigh, tucked her hair behind her ear in a gesture that was oddly girlish. "This job is imperative."

"An' 'e can do it – better than any fucker else!" Lugan pressed the point. "Three months! He's done his prospectin' –"

"The days of your bike gangs are gone, Lugan." She tapped her lips with her finger, long nail gleaming.

The days of your bike gangs…

Suddenly robbed of words, Lugan eyed the faded-blue ink that decorated his muscled forearms – a reminder of the way things had been before Pilgrim's Fifth Horseman had doled out the pharmaceuticals and smothered the world in happy grey smog.

The days of your bike gangs…

The ink reminded him who he was – who he'd been. It was youth and fire, experience and wisdom. Not only was he Alexander David Eastermann, retired biker, he was still the Lugan he'd once been.

When the world'd had the time for such things.

Tapping her index finger on her chin, she said, "I will admit that Ecko's fear of authority means his hatred of Pilgrim is sincere. And he remains remarkably untouched by the changes of today's society." Her eyes flickered as though she was watching something. "Eliza's initial psych report details the massive damage inflicted by his Tech – he calls her 'Mom'?" Her eyebrow raised slightly. "She also lists the physical and neurological adjustments he bears – and some very interesting psych reactions to his being effectively more than human." A smile touched her lips. "When so many people are now less."

Lugan said absolutely nothing. Unless he missed his guess, she was right on the fucking verge…

"All right – the details on Grey's location are cleared. Collator gives me 84.61 per cent success if Ecko runs solo reconnaissance and retrieval."

Lugan said, "An' if he don't?"

Her smile was cool. "Significantly less."

The lights shifted more swiftly, Collator was irrefutable. Lugan planted a boot against the table edge, pushed the chair back and stood up.

"If 'e succeeds –"

"Lugan, I've spent over a decade working against the world that Pilgrim has wrought here, fighting for the return of our social freedom, warts and all. If he succeeds, Eliza will run her full – and proper – psychological diagnosis. She'll design her Virtual Rorschach just for him, and he'll get the treatment he actually needs. If he fails –"

"If 'e fucks this up, I'll slit 'is throat myself. I already said so."

In the silence that followed, he became aware that the Boss had turned her face, ever so slightly. She was looking over her bare shoulder at him in a manner that was almost... flirtatious.

"Lugan, you have so much alpha you leave a bollock dent in your fuel tank – but even you may find that difficult."

"He's my respo –"

"Collator will process and download the full mission briefing to Fuller at 21:46." She turned back. "Ecko will move at 23:33. If he fails this mission, he's mine. Go back to the Bike Lodge, Mister Eastermann, and explain to him, in words of one syllable or less, what I have just told you – and what will happen if he messes up again. You say you can manage him? Go and prove it."

The screen went blank.

In the sudden darkness, Fuller's voice came over their personal link. *Do you trust this, Luge? She could as easily set him up...*

Lugan didn't answer. He wasn't sure he could.

2: RECONNAISSANCE

PILGRIM PHARMACEUTICALS RESEARCH FACILITY, LONDON

Ecko crouched against the back wall of the roof garden.

The cold March wind shrieked the length of the Thames, driving the grey water to white froth. The weather had grounded drones and aircars; on Blackfriars Bridge rain slashed viciously sideways into bright glass. Up here, acrylic greenery was driven to madness by the howling weather, it thrashed round where he hid as if it were trying to give him away.

He'd been cornered like a fucking rat – stuck here, with no way out of the shit Lugan'd landed him in.

He'd like to see Collator's percentage on *this*.

Ecko's recon was fucked and now he was trapped, eight storeys above the sidewalk, with no firearm, no aural link and no radio. The wall of the building below him was sheer glass, running with rain – too tough to break and too smooth for his vacuum suckers to hold. His usual Spidey tactics useless, the only way out was past the guard-'bot that blocked the stairwell door.

Yeah, like that's gonna happen any time soon...

Through the rain, he could barely see it. Like his suckers, his oculars were trashed by the weather – the 'bot was a dark-grey blur against a bright-grey background. It'd set up camp like it was waiting for the opening of a BiFrost gig. Watching, Ecko hunched against the wall and wondered if Lugan would send the cavalry in time.

Salva, goon commander, knew he was up here. She was coming.

And once she found him, he was fucking toast.

"I know you can do this," Lugan'd told him quietly after the initial briefing. "But listen up. This run is just recon – you get in, you get out. No mess. Fuller uploads the report at 06:48. *Don't* fuck this up."

Ecko'd barely listened; he'd been so fucking cocky. He'd been given a chance to show what he could really do – and he'd grabbed at it like a dangled carrot.

"Like I'm as dumb as you look."

"I mean it." One of Lugan's hands had clamped hard on his shoulder, holding him back. "You don't understand 'ow important this is – an' I ain't explainin' it, not now. Behave yourself."

Yeah right, Ecko told the memory. *That's why you didn't gimme a radio you –*

One of the potted trees went over with crash, ceramic shattering. A blood-red sheet of target-scan seared through the rain.

Ecko dropped flat in the lee of the wall and belly-crawled backwards, the puddles soaking his skin. The scan passed over him.

Jeez, he thought at the 'bot, *Get it through your metallic brain willya, there's no one fucking up here…*

It was his only plan: if the 'bot scanned one hundred per cent of the potential hiding places and found nothing, it might just go for a cappuccino.

All right, already, so it was a long shot.

He'd thought this job was going to be so fucking simple!

Collator had pulled everything it could on Doctor Slater Grey; it had plotted Ecko's approach carefully. They'd seen sat-cover of the South Bank – cafés, bars, galleries, theatres. Tourists and yuppies, he'd thought, a piece of piss, placid after dark. Grey's pad was a zigzag of blue glass rising above its surroundings.

Getting in had just been too fucking easy.

He'd been a flicker of obscurity; they'd never seen him coming. His chameleon skin tone concealed him from visual security, his small physique radiated no heat, his stealth-cloak blurred his outline. His black-on-black eyes and black grin reflected no light. Mobile or stationary, he made no noise unless he chose to, he left no scent –

That fucking 'bot was moving.

Flicking his vision over to starlites, Ecko struggled to make it out. It showed up like a blotch of grey-green, one arm rising to point across the landing pad. Through the screaming weather, he made out a faint whirring noise.

Like a gyrocopter. Or an arm-mounted –

Shit...!

Unable to do anything else, he hugged the soaking gravel and prayed to the Bogeyman for luck.

The noise was phenomenal. Muzzle flashes dazzled his adjusted vision; rapid explosions chewed chunks out of the ferrocrete wall, dust and debris covered him. Already battered by the gale, the trees were shredded, pots exploding into splinters. Flying shards slashed at his face.

It stopped.

Breathless in sudden quiet, Ecko realised he was okay.

His first thought – *Missed me, sucker!* – was followed by a furtive scan of the sky. Was Grey two cogs short of a full fucking gearbox or *what*? Belly-flat on the freezing rooftop, he wondered who the cops would shoot first.

And if he'd get the chance to explain how the fuck he'd gotten himself up here...

* * *

Initial recon found Grey's lair just as the briefing had described – soft carpeting to cushion footfalls, framed prints to inspire loyalty, a join-the-dots of pretty, neon pinpoints to light the corridors and conceal the security.

Shadow within shadow, Ecko waited, counting the time readout in his field of vision, watching the mottles of his skin shifting like disease. His black grin went unseen, his superiority unspoken. He mentally marked the IR trips, the UV tags. Then, without a breath of sound, he slid past the cameras and headed upwards.

He was the Bogeyman, the nightmare, the fantasy. Grey could dream on in all his plush Pilgrim naïveté...

Until – *boom* – it was too late.

Goons passed him on a back stairwell; he heard them long before they came close. Their kit was good – gas-powered, close-assault weapons, nerve-contacted shades that imitated ocular scans – but they sauntered oblivious, unaware of the dark spider that crouched on their dark wall.

Ecko watched them as they passed him and then strolled, ignorant, round the angle of the stairway.

After a moment, their booted feet paused.

"Stairwell clear; time 01:14, moving onto floor three." A door opened and closed.

Then silence.

Over his head, the camera whirred softly as it changed angle. He lifted his chin and pulled a face at it.

Timing his movement carefully, he landed silently behind its arc and flitted, ghostlike, up the stairs.

Straight to Grey's nerve centre.

Yeah, he thought, *this is like takin' cellphones from street kids*. Lugan had made such a fucking fuss – and Pilgrim's security stank. He was amazed at how easily he'd reached his target; how simple it was going to be to penetrate Grey's innermost defences.

Just like this.

At the top of the stairs, the door to Grey's lab. Beside it, a small security alcove with a mirrored back wall. The briefing had said it would be occupied.

Sitting in a swivel chair: another goon – weapon, shades and earpiece.

Standing, arms crossed: a small, blonde female, Slavic cheekbones and hard eyes – Salva, goon commander.

The third was tall, skinny and long haired. There were flesh tunnels in his earlobes and knotwork tats down one side of his neck. Over a black tee and jeans he wore a lab coat that looked like he'd slept in it. Half a reefer was firmly stuck between his fingers as he pointed at one of the flatscreens.

Brilliant, radical, total fucking sell-out: Doctor Slater Grey.

Behave yourself, Lugan had said.

Got no radio, asshole, Ecko told the memory. *Howya gonna check up on me?*

It was just too tempting. Coaxed by the apparent simplicity of Grey's security, Ecko gathered his concentration and focused on the mirror.

He began to breathe.

Slowly, softly.

He breathed through the back of his throat and nose: a heavy, wet noise that was half Darth Vader and half rotting-liquid-corpse. It was a dank sound, a sound of absolute darkness.

And, like the rising miasma of something dead on a hot day, it was getting worse.

The goon was closest, he shivered and rubbed his shoulders. "What the hell was that?"

Ecko had practised this as a kid, sending his clamouring, spoiled sisters screaming for Mommy. He focused again, staring intently.

Raised the volume.

It was desolate, empty breathing, spectre cold and carrying a hollow note of laughter. The goon shoved his chair backwards, bringing his carbine up to cover the mirror.

Ecko gave him a flash of red eyes.

As dumb as you fucking like, he fired.

The mirror frosted, opaqued with cracks. Grey swore.

No fool, Salva had spun to cover the landing. She barked commands, clipped and cold. The goon just stood up and turned, wide-eyed at his own stupidity.

A moment later, the heavy boots of the patrol were pounding back up the stairs.

On the roof, the minigun suppressed again, heavy calibre rounds detonating further along the wall – it was shooting blind. Ecko snuck a second glance upwards, but the only light was the rotating LED that topped the Tate Leisure...

No cops. No 'copters, no aircars, no drones.

So – what? Grey could just let off suppression bursts with miniguns whenever he liked?

The firing stopped. Through the howling weather, Ecko heard the whirring of the barrels wind down, then cease.

Yeah, he thought, *maybe that ain't so smart, RoboCop. Now, what else you got?*

Their impasse was unchanged: the 'bot couldn't see him, he couldn't get past it. Without Lugan to run a distraction, Ecko was going to be stuck here when Salva and her goons reached the top of the stairwell...

Where the hell had that biker bastard got to?

Ecko wondered if Collator knew that Grey'd got a fucking *Takeshimi* combat machine. Lugan's Tech had been babbling the other day, "Experimental," he'd said. "Not ready to leave Japan," he'd said...

So what was this one – on fucking vacation?

The vertical red slice of the scanner swept again. The rain glistened like falling blood.

It knew where he was, huddled in the shredded remains of the roof garden – it was just gonna keep scanning 'til it got him. Salva couldn't be far behind… Lugan was *so* not gonna reach him in time.

Where was Collator when you needed it? With its percentages and fucking scenario analysis? Ecko held down a sense of panic, he didn't want to know the odds on what he was about to do.

You're not, he told himself.

Yeah, I am.

The wall behind him had been shattered, pieces of rubble were still tumbling to the sidewalk far below. No security defended the roof's edge. Not thinking about the drop, not thinking about it, he let his outrage at his own stupidity focus into white determination.

Swallowing a mouthful of insanity, he slid backwards over the edge.

There was no fucking way he was letting some experimental tin can get the better of the Bogeyman.

The goons burst, breathless, onto the top of the stairs – and they'd found only Salva. If she'd heard their confusion she ignored it, she was scanning, slit-eyed and unfooled.

The landing was the size of a food-cube; if there was something here, she appeared intent on finding it.

She glared round the walls, studying every millimetre. When she found nothing, she looked up, raising the muzzle of her rifle.

Still nothing.

Her expression narrowed.

Gotcha, bitch! With a grim smile, Ecko watched her ocular scanners flicker. Less than a metre above her head, he was backed into a corner, crouched like a nightmare with his shoulders crunched against the ceiling.

Her gaze went straight over him.

He didn't dare move, she'd feel the air. He stayed as still as stone – even when she squeezed her trigger and loosed a short, sharp burst of ammunition directly upwards.

He stilled his breath. Dust and plaster scattered.

"Sal!" Grey stubbed his reefer out on the security desk. "Don't trash the place. You lot, get a grip. Maynard, stay here and watch those readouts. You two, keep an eye on the stairs. Anything comes near you – shoot it."

"Doc, if the building's compromised, shouldn't we –"

"If you patrol, it'll take you out one by one. Stay put – and stay together." He shrugged off the lab coat, revealing pale arms and more tattoos, blue with age. Old needle marks decorated his forearms. "Sal, time to hit the panic room."

Ecko stayed still as the chemist moved to open his sanctuary door. Beside him, a hatchet-faced Salva still watched the ceiling.

As the goons settled down to squabbling about who'd seen what, the door into Grey's lab swung open, then slowly closed.

Before it resealed, Ecko was through it.

One hand.

Two.

Flattened by the wind and hammered by the driving, freezing rain, Ecko clung to the edge of the roof.

The flexiweight in the cloak hem kept it from tangling his legs but its folds billowed and flapped as if threatening to drag him loose. His hands strained to hold him – his reinforced skin didn't cover his fingertips and they stung with pain on the broken stone.

Ecko's Tech – he called her "Mom" – had fashioned him many things. Laying a complex system of wiring into the motor nerves of his hands, she'd turned his fingers into inhumanly accurate callipers. Arrayed with tactile sensors, his bare fingertips could tell him the location of wiring in a wall, the movement of tumblers in a lock, the exact moment the breath stopped in someone's throat...

But they also hurt like bastards if anything damaged them. He could feel all of it: every lump, every splinter, every crack, every chip and fragment of the broken wall. He could have mapped the destruction to the last half nanometre – the pain etched the landscape of the stonework into the blood on his fingertips.

His resolve set like cold steel, Ecko swung sideways along the roof's edge – away from the can's target arc. His jaw jumped with the hurt of every handhold, but he kept his oculars focused on the dirty, pitted ferrocrete before him. He closed his ears to the demented yowl of the wind, ignored the rain as it battered into his flesh. If he fell...

...He was playing Bogeyman, playing Bogeyman for real. Bogeyman didn't mess up – and he *didn't* fall off the fucking wall. For Bogeyman to end up as Pavement Pizza was inconceivable.

He sniggered like the first sign of panic.

One hand then two.

His feet swung loose, billowing uselessly as if his legs were broken. He could get no purchase on the slippery glass. After another metre, the pain in his fingertips was sparking stars across his vision. His hands were cramping, his arms and shoulders shuddering with strain. As the hurt increased, his fingers lied to him. A whole chunk of wall came away under his grip and he dangled precariously from one hand, the wind blinding him with his cloak hood.

For chrissakes, he thought to himself, *get a fucking grip*.

He sniggered aloud – then strangled it before it rose to a scream.

Desperate fear gave him strength. With a simian swing, he secured the second handhold and hung there, sick with relief. He dared not raise his head above the lip of the wall – that fucking can would blow it clean off.

Another two metres and he'd reach the corner.

* * *

Ecko's briefing had covered only the corporate basics – approach, building security, office space – it hadn't listed the contents of Grey's lab. That shit was target *numero uno* on the list of stuff Ecko had to recon.

Gotcha!

Behind him, the door clanged shut and sealed with a slight hiss. Oblivious to the additional presence, Grey and Salva headed swiftly away across the gloom.

Leaving Ecko crouched at the bottommost edge of a nightmare cavern.

He'd been expecting the usual – some elaborate medical set-up. Computers, cryogenics, glass tubing, dry ice, some twisted lab assistant with genetics issues... The span of the entire building and four floors in height, this place had none of these things.

It looked more like a prison.

In the moment of confusion, he paused to check for security – just scanning the gloom as though nothing was wrong.

And then he realised what he'd found.

It left him breathless – staring above and around him in a choking swell of awe, fear and scorn – a rising, throat-closing claustrophobia that all but had him scrabbling at the door.

Down each long wall, stacked like crates and stretching into the gloom, there were chambers. The layout was utterly familiar – and terrifying in its banality. Now utilised by every major corporation to house its staff, these were bog standard, completely recognisable Human Resource Containers – commonplace city habitation, sold on by Pilgrim to the big corporations. They were marketed as "bolt-holes" to those that lived in them – known as "shit-holes" to those that managed not to. Each had a bed, a cupboard, a toilet, a fridge and a console loaded with The World of Anywhere-But-

Here... Yeah, each one had everything the mindless worker drone needed.

Grey and Salva had purposefully vanished. Ecko didn't care. Hunched under the weight of the room, he stared from door to door to door, his lungs filling with repulsion and horror. *This* was social perfection – pure order. This was what Pilgrim strived for, *this* was how they'd become the single most powerful corporation in the world. They'd delivered a quiescent, contented population, a totally peaceful and crime-free society.

Yeah right. What they'd delivered was fifty million little plastic bottles labelled "Mood Stabiliser".

Instant contentment. Happiness in tablet form.

Yeah, it may as well have been fucking cryogenics, Ecko reckoned. At least the bastards shut in those didn't have to *work* a nine-to-six.

The place stank like a week of backed-up shit. As Ecko remembered to breathe, the stink was a sharp punch in the nose. He found the room smelled of piss, unwashed skin, rotting food... It reeked like a bunch of junkies had been using it as a crash space.

Ecko quelled his anger and checked again for the room's security. Then, as wary as a black-eyed rodent, he moved to the door of the first shit-hole.

He'd had a horrible fucking idea he knew what was coming.

At last, Ecko reached the corner of the building.

Feeling the openness of the sky to his side, he hung there for a moment, willing himself to continue. His blood screamed louder than the wind in his ears.

As he eased precariously round the angle, the weather hit him like a train and he found himself scrabbling frantically for a foothold. From being plastered to his back, his cloak became a parachute, pulling at his throat, hips and elbows – its loose folds inflated and the wind shrilled through carefully seamed rents.

For an instant, it nearly ripped him clean off the side of the building.

The thing was a mass of folds and slits and loose ends of fabric... all now trying to pull him loose. Ecko twisted his back to the wind and the thing deflated like a dying animal.

His fingertips were slippery, leaving bloodstains; he could feel the palms of his hands oozing with stickiness. He didn't dare release a hand to move onwards and the cloak was too complicated to release, so he hung, pain, fear and savage resolve all yammering for attention in his head.

Whatever you do, he told himself, *don't fucking look down.*

Fucking Collator and his fucking odds, fucking Lugan and his fucking plans. *You get in, you get the data stick, you get out...* Yeah, right – more like, you get in, you get screwed, you end up target practice for a *Takeshimi* tin can that's not even supposed to *be here...*

His feet slipped and skidded; his arms and fingers cramped like he'd never uncurl them. The cloak still tugged at him. He shook the cowl from his head and the wind slammed into his cheek.

The temperature was dropping – the rain was turning to sleet.

With an effort that nearly broke him, he swung his weight into motion once more – one hand then two, just a little further...

The first shit-hole wasn't locked.

On the bed, the recumbent figure wasn't restrained. As the door inched open, she turned her head to smile, although she didn't sit up.

Her cupboard door stood ajar, spilling soullessly creased

garments onto the carpet tiles. Her gaming console was on standby, the eyewear discarded. Beside her was a metal mug – as Ecko slipped around the door, he saw it contained puddles of white, furred mould.

Stink and revulsion flooding his system, he realised she hadn't left the bed in days.

But – she wasn't restrained. No one was forcing her to stay. She was lying there because... his heart cowered in his chest when the full depth of Grey's achievement hit him... she was lying there because she *wanted* to.

She was *happy*.

Peace: a population that voluntarily incarcerated itself, that had no interest or need outside the workplace –

No passion, no fear, no desire. No anger. No frustration.

They didn't even know to fight back; they no longer cared.

They wanted *nothing*. They were just *content*.

Stealth forgotten, Ecko stood in the centre of the little box, his blood congealed to fury. Around him, above him, across the room from him there were more boxes and more boxes...

How many people had Grey got in here – his control experiments, his gauges? Were they better than this? Were they worse?

The woman was – what – maybe thirty-five? Her well-cut suit was crumpled to a rag, her well-cut hair grown to an unruly tangle. She had clothes, food, entertainment – a door out of her box whenever she chose to take it...

But she was fine where she was.

Ecko found his face twisting round a sneer that felt like pity.

With a red flash of contempt, he wanted to make her react, to defy her own conditioning and stick one in Grey's throat. He pulled the door from the cupboard, yanked out her garments, tore them to strips, kicked over her fridge... She followed him with her eyes, smiling at him.

He turned and snarled at her to move, to get the hell up, to say something, to cry, to curse, to fight, to beg him for help.

Her mouth moved, but it was only for a moment. She returned it to the smile.

With a short, sharp impact, he punched her in the face.

Her nose crunched, her lip split; blood splashed across her skin. She spluttered surprised red bubbles. Her hands half rose in an effort to cover her head against further blows.

But even that wasn't enough. After a moment she fell back, arms tumbling slackly to her sides – like her fucking batteries had died.

Fight me, you fucking – !

With a surge of absolute savagery, hating the drone for being a victim, hating Grey for what he'd done, Ecko drew in a breath and exhaled.

He breathed pure fire.

It was Mom's greatest trick, one he'd asked her to design for him. It was more a toy than a weapon – only lethal at very close range.

Like this.

The drone died without a sound, her face blackening, blistering and sloughing down into the pillow. Hell, she had to be better off. Beneath her, the unclean bedding coughed, spluttered flame and flared into life.

Ecko was just wondering if he had time to total the rest of them when he heard servo-motors, loud across the cavern's quiet. His vision spun as he focused his telescopics in the direction Grey had taken – the other side of the room.

It was then, of course, that he'd seen the 'bot.

On the roof, the 'bot could no longer see him.

With a mouth full of terror and indignation pounding in his temples, Ecko pulled himself upwards until his forearms and elbows rested along the top of the wall.

His shoulders sang relief. He didn't dare look at his fingertips.

Here, the stone was unbroken; here, he was shielded from the arc of attack. For a moment, he paused, feeling the sleet on his skin, the blood on his hands, the cloak flapping like a dead thing round his legs.

So much for the fucking cavalry, Lugan. The thought was a bitter one, but there was a savage sense of righteousness in doing this by himself.

What had Lugan said, after his interview with the Boss? *"You get this right, mate, an' she's promised she'll have Eliza fix you up proper, d'you know what I mean? No expense spared."*

Ecko responded as he'd done that morning, *"What'm I, your fuckin' bike, now? You think you can customise me any which way? You fuckin' hypocrite! You leave my cyberware alone an' you stay the hell outta my head."*

There was motion. A door, booted feet. A clipped, military voice.

Salva.

Holding his breath, he watched.

Salva was coldly efficient, covering the shattered remains of wall and roof garden. Ecko didn't need oculars to clock the precision in the way she scanned the area, ducked back, paused, and moved to the next checkpoint.

It'd be about sixty seconds before that checkpoint was slap-bang in his face. If he was gonna pull this off, he needed to move. Like, now.

He let the wind swing his body sideways, got one foot on the top of the wall. Not thinking about the drop below him – thinking about the 'bot, the *'bot* – he rolled silently over the top and down onto the gravel.

The wind suddenly cut off as the stonework shielded him, his ears sang with cold. He stayed still, waiting, watching.

As Salva moved to cover the trashed remnants of the roof

garden, Ecko realised that she was alone – her goons had not come with her.

At last, the Bogeyman's luck was with him; he might just fucking do this after all.

Hope and adrenaline flooded his system.

Mom had built Ecko to be many things – stealther, spy, thief, tech – but her vision and genius had not stopped with reconnaissance and Bogeyman trickery. He had also been constructed to excel at something else.

Assassination.

Guilt, fear, compassion; these had little meaning against the adrenal boosting that supercharged his coordination and reflexes, against the ocular targeting that cross-haired the most elusive objective. His mottle-skin was spider-silk woven, lighter and tougher than Kevlar; biospheres in his bloodstream doubled his healing rate and fought infection. Increased capillarisation improved his body's ability to transport and process oxygen. He was as strong, as tough, as fit as the characters he'd grown up with.

As Salva came closer, so Ecko went from joker to combat machine.

He had one shot at this.

The first kick hit her knee and snapped her leg. The same foot flashed again, connecting with the side of her head as she fell. Doctor Grey's elite fighter never knew what'd hit her – she was dead before she hit the gravel.

Her rifle was in Ecko's hands.

But the 'bot was moving.

He heard the high-pitched whine of the barrels, saw the thing turn into his field of vision. He raised the rifle butt to his shoulder; his targeters cross-haired the sensor array in its head. With a snarl of defiance, he squeezed the trigger to blow it away.

He missed.

His arms were shaking too badly. Overstrained, he wasn't strong enough to hold the weapon and it climbed, rounds flying high and wide of his target.

In the split second he had before the tin can opened fire, Ecko knew he was screwed.

There was no cover up here; nowhere to go. Turbocharged or not, he wasn't a fucking action-movie hero able to dodge short-range rifle suppression with no cover.

He did the only thing he could do. He went over the edge.

And fell down, down into the screaming and the dark.

3: THE WANDERER

Ecko drifted through layers of consciousness.

"...Why he even brought it inside." The speaker was young, female. His head was clouded with fug; as the voice hazed into focus, he groped for a name. "We've got enough strays: new cook, new bar staff. Oh come on, mush, I'm *never* inhospitable..."

"The Bard said he knew what it was." The second voice was male, clear and deep. Soft footsteps moved somewhere behind where Ecko lay.

Behind him...? Where...?

He couldn't think. His limbs and head felt heavy: he'd been sleeping very deeply. The last thing he remembered...

The roof garden. Bloody handprints across the shattered wall. Insanity screaming in muscle and weather.

Falling.

Stupidly, his first solid thought was that Lugan never reached him in time.

They must've scraped him off the tarmac like so much roadkill. In the thick, sheltered blanket of awakening, he wondered: why was there no pain?

"Anyway, we can't leave it up here." The woman was brisk, authoritative. "I don't even know what it is – we can't have it running around, it'll scare the customers."

"This is Roviarath," the man answered her. "Their only concern would be what they could trade it for."

She giggled.

No pain... Ecko tried to focus on that realisation. No pain. Only his hands... Gradually, pushing back the smothering warmth, he allowed his awareness to expand. He wasn't restrained, though his webbing and cloak had gone. His cheek rested upon something supple, cool to his skin. He had no injuries. A brief, subvisual check showed all systems normal, although the flamethrower tanks in his chest weren't full. His memories were washing up slowly, garbage on the riverbank – Doctor Grey with his half a reefer, a scanner, blood red through the rain...

In the bottom corner of his field of vision, his digital time readout was jittery: he'd no clue how long he'd been out.

Even Grey wouldn't've seen anything like Ecko before. Dimly he wondered: maybe they were gonna do *experiments* on him?

Humour flickered. Heh... would *they* be in for a surprise.

He remained still, his breathing unchanged. The air was clean – but there was no hum of purifiers. He could hear a party – but there was no music. More fragments floated belly-up to the surface – the woman, burning on the bed; Lugan saying, "You get in, you get out. No mess."

Yeah, right. Whatcha gonna do about it *now*, biker-boy?

The female voice tutted. "Look, do you think it's all right to leave it? I need you downstairs, we're in the wrong part of the city here." She walked round where Ecko lay, her footsteps soft, indicating carpets or rugs. "Roviarath can be difficult – c'mon, Sera."

Ecko waited for a third voice but the man answered, "It seems quiet for the moment... yet it seems you are not giving me the choice."

Sarah? A guy called "Sarah", for chrissakes? Ecko tried to pull his concentration together. What was downstairs? And where was "Rovi-ar-ath"?

Were Grey's goons talking like this when they'd passed him on the stairwell?

He heard a door open.

The sound was two, maybe three metres away. Though still unseen, the room took on shape and size. For a moment, the noise of the party became louder.

Then long, easy bootsteps crossed towards him.

A sudden, peculiar tension brought Ecko fully awake. He lay motionless, stilled by incomprehension. Who...?

The footsteps stopped; the newcomer was right over him.

Salva was dead; it had to be Grey. What was he carrying – pistol, hypo? Ecko's targeters twitched although his eyes were still closed. Could he spark and flame before – ?

"Karine, Sera."

The voice was male, warm, light and fine; it had a timbre and vibrancy so compelling that his questions braked to a screeching halt. It wasn't Grey; the subtle accent was completely alien. And yet...

"It seems the traditional brawl is brewing early." Where had he heard it before? That hint of wry humour was familiar, so familiar...

...was this the deal – were they gonna *talk* him into submission?

Shit. He remembered that Lugan'd sent him on this fucking mission without a radio. He'd have no help getting out of here.

"They should be drinking, not fighting," the woman said. There was a faint scuffle. "Go on, you dirty great bouncer, get your arse down there and sort them out. I don't want the place trashed."

"Will never happen." "Sarah" headed for the door.

When he'd gone, there was a pause.

The long footsteps of the guy with the voice crossed to another point in the room. There was a shuffling of what sounded like paper – *paper*, for chrissakes? – and the woman said gently, "What's up?"

Ecko heard the guy inhale, let his breath out again in a half-muffled sigh like he was rubbing a hand over his face.

"How I wish I understood," he said. "This is so unexpected, and yet it brings me hope." The voice held – what was that? Anticipation? Fear? "My dear Karine, you know the tales as well as anyone –"

"You're a nutjob, looking for something that isn't there."

The man chuckled. "Perhaps." His voice danced with irony as he added, "Perhaps I'm the only sane one."

"You're a nutjob – and an egomaniac." She tapped fingernails. "Come on, Loremaster, we've got an alehouse to manage."

"*You*'ve got an alehouse to manage."

"Don't even think it!" Her footsteps crossed the room.

He laughed. "All right, all right. Lace transitions are traumatic – our friend here won't be conscious for a while." Furniture moved. "And I may be insane but *you* are a bully."

"Which is why you gave me the job, as I recall. Go on – out. I'm coming too."

"Riddle me this –" the man was heading for the door as he spoke "– what's pretty, aggressive and going to be my absolute undoing?"

"I'll be your absolute undoing in a minute," the woman said. "If you don't get down those stairs, I'll –"

The door closed behind them.

When they'd gone, Ecko lay still.

His head was a glaring question mark. The beautiful, alien voice; the words it spoke. It was all wrong; sounded wrong, smelled wrong, *tasted* wrong.

He listened.

No howling weather. No traffic, no sirens, no pounding nightclub bass. The party noises were coming from a lower floor, he must be upstairs. The air was quiet; yeah, it was too damn quiet and it was freaking him out.

The obvious conclusion – that this was one of Grey's shit-holes – he'd dismissed when he'd realised the room was too big.

The voice had said he wouldn't regain consciousness for a while, they'd probably left him alone. Turning off his flickering digital clock, he counted: *one* dead corporate, *two* dead corporate...

When he hit six hundred without noise or motion, he slitted open his eyes.

And the big question mark got one helluva lot bigger.

It took him a stunned moment to realise it was a set-up, a *set-up*. It was some kind of simulated environment.

Had to be.

Ecko was on a couch, one of three that surrounded a small table in the centre of a large, low-ceilinged room. On the table sat his webbing and cloak. Light came from some kind of writing desk that sat by a long drape – two further drapes presumably covered more windows.

There was no guard.

There was no security of any other kind: no cams, no mikes, no weapons, no trips, not as much as a cable. There was no console, no flatscreen. There wasn't as much as a fucking datasocket – like you could fit one on a wall of bricks and beams. His heatseeker showed warm ambience, only the light source raised the temperature of the air.

What was this – the set of some Sauce'n'Swordery routine? Was fucking Robin Hood going to come prancing through here any second? This was like some loony-trick spook-interrogation thing. If this was Grey's idea of a head game...

Maybe they'd left him free, with his kit, just to see what he'd do – there had to be a vid-feed somewhere.

Yeah? Well, he was gonna take that bluff.

His webbing and cloak were untouched. As he kitted back up, he realised two things – that he had no injuries other than his ripped fingertips and that there was no sign of Salva's rifle. Warning alarms rang in his head, but he flicked his hood to cover his face and headed for the nearest window.

First priority – find a way outta here.

The desktop offered no information – just curly papers and a feather-in-a-pot cliché that made him wince. The feather was a bright, UV-brilliant white. The room's light source appeared to be a rock, for chrissakes. Shaking his head at Grey's apparently whimsical nature, he tweaked back the edge of the curtain.

A slice of bright illumination made the colours of his skin recoil.

His oculars defending his vision, he looked out at the polluted, halogen-blazing –

The sky was dark, untouched by advertising – unobscured by clouds or buildings, by the Tate's ever-cycling LED. It was pitch-black, crystal-vision clear and completely starless.

What?

That wasn't right.

The moon was half full, low, brilliant and shimmering silver. It was way too close and way too bright – that wasn't right either. The second moon, a little higher and glowing a fantastic yellow gold, was also half full. That was getting beyond not-right.

What freaked Ecko right out was that it was the other *half*.

He blinked.

No fucking way.

Reality took a half step sideways, staggered, and fell on its ass. Panic rose in his throat and he found himself fighting to breathe – what the *hell* was going on? His adrenals had instinctively kicked; he was shivering with fight-or-flight tension and it was making him queasy.

It was a picture, a projection of some kind, it *had* to be. They were just messing with his head...

He was losing control of his gut. *Think*, he told himself. *Get a fucking grip for chrissakes.*

He'd been sent on a recce. He'd jumped off the roof. He'd splatted on the tarmac like a lump of strawberry jam. Grey could've done whatever he wanted...

Fucking Grey.

The memory was like a reprieve, he found his knees going. This was a simulation all right, they'd shoved him in one of those boxes and plugged him into the fucking console. It was a *game*: a few rounds of interrogation in The World of Anywhere-But-Here, soften him up a bit. It explained why the fall hadn't mashed him.

But then – how the hell did he get out...?

Shielding his skin from the light, he backed into a crouch half under the desk and fought a sudden, choking clamour of panic. Even the drugged-up-zombie workers were allowed to game, it gave them an approved – and supervised – recreational outlet. Bread and fucking circuses. But if he'd been put in here, and he couldn't unplug himself...

It was an inescapable gaol. He was helpless.

Yeah, Ecko lashed at his fear with savagery, *but that don't fucking mean you hafta just sit here.*

Annoyed at himself, he twitched the curtain. The window was long and narrow, tiny panes of – was that mica? – stretching floor to ceiling and allowing him to see outwards into the weird, pale-yellow light.

Stone walls, dark archways, narrow, twisting streets. The moon... moons... gave everything a bizarre, cross-hatched shadowing that warped the scene into a comic-book fantasyscape, something unreal – a world as beautiful and alien as the voice had been –

He was gonna puke.

He let the curtain go and edged right back under the desk, cloak covered, his hand over his mouth. His gut was churning like the back wheel of Lugan's bike, the adrenal rush had left him shaking like a –

Again, he heard the door.

What *now*? This place was like fucking Clapham Central. Secure in his stealth mode, he raised the front of his cowl high enough to watch.

It was the owner of the voice.

That same not quite familiarity shivered in Ecko's skin, made his heart lurch with anticipation. Like seeing a brain-rig actor in the street – or a celeb you'd once had a crush on – you knew them though you'd never seen them before.

The man who came into the room was tall – as tall as Lugan – but rangy, long legged and dressed like a ponce. Black boots and black pants looked like the bottom half of a highwayman costume; a loose pale shirt was stark against deeply tanned skin. Long, heavy black hair was tied back in a tail – in the light from the rock, it shone almost blue.

Ecko's heatseeker showed no weapons, no enhancements, not even jewellery – fucking diddly-squat.

He needed his Tech – Mom – to run a full diagnostic.

Yeah right – and he needed a radio. And Salva's rifle. And a coupla grenades. And maybe some plastic explosive...

He needed forty thousand hit points and a sword of bad guy slaying.

What he *needed* was a fucking way out of here.

The man stopped, apparently scanning the room.

"The nausea's a side effect of your transition," he said. "It'll pass. Kale's cooking something that'll help you – but you're strong. It won't be ready just yet."

That was the second time Ecko had heard the word "transition". He swallowed convulsively; they had to be pulling his chain. They'd boxed him up for sure but they wouldn't try anything that dumb...

The man closed the door. The sound had a distinct finality.

Ecko shuddered.

"I'm Roderick of Avesyr," the man said, "usually known as the 'Bard', though I fear the moniker is somewhat ironic. This illustrious drinking establishment is The Wanderer, it has the occasional habit of collecting strays – both local and otherwise. And you, my friend, would seem to be an 'otherwise'. If you let me, I can help you."

An "otherwise"? What was that: a Connecticut Yankee in the King Arthur's Arms? Silently, he watched.

Roderick crossed the centre of the room, stopped. "Know that neither I nor anyone in this building will threaten you. Please, I understand you're confused, but there's no need to conceal yourself."

He said, "Trust me."

"*Trust* you?" In a snap decision that surged ahead of nausea, fear and incomprehension, Ecko exploded from under the desk. "You work for Grey, don'tcha? You plug me into this shit, you question me, I tell you everything, then it's Experimentation Time?" He leapt four steps and was on the table, crouched like a confrontation. "Yeah, well, I've seen through your little ruse. Bring it on, asswipe, let's see whatcha got."

"Answers." The Bard was neither startled nor slow; he spread his long hands in a shrug. "I'm welcoming you, trying to help. Your anger and disorientation are completely understandable – I'd like to try and make this easy, if I can. Sketch out the basics."

Ecko bared his teeth. "Don't turn your fuckin' vocal charms on me or I'll use your skull for a piss-pot."

"I know you're confused –"

"Confused! You got five seconds to tell me what's what or I start breaking shit. An' you can begin with those *moons*."

"The light's making you queasy?"

"The light," Ecko said, "is reflected sunlight –"

"The light," the Bard said with a half-smile, "comes from the Gods."

"The moons are gods?" He had to be kidding. "That's one hell of an interrogation technique. What, d'you sacrifice virgins to the *sun* in your spare time?"

"Round here, I'd only have to trade for them first." His supple voice made the statement rich with amusement.

"You're a fuckin' scream," Ecko said. "Now. You tell me what's goin' on or I start burning shit *down*."

"Take it easy, there, my friend." The Bard's tone was humorous, gentle. "There's no need to be burning anything. I understand this is bewildering, and I came in to help make you welcome – firstly to The Wanderer, purveyor of fine ales, and currently in the city of Roviarath."

Without taking his eyes from Ecko, he gave a half bow, spreading his hands, and his expression flickered mischief. His face was lean and bore a tracery of age lines; his eyes were violet and so long lashed he looked like he wore make-up. Watching him, Ecko had no clue how old he was.

But he was still speaking. "Roviarath is our culture's pivot and lynchpin, the heart of our trade. All around it are the Varchinde, the open Grasslands. Beyond that, I come from the north, the Khavan Circle. The Kuanne to the west is lifeless; the Archipelago to the east scarcely populated. To the south, the Red Desert is home to nomads, a hundred banners with a hundred cultures. They're a short-lived people, but fiery."

As the Bard spoke, so Ecko's surroundings took on shape and form, became more solid. The nausea began to ease. Yet the map the man drew made the whispering realisation louder... this was already far too complex, far too real...

Real? Chrissakes, this was insane – even more insane than two fucking god-moons that disobeyed every physical law...

They'd never make him believe this shit!

"Okay, smart-ass, what's the time: what year is it?" Panic in his throat, Ecko pressed for flaws, watching the Bard, the room. "Year? Jeez, three hundred and sixty-five an' a quarter days, one cycle of the seasons?"

"The Count of Time will be different for you – perhaps that's no real surprise. Here, we call the seasons a 'return' – a Return of the Spring – broken down into cycles and halfcycles, twenty days and ten, each measured by the Moons –"

"All right, already; enough." Ecko tried another attack, pressing for the flaw, the crack, anything that would bring the walls down. "So – what – I just 'woke up' here?" He snorted. "An' I'm s'posed to think this shit is *real*?"

"I'm supposed to think it's not?" The Bard sat back, lines of amusement creasing around his eyes. He stretched long legs under the table. "Perhaps you aren't here. Are you a pathwalker, or a lucid dreamer? Or has someone placed you here for a purpose?"

A purpose... the understanding was a fist in the face.

Oh, for chrissakes.

You get this right, mate, an' she's promised she'll have Eliza fix you up proper...

Ecko found he'd forgotten to breathe. In the ice calm of realisation, everything froze perfectly into place.

You don't understand how important this is – an' I ain't explainin' it, not now. Behave yourself.

It hadn't been a recce – it'd been a fucking *test*.

No radio, no rifle. No back up. A piece of rare and experimental robotics that he couldn't hope to take down. A top, corporate, City location where gunfire would be ignored by the cops.

How could he have been so fucking dumb?

He was plugged in all right, but not to some drone entertainment game, some amateur role play... *This* was the real fucking deal.

This was the full-on Virtual Rorschach, the mutt's nuts, the fucking cat's pyjamas. Designed by the Boss's pet psychotherapist Eliza, controlled and run by Collator's massive mainframe – a perfect blend of human instinct and mathematical algorithm. This "world" was made for him and from him – it was the extrapolated fractal landscape of his own brainwaves, a completely functional and unique reality, mathematically remodelling itself around his every decision and reaction.

In short? It was his head.

And he was stuck in it.

The *hypocrites*. The lousy, rat-shagging, mother-fucking *bastards* – they'd sold him straight down the Thames! They'd flogged his soul for thirty pieces of ammunition! *How* could he have been this stupid?

"I see you're seeking your truth." The voice was calming. Ecko focused on Roderick's expression – wariness, compassion, concern. "The culture shock can be a hard thing to assimilate –"

"*Culture* shock?"

Naked, black-toothed savagery made the Bard start back. Ecko came off the table, his adrenals swift as a pounce. He had the man by the shirt and was snarling in his face. "They didn't fucking do this to me, they didn't *do* this! How the hell do I get back out?"

"I'm sorry…"

"Shit!" Throwing the Bard back against the couch, he lashed out with a foot and crashed the table into splinters. He spun back, targeters flashing.

"This is *insane*!"

Roderick leaned forwards to lay a hand on his arm. "Please. You're welcome to stay here as long as you wish. And if you let me, I can help you."

"Get the hell off of me." Ecko shook off the contact like a poisonous insect, backed up. It was too much, swamping him. He was sinking in insanity and disbelief. "I need – security.

I need – my Tech. I need my fucking head examining. That wasn't meant to be funny. Jesus, I don't even *know* what I need. Why the fuck would I wanna stay here?"

A ghost of a grin flickered on the Bard's face.

"You'll have to stay somewhere," he said. "This building was given to me by the Lord CityWarden of Amos. It's a tool, a catalyst and a nexus. And it has very good beer." When Ecko said nothing, he continued, "Look, I've spent my life seeking answers to certain questions – and, slowly, they have all come here, they've... coalesced. And now you're here too." When Ecko still glowered, the grin spread. "Where else would you wish to be? We ride fate, here. Tonight, we're in Roviarath. Tomorrow morning, we find a new location, another city perhaps. And the day after that..." The sentence ended in limitless possibility.

"That's bullshit," Ecko said, "you can't just fucking *teleport*. What about your water, and –" he stopped short as he realised that if this was a constructed reality, the pub, like the moons, could do whatever the hell it wanted "– stuff?"

That made Roderick chuckle. "Our water comes with us. We move just before dawn and nine nights of the halfcycle it's to somewhere we can trade. Occasionally, though, we do get a surprise. Eight days ago, we found ourselves in the ruins at Tusien, all our customers had been dead a thousand returns. Very bad for business."

"Christ – they've dumped me in The Magic Faraway Pub." Cursing, Ecko spun from the couch to kick at table bits and pace the room like a caged creature. He eyed his surroundings with a growing sneer: no weapons, no plastics, no electronics. In fact – he noticed this after a moment – no metal.

This was *insane*.

Eliza's Virtual Rorschach was supposed to be *therapy*, for chrissakes – a long-term, total-immersion solution for the Boss's more difficult personality cases. He didn't know how it worked, but he knew that they'd clock his every reaction, and he knew that somewhere, there was gonna be some path or puzzle, something he had to solve or achieve or piece together. Maybe he could find it, get it the fuck sorted and get out – and maybe if he did it fast enough, he might even make it back with his brain intact.

Before they *fixed* him.

Chrissakes.

Once upon a time, Mom had made his body tamper-proof, unbreakable. Hell, maybe she'd made his head the same.

Roderick said, "You haven't told me your name."

"I'm Ecko, silent 'G'." He stopped his pacing by the desk and picked up a random piece of curly paper. He exhaled a tiny touch of flame. The paper flared eagerly then crumbled to black ash. "Though you really wouldn't get the gag."

"Ecko." The Bard thought for a minute then continued, "You're –"

A smart rap on the door cut him off.

Ecko turned, half crouched, his cloak mantling, ash scattering, but the Bard extended a calming hand.

"It's all right," he said. "That'll be dinner. Having no idea what you eat, we thought it best to start simple."

Recoiling, biting back a sarcastic response, Ecko stared at the door, his oculars cycling.

It opened to reveal a young woman with a tray propped on one hip. She was curvy, with shining brown hair and a cleavage you could've parked a bike in. Like the Bard, she had no enhancements, no weapons, no metal. There was something impertinent in her stance.

Lugan would've been all over her like a tattoo.

For a split second, Ecko had a vision of the young woman slapping the huge biker round the face. He almost grinned. Then the grin fractured and broke – Lugan was a million miles away, in another world, walled apart on the outside of Ecko's skull.

Lugan was lost.

Lugan had sold him the fuck out.

Lugan was in deep *shit* when Ecko got outta here.

He shook his fingers and the last flakes of ash drifted to the floor.

The woman said, "What did you do to my table?" It was the same voice that Ecko had heard earlier.

"Karine." The Bard stood up. "Meet Ecko. All things considered, he's adjusting remarkably swiftly. Perhaps, when you have a moment…?" Roderick left the question unfinished but the young woman seemed to know what he meant.

"When do I ever get a moment?" She put the tray down on the arm of the couch, then straightened up to treat Ecko to a broad wink. "I run this building, and don't let him tell you otherwise."

"I wouldn't dream of it," Roderick said, eyeing the rafters.

The tray contained some sort of pottery bowl that steamed with a surprisingly rich, meaty scent, and a hunk of something that looked like real bread, grainy and rough. Ecko had an odd urge to pick the bread up, break it, understand its texture. His belly growled, distressingly human.

Karine chuckled. "Don't worry, you can eat it safely, we're not going to try and poison you or anything." She treated Roderick to an arched brow. "Though *you* are going to have to haggle for the table. And when you've picked up the bits, you can turf out the big room under the roof. You know the one. It's got all your *souvenirs* in it."

The Bard grinned at the gibe.

She harrumphed at him, then said, "There's also more news… But that can wait for now."

Roderick shot her a look. Her responding gesture was tiny, but Ecko's targeters tracked it like prey. He picked up a second piece of paper from the desk, and turned it between his fingers.

Karine said, "I'll come back in a bit, make sure you're settling in okay, let you meet the others. In the meantime, don't let this one talk your ears off. He's a good man, but he is a bit crazed."

With a twitch of her hips, she was gone, hooking a foot to pull the door shut after her.

After a moment's quiet, Ecko said, the words biting, "'Crazed' huh? Maybe you're the one in therapy."

The Bard picked up a piece of the table, then threw himself down on the couch.

"I was given this building because I believe in a certain future – a vision, I suppose. And when I found you, I brought you in here because I believe that you're a part of that vision. That future." He held Ecko's black eyes for a moment. "I've seen you before."

...A path or a puzzle, something he had to solve or piece together...

A chill of inevitability skittered down Ecko's spine, then a flare of anger like panic, like the closing of a trap.

"Fantastic. So – what? You gotta prophecy that says I kick the ass of the God of Evil? A Major McNasty that's about to wake up? How 'bout a World-Shaking War?" His sarcasm was vicious. "Where do I start?"

With a wry chuckle the Bard replied, "Sadly, it's not that simple. There is no 'prophecy' – I wish there was. There is no 'God of Evil' – no 'Major Nasty' – not really one that does house calls. And the last World-Shaking War was a very long time ago." He stood up, shot a rueful glance at the remains of the table and then shrugged. "If it'd been that easy, this would already be over."

"*What* would be already be over?"

"That," he said, "is what I've spent my life finding out."

"Jesus shit." Ecko stared. His stomach grumbled again. He ignored it. "You dunno, do you? Loremaster, my ass."

Roderick said, "I know enough to know how much I don't know – and with every return, it becomes clearer. Look, like this…" With a dextrous flick of his fingers, he was holding a flash of metal. "Is this familiar?"

Ecko's targeters flashed, he was away from the desk in an eye blink. He snatched it from Roderick's hand. His flicker of inevitability – helplessness, almost claustrophobia – rose to a thunder. A wash of returning nausea made him breathe, *breathe*.

He looked down at what he'd grabbed.

It was a lighter – heavy, square, chrome plated and, so far, the only piece of metal he'd seen. On one side was engraved the Harley logo. On the other…

On the other, it said: *Alexander David Eastermann.*

"This is Lugan's." He gripped the lighter harder, as if it were the only solid thing in existence. "He lost it, like…"

Like yesterday.

For a moment, the complete insanity of the situation screamed at him – he wanted to push the walls down, like a film set, tear the scene from top to bottom as if it were only fabric, reveal the Bike Lodge that lurked just behind it… didn't it?

Didn't it?

But the Bard was still speaking, as if nothing strange had happened.

"The Wanderer finds many things," he said. "Just like it found you. It's a portent, I think. And it's white-metal, *muara*, extremely rare and of a quality I've never seen. Its value is considerable."

With a sense of absolute surreality, Ecko chinked the lighter open and flicked the wheel. It sparked and died.

"Outta gas." Somehow that wasn't the point.

The point was that it was here. Like a swat round the head, Eliza had clearly marked the opening point of the pattern. She'd given him the "Go" signal: "Ecko Start Here". Amid the tension that still thumped in his throat, the thought was fantastic enough to be ludicrous.

"So you're tellin' me the adventure starts in the tavern. Cute.

I'll give Collator 86.24 per cent there'll be giant flying lizards by the end of the week."

He glanced at the Bard. "Fuck!"

In a flash of frustration, Ecko threw the lighter viciously across the room. He was manipulated, betrayed, powerless, caught like a fucking street urchin. Somewhere, Eliza sat watching this on some huge fractal flatscreen – maybe she was behind the Bard's violet eyes, maybe she'd be behind the eyes of everyone he passed. Somewhere, Collator calculated odds, mapping, generating, predicting. Every movement Ecko made, every decision, every word he spoke – hell, maybe every thought in his head – was going to ripple outwards to affect the world around him – and those ripples would be broadcasting his behaviour. They'd be analysed, interpreted, judged.

Ever get the feeling you're being watched?

He wanted to rail against his fate, show that damn psycho-the-rapist bitch who was boss – but she had him by the grey matter and there was no way out of his own head. Bitterly, his mind spat at him: *Will you stay with the tavern? Turn to page 102. Will you flee? Turn to page 94.*

Or will you torch the place and watch it fucking burn?

The blazing temptation just to destroy everything... because he could. That'd fucking show her. Hell, what did it matter if he trashed *cities* – none of it was real. *Keep your fucking breadcrumbs; I'll do this my way.*

The answering thought was so flawlessly enmeshed, he wondered if it was even his own: *Turn back to page 1.*

Would they really loop him, endlessly, if he didn't succeed? Or would they just – *Jesus* – would they just turn him *off...*? Could they really do that?

For a moment, his intellect battled his emotional, knee-jerk instinct. Then, slowly, like it was the hardest thing he had ever done in his life, Ecko walked across the rug and picked up the lighter.

He felt dirtied – like he'd taken the first psychological step to sympathising with his torturer, like he'd already let them beat him.

But he was conceding the battle, not the war. He would so pay them back.

Roderick stood silent amid the shattered remnants of his table. Vocal enhancements or not, he made no attempt to push Ecko's decision one way or the other.

If Eliza was behind his eyes and had witnessed Ecko's acquiescence, the Bard did not show it. Yet strangely, his wordless comprehension was almost harder to bear. He held out his hand for the lighter and, with a flash of his more usual cynicism, Ecko brandished it like a dare.

He threw the words. "Only 'til I find the way outta here."

Remarkably, Roderick managed to say, "Of course," without sounding remotely smug.

PART 2: RIPPLES

4: THE MONUMENT THE CENTRAL VARCHINDE

Across the vastness of the Grasslands, the sun was setting.

The low rays were warm on the riders' backs, around them, the open Varchinde glowed in celebration of a summer's day done. Soft brown shadows grew from the hooves of the creatures they rode.

Their progress had been steady – they would make the Monument on time.

Around them, insects were beginning to sing. Ears chilled from endless wind, Amethea spat out the stalk she'd been chewing and reined her beast to a patient halt.

"Thea?" In the final stages of his 'prenticeship, Feren stopped beside his tutor.

"Just stretching." She lifted her pale braid of hair away from her neck. Under her, her heavy, slope-shouldered chearl leaned his ugly head down to snort among the grasses. Tiny flecks of life scattered. "Long day."

"Aye." He looked behind them, maybe at Roviarath's distant Lighthouse Tower, the safe city world he'd left – maybe at the great shadow of the Kartiah Mountains growing over the empty plain – Amethea couldn't tell. "And off the trade-roads."

"Nervous?" She smiled.

He shrugged. "Just tales." Running his hands through his shock of orange hair, he shook the dust out of it. "My cousin Redlock used to scare us kids when we were knee-biters. How the Kartiah are haunted and some such... Got any more water?"

"Told you not to guzzle all yours." Leaning over in the high-backed saddle, Amethea passed him her waterskin. "You said yourself, we're off the trade-roads, no one comes out here – even assuming we're lucky with the taer, it'll be late tomorrow before we get back to the river and any hint of civilisation."

Feren took a careful swallow of lukewarm water and gave her a cheeky, sunburned grin. "You wouldn't fail me. Not after everything."

He had a point.

Taer was dusk blooming, found in only three places across the Grasslands and sought for a pollen that knit bones like hide glue. Crossing the open plainland herself was a huge undertaking – taking her 'prentice on his final test was as much an assessment for her as it was for him. "Go with caution," Vilsara had said, "and return with wisdom."

All very well for Vilsara, far to the north-west in Xenok's hospice... Amethea and Feren were two days out of the Great Fayre at Roviarath, nearly a full day from any kind of safety. The vast emptiness of the open plainland was powerful, unknown, dangerous. Only the Deep Patrols came off the trade-roads – and they were an odd lot, somehow changed by the desolation.

"...Days since we've seen a decent tavern." Feren was muttering under his breath. He suddenly interrupted himself with a pleased grin. "Unless The Wanderer comes out here."

"The Wanderer?" Amethea chuckled. "Wasn't it in Xenok? You think it's following us?"

"I wish it was." Feren's grin broadened.

The teacher shook her head.

"We see it out here, I'll eat my saddle and ride home bareback."

"Really? Now, who told me the Gods had a sense of humour…?"

"You want me to finalise your 'prenticeship?" Checking about her, Amethea swung one leg over the chearl's spike-maned neck and slid, with a groan, to the ground. The grasses reached past her knees and she leaned forwards to pound stiff thighs with her fists, making dust and pollen fly. Her chearl turned and blew noisily on her breeches. Absently, she scratched his great head.

"Are they? Haunted, I mean?" Feren was back to watching the distant mountains.

"You are nervous." Amethea, too, turned westwards – the setting sun, the rising shadow. "It's superstition, that's all – that and your cousin pulling your strings. The Kartiah are just mountains – people live there."

"People." Feren's scepticism was typical Grasslander wariness. "They're slavers."

"They're craftsmen, Feren, metalworkers, part of the trade cycle. 'People.'" Her voice held an edge. "Neither the Kartiah nor the Monument are saga-borne myths."

Feren, too, slid from his saddle. "So why don't they know what it was for? Or what destroyed it?"

"The Monument?" The chearl was slope-backed and carried her panniers on his withers. Amethea reached into one of them for a handful of dried fruit. "You want to know if all that hairy-scary 'Souls of the Elements' stuff has its feet in the truth? Only the Gods know that. It was probably just destroyed by the Count of Time."

"No one knows." He accepted a piece of fruit.

"No one cares," Amethea told him. "Vilsara says we used to keep records, once – going back to Xenok's builders. But they're rotted, almost mush. Gods know what the real tale was."

"So… the mountains could be haunted – we've just forgotten?"

Laughing, she threw fruit at him.

"'Haunted'! You've been listening to those idiots in the market. Come on, if the shadow's bothering you that much we'll stay ahead of it... that way the mountains' twisted spirit can't get us and turn us into something icky." Swearing under her breath at stiffened muscles, she swung herself back into her saddle, settled against the back. "Besides, if we don't catch the taer right the pollen'll be all gone."

"Aye." Feren returned her waterskin and mounted the broad back of his chearl.

Soon, the two creatures were tirelessly running, broad hooves thrubbing on the baked soil, grasses dancing about their thick, muscled legs. They were heavier than horses, not as swift, but stronger over distance and steadier of nerve. Tales told that their ancestors had been crafted by some kind of alchemy; in the high days of Tusien, they rumoured, such crafting had been familiar. Amethea had sometimes wondered if those records were among the mouldering piles in Xenok's hospice.

Now, though, chearl were bred normally, and so common that people had long since forgotten the tale of their origin.

Before them, their shadows lengthened; behind them, a greater shadow rose. As the sun sighed into the mountains, the creatures ran tireless, smooth gaited and placid in obedience. They had come a long way – following the ribbon-towns and trade-roads from the sprawled city of Xenok to the forested Irahlau, along the edges of the Rhamiriae to the huge Fayre at Roviarath. Following the growing swell of the Great Cemothen River, they had at last turned across the open plain – off the safety of the road to a place now known only to Deep Patrol beer-tales and reckless, almost-senior apothecaries.

Apothecaries like Amethea, wondering what in the world she thought she was doing, bringing her 'prentice this far from home.

She stole a sideways glance at Feren as the light faded. He

was sitting upright, refusing to rest against the high back of the saddle – a position that strained his legs, as his feet were forwards in their stirrups. He was young, his soft beard new and a shade lighter than his shock of hair. Feren was freckled and a little wild-eyed. He'd given the chearl its head and his hand strayed often to the javelins slung down the side of his saddle. His cousin Redlock was famous – perhaps infamous – across half the world, a man of fearsome reputation who had abandoned his land, lady and daughter to become a warrior without peer. Was Feren a fighter? As a distant yammering made the 'prentice jump, Amethea chuckled. Feren was hardly warrior material, but road-pirates stayed where the pickings were rich – and the chearl were big enough to deter most predators.

Like the bretir, the wide-winged flyers of messages, and the couriers' companionable, guardian nartuk, now extinct, the chearl had been crafted with flawless efficiency.

If the tales were even true.

Slowly, the twilight caught them, rose around them. Above them, the moons were in perfect halves, they lit the plains to a vast, eerie emptiness where the ghosts of the Kartiah gibbered under every thought. The air grew chill and the grasses swished as the chearl ran on.

"Feren." Amethea reined her beast and pointed. "There."

He paused beside her. For a moment, they both stared in silence.

Before them, the ground swelled into a low hill. Against the deepening blue of the sky, the massive, tumbled stones glimmered faintly with their own light, giving the Monument a peculiar, skin-crawling glow. Amethea could make out the heavy black ridge of the surrounding bank – soil upon which no grass grew.

Compelled to an awed silence, they rode slowly upwards.

Surrounding the bank, a huge, empty ditch held only

darkness. No creatures lived here. Yet the fallen stones themselves still towered over bank, beasts and riders and commanded breathlessness and wonder.

His voice barely a whisper, Feren said, "It sings."

"Yes." In the faint glimmer, Amethea could see that the massive, fallen sarsens were lichen-free. Faintly, they hummed in the deepening dusk. Her skin shivered.

"Why?"

"I don't know." Oddly, the hum held a sense of patience – as though the whole Monument had simply settled to rest. "Maybe it once was some celebration, some ancient elemental temple; maybe the stones just observed the Count of Time. Maybe it was a memorial, or a tomb. I heard once that the hill we're standing on is a great passage grave, commemorating some lord or hero." Catching Feren's expression, she smiled and made an effort to speak normally. "Maybe it's all rubbish. Come on, you, we're losing the light."

"Aye..." He didn't move.

"Feren."

"Coming."

She turned her chearl, listening for him to follow.

Still, he didn't move.

"Feren?"

"Thea." His tone was flat, ice-cold. "Wait."

"What?" She twisted in her saddle.

"Horsemen, coming this way." His hand rested on the knife hilt. "They bear no light."

A chill shivered her shoulders. For Feren's sake she said, "Vilsara said the Patrols do come here; they're probably checking to see we're not chiselling the names of old lovers into the stones."

But she turned her beast to look.

Surprisingly close and coming fast – *fast* – up the other side of the hill were three mounted riders. In the almost-dark, they were barely more than shadows – the hauntings of the Kartiah brought to life. The glimmering of the Monument hampered her ability to see. She blinked and tapped heels to her chearl to move forwards.

Behind her now, Feren said, "That's not a Patrol…"

The riders were swift and silent. They showed no signs of slowing as they came closer. Moonlight glinted from smoothly flowing horse muscles and –

Goddess.

As they came towards the top of the hill, she saw them clearly and she realised…

They weren't riders.

They were *attached*.

Too stunned to move, her placid chearl ever-unworried beneath her, Amethea gawked. In the failing light, they were all but on top of her before she could understand that what she saw was real – those were horses all right, big ones, heavy legged and strong…

…but they had no heads.

No *heads*!

From their equine shoulders came the upper bodies of people – as smoothly muscled and powerful as the horse bodies beneath. The creature in front was larger than the other two; he bore a longbow as thick as his wrist and fully as tall as Amethea's chearl.

He was fast. Between her realisation and her very next heartbeat, he was before her and looming over her – chearl mounted as she was! – he was close enough for her to feel his breath.

For the briefest of moments, she met his eyes, human eyes, gleaming in the Monument's light. Stupidly, her mind told her he was beautiful, wild haired and potent, the blood in his skin pounding with outrage. As he opened his mouth, she saw long incisors glitter.

He screamed down at her, a sound of pure fury.

Shocked out of her disbelief, she was trying to back up and turn her beast, slamming her heels into its shoulders, shouting at Feren to do the same. Hopelessness laughed at her. Big as they were, chearl couldn't outrun a good horse on a short distance and that... thing... was bigger than any horse she'd ever seen. Fear hammering in her chest, she leaned back against the saddle support as he gathered his legs to turn and run.

Feren, too – she caught a flash of his ghost-white face as she passed him – was turning his beast to flee. Perhaps he prayed. She screamed at him to run, *run*.

The first fletchless shaft hit his chearl's hindquarters.

It squealed, skidded, lurched sideways and kept moving. Feren cursed, his voice high with fear. Amethea paused to wait for him, and dark shapes flickered past on either side of her. And stopped.

Trying to trap them.

"Fe-*ren*!"

He looked, but his fear-crazed eyes went straight through her.

A second shaft hit his beast's other side. It skidded again, its back legs faltering. With an inarticulate shriek, Feren crashed sideways to the ground, the rein still in his hand.

"Don't let it drag – !" Amethea called. The height of the fall tore his hand free. Instinctively, she stopped.

But what could she do?

In the emptiness of the plainland night, she turned her beast to face the creature. Lost in the grasses beside her, Feren moved, fear and pain spilling from his mouth. With a faint feeling of ludicrousness, she drew her own belt-knife.

"I'm a healer, I belong to the Hospice in Xenok – what do you want?" Her defiance was shrill, blade and voice shook. Did this thing of madness even understand?

"Little lady."

What had she expected? Not this masculine elegance; this

sensually perfect voice that shivered her ears. Her chearl watched the mighty creature, his head up and ears cocked forwards.

"We only came for the taer…"

"The taer is *mine*!" His flare of passion made her jump. "The grass is mine, the great stones are *mine*. Creature-created I may be – but I am crafted to mastery, to leadership. I am better than these stupid beasts that let you sit upon them. They, too, are now mine."

Crafted to what? Knife forgotten, she stared. Behind her, there was a flurry of movement and a high, skin-crawling scream. Something big struggled, coughed liquid and fell. Feren's chearl?

"Please…" This was crazed. "…I'm an apothecary, a healer –"

The creature glowered at her, his predator's teeth flashing, the light shining from his smooth skin. "Heal and Harm, little lady, the oldest rule. Apothecary or alchemist, you must obey. Do you understand?" One foreleg raked, tearing the grass. She saw that it was tipped, not in a hoof, but in a huge three-toed claw.

"None can learn one without learning the other." It was a child's lesson. "But – alchemist? What made you, what – ?"

"The craft is found," he said to her. He paced forwards until he was almost close enough to touch. His presence was stifling, even flattened against the high back of her saddle, she could feel the heat of his skin. Her chearl whickered at him, bizarrely unafraid. "We return. But do you know what it means?"

"It means…" Overpowered, she wanted only to back away, but did not dare move. "No, I don't…"

"I am alive!" Rage burned from him like madness. "Creature-created, I am, crafted for perfection – better than these foolish beasts. And it makes my life more important that yours."

What…? She did not find the opportunity to articulate the thought.

His voice dropped to a thrum. "Have you saved a life, little lady?"

Barely a whisper. "Yes."

"Have you taken a life?"

She had hunted creatures for food, much as anyone. "...Yes."

He laughed at her, cavernous and chillingly perceptive.

"Can you wield that little blade you bear? Yes – or you would not be out here alone." Stepping back, he crossed muscled arms over his chest. "Take the life of the young male that cowers beside you."

"No." Her reaction was immediate and without question. Feren was struggling to stand, his face white. Behind them, the other two creatures closed in.

"It is weak and injured, it serves no purpose." The creature nocked a huge, flightless arrow and began to bend the limbs of his longbow. "It pollutes the whole. Its life is mine and I say it is *done*."

"Thea..." She found Feren's hand on her leg and covered it with her own. He was shaking, sweating. Dimly, she understood that the fall had injured him – yet, somewhere, her fear and disbelief were starting to smoulder into anger. "Maybe... I was right... about the mountains..."

"Take its life, little lady," the creature said. "Show you understand."

"Or you'll take mine?" She found there was an edge in her voice.

In the pale light, the great bow flexed and loosed.

Feren gave a faint cry. His hand was gone from hers as he fell.

So sudden. So utterly final.

The flickering of her defiance drowned in total incomprehension, she shook her head. *No.* Instinctive, pointless denial. *No.*

Her chearl shifted, snorted at the metal smell of blood.

"Leave the male to die, bring this one." The great creature ran a hand though his mane of hair – a disturbingly ordinary gesture. "There is need of a healer."

Reeling from shock and nausea, the blow to her head somersaulted her forwards into the dark.

His face itched.

When he moved his arm to brush the grass away, other sensations shot through him – sickness, cold.

Pain.

His stomach lurched and he retched – a dark, liquid splash on the grass stalks before him.

Inanely, he heard Amethea's voice, ...*told you not to guzzle it all*, and it came with the realisation he wanted water.

He retched again, a thin stream of bile and blood.

Above him, the air was cold.

With an effort that spilled tears down his cheeks, he got his hands under him and pushed his face and chest away from the bloodied grass. He looked up.

Far, far above him, the sky glimmered faintly – it was almost dawn.

Across from where he had fallen, the body of his poor chearl still bore saddle and panniers. Black specks buzzed sluggishly about its eyes.

Fighting the urge to retch yet again, he tried to sit up.

And collapsed, biting his lip against a scream.

The pain was in his belly, just over one hip, focused about the arrow shaft that had spiked him front to back. One hand found it; carefully explored it. It was a broadhead, he could feel the point. At such short range, that monster bow had simply punched it straight through him.

Okay – the Gods were with him. He knew how to deal with this.

Chearl, panniers, healers' kit.

Apothecary, heal yourself.

Stupidly, he started to laugh.

His laughter scaled upwards and he found himself fighting for control. He was shouting, shrieking, "Thea, help me!", yet knowing that the creatures had taken her. He raised his hands to cover his face and sobbed.

He was going to die out here, under the haunted mountains, and the insects would eat his eyes.

Yet the tears subsided and, oddly, he felt better – calmer. Chearl, panniers, healers' kit. Swallowing nausea and mindful of the arrow shaft, he tried again to sit up.

As he moved, white anguish seared up his leg and he felt a muffled, sickly grinding.

He stopped, panting. Using his arms and hands to support his weight, he forced himself into a half kneel, his right leg out before him.

His foot was badly twisted. Breathing hard, now – focus, *focus* – he slowly tried to move his knee, his ankle, his toes.

Distantly, a high-pitched yammering was echoed by a second, closer by. Realising he must stink of blood, he tried to order his thoughts.

His ankle was broken. His tight, laced-up boots – a gift from his cousin – would hold the injury, but he needed a crutch if he was going to move any distance.

Distance…

It was then that Feren realised he was going to try for the trade-road. Surprised for a moment at the clarity of his resolve – and at the impossibility of crossing the plains, alone, injured and without water – he looked down at his tough, dusty boot.

"It's not about courage," Redlock had once told him, "it's about *necessity*. When you have to face something impossible, you'll find you will – because you don't have a choice."

Chearl, panniers, healers' kit.

Moving with incredible care, he shifted on his hands and backside over to the poor, dead beast that had carried him from Xenok. The insects rose resentfully at his approach, several larger things scampered – and slithered – into the grass. He didn't want to think about it. In the uppermost pannier: road rations, empty waterskin, spare foot coverings, herb bag, dry kindling.

Javelins.

Dried fruit took the taste of blood from his mouth; its sweetness gave him a sudden rush of energy. He had a momentary flash of Amethea, passing him a piece only hours ago, but blinked back the image and turned instead to tearing his linen foot bindings into long, narrow strips.

The last strip he tore in half, folded into two pads, and stuck both between his teeth.

One deep breath.

Two.

Snapping the front of the shaft was easy – it just hurt. The wound was wide and ragged. Snapping the back was awkward and had him sobbing, grinding his teeth into the linen.

But he did it. Leaving the centre of the arrow still in his flesh, he took the pads from his teeth and added a scattering of herb to his own saliva.

Oh, yes. Graduate me now.

Carefully, he bound them, front and back, to hold the arrow in place.

Then, shaking, he retched again, pieces of bloody, half-chewed fruit.

As his coughing subsided, he wiped water from his eyes and focused instead on his ankle. He needed a piece of wood long enough to make a crutch, but the javelins were too short and, this far from the river, what trees that grew were stunted and bent by the endless wind.

The distance to the trade-road was suddenly tremendous.

Despair threatened him – he couldn't walk, he had no water. How – ?

Necessity, Redlock had said.

But what he did have…

He and Amethea had both been carrying small bundles of dry firewood. The trade-road sites were tended and deliveries regular – but out here, wood was difficult to come by. Only a little – just enough to cook on – but maybe…

They had been going to make camp in the Monument itself – a kids' adventure. Funny how crazed that now seemed.

Bound across the back of the chearl's saddle and covered by a length of waxed calico, a small bundle of wood. A couple of pieces were maybe the length of his arm, but again the Gods were smiling – one piece provided him with a forked rest for his armpit and if he was careful, he could bind it to the javelin shaft…

It wasn't perfect – the wood was too dry to take his weight for long – but he bound it as tight as he could with what remained of his linen and prayed that it would hold to the road, at least.

By the time he was done, the sun was rising into a clear, bright summer sky.

His mouth was parched. He drained the last drops from his waterskin and slung it over his shoulder, just in case. Then he took his fruit and his herb bag and bade a farewell to his silent chearl.

He knew he would never make it.

5: LIVING THE NIGHTMARE

THE WANDERER, ROVIARATH.

With a final reminder of his offer of help, the Bard left Ecko alone.

To think.

Ecko waited until the door had closed, then picked up the bowl of food. For a moment, he was tempted to sling it across the room, but his belly grumbled again and, gracelessly, he started to shovel it down. He'd probably give himself indigestion, but he was fucking starving, and twenty kinds of freaked out, and frankly, he didn't care. Hell, for all he knew, his stomach wasn't even real.

This was fucking ridiculous. Wasn't it?

Yeah, like now the shock is settling in...

His brain was doing a wall-of-death, spinning and chaos and noise. Some part of him wanted to jump screaming from the window and just pray that he'd land with a splatter on the south bank of the Thames...

...wake up in a nice, safe hospital. White walls and blankets and shit. He'd even deal with the intravenous happy juice, at least until they came to get him.

And the window was right *there*, for chrissakes.

Right.

There.

But that would be quitting. And if there was one thing Ecko wasn't, it was a quitter.

He paced the length of the pattern-woven rug, kicking angrily at bits of broken table. He spooned more stew. The rocklight slid over him as if it were trying to make him welcome, and his skin shifted with its colour.

The stew, whatever it was, was unexpectedly good – he found himself cleaning the bowl with the breadcrust. It was rich and warm, and it left a feeling of fullness, a luxury that seemed to uncoil through muscle and nerve. He'd been a child the last time he'd eaten anything like it.

It slowed him, helped him clear his head.

Think.

His frenetic pacing eased, then stopped altogether. He put the bowl back on the tray, and tried to focus.

So, here I am then: the Little Pub on the Prairie.

He turned back to the window, to the starless sky and the batshit moonlight. The urge to jump had faded, but the smoulder of resentment had not.

Just remember: I ain't your bitch, bitch, an' I ain't gonna be a rat in your maze. I'm gonna beat this.

From somewhere outside, there came a throbbing of hooves, a squeak of wheels that retreated into the night. He groaned.

Horses? You gotta be kidding me...

For a moment, Ecko had a horrible vision of trying to ride one – he could ride a bike, but anything with legs was taking the fucking piss already. *Jesus, Eliza, you're not funny...*

Chances of success at...

Without warning, he was hit by a return of his claustrophobia, a rising, panicked mental shriek. *This can't be happening!* He needed to understand, he needed to know where he was, how he got here, how he fit in – or didn't – how much free will he had to make his own decisions. Was Eliza watching him, marking him, managing him? Could she pull his strings and make him dance? He had his start point, but how did he get even the basics – a cache of kit, a hiding place?

A fucking *map*?

What the hell was really out there?

For a second, his boosted adrenaline meshed with his fear and they screamed engine loud, thundering a pulse beat of blood in his ears. He had a sudden mouthful of stew and bile.

I have to – !

Have to – !

No!

Choking on the effort, he stayed where he was, fists clenched, fighting the rage impulse back under control. He stood, shaking, swallowing. His throat burned. He could almost hear Eliza laughing at him.

Chances of successful adjustment: 17.84%... 17.83, .82...

But she could laugh all she wanted, he was gonna sort this thing, and she could just sit there and fucking *watch*.

Somehow, he was gonna do this shit.

He was standing at the long window by the desk when there was another knock on the door.

Outside, the moons shone silent, alien and compelling. They lit the square and faded sign at the foot of the building's short foregarden. It had no design, no creatures rampant or rearing, it said only "The Wanderer" and it squeaked back and forth in a breeze that tickled his skin through imperfections in the window seals. Tight streets were paved in glistening cobblestones; an empty square seemed to indicate some sort of gathering or market space. Figures hurried, heads down, cloaked and hooded – every fucking one of them looked like the poster boy for the local Guild of Assassins.

Willya look at that. Ecko thought, with a grin. *I'm gonna fit right in.*

The knock came again. Still flickering with the last shreds of his antagonism, Ecko took three steps across the rug and banged the door open. He snarled, "What?"

Karine stood outside. With her was an older guy, slightly stoop shouldered and only a little taller than Ecko himself. He was in his fifties or more, with a worn, sun-leathered face and brown eyes flecked with an odd orange-gold.

Tiger's eyes.

Behind him, there was a low-ceilinged, brick-and-beam passageway that hinted at more doors and some sort of stairway. There was a small, moonlit window, but nothing else.

Karine elbowed the brown-eyed man forwards.

"Ecko, this is Kale," she said. "Kale's just started with us, he's still finding his – ah – feet."

Ecko said nothing, didn't move. He watched them, his oculars in overdrive and a peculiar, nebulous wariness starting to prickle at the back of his neck.

Kale's core temperature was wrong, too high.

And as he met Ecko's empty gaze, it jumped.

It *what*?

Ecko resisted the instinctive, wary urge to back up. Instead, he stood poised on his toes, blocking the doorway, waiting for the assault, the change, the demon, the dragon, the manifest deity, the whatever-the-fuck it was...

Yeah, you just bring it the fuck on...

Right now, he'd welcome the release.

But the man said, quite affably, "Ecko. How was the food?"

"Fan-fuckin'-tastic." Ecko didn't budge, didn't back down. His adrenaline shivered, eager. "So what the hell're you? Security?"

"He's downstairs," the man said, smiling. "I'm the cook."

"You like vindaloo?"

"What?" Kale didn't get the joke. They watched each other, unspeaking.

"Ecko, get out of the doorway, for Gods' sakes." Karine chuckled and slithered with remarkable dexterity around where Kale was standing. "If you're going to be all bristly and paranoid, at least retreat far enough to let me get the dishes." She flicked an eyebrow, all pert indignance. "Unless you want to clean them yourself."

Ecko blinked.

Karine's brusque affection apparently gave her an uncanny ability to take charge of a situation – before he'd even realised it, she'd slipped past him and was picking up the tray. "How you coping, anyway?" She winked at him. "Has Roderick started pontificating yet?"

Huh? Ecko was getting overwhelmed, confused, he didn't need this. Keeping both of them in sight, he retreated from the doorway. There was a whole new set of social rules and shit going on here...

Chrissakes, this just wasn't *fair*!

Their inability to understand his banter bewildered him. And they hadn't reacted to his appearance – it was like they hadn't even noticed. His enhancements had been deliberately crafted, bought with pain and endurance beyond human limits – he'd given everything to look the way he did. On some level, it was supposed to give him *space*, for chrissakes, emotionally and physically...

Yet neither Kale nor Karine seemed to give a shit.

His oculars still working, scanning, searching, watching around him, watching Kale's every move, every flicker, he reached for something else to say.

"Yeah, he's crazy. I'm crazy. We're all fuckin' crazy. An' you didn't answer the question."

Kale replied, quite calmly, "Why do you have no scent?"

"Chris*sakes.*" Ecko was lost, he was out of place, he was

baffled, his adrenaline was hovering on the edge of a full-on ass-kicking – there was a smouldering volcano of pressure under his skin and these two were just bumbling the fuck about like there was nothing the matter. His oculars targeted the tray, the cook's eye, ear and heart in four successive seconds.

He snarled, "Look –"

"Ecko, ease down before you strain something," Karine told him. "The Bard's gone to sort out a place for you to sleep – a space of your own for as long as you need it. And I'm here – we're both here – to help you. This is The Wanderer, and you've landed on your feet, well and truly. If you'd calm down for two ticks, you'd realise that."

He glared at her. "Don't fucking patronise me." The moonlight gave her hair a bright brown shine. She was exceptionally pretty, but he could never think like that, never go there, never again.

"Oh all right, enough," she said. There was an edge of irritation in her voice. "No one's going to stop you leaving, if that's what you really want. But you need to understand, acclimatise. And let's face it – where better than the pub?" She flashed him a grin. "Where else can you explore without having to sleep in ribbon-town inns; eat the best damned food in the Varchinde without having to hunt it yourself? Where else can you find every luxury traded by tithehall and marketplace? Where else can you see something new every morning? You stay here, Ecko, you'll see the whole world – and the road-pirates won't pick on you and the beasties of the deeper plains won't think you're lunch." She winked at him. "*And* you'll get to drink in your local every night."

"Answer the fucking *question*."

Karine said, "He told you – he's the cook."

Kale's core temperature jumped again, it seemed to flare like rage, almost like Ecko's adrenaline. Ecko snorted. "So – what – you cook dinner with your fiery temper?"

That made them exchange a glance; something passed between them that Ecko couldn't begin to fathom. His adrenals shivered again and he found himself on the balls of his feet. He'd touched something – but if they didn't fucking cough this shit up, whatever it was, then he was outta here.

He'd take his chances.

The cook shrugged, seemed almost resigned. His shoulders slumped further, then he said, "Will you trust us if I do?"

"Sure." Ecko glared, tasted stew, swallowed.

Kale nodded, slowly.

"Please understand," he said, "that I was born like this. When I was younger, it was a jest, a game. And then I got older, and it wasn't funny any more. I won't hurt you, but..."

Born like this...

The heat started in Kale's skull, in the back of his neck, ran like liquid fire into his face and down his spine. Patchy fur burned his skin as it spread. His shoulders hunched, his face twisted around his elongating teeth. His arms gnarled, strengthened, his toes and fingers knotted and claws tore through his flesh. His knees bent inside out and he crouched forwards, the end of his lengthening spine burst from his back, lashing furiously.

There was a snarl that sounded like pain.

The transition took seconds. Then a feral, savage thing with asymmetrical green eyes and fangs as long as knives bubbled pure hate into Ecko's face.

Holy fucking shit!

Despite himself, Ecko was retreating. His adrenaline shrieked but he didn't know whether to scream, puke, run like fuck or kick the thing's head clean out the fucking window.

What the hell...?

And then it was gone and Kale was standing there, scratching at his neck where fur had melted into skin. He was shuddering violently, steadying himself on the wall. He said, "Pain is a stern teacher."

The phrase was a like a friend.

A stern teacher.

Ecko knew... *knew* what that meant, how it felt...

But Kale was still speaking. "If you ever need to stop me, you need white metal. It upsets the balance of the beast in my blood – the wounds don't heal."

Karine said softly, "Kale came here to find help, Ecko. And we can help you too –"

"Just wait... wait." Inundated with impossibility, swamped by everything that was happening around him, Ecko'd backed right up to the wall. "What're you, some kinda werewolf? With *those* moons? How the fuck does that – ?"

"It's not the moons," Kale said. "The beast... gets away from me. I came here to find help, to learn control before..." His expression twisted, but not with anger. "I suppose we're all crazed, in our own ways."

Karine said gently, "Believe it or not, you're among friends."

Ecko said, his mind still reeling, "Shit, this place is a fucking loony bin."

She grinned. "Kale's a beast. I'm a political outcast – small matter of an – ah – admirer I really didn't want to marry. Sera, downstairs, is a Games Champion – he killed nine opponents in a bout he was told to lose. Silfe's a runaway. Everyone here has a history."

"I feel so much better."

"Look, we'll leave you in peace for a bit longer," Karine said. "You've got a lot to take in. I'll go see how the Bard is doing with your room. In the meantime –" she went to lay a hand on his arm, but he backed up "– trust us. Whatever else happens from this point on, this can be your home. If you want it."

Ecko's room was high under the vaulted beams and looked like something off some medieval film set. The wood was warm and rich – floor, beams, an old table and bench. There was leather on the seat coverings and pale wax candles. Wooden shutters covered the window and an old rug covered the floor. Between the beams, the walls were brickwork, decorated with old pictures, and with hooks where the Bard had taken down his "souvenirs".

Half enchanted and half scathing, he checked it for hiding places, verified and listed his equipment, swung himself onto a beam and waited.

As soon as this place settled down, he was gonna get some fucking bearings, case it from penthouse to basement. He needed understanding, needed to know what was out there. And he needed equipment. Currency. Weapons. Food. Maps. Kit to flee with – or to build a cache.

Too many surprises. He wasn't being caught with his kacks down again.

Carefully draping the folds and curves of his cloak, he dissolved silently into the room's darkness.

And he waited.

It was warm.

Locked into his stealth position, he remained still as the building slowly softened into silence around him. He heard doors opening and closing, voices laughing outside. After a while, feet moved up and down the creaking stairs and Ecko labelled them mentally – the implacable stamp that had to be Sera, Karine quick and light footed, Kale unhurried. The Bard's boots were easy to identify – though heavier than he might have guessed.

Upstairs, doors banged. One by one, the tavern's staff returned to their rooms and settled for the night.

As the quiet swelled, his throat started to close with rising pressure. He began to doubt, pointless fears dancing at the corners of his awareness. *Am I dreaming? Am I fucking dead?*

He told himself it didn't matter either way – he was here and he'd better just get on with it.

Food. Weapons.

Understanding.

The doubts laughed at him again, in the darkness they sounded like Eliza, like Lugan. *Chances of successful adjustment increasing: 34.74%*

Would he even recognise what he needed? He was lost, betrayed, naked in the field once more. He was missing the cornerstones of his existence. No plastics, no metal. No communication, no information. No drugs, no pharmaceuticals. No branding, no packaging, no labels. Where did they get clean water? Where did they go to the john?

Mockery rang increasingly loud in the hush. The room's very simplicity became unsettling. He clung to his beam as if everything else would fade into nothing around him.

Where the fuck was he?

A feminine voice cursing made him start. He heard the Bard's rich, distinctive chuckle, and the faint glimmer of light beyond his room went out.

Sudden, utter blackness.

Silence.

He was swallowed by them, abruptly alone, so fucking alone – an illegal alien in a crappy backwater culture. He froze, stock-still. Childhood fears – he dare not move or speak or turn, because if he acknowledged the beast of the darkness, it would pounce...

He was holding his breath.

His heatseeker showed him only infinitesimal, subtle shifts that made the darkness deep as nightmare – there wasn't enough illumination for his starlites.

He couldn't even see himself. Only the wood under his fingertips told him he existed, that Eliza hadn't flicked the big red switch marked "OFF".

Was she watching him? Out there in the darkness? Could she feel what he felt? Was this... was this supposed to teach him a fucking *lesson* of some kind?

Yeah.

You.

Bitch.

The snarl of defiance was reflex, it rippled through him like the first whisper of the tsunami. His expression twisted, he inhaled and his adrenals kicked. The lightning thrill of energy slashed a sudden, whetted grin across his face. Challenge *him*, would she? The muscles through his back and legs coiled, anticipating.

Were you fucking laughing? At me?

Sudden, sharp focus. Comprehension. *Sartori.*

There was no fear here!

The blackness was home, it was his and he understood it – he *was* the beast in the fucking darkness. It had been his cover, his cloak, his friend, his best weapon. One more thing to add to the list of shit he'd left behind...

...ohhhh yeah, the fucking *light.*

No streetlights, no aircars, no hoverdrones, no cameras, no fucking *electricity.*

He found himself trembling, elation and adrenaline making the corners of his vision spark with realisation – a realisation of total, unmatched ability.

He was unique; he was all-powerful, superhuman. He could pull shit this world had never even fucking *heard* of. All the dark, Bogeyman dreams of his childhood were here. They were in the darkness round him.

Only waiting for him to take hold of them.

Oh yeah.

As he dropped silently from the beam and carefully paced the distance to the unseen door, his blade-sharp grin cast a black reflection in his thoughts. This was it all fucking right.

This was Living The Nightmare.

* * *

Turning through an approximate L-shape of ground, The Wanderer was too simple to even offer him a challenge.

It slept oblivious – the only warmth a blur of feline, creeping on silent paws. The critter's ignorance amused him. Navigating by heat, touch, simple mathematics, years of recon memorised the layout and brought him down to the bar.

Pub.

Taproom.

What-*ever*.

Yeah, like whoever designed this should've left neat, clearly labelled ration packs laying in obscure corners, plus hard cash and some sorta silent missile weapon that didn't involve *feathers*.

Hey – and how about a couple of handy medikits and a ten-foot fucking *pole*?

He emerged through a door behind the bar and his anti-daz flicked nanosecond irises. The taproom was bright, cross-hatched moonlight streamed through two front windows like the Bard had parked slap-bang in the middle of Leicester Square.

His crouch was instinctive, but the room was empty.

Motionless, he scanned.

Wood. More fucking wood than a hot first date. Barrels, tables, benches, wine racks, floor. This place'd go up like a fucking Fawkes' Night party. For a second, temptation gibbered at him, dancing like a lighted match... Then he got a fucking grip and shut the door.

His adrenals were waning, unused by fight or flight, their fading left him cold and hollow. Shivers twitched his shoulders. The colours of his skin squirmed under the light and he swallowed nausea.

The taproom was silent, flanked by a gazillion alcoves you could hide a fucking army in – but his heatseeker picked up only the fading warmth in the fireplace. Next to its faint glow, a table was scattered with paper, curled into rolls or weighted with oddments. His telescopics picked out tiny, intricately detailed brown writing – sketches, even – but no map.

Remote sounds tickled the outer ranges of his hearing. Voices? Feet? Horses' hooves again, somehow sounding wrong... Shouting and a sudden clatter that might've been a fight. More feet in a pounding and familiar rhythm.

Oddly reassured, he checked quickly for currency – gold, surely! When he found nothing, he snaked onto the bar top and crouched there, gargoyle still.

But there was no cash, no glitter of coinage. No pumps or optics, but hey, that one was obvious. *Still* no fucking metal.

He found wooden barrels and racks of pottery. And he found papers, loose rolls in differing colours of ribbon – they were off-white and rough to his touch. When he unrolled one, he found it was etched with some kind of tally marks, an elaborate record system he couldn't begin to fathom. And under them, there was a squat, locked box – a box that his agile fingers took less than six seconds to prise open.

Whaddaya know. I hit the Vegas jackpot.

It was full of *stuff*.

Fragments of bright stone, ceramics and wood, pinches of powder in twists of fabric, white stuff that might've been horn or bone, jewellery braided from thread and colour. And most common of all, a kind of solid resin that looked almost like amber, almost like plastic. It was oddly smooth to the touch.

It wasn't the only thing that he didn't understand.

He went through the box, carefully.

Some of the resin was carved, or dyed, or both; some of it was just loose chunks. Some of it was crafted into more jewellery, or tools. Some of it had fibres running through it in elaborate patterns.

Laying a pendant thing back in the box, Ecko looked up and

around the room, a realisation suddenly crystallising.

Jesus shit...

Hung on the walls and pillars was a half-ton of local swag –
swords, scythes, tools, big ol' spears with heads like half moons
and axes the size of his head. Reaching out, he took one of the
smaller blades down.

And it was the *same*.

It was the same resinous, wood-warm, glass-smooth, metal-
hard stuff that was in the box, incredibly light with a pattern
of fibres running up its centre – reinforcement or decoration.
It wasn't sharp, though his sensitive fingers found old notches.

What the hell was this stuff? Was it like their gold, or steel?
Or both? Now he looked round properly, he could see that it
made everything from weapons to rivets to cutlery – whatever
the fuck this stuff was, it was critical.

Curious, he took hold of the blade with both hands and
applied a little pressure.

With a sharp retort in the still air, it shattered, fragments
flying, but fibres holding the two halves crazily together like a
snapped limb.

Over his head, there was the scraping of furniture.

Which room?

You stupid fucking –

Kale.

Cursing Eliza as the great-grandmother of all head-fucking
bitches, he threw the busted sword back onto its hooks, closed
the box, aimed a savage axe-kick at the pillar, then picked up
the bits – all of them – and evaporated like a nightmare in the
glare of a halogen torch.

6: FLESH UNKNOWN

Feren!

Her skull was coming apart, Amethea lifted shaking hands to her face and found crusted pain under her fingers.

Her hair was matted with it, it was gritted in her eyes.

Feren?

She tried to move; her legs betrayed her. She fell hard to a stone floor, heat and darkness clanging loud in her head.

The impact had split her eyebrow. She was wobbly – the gash was wide and shallow; it had bled profusely, but was not serious.

With each clatter of pain, images came like echoes: the plains, the Monument, the... *creature*...

The tears came too, as they had to. She let herself cry for a few moments, then, irritated, she scrubbed at her wet face with her palms. Her tears washed the blood from her eyes and face.

"Feren?"

She ground her gaze into focus and looked about her.

"'Fraid not, love."

The voice startled her – she'd no idea that there was anyone else in the room. It had come from behind her, deep and masculine, the accent utterly strange. Stumbling up to her knees and wiping her face she turned to see who it was.

Her head hammered like her chearl's thudding hooves and she remembered...

Leave the male to die, bring this one... There is need of a healer.

"Who...? What happened to...?" She stumbled over her words.

Heavy shoulders shrugged, uninterested in the question. Above them, a tangle of dark hair framed tanned, work-roughened skin, spotted with ingrained dirt like that of a miner, or a drover walking too long at the end of a column of beasts.

"Nice of you to drop in," the man said.

She stared. Short beard, full mouth, half-smile; eyes as dark as that creature's had been, but flecked with fire. Nervousness shivered her skin. She had no idea who he was, but he compelled her for reasons she couldn't even begin to comprehend. Unconsciously, she raised a hand to her blood-streaked hair. *Who was he?*

He made her heart tremble in her chest.

Other realisations tolled through the clangour – a tiny chamber, floor and walls of worn rock slabs, but air tense with unidentified heat; pack and belt-knife gone, but pouches and neck thongs untouched; hair and garments, sticking uncomfortably with sweat, blood and fear.

There is need of a healer.

"Who are you? What happened to Feren?"

"He flew to the moon, sweetheart." One callused hand extended to help her to her feet. The fingers were hot and strong, several had been broken at some time; he wore heavy, white-metal rings. There was old dirt under his nails. "C'mon, love, you've got a lot to catch up on."

His tone was gentle, but those *eyes*...

"Hold on... hold on a moment." She held up her hands

to ward him off. "I'm leech and apothecary to the hospice in Xenok, Feren's my 'prentice. I – we – came out to the Monument for taer and there was this... thing –"

"The stallion? Don't let him upset you, he's just my – ah – watchdog." He lifted her chin, made her look up at him, smiled. "Like all fanatics – more ideal than intellect."

"He shot – !"

"I'm sorry about your mate... but he didn't suffer. You, little lady – you're important."

He didn't suffer. For a moment, Feren's death held her poised and breathless, disbelieving – but this man, whoever he was, was looking at her, into her, holding her heart and soul in his gaze. The flecks of fire in his eyes were warming. She sniffed, like a child, and his callused thumb stroked a stray tear from her face.

"It's all over, love, all over. No need to worry now. Let's get you a wash, and some clean kit – look at those big blue eyes and all that pale hair, you're too pretty to be this much of a mess."

Feren had fallen to the grasses, his hand gone from hers. "No..." She shook her head, breaking the contact – the thud of renewed pain helped her focus. "And... anyway... get *off* me."

For a moment, it seemed the man chewed the side of his mouth. Then he caught her eyes again and smiled at her.

"Poor love, bloody stallion hit you like a wrecking ball – you're confused."

She was backing away – but the chamber was eerie, too close, too small. The sweat on her skin was like a glaze. "And why's it so hot in here?"

"All right, all right, look." He reached to close the gap between them, but she twitched back further – the stone in the wall was warm. "Baythunder – that great beastie you met outside – is barking, right? He shot your mate, liberated your chearl and left you with a dirty great clonk on your skull. You can't get home to Xenok like you are."

She found she was looking at him, feeling the warmth of his sympathy and watching his expression. As he reached again to brush the tears and blood and dirt from her face, she allowed him to touch her – and his heat shot through her flesh.

She caught her breath.

"That's more like it," he said softly. His smile deepened, showed the tips of his teeth.

"Who are you?" The question was quiet, her attention was all in his eyes.

"Maugrim," he said. "I've had other names – but that one... suits me." His hand stroked the side of her throat. "Welcome to the world's new beginning."

There is need of a healer.

For a moment, she held the strangest feeling that something had gone amiss. The plains, the Monument, a hand slipping from hers...

But she couldn't remember. Maugrim's hand was in her bloodied hair, his eyes like embers. He closed his fingers about the strands and pulled her head back – abrupt, not quite painful. She found herself breathing hard, his fire lighting her blood, a sudden, hot sensation of *want*...

"All you have to do," he said, "is help me."

She heard herself answer him, "I'll help you. What can I do?"

The predatory smile broke through his beard like a blade.

Amethea dreamed.

She dreamed of heat. And lust. And passion. And power.

When she awoke, her vision was so full of flame she had to squint to realise the small stone chamber was dim, the rocklight faltering.

The palette beside her empty.

She was still wet, sweetly aching from the repeated impact of his body on hers, skin and sheets were soaked in sweat.

The thought of him brought a lightning shiver of adrenaline, a rush of excitement, exultation that was new.

She sat up, his smile on her face – and there was no headache. Raising her fingertip to the wound in her eyebrow, she was unsurprised to find it gone – a scar like a sear in its place.

Heal and Harm, little lady, the oldest rule.

She had been going somewhere – had lost something, was looking for something? A faint sense of disquiet tickled her cheek like a moth... then – *flash* – was gone.

Whatever it was had been cleansed, inside and out. For the moment, her wants were assuaged, she needed only to brush work-roughened fingers over smooth sheets and recall the blaze of Maugrim's need.

He had gone; he remained. She could smell him on her skin. Her head was full of him.

Disdaining to wrap her slender nakedness, she stood up.

About her, the chamber was even smaller than she'd thought, perhaps five paces in each direction. If she raised her arm, she could touch the ceiling. The walls and floor were all flat stone, wide regular shapes set in soil, smaller shapes packed in corners. In places, there were carved patterns, but the markings were unclear in the faltering light. That she was underground was evident – but where?

The air was hot and still. This was not the vast rock networks of the Kartiah Mountains, nor the open stone quarries of Belegandyne or Darash. She laid a hand against the wall, feeling the blood-warmth. The room was too small, yet there was a vastness around it that lost her; it felt...

In spite of the heat, shivers prickled her skin. A sudden, hollow rush sucked the memories of Maugrim from her and left her standing, minute and utterly alone, a fragmentary mote against the all-might of the stone arrayed about her.

It felt like a tomb, ancient, vast and infinite. It felt like a church. It felt as though Maugrim's mesmeric presence were too tiny to be noticed.

It felt as though it was *waiting*.

With a shudder as deep as her soul, she pulled away from the stonework, picked up the sheet and cloaked herself in it. She was chilled through, inexplicably miniscule and terrified.

She *had* been looking for something – !

"You're awake, love." The wall was rolling closed behind him. "I've got you some water and some clean kit."

In his presence, the chamber was warm, her fears ashes. The sheet tumbled to the floor and she welcomed him with open arms and lips.

He kissed her briefly, squeezing a buttock, and pushed her back.

"You need to wash and dress, sweetheart, and quickly. And you need to listen."

"Of course." She took the jug, the garments he had chosen for her and hoped she could please him. The embers in his eyes stroked her naked skin, leaving the warm touch of trailing fingertips.

He turned away.

"You're a healer, little lady, herbalist, apothecary and teacher. And Xenotian – meaning you've worked your sweet arse off for those qualifications, and you're tougher than you look." He turned back with that predatory smile, taking the sting from the comment. Then he said, "Answer me something, love. Does it ever get to you?"

"Get to me?" The phrase was unfamiliar. She took a cloth from the jug and tried to unclot the bloodstreaks from her hair. Chill water ran down her hot skin, evaporating before it stained the floor. The air thickened.

Maugrim raised one hand and his metal rings flashed in the rocklight – one was the fanged skull of some mystery creature, one a grey-black stone that gleamed oddly metallic.

"Get to you, love." His expression twisted, though the casual tone of his voice didn't change. "The whiners, the needers, the hypochondriacs, the neurotics, the weak-willed and the desperate. 'I'm depressed, I'm lonely, I'm fat, I've got to stop smoking – but I'm too bloody feeble to do it myself.' They don't try, they don't learn. They wallow in self-pity. They come to you so you'll take it away – but they don't really want to give it up. Because it's all the meaning they have." His smile deepened, a rush of warmth made her gasp. "C'mon love – you have them here too. It's not wrong to resent them."

Resent – !

In the heart of the heat, a flare of shock and shame – then all lost to wonder. She found herself laughing like release; she wanted to kiss him.

"Yes, yes, sometimes." How had he understood? The darkest corner of her healer's soul – illuminated by his firelight and it was all right, it was all *right*. "When your life is others… sometimes you do just want to say to them –"

"Get a fucking grip!" He took her shoulders, enthused at her. "You're no saint, little priestess. In your heart, you're just like I am. Don't you look at them and just… wish…"

The sentence tailed into a silence laden with suggestion. He smiled, kissed her, withdrew. She wanted to reach to him, to – *oh Gods* – tell him the secret place he'd just touched, but his gaze had gone. It was on the chamber, stroking the faint marks on the walls.

"So many years as other people's confidence," he said softly, "their crutch. And then I became obsolete, outmoded by a prescription. Now, here…" When he turned back, his smile was a welcoming campfire on a chill night. "Here, little priestess, I can do *magic*. Miracles. I can make this world anew!"

She watched him. He was compelling, exotic, his words alien. Transfixed, her response was a whisper, almost as if she feared what he'd say. "If you're such a healer, why do you need me?"

"Finish dressing, and quick." He grinned, predatory and savage as a Varchinde bweao, and his gaze flicked to her eyebrow. "I need you because I can't heal flesh, sweetheart. And they keep *dying*."

Dying.

Against Maugrim's ardour, she couldn't focus the thought.

As her last garment was laced, he caught her upper arm in a grip like red-hot metal and propelled her from the chamber. Fragments of rocklight threw random shadows over stone walls. When she stumbled over her skirts, he gripped her harder, marching her through a tight, twisted underground maze. In places, he had to stoop, hunching his heavy shoulders against the stone; she was small enough to walk upright – just – but stubbed her toes repeatedly on an uneven floor.

Dying.

"Stop, Maugrim, stop. Wait…"

He pushed forwards, took a corner, a side passage, another. His hold on her arm was merciless.

"Where are we going? Who – ?" *Who keeps dying?*

"No time for explanations, love. I needed a healer – need you to do something for me."

"Do what?" She tried to halt, tried to tug her arm out of his grip. "What do you – ?"

He spun her against his strength, kissed her with a compelling brutality, then drew back to smile at her.

"You'll do what you're told, sweetheart."

Her body surged in response – she couldn't help it. When she kissed him back, curling against him in silent need, he loosened his grip, stroked her chin with the back of his knuckles. His rings were hot.

"Trust me," he said softly. He was fervent, alight with belief. "Your culture's stagnating, love, no challenge, no growth, no progress – and I know what that can do. I can change it, fix it. But you have to let me *finish*!"

"Finish what?"

He leaned his weight against the stone beside them and it swung inwards. Amethea felt a rush of air cooling her skin but not cold enough to be fresh. Beyond the door, she sensed, lay a large, dark chamber – a cavernous belly of potential.

A crystal-cold voice, oddly atonal, said, "Maugrim. You have brought an apothecary."

"I can't see shit."

"I shall give you light."

Amethea listened, but the chamber was silent. A moment later, white rocklight flooded the passageway.

She blinked, holding an arm to shield her eyes.

He thrust her through the doorway. Unable to see, she caught her foot in the hem of her skirt and tripped, fell hands-down to the floor.

He was over her, his strange, black boots surrounded by...

Metal. Tiny, round shapes of white-metal, a swath of them across a flat, stone floor. Instinctively, she realised this room was not part of the passageways – it was newer, larger, colder. As she blinked dazzle spots from her vision, she reached for one of the discs – flat, with a hole through the centre. It was one of dozens, hundreds, casually discarded across soil and stone.

Riches to make her head reel.

As if she had blundered through some saga and found his treasure hoard.

Maugrim leaned down, caught her arm and hauled her to her feet.

"This is for you, little priestess," he said, gently. "As much wealth as the world has ever seen – as long as you help me."

She looked up from the disc in her hand.

In the centre of the chamber stood a young man, rigid and silent. His back was to the door and the light reflected oddly from his skin. Scattered haphazardly about him were other, much larger, shapes of metal, utterly nonsensical. They were stained and dirty, some of them had powdery brown rot growing across their edges. The dark, liquid splotches had spread onto the floor, where she could see discarded cloths, oddly shaped tools, unfamiliar liquid containers. At the room's far wall, one long, low shape was covered by a waxed calico sheet.

There was no sign of the owner of the voice.

The chamber smelled strange. Blood, metal – and a tongue-tang of something she didn't recognise, something that tasted... *wrong*.

When Maugrim touched her shoulder, she lifted the hem of her skirts and picked her way across the floor.

The young man didn't move.

As she came closer, she slowed, stopped, stared.

He had no skin, no hair. Rather than flesh, he was a sculpture of carefully shaped metal plates. Over his skull, across his face, down the strong lines of his body, he wore an exquisitely detailed carapace, intricate and beautiful, metal fused to him as if he were a saga golem.

The work was not the same as the metal on the floor. It was Kartian – crafted with only the extraordinary detail that the mountains' artisans could create. Raised and trained in all but absolute darkness, they had a sense of touch no Grasslander could match.

"He can't hurt you, love." Maugrim's reassurance let her step closer.

Closer still.

Then she stopped, horror crawling across her skin.

Under the plates, his skinless muscle was raw, red flesh blistering, bubbling through the cracks. She could see searing torment in every line of his being, feel a silent scream that came from his twisted stance, his fast, shallow breath. His eyes – eyelids plated like everywhere else – were closed, but behind them, he twitched visions of agony.

His lips were sealed with a large, single plate. The skinned muscle of his face was torn where he'd tried to scream.

Oh, Goddess...

Black scabs split like lava, never healing, leaking trickles of red and yellow suffering. There was a caked pool around his feet. Even as she watched, a fresh swell of blisters erupted, rippling across one cheekbone. They oozed, swelled, burst, subsided. The plates shifted. She heard him whimper between lips that would never move again.

And it spread, flowed down his face and throat in a caress of anguish. Under his plating, his flayed body boiled as if he were being cooked alive.

Hand over her mouth, denying tears of revulsion, she understood he was trying to scab and heal – and couldn't. He was one, vast, conscious wound. Maugrim had replaced his skin with pure pain.

There was a smile engraved on the plate that sealed his mouth.

They keep dying.

"Nonononono..." Her denial was unconscious, she was shaking, backing away. Every healer's instinct she had told her to do one thing.

A heavy, ringed hand landed on her shoulder.

"No time for cold feet, love, he needs you – and soon." The hand was warm, it steadied her. "I get the empathy thing, you feel his pain and you want to help. I'm telling you, you can. He's a prototype, strong; a fusing of flesh and metal into the perfect warrior, the perfect conductor. Amethea." She turned to stare at him as he used her name. "I believe in what I'm doing, I believe in you. Heal him. Complete the fusion. If you do, we can make the world a new and better place."

The world's fine... isn't she?

The thought was tiny, lost under the potence of Maugrim's

passion and vision. What was one soul in pain against his belief? She ached to please him, to win his approval and earn his touch. Almost without realising, she yearned towards him and he smiled at her, igniting her blood in a flash of pure, physical hunger...

He turned away.

The young man's eyes flicked open. Cool, grey. He couldn't – or didn't dare – move, but his gaze caught Amethea's and his plea needed no words. Her heart convulsed in her chest, she swallowed tears. She *couldn't* leave him like this... it was pure horror, way beyond Heal and Harm, beyond the ethics of the hospice that had raised her. Somewhere in her soul settled flakes of revulsion.

But – !

Maugrim pushed a dirty fingernail under one of the plates buried in the blistered, skinless mess of the young man's face and tore it free. Blood welled in the hole, then ran down the myriad cracks to his jaw.

Under the horrific metal smile, his upper lip tried to curl, tugging bloodily at his bared muscle. His look was pure insolence – skinned alive he may be, but he was still fighting.

"This is crazed," Amethea said softly. She was torn, she ached to help. Words tumbled from her. "Even if I wanted to, I couldn't fix this. His skin can't heal. You have to take them off. And... I don't know how he's even alive, blood loss, shock..." She heard herself sob. "How did you do this? It's madness – how did you – ?"

"I call it 'magic'," Maugrim said quietly. He held the tiny metal scale out to her but she shrank back. "A little psychology, a little craftsmanship, a little luck." He chuckled, took her wrist, pressed the plate into the skin of her palm. "This world has forgotten many things, little priestess, but they can be found – the elements and the Powerflux can be awakened. And then they can be channelled and moulded; a new might wrought from power that's vast and ancient and screaming for release." His voice thrummed with heat. "And that power is *mine*, it was given to *me*. It lives in my skin, in my very heart." She blinked at him, not really understanding but carried by the force of his belief. "Look, 'Thea, this one's a fighter. Pain, loss, terror, defiance – they're teaching him strength, perception. He should be dead, but I can channel the very Powerflux through his flesh, just as I can channel it through myself, through you – down here, the elements are *alive*." For a moment, they were eyes on eyes, then Maugrim closed her fingers over the metal. "You'll heal him, sweetheart. A fusion of flesh and metal – a new creature that will save your world, that will bring to light the lore you have left to rot. You know you have to!"

Firelight. Scorching. Stone blackening. Her home was burning. But she was freed – from the sheltered life of the hospice and its rules and its ethics and its litanies and its moral restrictions. Her past crumbled. For the first time, she was free to make her own choice.

Maugrim had freed her.

The young man watched them, his grey eyes an overspill of plea, pain and defiance. She opened her hand and looked down at the metal.

We can make this world a new and better place.

As she surrendered, the young man slumped, almost imperceptibly, his moment of hope burned away. *I'm sorry*, she mouthed at him, helplessly, *I'm sorry.*

Beside her, she felt Maugrim glow, expand. As the young man watched, he slid a hand round the back of her neck, pulled her to him and kissed her with a passion and skill that burned everything else away. Impossibly pliant, she wrapped herself around him, lost herself to his touch, his mouth, his hands.

The grey eyes of Maugrim's victim watched them as they tumbled to the bloodstained floor.

7: MYTH VANKSRAAT

Cold and silent, Ecko was crouched on the roof.

About him, the night air was clear, sharp enough to cut his lungs like splinters of glass. The sky was starless black and the batshit moons were slowly sinking. Under him, the building was silent, still sleeping blissful and content. He'd been up here a while, curled against the chimney like a street cat, waiting.

Below him, scuttlings of critter-warmth crossed the tavern's backyard and vanished into the walls' creeper and moon shadow. Occasionally, people scurried past along the cobbled street.

They didn't look up.

Far away, hopefully to the east, he'd watched the growing sliver of light along the horizon – the hint of grey and pink and silver that heralded the rising sun. The night's stillness had not calmed his thoughts nor offered him answers – and frankly, if this building was going to fucking *teleport*, then he was going to ride the damn thing all the way.

Now, that time had almost come.

The roof was slate, the chimney still faintly warm. As the sky paled above him and the very first light crept along the narrow, stone streets of Roviarath, his skin shifted softly as if to welcome the dawn.

He sat up.

His adrenaline was poised, beginning to shimmer with anticipation. He pitched his cynicism against it – surely there was no way this building was just gonna *vanish*.

Come on then, I dare ya, I double dare ya –

And then – *whoosh* – it all went horribly wrong.

That first, soft light was suddenly slewing sideways, smudging abruptly out of focus – it was smearing across his vision into a sparkling grey blur –

Shit!

He barely had time for the thought. Suddenly, his adrenals were fired and he was clinging to the chimney stack, his heart pounding.

What the hell...?

The light convulsed, heaved. It knotted about itself; it swallowed its own tail and spiralled away down the plughole. There was a nanosecond of scrabbling, of wild-eyed panic, as the chimney and the roof were both gone and he was sucked helplessly back into...

Nothing.

No bricks under his fingers, no sky, no sunrise, no biting chill of air. He was not alone, nor afraid – he was just *gone*.

He'd never been.

Then there was ripping, like flesh; a thin, harsh scream. Falling, he tumbled through the tear. He was breathing, moving. He was Ecko.

There was slate, scraping beneath his fingers, dawn light on his skin. Dimly, he became aware that the thin scream was his own.

"Holy fucking mother of god..." He controlled his vocals with an effort. "What the...?"

Incredible, impossible, it'd all happened way too fast – he

was there and he was gone and he was back and now he was trembling, skidding down the roofside and clinging to the tiles like a half-dead rat. He reached for breath, shaking. Around him, the world spun gently, winding down – the building was still, the jump, transition, *whatever*, was over.

The world slowed, sighed and stopped.

So what the hell was that? A bad trip? Fucking hyperspace…?

He skidded to a tangled halt by the guttering. He lay there for a moment, breathing hard and blinking as his sight and mind cleared. Around him, the air was pale and cool, a faint breeze tightened his chest and made him cough. He curled over the noise, smothering it. His hands at his mouth tasted of blood where they'd scraped on the roof tiles.

…Translocation? FTL travel?

How the fuck did it just do *that?*

He'd been half expecting to be free. To come out facing Lugan, or a cryo tank, or a nest of otaku wiring and Eliza in a lab coat. Maybe he'd find himself in one of Grey's shit-holes – or in some other champion-needing world. *Hey, howdja fancy Ecko as High King of Narnia?* Part of him had even expected to not come out at all – but no, the quantum roller coaster had dumped him at the station and the sissy bar was rising on cue.

Carefully, his heart rate slowing, Ecko raised his gaze to look round.

The stone streets, the narrow buildings, the crepuscular light – all gone. Instead, the sky was high and clear and pale. Ahead of him, there was the metallic sheen of sunlight on water and on its far side, some sort of town, still misty with the early hour.

Teleporting, for chrissakes. What next – magic fucking wands?

Twinging with unease, he untangled himself from the mass of fabric, rubbed his bloodied palms on his thighs.

This can't be good…

As his anti-daz filtered the brightness, he could see the tavern itself was intact – garden and sign and all – and that it was now on the grassy edge of a river. On the far bank there was a tessellation of roofs, rising to a tower that didn't quite look like a church. The breeze flickered the many ends of his cloak, taunting him.

The air was wild, somehow, sparkling like old-school fizzy pop. He'd never had a lungful like it.

And there was movement. A harbour that wrapped the townside, larger that he might've expected, rowing boats out with the morning.

Ecko untangled himself fully and sat up. His adrenaline had washed out of him, down towards the guttering, he found he was hunching his shoulders against the vastness of the sky. The ride had kicked him into high gear – towards hopes and fantasies that this really had all been only a joke…

But this was the same roof, the same chimney, the same front yard.

And something in him said: *That's it, then.*

The teleport had been his last gasp – he felt as though he'd lost his final grab at freedom. Watching the rising dawn, the shining water, he found the certainty closing over him, once and for all – this was it and he was drowning in it and he was stuck, and there was fuck all he could do.

Oh, you bastards.

As if in answer, a water-rat thing scampered across the front path and he bridled at the symbolism.

You just wait.

The rat critter turned sharply, long tail twitching, and vanished. Ecko shifted into the shadow on the other side of the chimney and spun his oculars to watch the town.

Okay then, bring on the pointy-eared bastards with the bows…

But the town was not some ethereal, crystalline dream,

some screensaver vision, it was stone and wood and solid and functional. It was also absolutely miniscule – hell, he'd got no idea how big these things were supposed to be. With no high rise, it maybe held six thousand people, seven? It had no defensive wall, only the harbour, and the tower seemed to hold some mega version of the rocklight in his room. It was hardly gonna be a lighthouse for the water.

To one side, following the direction of the river, the plains stretched away into the morning, a fantastical swath of colour under the sky. To the other, to the south and west, there was a slope of misted forest that rose into...

Jesus.

Rose into *mountains.*

Even in the bright dawn light, they were harsh, dark headed and remote, high and jagged as though they cut into the very sky. They made him shiver with some odd sense of anticipation, though he'd no fucking clue why.

He'd never seen mountains, not this close, and they towered over his presence and silenced his jittering brain. For a moment, he was lost for a sarcastic thought, and he stared with something approaching awe.

Then his attention was pulled back by a shout that carried clear across the water.

"The Wanderer! The Wanderer's here!"

One of the fisherboats had seen the tavern manifest on the bank like some insomniac's hallucination. In a moment, the rest had taken up the cry and the boats were being rowed hard back towards the town.

Great. For today's therapy-session role play, I get to be a barmaid.

He was measuring his chances of staying the fuck on the roof when the skylight below him creaked open.

"Ecko. Good morning – surprised to see you still here." Hair loose and bare shouldered, the Bard glanced at their surroundings and grinned. "Well, this could be a great deal worse. Enjoy the trip?"

"Yeah, like a laugh a minute." Ecko's cloak and skin had shifted with the colours of the dawn, but his eyes stayed black as pits. He indicated the riverside city. "Ain't exactly Minas fucking Tirith is it?"

"This is Vanksraat. We've come south-west, Roviarath is directly downriver." Lifting the skylight further, Roderick peered over the roof's edge. "Good place for us, there'll be gossip and trade. We'll have a busy day, I think."

"They've spotted us already." Ecko returned to studying the town.

"They do that." The Bard grinned, his ridiculous goth hair rising loose in the breeze. "We're a breath of life. We don't only bring ale – we bring tales of the Varchinde, news of the terhnwood crop, trade-goods and information. In some ways, we bring the world."

Okay, not a barmaid, a mailman. Hell, maybe I get a hat.

"There are also some questions I need to ask you – and something... well, maybe something you can help me with."

Ecko snorted. "You reckon I'm gonna stay?"

"I've already said that's your choice – though if you're going to jump wagon, there may be better places. You'd like Xenok, or Padesh..."

"Jump *ship*, you jump *ship*."

"Why would anyone jump off a ship?" Roderick had thrown the trapdoor all the way open and was now sitting on the lip checking out the view. "Come down. Tundran-blooded I may be, but I'm getting cold."

Ecko twitched his shoulders, discouraging the emptiness of the sky. Ignoring the Bard's offered hand, he scrabbled down the roof. As he reached the skylight, though, something snatched his attention.

The Bard was stripped to the waist. He was lean, a wire-work of steel muscle. What stopped Ecko was the ugly mess of white scar that tore into Roderick's chest under his outstretched arm. It was a messy, patchy wound – it looked like he'd been half munched by a shoal of piranha.

It was an ugly wound.

It was a *mortal* wound.

Suspicion paused him on the edge of jumping. He pointed.

"What the fuck did that?"

The scar was old, long healed – but its severity was as loud as a scream. Razor-wire teeth had shredded the Bard a new one the size of the fucking Grand Canyon. And it'd healed hollow – as though too little skin had been stretched to cover the damage. Busted ribs and half-eaten lungs were the least of its problems out here, where the fucking *leech* was the height of hot meditech –

How had he – ?

"Seeking lost lore, on a reconnaissance mission to Rammouthe." Ruefully, Roderick looked north-east, ran his fingers over the scar. "I was running scout, and disturbed a knot of sleeping magharta. Not something I'd recommend."

"You oughta be dead." Ecko studied the Bard's pretty-boy face for signs of rotting. "You're not, are you? You're not gonna pull some fetid zombie undead bullshit?"

"Fetid zombie undead bullshit?"

"Oh for chrissakes. I mean: why the fucking hell're you still breathing?"

"I won't get let off that easily?" Roderick grinned. "Once magharta start eating, they're not easy things to stop."

"Don't gimme the smart-ass remarks – if you got monster issues, I'm your fucking exterminator. Tell me where they're at and it'll all be over by dinnertime."

And I can get the hell outta here.

"Only monster in here is in the kitchen, cooking breakfast." Leaving Ecko to catch the skylight, the Bard jumped down onto the landing. "C'mon, let's go give Kale a hand." He glanced back up, gave a brief chuckle. "He might even let you start the fire."

Downstairs, the front doors of the taproom were propped open and the sounds of water and birds were carried in on sweet, clean air. Karine was already there, counting a stack of pottery bottles on the bar top and making marks on the papers that Ecko had seen the previous night. Beside her was a slender, wide-eyed waif who looked no older than sixteen.

Standing in the open doorway, arms folded and watching the river, stood a silent, self-possessed man who turned and nodded at them as they came in. His pale hair shone in the sunshine and, like Karine, he seemed far too young.

There was a long scar across one of his ears.

"Ecko." His voice was clear and calm – it was the voice that Ecko had heard when he'd awoken. "Welcome to The Wanderer. I'm Sera – I didn't see you last night as you had so much to take in. Though, this morning, I fear you may have rather more." There was no trace of humour in his expression or voice. "The city is about to land on our doorstep."

City?

Almost in spite of himself, Ecko craned to look past where the man stood, flicking his anti-daz against the sun's shine on the river. There was a boat full of people already halfway across, figures at the bow pointing and talking.

He groaned. "Jesus, do you people sleep?"

Karine said, "Forty-one, forty-two, forty-three. We're two short. Can we get a messenger to go back to the bazaar – I'll need at least fifteen more of the spirits and all the ales they've got. And wine – we're close enough to Padesh to make it the good stuff. Kale needs fresh veg, whatever the farms have brought in."

Roderick caught Ecko's black gaze, and winked.

But Karine was not slowing down.

"Silfe," she called to the waif, "can you get me the loose terhnwood? And the scales? And Sera, can you sort the loading? I don't want the chain through here, take them round the back and load directly. When they're done, send them to me."

"Ecko," Sera said. "How d'you fancy joining me on a loading crew?"

"How d'you fancy a new asshole?"

The pale-haired man turned fully from the view of the water. Ecko watched him, daring him to start – what'd they said about him killing nine people? – but he said only, "It seems we already have one."

That one caught Ecko clean under his guard. He spluttered, "You –"

"Whoah." Roderick placed a hand on Ecko's shoulder. "It's far too early to be starting fights. If you wait until after breakfast, we'll all come outside and watch."

"Yeah, maybe you can make a *wager*." Shaking off the contact, he looked for a corner, somewhere away from the door and the light and the banter and the incoming people. "I still dunno if I'm even staying... Jesus *Christ* enough already!"

Another door had banged open, startling him. This one loosed the scent of cooking flesh – blood-rich and suddenly, strongly reminiscent of his early childhood. Meat – real animal, raised and killed and carved and sold... The smell was powerful, enticing, slightly sickening. Echoes of his mother's children's home swamped him, too many people, too much noise, too much to take in...

For fucksake!

It was overpowering. He gripped the hard edges of Lugan's lighter and backed to a table at the edge of the room.

Gave himself room to breathe.

The Bard ducked into the kitchen. Crouching on a corner

seat and shrinking under his cowl, Ecko stared round at the taproom, at the sunlight, at the people, at the resin stuff – had they called it terhnwood? – hung on the walls.

Analysing. Critical.

Claustro.

He didn't need this – if he could grab *that*, *that* and as much of the meat as he could carry...

...but he couldn't bust outta here 'til he knew his ass from his elbow – some random critter would crunch him for a mid-morning snack. He had to get the Idiot's Guide, the one-oh-one download as to what the hell happened next. Then, God of Evil or no God of Evil, *something* was gonna get its ass kicked.

"Are you hungry?" The Bard had returned with a pair of leather mugs in one hand. "Or are just wondering how much you can steal?"

Ecko glowered at him – shadow skinned, black eyed, black mouthed – his look could send hardened street warriors screaming home for Mommy.

Putting the mugs on the table, Roderick spun a chair round and sat astride it, its back between Ecko and himself.

"So," he said, "welcome to your first morning." When Ecko still glared, he grinned. "What can I tell you?"

"Gimme the short version. What I can eat, what's gonna eat me, and where the Bad Guy's at."

"It's a little more complex than that."

"What – the God of Evil doesn't have a bar tab?"

"He's notoriously bad at trading for his ales... Look." The Bard picked up his mug as if checking exasperation. "You understand the importance of reconnaissance, intelligence. Knowledge is something I've spent my life seeking, and the little I have is –" he gave a wry chuckle "– not nearly enough. I have only rumour, stealthing in the grass like a hunting bweao, and its source eludes me."

Ecko bit back an immediate response and picked up his mug.

"Rumour of what?" The stuff inside was herbal, it smelled like old socks and green tea. He took a mouthful and scalded his tongue.

Outside, there were voices coming closer, and Roderick, with a glance over his shoulder at the door, began to speak more quickly.

"There is much lore you should know, Ecko, lore that I alone have use for – but I fear this morning, the Count of Time is against us. For now, I will say only this: that we of the Grasslands are no longer warriors. Our last war is forgotten, the memory discarded. Our Elementalists, the priests of the people, once teachers and guides, have long since faded into tavern-tales and trickery. The Powerflux, the surge of element to element across the world, is gone and lost." He reached up, took a resin blade from the wall and laid it across the table. In the morning sun, it shone like gold; it was exquisitely decorated and there was a mark, a symbol of some sort, carved into it at the crossguard. It was significant, but for the moment, Ecko did not know why.

The Bard glanced again at the door. "With this long freedom from both strife and learning, we have become a culture dependent upon the cycles of our trade. Upon *this*." He turned the blade to catch the light. "As Fhaveon took power in the Varchinde, so she became the greatest source of terhnwood – this resin and fibre that makes our every quintessential craft and tool. The GreatHeart Rakanne gifted Fhaveon's terhnwood to the plains in return for trade of wood, and stone, and food, and spice – and now, that trade is our lifeblood. To maintain that circulation, much of our population roves free, carrying craftmarked goods from bazaar to bazaar, from city to city, and this has swollen our trade-roads into ribbon-towns and markets and caravanserai. There are pirates, of course, and there are soldiers to face them; there are farmlands that tithe into the cities for terhnwood of their own. The system is complex, warded by craftmarks and tallies and tithehalls –

Karine could explain such things to you more than I."

"What – terhnwood makes your world go round?" Ecko wasn't laughing. Something about the Bard's plea was chillingly familiar.

Our last war is forgotten, the memory discarded.

There were feet getting closer on the path outside.

"We are complacent in our comforts," Roderick said, "and ruled by our merchants. Our satisfaction is surpassed only by blindness. Yet now, rumours rise like figments, hauntings of imagination. And without our lore…"

There was a shadow in the doorway, the sound of feet on stone and an awkward throat-clearing. "Um. Hello?"

"Without our lore," the Bard finished, "I fear they will surpass us and we will be lost."

At the door loitered a small gaggle of locals who'd paused, peering into the building as if it would haze out of existence like a mirage. As the Bard turned, they shoved one of their number forwards – a young man, a heavy bag in one hand and a hat wrung to a rag in the other. From his garments, Ecko's mind instantly labelled him "farmer".

Sera stood like a wall, unspeaking.

Karine called from behind the bar top, "Morning! Are you trader or worker? If you're here to get legless, you'll have to wait until highsun when we're fully stocked."

"Please," the young man said, looking from face to face. "I'm neither. I came to ask a question."

And he-eere we go… With a mirthless smirk, Ecko shrank back, watching. *So – what's it gonna be? Great Mage? Demon? Dark Druid? Put your cards down, Eliza, let's see whatcha got…*

"Of course." The Bard came to his feet. "What can we do for you?"

When a fellow behind him gave him a nudge, the young man swung the heavy, drawstring bag onto the nearest table. It hit with a thump. Ecko's oculars kicked and tracked, but the contents were heavy, motionless and cold.

Dead, or he was a monkey's asshole.

The boy opened the string. With some effort, he pulled free a creature.

Ecko spun his telescopics.

The beastie was unfamiliar, but dead as fuck. It was doglike, long legged and skinny, though deep chested with powerful back legs and a balancing tail. It could probably stand on its hind paws if it had to, or spring extremely high – certainly high enough to see over tall grass.

Intrigued now, Ecko shifted so he could see it properly. *Oh c'mon, what's it gonna do? Animate? Skeletal lich dog? Oh, you so know you wanna...*

The thing just lay there.

Karine bawled, "Oi! Get that off my table!"

But Kale was in the kitchen doorway, his face bothered and frowning.

Ecko tensed, but the cook's temperature was normal. He seemed puzzled, intense.

Roderick ran a hand over the thing's flank. He said, "Where did this come from?"

The young man bobbed his head, twisted his hat. His friends had crowded in through the door and they jostled each other to see.

"Please, we found it. It was alive – quite friendly really." He looked upset. "We tried to feed it and it just died. My family're farmers, we're tithed to Vanksraat and our manor's good to us, we're only here for the fiveday trade-market. No one knew what it... we tried... and it just toppled over."

"All right, all right, easy." Roderick shot a glance at Karine and she reached for a pottery goblet. "Have a seat and let me... dear Gods."

The smell was enough; it brought Kale right out of the doorway and drove Sera into the sun. The Bard, though, didn't move a muscle. He stared as though his boots had been nailgunned to the floor.

Ecko craned.

The thing was *rotting*.

Right there on the table – as the light touched it, it was superheating and dissolving into mulch. Its skin peeled back to muscle and sinew, black creatures invaded its flesh and ate it from the inside out. Organs swelled and burst and stank and dissolved, bones cracked and twisted. There was the faint smell of burning wood, a thin wisp of smoke.

The scream was Silfe, the outrage Karine, but Ecko was transfixed, his oculars working, working. The heat was localised – some kinda spontaneous beastie combustion. Okay so it wasn't a skeletal lich dog, but hey, it was still pretty fucking cool.

The young man shook. His friends patted him as he turned away.

But Roderick watched as the thing dissolved to ash and memory, as the invading creatures starved, perished in their turn, and were gone. There was a char mark on the table.

The Bard said, his voice like stone, "Get me a brush."

His expression was bleak.

As the young man was hustled outside and given a mug of green stuff, Ecko rather thought that shit had just gotten serious.

Ecko said, "So? What the hell was that?"

The front doors of the tavern were closed. Sera was outside, talking to the boy; Karine and Silfe had vanished with stocklists. With Roderick now was Kale, his worn face troubled.

"It was a nartuk," Roderick said. "An alchemical cross – they've been extinct for hundred of returns. It's also not the first... oddity... that's been seen." His fingers were tapping tattoos on the table. He glanced up at Ecko. "We're unique here, we amass rumour from all places, much as we amass trade-goods. We're a node, and our catch-net is very wide."

"So? What's one dead critter?"

"So, we were talking about myth, and rumour. I hear things from all over the world, and I piece them together. This isn't just one creature."

Kale said, "It didn't smell right. Even when he brought it in. It smelled –" he searched for a word and came up with "– wrong."

Ecko snorted. "That's some nose you got there."

"I don't understand." The Bard stood up, fingers now rattling against his thigh. He was restless, pacing. "This is the first time our rumours have been realised. And nartuk... that lore is lost. We've not practised such alchemy since the high days of Tusien. This – all of this – both defeats and intrigues me."

There was a flare in the Bard's amethyst eyes, a flame of something less than sanity – or something more. Hell, this place was getting more like a home-from-home asylum with each day, for chrissakes. Ecko watched, barely suppressing a grin.

Maybe I'm not the only one who needs a shrink...

Roderick took a breath. "Our world is afraid. In her thoughts, she fears something she can neither name nor remember. I've spent my whole life, everything I have, seeking to understand that fear. It's why I have The Wanderer." He picked up the small terhnwood blade that he'd shown Ecko earlier and gestured with it as he spoke. "I'm Roderick of Avesyr, Guardian of the Ryll, once hailed as the hope of my people. All my life, I've searched for lore and insight, and still, I don't understand."

"So? Enough with the OCD shit. The guy's outside, let's interrogate the crap outta him. He tells us where he got it – we're good. Let's go."

Roderick said, "The Ryll is a waterfall, far to the north of here, where the thoughts of the world are manifest – and where her nightmare was shown to me. And you're not going anywhere until I understand how this *fits*."

"How 'bout we just get off our asses –"

"I'm not jesting," Roderick said. He pointed with the blade, his expression cold. "The world knows *fear*. And this, this is a tiny fragment of that larger picture. There have been sightings and rumours all through the central Varchinde. It's not just one nartuk, it's more than that. It's the beginning of something *huge*."

"Says who? It's one fucking critter!"

"Did you not listen? I am – was – a Guardian of the Ryll. I watched the thoughts of the world in the water. And I saw –"

"Yeah, a nightmare, I got it already." Ecko grinned. "How many mushrooms were you doing?"

The Bard went white. He said, slowly and very carefully, "It's not just one creature, Ecko. It's the *beginning*. The world has a fear that she had forgotten – and we must assemble the pieces."

"Chrissakes." Ecko came up to a half crouch, facing the Bard across the table. His targeters crossed Roderick's forehead, the weapon in his hand. "It looks pretty fucking simple to me: wherever that thing came from, that's where we go. We follow the trail, we do the Grand Quest, I get my hands on the God of Evil, he's shish kebab, I go home." He grinned. "This should be as easy as... hey, let's say 'a booze up in a brewery'."

"By the Gods, Ecko! Where do you think I got my scar? You talk so glibly of a 'God of Evil' – legend tells that there indeed was once a creature who may fit that description. I went looking for him – and I found *nothing*." The Bard's passion was powerful, but Ecko didn't care. "There is so much more we must know. The soil of the Varchinde does show remnants of some ancient war – but I know not how the pieces fit together!"

"This is *bullshit*!" Ecko snarled back at him. "You can't just sit on your fanny in here doing shit-all, waiting for... what? The sky to fall on your head? Your God of Evil to drop in for a chat and a pint of the good stuff? Go question the guy with the nartuk. You should be doin' your investigation or whatever, not –"

"Investigation?" Roderick's snarl matched Ecko's own.

"Ecko, I've been searching almost a hundred returns – I have dug every ruin, I have found every treasure, I have learned every tale, I have faced every foe. Wherever these alchemical creatures are coming from…"

"Gimme a map, already, I'll tell you where they're comin' from. Where's your realm of death and decay? Your pits of fire and mountains of ash? That's where the source is, that's where the Bad Guy always hangs out – hell, his shadow's rising even now." He sneered. "Let's get our butts down there and wake him the fuck up. We can take him an espresso."

"A *what*?"

The tension in the room crested, paused, and shattered. Either side of the table, Ecko and the Bard were intent on each other – Ecko's small, tight frame coiled in a crouch facing Roderick's height and presence. Kale had quietly slipped away.

Then, as if Ecko had snapped his back like the fibres of the resin sword, the Bard dropped into his chair.

"I'm sorry," he said, softly. "Sera is asking about the nartuk, and we'll learn what we can. But unless we see something more, I fear Vanksraat can't shed the light we seek."

"Save it." Ecko's snarl was subdued. "Feeling sorry for yourself won't get you shit. Unless Eliza's stuck me in some *Kobayashi Maru*, there's a solution. Let's go get it." He blinked. "Unless you're any good with pentagrams and goats?"

"When we come to the capital city, to Fhaveon, we can speak to Rhan. He is…" He stopped himself, then said, "…I shall be interested to see what Rhan makes of you, Ecko. Or perchance, if The Wanderer allows, I can take you to my home city, Avesyr, and the Ryll's ever-falling water." He stared at the broken sword for a moment, perhaps not even seeing it. "They will not welcome me." Then a ghost of his former chuckle danced from the walls. "In the meantime, we can pray that our nartuk will give us some answers."

8: TRIQUETA THE RIBBON-TOWNS OF ROVIARATH
AND THE CENTRAL VARCHINDE

The Wanderer thumped with noise.

The taproom was heaving with bodies and shouting and drunken laughter. The air was hot and close, it reeked of sweat and animal.

Crouched like a bilious gargoyle on the end of the bar, Ecko reckoned he was going certifiably fucking loopy. The noise and the stink were overpowering, nausea had closed his throat and his nerve endings were sparking with exasperation. All he wanted to do was get on with this, track down the Uberboss and kick the shit out of it.

Wasn't that how this stuff worked?

The nartuk's owner had told them a simple tale – that the thing had befriended them en route to the fiveday market at the local tithehall. The poor, clueless bastard seemed more upset by its death than by the fact that it was apparently a thousand years old.

Hell, wasn't like they could even dissect the damn thing. Ecko would've given a hefty weight of that terhnwood stuff for some decent forensics.

Communications.

A fucking *library.*

That morning, they'd jumped from the Vanksraat riverside to the ramshackle unrolling of a Grassland "ribbon-town": one of the twin, thin stretches of deadwood that bled out along the trade-roads from the major cities. The place was a dump, abundant in two things: dirt and poverty. The roadway looked like some jingle-booted sheriff should have a high noon shoot-out and leave the bodies to rot like the nartuk had done.

But noon had come and gone and no sheriff had manifest to demand his sippin' whisky. Now, the evening was warm, the sun low and red and fat. It rested on the rickety roofs and sent long, bloody shadows through the dust.

And Ecko was crouched on the bar top like a silent and stone thing, realising something that annoyed him…

He missed Lugan.

Missed his humour, his decisiveness, his forward motion. Lugan would've been on the move already, shaking shit down, sorting shit out. None of this "the world's had a nightmare" crap.

Hell, he'd've been the one causing it.

Across the heave of bodies, the front doors were propped open and revellers spilled out into the dusty roadway, laughing. On a nearby bench, leaning back with his black boots on the table, Roderick lived up to his moniker with a stringed something-or-other that he apparently played with some skill. His listeners stamped their boots in rhythmic appreciation and sank more booze.

Ecko wanted to rail at him: *Get up, already, ask some questions, detain someone, torture the shit outta something – just move!* His adrenal boosting was misfiring, twanging on his nerve endings like anxiety. He flashed random crosshairs. *Go on, kickstart it, you know you wanna!* Hell, a bust-up might shake something loose.

Lugan would've known the danger signs, distracted him, given him something else to focus on – in here, no one even looked up.

Behind the bar, Karine had a sweat on. She and Silfe tapped barrel after barrel. Every so often, Sera would stir himself to roll one away through the kitchen door, and then come back with a full one on his shoulder. There was no sign of Kale – only the lush food smells that the door wafted in Sera's wake.

More stink.

Jeez, it was *suffocating* in here.

Ecko was used to people, the crush of the crowd, the press of flesh – but this? Too much reek, too much skin and dirt and resin and critter. The smells were closing in around him like street kid bullies; his guts were still playing up from the change in diet. Chrissakes, he couldn't *breathe*.

You gotta love the grand-quest-fantasy-romance. No one tells you it comes with stink and gut ache and a lack of sanitary plumbing.

"Oi. Make yourself useful, mush. I need water." Behind him, Karine lunged for another ceramic bottle. She was sharp as a knife, fast as a circus juggler. Arachnid eyes and feline reflexes and hands that were everywhere at once. Remembering to wink lasciviously at the lad ordering drinks, she chased Ecko with a foot. "Well go on then!"

"Who died and made you Empress?" Ecko half turned, found himself with a rope-handled bucket in his mottled mitt. He glared, his oculars flickering fire. "What am I, fucking staff now?"

"You live here, mush, you work."

The lad paid for his drinks with a twist of something in a tiny cloth bag.

Salt? Sugar?

Columbian?

Ecko curled a black-toothed grin.

The lad grabbed his ale and retreated to safety. Muttering, Ecko took the pail and ducked out into the yard. Fucking with the drinkers was at least one way of cheering himself up.

* * *

When he returned, the room had stabilised, grown a tight edge of focus like the silent rasp of a whetstone.

His reactions instinctual, he handed over the bucket and was back on the bar top, crouched, cowl down, one shoulder tight against the wall. He curled still, adrenaline wary, nerves shivering with anticipation – but Sera stood casual, arms folded. Chrissakes, the doorman'd almost cracked a grin.

Curious, Ecko followed his gaze.

Well, he thought dryly, *whaddaya know.*

In the centre of the room, ten or so drinkers had collected loosely round a clutter of tables, others had gathered to watch. Flicking his targeters, Ecko took note of emblems stitched onto jackets, woven bands around wrists and forearms. Some of the drinkers had standardised weapons, bound into belt-rings by lengths of braided string.

Military? Name, wristband and serial number? They sure as hell drank enough.

Some of them, though, looked like something else entirely.

"Who's up then? Go on, you know you want to." Commanding the tables was a small, tightly sprung woman, rattling a leather cup in one slim hand. She was the first exotic Ecko'd seen: skin, hair and eyes all different shades of bright yellow-gold. She almost glowed in the sunset. His heatseeker showed skin-warmth, a fierce energy that burned from her like she was radioactive. In each of her cheekbones was embedded a pale stone like an opal, cooler than her skin, but shimmering in the dying of the light.

She wasn't beautiful, but the force of her presence was undeniable. Her deft fingers cleverly flicked the angles of the cup.

Almost in spite of himself, he grinned, a slash of darkness buried deep under the cowl. *Looks like we got us a card sharp.* He spun his telescopics and watched.

"C'mon, then!" She was daring them. "Doesn't Larred Jade compensate you? You can't all be cleaned out."

"CityWarden doesn't compensate us!" Ribald challenge and friendly abuse answered her, the gaggle of onlookers called for drinks, bets.

At the bar, an older bloke nudged his mate and called, "Go on, Triqueta, take 'em all on!" There was laughter.

Still flicking readouts, Ecko watched.

Across the scarred tabletop, one man unwrapped a red, metal bracelet – copper? – and chucked it into the pile, another had a chip of stone, striated with colour.

The woman, Triqueta, chuckled and rattled the pot again. The slanting sunset edged her in bright neon – she was a holo-projection, a fantasy. She had the room and she knew it. Grinning, she threw her hair over her shoulder – but the move was a distraction. Ecko's targeters caught it: her other hand was twisting the cup with a long-practised gesture.

You cheeky fucking bitch…!

She was cute, all right, smart, fast and intrig–

Oh for chrissakes.

In his head, brakes screeched. Long wheals of rubber scarred his thoughts as they careened to a dead stop.

You hafta be kidding me.

The blatancy of the gameplay floored him completely. For an endless, timeless moment, Ecko's breath was a ball of disbelief tight in his throat.

Basic instincts… no way…

In front of him, the woman called, "Any more?" She mock recoiled, laughing, as they cussed her.

On the bar top, Ecko watched, now captivated for a completely different reason. He could see what Eliza was trying to do, see the moves that she was making…

Oh no you fucking don't. This is one damned psych test I can't take.

A leering patron whispered something in the woman's ear.

She laughed, but her elbow in his chest sent him crashing to the floor, his ale – *splosh* – in his face. Around him, guffaws and slow handclaps celebrated his fall.

The blow wasn't malicious – but was hard enough to make the point.

Sera shifted, a gentle ripple of warning. Ecko stayed exactly where he was, barely daring to breathe in case she looked up and that cleverly orchestrated gold chain snapped shut its last shackle...

C'mon Eliza, don't do this one...

The woman rattled the dice one last time, then threw them across the table. They clattered to a stop. A circle of groans echoed round her. A couple of gamblers scraped back stools and headed for the bar.

"Wish I knew how she did that." The older man at the bar shook his head and his companion chuckled.

"If you did, mate, we'd all be living like lords in a Padeshian brothel."

They turned back to their ale jugs, chuckling.

Unmoving, his cowl down over his face, Ecko watched motionless, as though he could see the very fractal ripples spreading from this single, poised moment...

So. I go one way, the pattern does one thing, I go the other, it does something else? Which way's right, for chrissakes? Which way gets this damn thing done?

Beside Triqueta, her admirer was picking himself up. He was clearly absolutely rat-assed: stumbling, muttering, his movements erratic. As the woman dropped the dice – one, two – back into the pot, he plonked himself by her side and reached for the jug.

His movements were slow, blurred by booze, but deliberate.

Watching the tableau unfold, Ecko was utterly silent, caught on a realisation – on the apex of a sudden, adrenaline rush of understanding.

It wasn't just this decision – it was all of them. His every choice, tiny as it may seem, would affect everything else that he did, everything else that happened around him and to him and so on...

Jesus. Trying to wrap his head round the sheer *size* of this was gonna drive him batshit.

"'Nother round then!" Triqueta rattled a cheerful, rhythmic tattoo with the dice pot, caught the sightline of one of the vets at the bar and winked.

The bets started again – and a round of jeers as several of the soldier types shook their heads and pulled out.

Beside her, the leerer had descended into glowering. He refused to bet, just sat there, hands round his mug. She gave the pot a final shake and threw the dice again.

The groans redoubled. A pile of treasure was pushed over the tabletop.

The drunk muttered, "I saw that." He came to his feet, swaying slightly, then sat back down with an unsteady thump. He was shit-faced, anger rose from him like whisky fumes.

Sera was already moving, swift and quiet. Ecko's targeters hit *there*, *there* and *there*. If he'd wanted to, he could've kicked the fucker into the middle of next week, rescued the damsel and made his decision, made the pattern ripple and change round him...

But he had a better idea.

No, Eliza, I hadda give up girls. My mom told me.

Grinning, he slunk from the bar top like a sliding shadow, a soundless, scentless patch of darkness that flowed across the floor.

"I said I saw that!" The drunk was up and reeling. "You damned cheating bitch." Turning to glare at her, he made a clumsy grab for the pot. "Damned Banned – you're all fil–"

Sera didn't get close. A sharp back blow of the woman's fist broke the drunk's nose. He spluttered and fell back, a hot rush of blood exploding down his already-soaked shirt.

"I warned you once, sunshine." She dropped the pot, stepped back from the impact, hands wide, but her sharp yellow eyes looking for the next threat. "You saw that, right?"

"Oi!" Another of the grunts was on his feet, stool going over. "You're out of line, bitch!"

"Don't sweat it, mate," a third one answered him. "He had that coming."

"Chearlshit. If she's not damned cheating...!"

"I'm not *cheating*, you sonofamare." Triq wiped her bloody knuckles on her breeches and grinned. "I'm just *lucky*."

They were all moving now, stools crashing backwards, raised voices, accusation and drunken indignation. The two older guys at the bar rolled their eyes and set down their mugs.

Ecko was close, so close, he was almost under the table.

Brawl kicking off in t-minus...

"Enough!" The doorman's bark reverberated from the walls. He had the bloody-nosed drunk by collar and belt – a moment later the guy was sailing out of the door and into the dust.

Triqueta backed up, hands still wide.

"Hey, you know he had that coming."

Sera nodded brief assent, rounded on the nearest and loudest. He closed a fist in the front of the shirt thing the bloke had on, and propelled him smack back into the wall, snarling. Karine reached for a bottle.

For a moment, Ecko thought she was going to smack the nearest patron over the head with it and he grinned. *Any second now...*

But she was smarter than that. With a deep breath that swelled her cleavage, she bawled, "Okay you lot! This round's on the house!"

Loose cheers scattered the aggression, the brawl dissolved before it began. As Ecko returned to his point on the bar, Karine winked at him. "Cost us less than the furniture."

In spite of himself, he chuckled, his adrenals uncoiling.

Okay, Eliza. Let's see what you do with this...

He had the goldie girl's dice in his lithe, mottled hand.

In the chaos, Triqueta of the Banned had slipped deftly – and tactfully – out of the tavern's front door.

Swift and silent, like the final flicker of daylight, she'd untethered her little palomino mare and left the dusty noise of the ribbon-town behind.

Free.

The sun had gone, sunk to its death upon the distant Kartiah, and rich blue darkness drove the last of the light to frame the mountaintops. Triq tightened her knees on the mare's warm, bare back and she rode away from the ribbon-town, from the Bard's ale and music, from the squabbling drunks of the Range Patrol and her own Banned family.

Much as she loved them, there were just times...

In the midst of the almost-brawl, she'd lost her fireblasted dice. She'd split her knuckles on that sonofamare's face and the young patrolman she'd had her eye on had wandered away... Triq knew when her luck had run out. It wasn't her night and she was better off wrapping her thighs around the flesh they needed the most.

As a kid, Triqueta had been fostered in the unrolling, ramshackle poverty of a trade-road ribbon-town. She'd been quick with feet and fingers before she could count. At six, she'd returned to her mother in the Banned – but held to the philosophy of her errant desert sire: celebrate your life, live for the now, take what you will, but hurt none.

Above her, two moons slowly rose to sail the ripples of cloud. Oblivious to the world below and ever in opposition, they lit the wild grass to a brilliant shimmer of light.

Like the stones in her cheeks, the desert was still in her blood.

She was wild souled and happiest under the sky.

She'd not seen her sire since she was a kid – not even when her mother was killed by scuffling road-pirates. As Triq's little mare cantered way out across the edge of the sleeping farmlands, she let drop only an idle thought – that family was what you made it.

It made her smile – a touch of the warmth of the red sands at the centre of the dark Varchinde.

In the far distance, she caught a burst of laughter from the rugged Banned campsite – doubtless Syke, Banned commander, was hosting the remaining Range Patrol soldiers in a booze-laden campsite party. Syke had many and interesting ways to stay on the right side of the local soldiery. Triq chuckled quietly and leaned windwards, steering the mare away from the campsite, the tavern, the river, the final scattering of Roviarath's tithed farmland. Uncaring of the danger – she was *Banned* for the Gods' sakes! – she headed north-east, for the open plain.

The little mare seemed glad of the run. She lengthened her stride, mane flying, shoulders churning with power and warmth. The grass parted for her, whispered as she passed. The wind raced cold past Triq's skin and her chuckle became a laugh, gleeful in the emptiness.

Sensing her rising mood, the horse put her heart in it and began to really run.

They left the roll of rural life behind them. The night was the sound of the grass, the strength of the animal that ran through it, her rhythm swift and clean. In the vastness of the dark, the moons, brother and sister cursed to be ever in opposition, rode with them, shining cold. Triq loved to lose herself in the Varchinde, the desolation elated her. She was tiny against the measureless grass, the infinite sky, yet its euphoria was with her and she wasn't alone.

The sounds of the campsite had all but faded. Triq leaned back, bringing the mare to a halt.

She sat, breathing.

Faintly over the sound of the river, she could still hear them – a scattering of distant hilarity snatched away by the wind. If she looked back, she could see the tiny, red fire-points of the campsite, and the faint, glimmering skein of the ribbon-town's windows. Brighter in the dark mid-air was the great, white eye of the Lighthouse Tower at Roviarath, heart and hub and lynchpin of the Varchinde's lifeblood trade. "Here is help," it said, "find me to find safety."

Triq turned her back on it and tightened her thighs. The mare moved into an easy walk.

Banned and soldiers faded into the grass.

Away from rocklight and fire, the moons dusted the sea of sward to yellow and white, washing past her like water. The mare walked calmly, her head up and her ears forward. Triq rested in the ease of her movements. She'd known this creature from a foal, raised her and trained her – and she was a friend.

Face turned to the wind, eyes closed, Triq rested her hands on the warmth of her soft hide.

At the gesture, the mare stopped, throwing her head up and back. One forehoof thudded uneasily. Triq tensed, eyes snapping open, hand going for her small belt-blade. Her thighs urged the creature forwards.

The little mare refused. She danced back several paces, snorting.

What...?

Nervousness tickled her skin, Triq trusted the animal's moods instinctually, relied upon her. If she smelled something, something was there.

She was chillingly aware of how small they were – herself and the horse, two sparks of life – tiny in the emptiness.

She had come out without her saddle, no tack, no weapons – only a belt-knife more useful for cutting dinner than pouncing bweao. Holding tight to her alarm and keeping absolutely silent, she stroked the mare's shoulder and allowed her to back up. It was a Range Patrol, perhaps, or maybe late-night road-pirates. The big predators didn't come this close to a ribbon-town – and the recent rumours of monsters were tavern-tales to scare the city dwellers.

Weren't they? There were no such things as monsters.

She listened.

Wind, water. Grass. She shivered – how had it got so cold? – and made herself sit absolutely still. Her shoulders prickled with tension.

Slowly, she turned around.

But there was only the white eye of the lighthouse, the rippling wash of the light.

Triq's heart hammered, but her gaze was steady. She inhaled and the slim muscles across her shoulders tensed, flexed. Belt-knife or no, she wasn't about to open the odds on being any beastie's late-night snack.

Silence.

Then something moved.

Close by.

She turned sharply but didn't see it, it was below the level of the grass tops. The gentle wind-ripple of light was uninterrupted – she had no idea where it was. The mare's ears were flat against her skull and she lifted her forehooves, skittering like a Padeshian dancer.

Was there a bweao, belly-down in the darkness? Some nightmare creature of legend and fang? Triq's heels were holding the mare – just. If she relaxed the command, she'd gather her legs and flee.

She was fast – could she outrun it?

"Please…"

The word was barely a hiss, and utterly unexpected. It froze the breath to the sides of her throat.

For a moment, she was so damned scared she couldn't move.

"Please...!"

It came from in front of her. She still couldn't see it. Any minute now it was going to call her by name...

That was it – she was getting the rhez out of here.

"Please help me!"

Instead of calling her name, the voice sobbed, gave the cry of something despairing beyond endurance. She heard movement, clumsy. The moonlight scattered as something shifted in the grass.

She tensed her hands, ready. Decl– ! No sound passed her lips. She tried again, "Declare yourself!"

"There is someone there, oh thank the Goddess!" Movement again, pained, terrible movement. "I can't stand up any more. Please, help me." The words dissolved into a gasp.

The voice was young, hurt, male – she had no clue what he could be doing out here.

But she was fireblasted Banned and if it was some forgotten monster or some phantom figment, she'd slit it straight up its daemonic middle. Keeping her hand firmly in the mare's mane, Triq swung one leg over her rump and slipped down into the long Varchinde grass.

It wasn't a monster.

It was a boy.

Perhaps fifteen or sixteen returns, shock haired, badly injured and alone. His skin was parchment white, his garments black with blood. Beside him lay a crude, scratch-built crutch.

He looked oddly familiar.

She stood stunned, shook her head helplessly when he begged her for water and wondered what in the name of the Gods she was going to do with him. She was no cursed apothecary – something about not shifting him because of his back?

"You're injured," she said. "I don't know –"

"I do." He shifted painfully, gulping air. "My ankle's broken – it's not serious. But my hip... please, be careful... I have to get to Roviarath... my teacher... need to tell them about the monsters... need to tell someone what they *were*..."

He was desperate, babbling, Triq didn't really hear him. She'd have to let go of the ever-more-skittish mare to retrieve the boy, she wasn't betting the horse would stay put.

The boy coughed and something liquid splashed over his fingers.

Annoyed with her own hesitation, she let the mare go and knelt by him. His eyes were glazed – pain, fear, relief – there was a heavy, dark stain soaking through his garments at his hip.

The mare had backed, but not bolted, the whites of her eyes were showing. As Triq called her, she came to whuffle at the boy's fallen form and laid her ears flat back. There was froth specking on her chest.

"What's up with you?" Triq wondered out loud. "Blood doesn't bother you, you've smelled enough of it."

The mare blew snot, ears flicking. The boy tried to smile, reached a hand to touch her mane. When Triq asked him if he could stand, he heaved himself to his good foot, hand on the horse's shoulder, and she boosted him over the little mare's back.

White faced under the moonlight, he passed out.

Triq fixed her attention on the lighthouse, aimed a little to the left, and began the long walk back to the tavern.

Her little mare sweated fear every step of the way.

9: STONE THE MONUMENT

Amethea's existence was nightmare and death, the smell of cold stone and hard metal, the feel of blood-wet flesh.

There had been something before this, something she'd been seeking, a friend she'd forgotten – but such things were worlds away, shadows of another time. She was a wraith, a ghost that flickered with loss.

Hollow, she watched listless as the girl died.

Her healer's hands were like strangers. The blood of others was crusted beneath her nails, caked in the skin about their outsides. She had failed – again. Maugrim would be angry with her, but her hands were helpless. They lay in her lap as if they were broken.

The girl was keening, last breaths thin with horror. She had collapsed, slumped and broken on the dirty stone. As Amethea watched, she shuddered once, tried to speak, and was still.

Reaching forward, Amethea closed her eyes. Her metal-scaled skin was cold. Perhaps she should have prayed, but there was no touch of hope in this Godsless place.

The girl was the third failure, the third tormented death, the third sufferer to succumb to Maugrim's burning passion, to the exquisite tortures of the Kartian craftmaster called Vice.

Maugrim was a blaze of vision; an architect so powerful that she'd not even felt herself fall. He pulled her, drove her, wanted her and inspired her. She hated him, but she needed his fire to warm the cold she had become. Nothing else seemed to matter – this was his dream and she existed only to make it happen, to bring his revelation to power and life.

She and Vice, craftsmen both, workers of flesh and metal.

Now, though, Maugrim had gone. Vice was stood behind her, his presence sharp and cruel. She turned, looked over her shoulder at the elaborate and deliberate scarring that carved patterns in his pale skin, at his thin white fingers blackened with blood and metal shavings. When he spoke, he was as cold and distant as the white moon.

"You've failed."

"Yes."

His chill voice was rich with a thousand layers of intonation that her blunt Grasslander ears would never pick up. Raised in almost pure darkness, Kartian culture communicated by sound and by touch. His scars were his identity, his rank and family, and the marks of his pure skill.

"It can't be done." Her voice caught on a sob and she found she was angry – with herself, with Vice's blame and scorn, with the insanity of what she faced. She had no sense of time – of day and night, of sleep and hunger – her sunless world had become pain and torment and failure. The screaming of flesh and the scraping of metal.

Maugrim's fire.

She feared him, needed him; she tumbled in his wake and she hated herself for it. When he was gone, she resented him and raged silently against him; in his presence, she would do anything to please him.

She looked at the corpse of the girl, at her glittering carapace of metal-scaled skin.

"It can't be done. The trauma's too severe, too much blood…"
Her voice was a whisper of horror at what she was doing.

Vice said only, "We start again. Maugrim should be told."
The accusation in his tone was as heavy as metal itself. He
turned and walked away, quiet as a final breath.

Watching him leave, Amethea felt her heart retract in fear.
Maugrim would be angry with her… but there was nothing she
could do, no way she could make this happen.

I can't do this… I can't…!

Helpless, she walked through the twisted, narrow tunnels to
her chamber.

She was drying her hands when the doorway rolled back.

His anger was tangible, she could taste it, feel it – it blazed
from him raw and red. Water dripped sparkling from her skin.
She backed away, found herself babbling, "I tried, I swear, I…!"

He wasn't listening. Two steps, he had one hand round her
throat, her back pressed hard to the warm, smooth stone. She
breathed swift and shallow, a caught animal, wild-eyed. His
predatory smile was primal, an unholy firelight burned in his eyes.

She knew that she hated him. And yet she was gasping at his
touch, and *wanting*…

Somewhere in her heart, there was a tiny fragment of
defiance, *Why do you let him do this why do you let him* do
this? But his intensity was beyond her. When he was this close,
she burned.

His hand on her throat squeezed; his expression a promise
of danger.

The pressure was just enough to show his strength. She
bared her neck to him as if he were a bweao.

"Please…!" she gasped, but no longer knew what she was
asking for.

He let her go.

Her knees went, she slid to the floor. Every time – every *time* in his presence! He robbed her of her thoughts – all she wanted to do was make him happy.

This had to stop.

The stones beneath her were blood-warm, oddly comforting. She spread her hands on them, steadying herself.

Maugrim slammed a fist into the flat rock of the wall. He spun towards her.

"Why?" he demanded. "I've got every resource, every insight. I've done all the calculations, I *know* this can happen. I'm missing something, sweetheart, what is it?" Blood oozed from his fingers where his rings had bitten his skin. "This damn world plays tricks on me!"

She knew she should get up, should get up now, but the stone beneath her hands was strong, oddly reassuring.

"What you're trying to do… is alchemically impossible," she said. "Flesh can't grow into metal. Metal's lifeless – all I've got is another *experiment*, dying before my eyes, I…"

"You'll fix this, little lady. You're the doctor, you can make this happen." He came to one knee, right in front of her. One bleeding knuckle raised her chin to look up at him. He was overpowering. "I need you, Amethea. I'll get you anything you want."

Need you. There was a bite in her voice as she said, "Or I'll be next?"

That made him smile, like the edge of a dirty knife.

"I'm running out of time. And patience. I know I can make this happen."

She heard herself defy him – "You wouldn't!" – even though she knew he absolutely would.

He laughed, a sound like a snarl. He put his hands on her shoulders, pushing her back to the wall and leaned in so she could feel his breath on her cheek.

He said softly, "It's why I'm here, Thea: your world's alchemy, your lost Elementalism – I am bringing them back to life!"

His weight was hurting. She didn't care.

"I *can't*, don't you – ?" she began.

One hand shoved, hard. She fell back, crumpling gracelessly to the floor. In a moment, he was astride her, turning her onto her back, holding her hands easily above her head. Suddenly afraid, she struggled, but he was far too strong.

"What are you…?"

For a moment, he did nothing – just let her realise how much she was under his control. Her fright was rapidly growing – this wasn't playing, she could feel his tightly controlled fury. She put her strength into it, writhing furiously. With a determined twist to his lips he held her down. As she subsided, his free hand stroked her jaw.

"Don't fight me, little priestess. You know you'll do what I want."

His kiss was fire and heat and poison.

She twisted away, turning her head, her back arched as she pitted herself against him. He shifted his weight, let his whole body drop full-length onto hers. She could feel how hard he was – and she still responded to him, the sunrise glow between her thighs, her hips moving though she didn't – couldn't – want them to.

His breath was hot on the side of her throat. She felt the soft scratch of his beard. She felt his teeth.

"Oh, Gods…" Had that been her voice?

He reached down with his free hand, pulling at her skirts, at the strange blue cotton trousers he wore. For a moment, she was fright and disbelief – yet her own body was betraying her, the anticipation of his touch was making her swell to meet him. She wanted this. Didn't she?

He purred words in her ear, it didn't matter what he said, the tone of his voice was flame and lust and her lips were parted, her breath catching on a whimper.

Gently, his fingers found her, found her more than ready.

With a deep, quiet chuckle, they eased into her.

Coaxing, stroking.

Oh, my Gods...

He knew just how to touch – there was no force, just a caress of absolute control. The pleasure was so intense, she could feel the blood rising in her face, feel her body quivering as he paused, then began again.

"You'll make this happen, Amethea."

Her hips ached towards him, muscles tightened around his touch, silently begging him deeper. But the resentment in her heart glittered, cold and hard and still. Somewhere, she remembered she wouldn't be controlled like this – not any more. Jamming her cheek sideways against his, she said, "I *can't*!"

He hissed exasperation; his fingers were gone. She gasped objection before she could stop herself. The wash of loss, the hollow ache of hunger...

But his weight was between her thighs, he was tugging her ridiculous skirts roughly out of the way. She was feet and shoulders and tailbone against the warm stone, eagerly welcoming his weight on hers, her legs rising to wrap round him even as her mind repeated, insanely, *Nononononono...*

Yes.

The first thrust was slow, full length – tension rippled through him at the contact, he was holding his own need sternly back. She cried out, struggling to free her arms so she could... what? Hold him? Fight to free herself? He braced his hands against her wrists, held his weight on his elbows and, still buried in her to the hilt, leaned up to look at her flushed face, her splashed hair.

Somewhere in his soul, he smouldered. Embers burned in his vision.

Your alchemy, your lost Elementalism...

She could feel his heat, over and in her; hear her own

breathing; feel her pulse hammering in her skin.

And beneath her, the rock was *warming*.

It seemed to thrum, as if summoned by his fire, by the drumbeat of her blood.

He withdrew – almost. Circling his hips gently, a tease, a tempt, he said, "You can. And you will."

She wanted him back. Her legs tightened but he was too strong. The thrum beneath her was becoming a reverberation, an echo and broadcast of her own hammering heart. Somewhere between the heat of the stone and the burning between her thighs, she found herself saying again, between gritted teeth, between breaths of craving, "All... the tricks... in the world... won't make it... any more possible."

His face set, then, his eyes gave a single blaze of fury. He pushed into her slowly, watching her expression, and she stared back, unwavering; yet her voice was catching in her throat – a feminine cry she couldn't stifle.

He withdrew, eased into her again, a long, smooth stroke. She gasped, wanted, needed still – couldn't help it. She unwrapped her legs to brace her feet against the stone.

The hot pulse of the stone.

Metal's lifeless...

The thought was incoherent – she hadn't grasped it, not yet. Once before, she'd felt the vastness of the rock about her, that sense of potence and patience and loss and age...

She had been looking for something!

The reverberations of her own pulse echoed back through her skin. In the stone, something *heard*.

Oh, my Gods.

It was rhythmic and deep, its might massive, yet not hostile. It was far, far bigger than Maugrim's petty lust, his need for control. It was bigger than her resentment, than her body or senses, the chamber, the passageways. She couldn't encompass it or comprehend it. As waves of sensation and pleasure broke through her, she surrendered herself – not to Maugrim, but to the stone.

And he felt it too.

As she let go, it pulsed through her skin, her movements and responses and sounds. He gave a breath of amazement as the heat found him through her and he started to move more swiftly, making her cry wordless appreciation. She moved with him, matched him. He, too, lost himself in it, in her. She grounded him and he was her focus.

And the stone grew hotter. The thrum became a pound and it was tangible in the sweating air.

Now, she wasn't fighting him any more. She found his mouth, craving as much contact as possible. He let her hands go and they were in his hair, over his shoulders, clumsily pulling his strange garments from him so she could feel his bare chest, the muscles move beneath his skin.

Leaning back, he tore the lacings down her top with one hand, bared her skin to his.

And the stone grew hotter.

She could feel it in her feet, bracing downwards against it as she pushed upwards into the impact of Maugrim's body. The wet slide of him inside her was almost too much, she gripped him as hard as she could and he, too, cried out, guttural and abandoned.

She began to shake. Waves of sensation robbed her of every conscious thought. Her lips parted in inarticulate sounds – her hands clung to him, refusing to let him go.

He growled at her pleasure, drank it in through his skin. Beneath her, around her, the rock was alive, burning with the heat in the chamber. She was caught between flesh and stone...

As she crested the wave – hips high, back arched, colours flashing through her vision – she was vaguely, oddly, aware of intense sensation in her feet. Maugrim came moments after she did, head back, eyes closed, teeth bared. Then his relieved weight fell forwards on top of her, strangely comforting, secure.

For a moment, she rested under him, feeling the stone beneath her slowly cooling.

The thrum faded from her bones.

After a minute, he propped himself upright, looked down at her with an odd smile. He looked – young, almost confused.

She had no idea what to say, what to do – no idea what had just happened. The stone was only warm; it was hard under her shoulder blades.

And her feet…

…her feet felt strange, like she'd been sat on them too long and they'd gone to sleep. She tried to move them – half expecting the pin-ripple of returning feeling…

…and couldn't.

Sudden alarm pushed the languor from her body. She pushed him back, tried to sit up. There was tearing across her shoulders, a rush of ripping skin and fabric, a sudden flash of pain.

Warm ooze down her spine.

Maugrim tried to roll sideways, but her knee was in his way. She could move her leg, but her blood flow felt cut off mid-calf, her feet were weird, distant – somehow not her own. Her shoulders hurt like she'd shredded her skin; torn bits of her top were stuck to her.

In increasing desperation, she craned to see past Maugrim's body. She tried, really tried…

They still wouldn't move.

"Maugrim…?" she said. "My feet…"

"Thea." The word was almost gentle. Frowning, he sat back on his heels and stared.

Then he started to laugh.

"Vice!" Massively jubilant, Maugrim raced through the entranceway to the chamber he'd humorously named his "lock-up". "*Vice!*"

The Kartian had gone – his latest failure was a broken heap, glittering under the rocklights. Once again, the melding of flesh and metal had yielded only death. Maugrim dismissed it and cast his eyes over the bike, the stuff he'd stashed here, waiting.

Now useless.

Aftershocks of pleasure danced sparks in his blood. *How* could he have missed something so obvious?

His old life had gone – the van a blackened carcass of steel. He'd been in the back – heard only the angry squeal of pressure brakes, shouting, the hoverdrone rebroadcasting orders.

Then gunfire. The *spang-spang-spang* of rounds chewing metal.

And the note changing as they penetrated the plating.

He was untouched by enhancement – he'd spent his career treating too many messed-up fashion-icon wannabes. In that split second before the tank went, he'd just had time to wish –

Mind and metal and flesh. He'd been trying to create, to *re-create*...!

Metal's lifeless.

The intensity of his abandonment, the shuddering, osmotic feedback of pleasure... The alchemical fusion he'd been busting his balls to find wasn't flesh and metal – it was flesh and *stone*. He wanted to bang his own head into the wall for being so bloody dumb. The time he'd wasted! He wasn't sure what he'd done – not yet – but he did know the bloody teacher had managed to attune herself to the cycling of Elemental Powerflux, to the south, to fire. She'd managed what only existed in myth... she...

...Exultance. Vast might and passion. Overwhelming sensation – drowning in it. The sheer power of what lay beneath him...!

...had attuned herself to the Powerflux...?

No, that couldn't be right.

Tightly controlling his thinking, he kicked at an old spray

can. It was empty. It skittered across the floor scattering washers as it went.

He had to focus!

Stone. In the midst of her orgasm, her feet had turned to stone.

Maugrim had uncovered the long-forgotten lore – the Elementalists, the priests of the people, were no more, their skills forgotten and abandoned like everything else. A few of them still lurked, way out in the farmlands and the ribbon-towns, but they wielded little more than herb lore and trickery. The Powerflux, the flowing of the elements through the grass and across the world's surface, once the quintessential lifeblood, revered and trusted, had long since passed into humorous folklore – like fairies.

But he, Maugrim, knew it was there. He knew that he could reach it, and he knew he could channel the sheer glory of what he found.

No, the stone had grown through *her flesh.*

This was the nexus, the Flux's central point – the plug socket, if you like. Down here, beneath the Monument, *real* elemental energy was tangible: it hummed through the stone, he could taste it in the air. Here, an Elementalist could find and learn what this world hadn't bothered to remember – how to take that strength and channel it, how to perform miracles.

If he were strong enough to be a living capacitor – to stand the charge that surged in his blood.

With sudden insight, he realised something fundamental.

Metal's lifeless!

Maugrim was the world's only Elementalist, as far as he was aware, the only true wielder of this forgotten and unseen might. He could attune himself to the great, electrical web of the Powerflux, the cyclic flow of the four compass-elements that controlled wave and weather and growth and season – the flow and balance of light and darkness, ice and fire. The energy he drew was a rush – heat and chill and lightning and thunderclouds. He'd always thought of the Powerflux like a matrix of taser wires, shocks constantly running from end to end...

But this world was metal-poor, ferrous metal almost non-existent.

As far as he could tell, the Powerflux existed in the very *grass*. Somehow, they were one and the same thing.

He picked up a washer, held it on the tip of one dirt-ingrained index finger. The rocklights gleamed from the surface.

The Powerflux's energy was constant. It moved continuously between the four compass directions – the anchor points, the elements' "souls". In spite of the loss of lore, the knowledge was deep rooted – that everything from sunrise to weather to personal illness was caused by elemental cycling or imbalance.

And so he'd begun to study.

Flesh could harbour energy, like a capacitor – a properly trained Elementalist could attune himself to the Flux and he could, literally, charge himself up. The term "Elementalism" described the pure, raw energy – fire, darkness, light, cold... There were varying degrees of potence and skill that were largely encompassed by the word "focus". The better your attunement, the more power you could absorb; the better your focus, the more discipline you had when throwing it about.

His eyes went to the rocklight, gleaming smugly in the corner.

Its illumination laughed at him. Like flesh, it was a capacitor – it absorbed and held sunlight, then slowly released it when in darkness.

He couldn't believe he'd never realised something so simple.

Stone and flesh; flesh and stone. Both capacitor, both conductor. *Metal's lifeless! His* fire – *his* strength and power! The attunement he had been taught, attunement that no other mortal human had access to – *his* attunement had called the elemental current from the site, through stone and through skin – that bloody teacher had conducted like a gold bar. Somehow, he'd called to the very core of the Powerflux.

And it had answered him.

Amethea had been his fuse – his dead man switch. She'd absorbed and taken the damage of the supercharge he'd summoned.

Saved his arse. Shown him the glaring bloody truth.

Elementalism was emotional – rage and glory like throwing an electrical paddy. Alchemy – putting those elements to scientific use – now that was a different and far more clinical matter. Creations like the centaurs – that took a huge amount of skill and learning.

"*Vice!*"

The Kartian must've heard him – but the chamber remained still.

Maugrim flicked the washer onto the floor. *Tink!* He was planning, thinking, possibilities unfolding. This had been a beginning, a hint of what he could achieve if he focused his energy correctly. He needed to move his workroom closer to the heart of the site, the nexus of the Flux itself. He needed to plug himself in, to understand *exactly* what he'd done.

And he needed a new subject – a conductor, a dead man switch he could afford to sacrifice for the increased might they would bring. There'd been a woman, strange blooded, not bloody Range Patrol. Vice had brought her in – said something about a Kartian half-blood.

He had to recreate the experiment. Once he understood what he'd done, he could take control. If he could summon that kind of power, he could *electroshock* this complacent, indulgent world into alertness.

And that was what he really wanted, why he had been recruited, why he had been given the centaurs as his guardians, why he had been taught the lore of this world in which he'd found himself...

This world was stagnating, just like his own. It was in

stasis; it learned nothing new, had forgotten its own legends. Its population wasn't growing, either in number or in enlightenment. In short, it had its collective head up its arse. Like a patient in his old life, he needed to make it wake up, change, kick over – that's what his teacher wanted, why he'd been trained and taught. Why he'd been working so hard to make that timeless vision manifest...

Remembering what the half-Kartian woman had looked like, Maugrim began to grin.

This time, there would be no half measures. He was going to understand this new power he'd awakened – the skill it had brought him. And then he was going to let it blaze across the Varchinde.

Amethea looked at a pair of stone feet.

They were beautiful, perfect, the most exquisite carved stone feet she'd ever seen.

But they were hers.

She was lost, still trembling with the aftermath of extreme passion. She felt strange, empty, abandoned – not only by Maugrim, but by the stone.

The memory of her exultation was bizarre – frightening.

What had happened?

If she tapped her toe, she could feel it – sort of. She flicked it, then banged it – the sensation was oddly nebulous, like her skin was half numb. Half numb – and gracefully smoothed rock.

If she traced her fingers up the front of her shinbone, she could see where stone crystallised into flesh, where her skin solidified, where the creeping calcification had paused. For a long time, she stared at it, touching it, horrified and morbidly fascinated.

Was it getting worse?

Gradually, she became more aware of herself. She was uncomfortable, damp between her thighs, stiff backed. When

she explored her shoulders with her hands, she found she'd –
literally – left the top layer of skin from her shoulder blades
stuck to the floor. *Part* of the floor.

As though the growth had started, but...

Her fingers found fragments of ripped fabric. Her feet had
been – were – bare, but her garments had covered her back.
Somehow, they'd got in the way.

Of what?

With an effort, she swallowed a mouthful of horror and
tried to sit up straighter.

Okay – that wasn't so bad. Neither her feet nor her ankles
would move, but she could reach the palette and drag it towards
her. She could sit on it, easing the pressure on her tailbone and
freeing herself of the shredded remains of the ludicrous frock
he'd liked.

His hands, tearing it from her, oh dear Gods...

Shaking herself sternly free of the memory, of the rush that
came with it, she tore a length of the fabric and tied it round
her calf – marking the fusion point. Then she ran her hands
over her shoulders to find out how badly she'd torn her skin.

Apothecary, heal yourself.

Who used to say that?

Her hands paused. Again, the sensation that she'd lost
something. Closer this time – a bowshot, a sense of grief, a hand
gone from hers. A creature, massive and masculine and wrong,
screaming insanity in the plainland night.

Mighty stones, fallen and gleaming faintly iridescent, like
grandfathers of rocklights.

She struggled to focus; a boy with a shock of orange –

Oh Goddess.

Feren.

Like the stone in her feet, her thoughts were suddenly solid,
her memories as certain as pebbles in her hand.

She'd been riding from Vilsara in Xenok, taking her 'prentice to fetch taer from the Monument. They'd been attacked – horses with the bodies of men, beautiful, crazed. Monstrous. Feren had been *shot...*

He flew to the moon, sweetheart.

Killed?

There is need of a healer.

As though the creeping stone had driven Maugrim's fire from her flesh and heart, given her gravity, she focused clearly for the first time. She didn't know what had happened, but she'd felt consciousness under her – *in* her – skin. Vast, slow, beyond her ken or her comprehension... something had been *awake*.

It had driven Maugrim from her body.

And in the crucible it had provided, there was a hardening crystal of focus.

Alert now, determined, her first instinct was to break up the palette, find herself a chisel or lever – but she'd no idea what damage she'd do if she tried to separate her feet from the floor. Systematically, she tried to tense one calf muscle, the other. Move one ankle, the other. Wiggle her toes.

There had to be a way out of this.

She was tensed, watching the door, heart thumping now with adrenaline and purpose. She scanned the room for clothes and kit, almost wanting to pile them up so she'd know where they were. She needed to move. Needed to move *now*!

And gradually, as though it heard her plea, the calcification withdrew.

Elation fired her. It was slow, so slow, and it left a cold, numb emptiness in her flesh; an emptiness filled by screaming needles of returning sensation, by dripping, caustic blood. It hurt like the rhez, but the pain was cleansing, cleared her head, chased the last tails of lust from her body. She became impatient, hammered at her skin to make the transition faster – she *had* to be out of this before he came back!

Oddly, she found herself cold. As her legs were freed, she

could stretch to reach her old garments – the shirt and overshirt she'd worn from Roviarath. They didn't warm her, but their familiarity was comforting. Pressed to her face, they smelled of chearl and grass and woodsmoke. With them on, she knew who she was.

How many people had she refused to heal? Stood by and watched die in agony?

Without Maugrim's heat haze, there was no way to soften, rationalise – or to forgive. *Metal embedded in skin, each a vast, raw, open wound, unable even to plead for their own death.* For one horrified moment, she wondered if she deserved everything that Maugrim had done to her.

Then she was angry. Angry for herself, for Feren, for the people who had died in pain unspeakable, for the ones yet to come. With her hands under her knees, she tugged at her feet until she felt they'd tear at the fusion point.

One way or another, she was going to pay him back for every wound he'd inflicted, every liberty he'd taken. For every *touch*!

The faster her blood flowed, it seemed, the faster the stone receded – after a few more moments, she found she could stand up, legs shaky but capable.

The needle sting reached her heels. It itched.

She leaned forwards, hands against the rock, tried to lift one foot, then the other. *Come on, come on!*

They still wouldn't budge.

Her finger brushed a mark, carved in the stone.

A smile etched on the metal plate that covered his mouth.

No. She told herself. *Stop it.*

She'd noticed the marking before, but the shimmer of Maugrim's flame had blurred her vision and she'd not seen anything clearly. Now, as the itch strayed over the soles of her feet and agonisingly into her toes, she crouched and leaned to reach the rocklight.

Held it up to the wall.

Light glittering from a carapace of scales.

The mark was old, shallow and faded – a spiral curve, elegant and ancient. It spoke wordless of the vast age and might that dwelled within these stones, these passageways. She traced the spiral with a fingertip, wondering what it meant – who had put it there.

What had she said to Feren? *Maybe it once was some celebration, some ancient elemental temple; maybe the stones just observed the Count of Time. Maybe it was a memorial, or a tomb. I heard once that the hill we're standing on is a passage grave, commemorating some lord or hero...*

The realisation was so obvious: she was *under* the Monument. She was stood within forgotten stones, on the outermost edge of a site so ancient it was lost to lore, abandoned for thousands of returns.

Oh Goddess.

Two sharp, bright points of fear – one for herself, caught down here with no idea as to what really lay outside this dim, dry chamber. The other for Maugrim, for the might he'd touched...

...and for what he'd do with it.

Skin peeling, strip by strip, layer by layer. Metal in muscle, shuddering, jerking nerves.

Not again!

Leaning her weight on her wrists, she found she could lift her heels. One side then the other, she could reach down to scratch and scratch and *scratch* them. She could almost feel flakes of stone coming away under her fingers. She could flex her toes, just. Mastering the urge to just rip the ball of her foot clean away from the floor, she threw the rocklight to the pallet and scrabbled for the rest of her kit. Belt, knife, pouches, neck-thongs – as soon as she could move, she was trousers and boots on and *out* of this chamber.

And then what?

She traced the spiral again. The fading of the stone through her flesh had left only memories of its touch in her soul. Its vast awareness had gone from her heart – but she was herself, at last, she was Amethea. The spiral was comforting, as though the stone had not forgotten her.

She was no warrior, no scout, she had been raised by the church, parentless – but never purposeless. As her feet came at last away from the rock and she stamped on them, hard, fighting the pain of returning feeling, she remembered her determination.

He had looked down at her, and he had laughed.

Triumph and realisation.

Whatever he wanted to do with his flesh-and-metal minions, she had no doubt that flesh and stone would be his next step – that, somehow, he would seek to tap consciously into the awareness they'd awakened.

Into the sheer Gods-power of whatever lay beneath.

She threw her legs into her trousers, her feet into her boots, laced them both shut. There was a twinge of loss as her feet finally lost their skin contact.

Settling her belt at her hips, she faced the chamber door.

She'd only ever travelled one way – but had seen enough to realise the size of the maze that lay down here, forgotten by all but Maugrim himself. There was no way out through the treasure chamber – and besides, she found she wanted to stay with the stone.

Alone, her feet stinging raw with the return of circulation to bloodless muscles, she drew a long breath and rolled back the door.

He was smiling at her, a smile of victory.

"Going somewhere, sweetheart?"

The Kartian metalworker called Vice knew his usefulness was over – and the price he would pay.

He was an artisan, born to craft, raised in almost darkness

and tuned to heights of hearing and tactile sensitivity no Grasslander could emulate. In Maugrim's voice, he'd heard clearly the nuances of hope, exhilaration, domination and death; in the warm, shifting air of the passageways, his scarred Kartian skin responded to the faintest breath of draught, to the raised awareness of what lay deeper.

Maugrim had cauterised the stone, he'd burned away the light-lichens, the stray grass roots, the loose soil and the errant, blindly curious creatures. The rock was warmed by his elemental alignment, but he'd still not yet touched the site's true nexus.

The stone had awoken, Vice had heard its pulse thrum in his skin, in the bones behind his ears. It lay quiescent now – but its potential left him breathless.

Further in. Somewhere.

Maugrim's chamber of wealth and death didn't interest him – it was a dead end in more ways than one. He took a little of the white-metal – not enough to be missed – and he slipped silently away.

This site had no fears for one raised under the dark might of the Kartiah Mountains.

Following the soft touch of air, his fingers tracing the stones in the walls, he began to understand that Maugrim had only cleansed a part of the passageways – that so much more lay untouched. Slowly, the stones about him grew cooler and the roots of the grass began to penetrate the rock, touching his face with creeping pale fingers. Fallen soil caught his feet; the air smelled chill and dry. In places, the walls were graven with sigils his fingers traced with curious incomprehension.

It grew moist and cold, the cold of soil and stone.

He closed towards the centre – the heart of the site that lay directly beneath the broken sarsens of the Monument itself.

Here, the passageways were crumbling, tumbles of rocks littered the floor, dirt fell with a hiss as he passed, dusting his intricate white hair. There was emptiness here, loss and ancient abandonment – now awakened and seeking understanding. No mortal foot had passed this way in perhaps thousands of returns.

The rockfalls grew deeper and older until they barred his way utterly – he couldn't reach the centre.

Whatever they defended, he needed to find.

He was Kartian, he could navigate with a breath and a touch. In the darkness of the passageways he tried again to reach the site's heart – and again – but each time, rockfalls or tumbled ceilings barred his way. Growths of dried lichen teased his fingertips and the roots of the grass hung almost to the floor, curtains of pale entrapment.

Then the air behind him moved.

And the rock came savagely to life.

10: FEREN THE WANDERER, ROVIARATH

The crash of wood made Roderick jump.

The tavern's doors had been kicked open, slammed back against the benches. Between them stood a silhouette, small and strong, haloed by the moons' glitter. The rocklight glinted on four pale eyes.

In its arms dangled a corpse.

"Gods!" Heart in his throat, he was moving before he realised it, skid-vaulting the bar and hitting the floor running. The last gaggle of drinkers fumbled for peace-bonded weapons.

The thing in the doorway staggered, cried, "Ress!" and the four-eyed shape stumbled forwards into the light.

Triqueta.

She was wide-eyed and shaking, sweat and desperation slid clean trails through the dust on her skin. The stones in her cheekbones gleamed – and in her arms hung the body of a boy.

"Help him!"

The few remaining members of the Banned were moving, shouting.

"Triq!" Stool going over, one of the vets was shoving his way to the fore, around him, his mates were drunkenly swearing.

Voices clamoured. "What the rhez?" "Who's *that*?" "Watch it, you sonofamare, that was my beer!"

Triqueta was folding under the weight.

"Ress! He's out cold – pretty badly chewed up."

The tide of questions rose again.

"Over here!" Roderick made a grab for the nearest rocklight, shadows leaped like figments through the room as he lifted it over a table. "Put him there, in the light. I'll get you water."

With a grunt, Triqueta hefted the boy onto the tabletop.

And stood back.

It was deep night, and the tavern's staff had long since retired. In The Wanderer's taproom, the Banned's final die-hards had gathered close to raise old songs and leather tankards, but the soldiers had finally reeled away and the rest of the room was empty. Cursing rolled from a nearby figure, snoring on a bench.

The veteran Ress, tall and lean, his short beard shot with grey, studied the boy's dirt-streaked face.

Triq's hands clenched into fists at her sides. "He was conscious when I found him, just. His ankle's busted – he's a mess. Think you can fix him?"

"Think I can try."

The remaining Banned had lowered voices and vessels.

As Roderick returned with water, Ress was cutting deftly through the boy's shirt and breeches and leaning in close, examining cloth bindings in the tavern's pooled rocklight.

Triqueta fidgeted, swiped a tankard from one of her cohorts and took a long swig.

Ress glanced at her, puzzled. "You treated him?"

"Fat chance!" She wiped her mouth on her sleeve.

"Oi, Triq!" A voice from the table. "Bit young for you?"

"Not funny." She threatened them with the tankard, turned back to Ress. "Found him out towards the Monument. He'd made a crutch out of a javelin, Gods know how he got this far."

"The Monument?" The Bard glanced at the doorway, an

odd, formless shock prickling along his nerves. "That's crazed."

Triq had another mouthful of ale.

The rocklight showed the boy's slim, pale chest was crusted in blood. His shirt, breeches and bindings were stuck to him. With calm, steady hands, Ress was soaking the fabric away from his skin.

"Tough kid," he murmured.

"He spooked my mare," Triqueta said. "Had a rhez of time getting him back here."

The Banned round the table were muttering superstition and ribald defiance. A hand grabbed Triq's wrist and, amidst laughter, the ale tankard went back to its owner.

"One thing at a time." Under Ress's gentle fingers, the blood-clotted fabric peeled away from the boy's wound like a scab. The apothecary wheeshed through his teeth. "Whoever treated him knew what they were doing. Only reason he's got this far. He's been *spitted*. Ready for roasting. Straight through, front to back."

No healer, the Bard could only stay out of the light and watch. The mention of the Monument had thrown him, and he found that he was trying to remember something, a figment that had long since faded into darkness and the Count of Time.

But Ress was studying the boy, neatly slicing off breeches and boots.

"The ankle – wouldn't've been serious. If he's walked on it –" he paused as if trying to encompass this information "– it's splinters. Only made it because he kept his boots on. It'll heal, but he'll be crippled." He rubbed one hand though his beard. "His hip – chips off the bone. It's gone through at an angle – sitting on the horse has scrambled it badly. If it's punctured his kidney... Gods, I don't even know what could have *made* a hole like this." He shrugged exasperation. "Anyone? Suggestions? *Serious* ones?"

Triq said, "Where do I know him from?"

"So many, you've forgotten?" One of her Banned cohorts made a foul gesture and she punched his ear without missing a breath. There were guffaws, like the releasing of tension. Understanding their need for humour, Roderick covered a brief grin.

But he moved the rocklight to study the boy.

The kid's face was sunburned, freckled, streaked with tears, there was an old scar in his eyebrow. He had crazed, orange hair and several days' growth of fluff on his chin. And yes, he was faintly familiar.

It teased him as though a breeze had chilled his skin. Silently, the Bard cursed the irony of his moniker – like the very world herself, his memory was flawed.

Then his eyes were pulled to the terrible hole in the boy's hip.

And he found his hand over his mouth, his stomach knotting.

The wound was huge, as though a javelin had been driven through the boy's flesh, but harder than any mortal hand could wield it. Around it, the skin was white, torn, crusted with old blood and fabric threads. Its edges were a vicious red and deep bruising had spread down the front of his hipbone. He could see the end of a piece of swollen, blood-black wood, splintered as though it'd been poorly snapped. "Spitted", Ress had said. It was too fat for an arrow, too narrow for a spear – and it had gone through the boy's body like he was thinly stretched hide.

The boy's courage and resilience bereft him of words.

Where had he come from?

The air rippled again, his almost-recollection made him shudder with imagined cold.

But the boy was stirring.

Ress moved to his side, voice and hands gentle. Triq came close, too, standing beside Roderick. She smelled of sun and spice and fresh sweat.

"In the desert," she said softly, "life's precious – to be celebrated. Saving that life's more precious still."

The apothecary flicked a glance at her, raised a curious eyebrow. But she'd turned away and the boy was awake, moving, trying to talk.

At the table, there were ragged cheers. Leather tankards thumped together as they raised a toast to Ress's skill.

His shaking hands wrapped around the neck of a waterskin, the boy was speaking.

"I made it – I really did it!" His breathing was ragged. "I feel like I'm dreaming, I just walked and I walked and it wasn't really me and I never thought –"

"Easy," Ress said softly. "You've got a lot to tell... it can wait for a minute. You're hurt, lost a lot of blood –"

"I did good though, didn't I? I did it right?"

"You did...?" Triq almost pounced on him, but Ress understood.

"You... treated yourself...?"

"This is The Wanderer." His expression softened, staring in amazement at the taproom round him. His gaze came to rest on the Bard. "Amethea... she said... she'd eat her saddle and ride home bareback... She..." His jaw shook as he fought back a surge of tears.

"Shhhh." Roderick laid a hand carefully on his shoulder. "We'll take care of you now."

"Wait." The boy caught his arm. "I have to tell you. You're the Bard. Maybe you need to know this more than anybody."

And then he told his story.

Like the cold, spiked spine of some vast and sleeping creature, the Kartiah Mountains curved a silent guard at the westernmost limit of the Grasslands. By tradition, they were the home of darkness, the element made manifest; sun and moons both sank to their daily deaths upon the bared stone peaks. Down their flanks, the last of the light was spilled like blood and there forests swelled and grew. In their bellies, metal lay quiescent, awaiting the tactile skill of the Kartian craftmasters.

From here came the first scattered springs of the Great Cemothen River, the plainlands' central waterway that gathered its tributaries at Roviarath and then carved long leagues of meanders to the estuary and the dark sprawl of Amos.

Winding more or less beside it was the faint, ramshackle glimmer of the trade-road – and there on its outskirts, surrounded by the moonlit ripple of the shimmering grass, was the tiny, bright square of The Wanderer, a flicker of hope in the midst of the emptiness.

This was the Varchinde – the air was vast and wild and chill, and unseen creatures sang in anticipation of the birth of the sun. A soft, grey breeze shook the grasses, and stirred the dust.

Sheltered from the pre-dawn chill by shoulder-high stone walls, they'd gathered in the tavern's rear courtyard: Roderick, Triqueta and Ress. The boy, Feren, was resting on a narrow, two-wheeled wagon. The Banned's apothecary had done everything he could.

Everything would probably not be enough.

Bathed by the square of pale light from the kitchen window, Ress's lined face held failure. He rubbed a hand absently through his beard.

Roderick was watching eastwards, the dark of the sky was lightening to a deep, rich blue that made the slightly ragged, creeper-crawling wall top as black as nightmare.

They didn't have long.

In the Bard's Tundran blood, his odd fear still prickled, a shimmer of alarm. And now it had form.

Monsters.

Like the nartuk, but bigger, far bigger, than he had ever imagined.

Beside him, Triqueta held the headstall of her little palomino mare. She was edgy, watching the pre-dawn with an echo of his nervousness. Picking up on her mistress's mood, perhaps, the little horse threw her head up and down and stamped a splayed forehoof, the sound a heavy, dull thudding that seemed loud in the softening twilight.

Triq stroked her neck.

With them was the one remaining member of the die-hard, dawn patrol Banned. Jayr the Infamous was not one for the noisy crowds of a taproom – she was something of a loner, very young, ludicrously powerful, oddly awkward in company. She was also one of the finest open-handed fighters the Varchinde had ever seen. Her scalplock and meticulously, brutally carved scars were Kartian, her dark eyes those of a Grasslander and she had a powerful, Archipelagan physique. Both sets of knuckles were permanently scabbed over and her nails were bitten to the quick. Her big, bay gelding stood with his head down, snuffling at the cobblestones for errant greenery.

The remainder of the Banned had ridden – just about – for their campsite, mounts finding their way when riders could not. Syke, sharp-eyed and gleefully sleazy, would want to know what had happened. Jayr, unspeaking, had stayed.

Her hefty, cross-armed stance said *just in case*.

Ress's skill was considerable, but Feren's body was tainted with harm – he had an infection that was eating him from the inside out. The boy had fought so hard and come so far; his only hope of succour lay in reaching the city's hospice.

"The Count of Time creeps upon us," Roderick said, eyeing the sky. "Perhaps more than you know. Good fortune ride with you, Ress of the Banned." He had so much more he wanted to articulate: he wanted to wrest his feeling of unease into visibility, to show them the tremble of anticipation in his heart.

But now, of all times, his eloquence had failed him.

"We're slow – days from city limits." Ress was sat in the front of the wagon, the rein in his lap. The heavy, slope-shouldered chearl stood quiet in the traces. "And we're as vulnerable as –"

"Ress," the Bard said softly, his certainty apparently absolute, "you'll make it."

You have to. You have to tell –

"Do my best." The apothecary took a breath, made an effort to smile. "Failure's a part of success – don't get to my age without learning that."

Roderick clapped his arm, moved to the great wooden doors that held the open grass at bay. "You have both heart and courage. Not to mention an escort that kicks arse. When you reach Roviarath, take Feren's tale to CityWarden Larred Jade and tell him everything – *everything* – that the boy has told us. The city needs to know – and they must surely seek the missing Xenotian girl, the teacher." His tone had a thrum of urgency, it curled like creeper in his throat. For a moment, he left the doors alone, turning as if to conjure the image of Feren's monster from the cold stone of the moonlit yard. "You'll have to make him comprehend…" He stumbled, unable to wrest this odd and shapeless terror from his mouth.

"You believe this?" Ress sounded surprised. "Half man, half horse – alchemical experimentation? It's loco." Feren muttered, and Ress twisted to look back at him. "He was dehydrated, in pain, his mind conjured figments. He probably saw a Deep Patrol."

"A Deep Patrol?" Roderick turned again to the wagon, door unopened. The fact that Ress had no time for Feren's creatures had taken him completely aback. "Whatever his monsters may be, their existence is –"

"You're jesting. Alchemy like that –"

"Hasn't existed since the high days of Tusien – I know at least that much lore." The Bard chuckled as if strangling the tension in his throat. "Such creations –"

"Are impossible. I'm an apothecary, I know the limits of flesh."

"And hasn't this boy just surpassed those limits?"

The question brought Ress up short. With a tight sigh, he

managed, "Hardly the same thing."

Triq looked up, the dying moonlight caught a glitter in the stones in her cheeks. "Larred Jade's a practical man – we can't go in there with half-brewed tales of saga-borne beasties."

Ress snorted. "He'd throw away the key."

Jayr frowned and tore at her fingernails with teeth. Agitated, the little palomino tapped her forehoof. Triq patted her shoulder. For a moment, tension spun the dust at their feet into scuttling whirlwinds.

"We should go," Triq said finally, "before we land at the arse end of the Gods-Alone-Know-Where."

"Sorry." Ress shrugged at the Bard, picked up the rein. "This is real, it isn't one of your stories."

The words were a dismissal, a request to throw open the gateway and let them go – but Roderick didn't move. There was urgency in him now – the monsters were real, they had to be, he *had* to make them understand.

"Everything's a story to someone," he said and before Ress could answer, he turned away from the doors completely and gestured at the wagon, at the restlessly sleeping boy. "And this one must have an audience. Whatever these things may be, their threat is most certainly real – alchemy, the creation of creatures like this – it's no myth. Just because you can't see it, Ress of the Banned, doesn't mean it isn't there."

Over the wall, the light was slowly paling, tiny wildflowers shook in the breeze. Almost trembling now, the Bard continued, "The Powerflux gives the world her seasons, her weather, her light and her darkness – you're Banned, you live with these things in your blood. That this power has other manifestations is surely only sense?"

"This'd better not be your 'Great Power that Ends the World' speech." Triq rolled her eyes, though tolerantly. "You can play Prophet Loco on your own time, sunshine. The poor kid's half –"

"I'm not playing." The edge in his voice was sharp. "I feel the truth of this, in my heart and in my skin. If these monsters exist, they're an alchemical formula left over from the days of Tusien – something we've not been able to create in a thousand returns. I have a visitor, a champion come to me from outside, a traveller to whom our whole existence is a story –"

"You have a visitor? From another world?" Now Triq was smothering laughter. "Oh dear Gods. Been at the smoke-weed, have we?"

"You're not helping your case," Ress commented bleakly. "Or your credibility." His expression was humourless. "My priority's the kid. And no way am I taking tales of monsters into a CityWarden's hearing without proof. You're jesting."

"No," Roderick said softly. "I'm not."

Tension rose like the edge of the sunrise. Feren cried out, wordless and laden with pain.

And then came the shock.

An edge of a memory, a cold point in Roderick's heart, something that was there-and-gone, terrifying but utterly formless. He knew it, he *knew* it, and he had no idea why. It was an after-echo of a nightmare, chill and tantalising, shivering through his skin – and even as he was reaching to understand it, it had faded into the morning.

What...?!

His breath had congealed and he found he was shaking, his hands palsied with a desperate need to grab this thing, to see it and name it.

Fired by a rush of frustration, he said, "This is no story! How can I find words to frame this? Ecko is *here*; he brings darkness and fire and strength the likes of which I've never seen! He understands my tale, my vision, the world's lost memory." The words had a bitterness he could barely suppress. "I feel the Count of Time at my back. Call me madman if you will, insane prophet – whatever name you choose to give me –" he came forwards, the early light in his eyes "– but take this tale to Jade – tell him everything!"

"Tell him yourself!" Triqueta said.

"I must carry this to Fhaveon – to Rhan, and to the Council of Nine. To the Foundersson himself!"

"Gods," Ress said, sharp as a punch in the face. "They'll lock you *up*."

The Bard's plea tumbled into silence; it fell like a grey pebble in the pre-dawn light and rolled, disregarded, across the courtyard. For a moment, he wanted to rail with hopeless, helpless, timeless fury, *I am a Guardian of the Ryll, such instincts are my training and my strength. I can feel the truth of them in my blood and bone. How can I make you understand?*

But he knew that such words meant nothing – that they would fall forlorn and spin forgotten across the stone of The Wanderer's yard.

Triqueta stared at him for a moment, then turned away.

"Roderick, with respect." Ress gave a short sigh. "Your sincerity is apparent – I'm trying to help you. You can't just walk into the Council in Fhaveon with some injured kid's loco rumour – 'here be monsters'."

"I have to. And equally, you must rouse CityWarden Jade," Roderick said.

"This is crazed!" Ress spread his hands helplessly. "Feren's badly hurt, his mind could have played any number of jests on him. Roderick, with respect, I don't understand why you're –"

"Then take it this way," Roderick said. "Such alchemy is no *figment*. Tales of ancient Tusien say the city sired monstrosities – creatures of crossed flesh that dwelled in captivity for the amusement of all. Those creatures were crafted, not born. Where do you think our chearl first came from? Our bretir? Our –" his lips twisted "– nartuk? Who is to say that the Monument doesn't hold Tusien's memory; that somewhere this lore has not been preserved, uncovered? If you will not heed my fears, then heed my facts."

"They're *sagas*." Ress's words were like the snapping of a trap.

Roderick's grin had an edge of mania. "There is truth in every tale."

"Look, I've had enough of this." Ress picked up the wagon's traces. "You can't attach half a man to half a horse. That's the end of it. No amount of regurgitated legend is going to make me stand in front of Larred Jade and tell him otherwise. If – *when* – Feren wakes up –"

"Then give me an alternative." Roderick smoothed the nose of the chearl in the wagon traces. "If there was no monster, what happened to the boy? Where's his teacher, Amethea?"

"Boys." Triq was watching the sky. "Quit squabbling, will you? We're running out of time."

Feren muttered again, his face was white and sweating.

Ress turned on Triqueta, the paling sky glittering like shards in his eyes. "Why didn't you leave him?"

"What?" Triqueta was rocked back by the question. "You know I wouldn't – not even by my desert blood, none of us would. What the rhez kind of question is that?"

Ress shifted on the wagon seat. "I'm not Banned-born. I was a scholar, learned a lot about people – before it went wrong and Syke gave me refuge. The Banned, Triq, you're forthright, you act before you think, you speak your mind, you –" a rat scuttled across the cobbles, making Triq's mare snort and sidestep "– sometimes, you can be very naïve."

"Oh *naïve*?" Triq spat, indignant. "I've spent my whole damned life with the Banned, worked for every CityWarden that'd compensate me and done dirtier deeds that I'd ever tell you. Naïve! What've you done?"

"Learned." Ress gave her a wry half-smile. "Enough to know that you can't achieve the *impossible*." He glanced at the Bard. "So what's left?"

Triqueta gaped. "You mean – Feren made this *up*?"

"Think about it." Ress cut her short. "He's a good apothecary – good enough to know he'll die. And certainly, something's happened to his teacher. So, what's more likely?"

"Oh for Gods' sakes," Triq said. "He's a kid, he's hurt and he's worried about his friend. Besides, that arrow shaft had to've come from the biggest Gods-be-damned bow I've ever seen. The Archipelagan *Redfeather* don't make bows that size! And you said yourself that taer grows at the Monument – !"

"You're *stupid*." The slightly sullen, sulky voice was Jayr's. "All of you." Startled, they turned to look at her, at her elaborate, deliberate scarring shining white under the dying moons.

The girl was looking at her hands – at the multitude of long-healed breaks in her fingers, at the calluses and scars. She spat out a chewed piece of fingernail and shot them all a resentful, adolescent look. "You know something?" She glowered around at them. "This is all horseshit. Talk, talk talk. He's young and he's scared, and his friend is still out there. We should ride to the Monument ourselves and tear it *down* if we have to." She looked fully capable of ripping it stone from stone.

"We can't," Ress said gently. "Not until Feren's safe."

"You must speak to Jade," Roderick said. "Persuade him to call muster. At least scout the location, find the source and the truth of this – find the missing girl. And you must *tell* me!"

Triqueta checked the bow at her saddleside and swung herself easily onto the palomino's back. She had no rein: she rode the mare by knees alone.

Ress snorted. "Gods' sakes, for the last time –"

"Listen! I said nothing of fears or figments or monsters." Roderick let go the chearl's soft nose and stepped back. "Only this: tell Larred Jade he has a threat on his border. Tell him a force rises against him. Tell him the Great Fayre has no defence. Tell him the biggest Gods-damned arrow you've ever seen made this boy's wound. Do whatever it takes, Ress of the Banned. But don't leave this boy's teacher to die – and, by the Gods, *tell* me what you find!"

"And how do you suggest we do that?" Ress's comment was barbed. "Or do you also believe in scrying?"

The little palomino mare scraped a forehoof on the cobbles, shook her mane and ears.

"Jade's not a warrior," Triq said. "His patrols secure his trade."

"His trade will be the first target!" The Bard had a hand on the gate, but hadn't opened it, not yet – he had one final bid to make. "You said your horse was spooked. What frightened her?"

The mare paused, nostrils flaring and ears up as though she knew they'd mentioned her. Ress lay the traces back in his lap. For a moment, the three members of the Banned looked at one another as if the truth distilled like spirits between them.

"She was terrified," Triq said eventually. "The scent –"

"Not blood." Jayr started on another nail. "They know it too well."

"Then surely something frightened her. Some-*thing*!" Roderick lifted the drop-key and the wood creaked softly as the door moved. "And whatever that something is, it has taken the girl, and the CityWarden needs to know. The Fayre has no *defence*; Roviarath herself won't stand some major assault. All legends aside, that's *reason*."

Jayr grunted. "Still don't know why we can't just trash it."

"Because we don't –" as the wagon started to move, Feren groaned again and Ress shot a glance at the Bard "– we don't know what we're dealing with."

Roderick shrugged as if the conclusion to their discussion had been inevitable all along.

* * *

"Yep," Syke said, thoughtfully. "That's one loco story."

The Banned commander turned from the paling, striated sky to poke the fire with a thoughtful boot. He was an unremarkable-looking man – not tall, not muscular, not handsome – but he had a quiet, taut presence that kept his gathered riders in a loose kind of line. They may have a jest at his expense, but there wasn't a member of the Banned that would cross him. His expression was sharp, thoughtful. "Ress rode for Roviarath?"

"Was taking Triq and Jayr with him." Taure, Ress's veteran friend who'd been helping him prop up the bar earlier that evening, was brushing the dust from his sleeves and thighs. Possibly more sober than his mates, he'd ridden hard to reach the camp. "Whole thing's horseshit, if you ask me – but you needed to know. Damned Bard's a loon. Pass the wine."

The Banned commander cuffed Taure's shoulder, grinning. "Half man, half horse, eh? Kid could've meant us." He watched Taure's eyes roll, his own sparking with mischief. "D'you believe him?"

"What?" Taure kicked the fire. "Some alchemical beastie nicked this kid's teacher and carried her off... to what? Be his personal apothecary? Knock her up with some quarter-horse offspring?" The dying embers turned to reveal a new glow, warm in the cool air. "I think the poor kid's mind has snapped like so much chewed leather. Hey, I said *pass the wine*."

"Maybe." Syke had been drinking for most of the night, but his gaze was as clear and grey as the dawn. "And yet, if there *is* hassle at the Monument, it's not beyond a certain CityWarden to try and make us scout it for him." He jerked his head at the Roviarath Lighthouse. "Canny bastard, old Jade."

"Jade wouldn't go to all this trouble, for the Gods' sakes." Taure nabbed the half-full wineskin himself and took a healthy swig. "He'd just pay."

"I don't like the smell of this." The commander turned to watch the paling sky. "Not one little bit."

"You reckon the Bard's onto something? We should go out there?"

Syke gave a short, humourless guffaw. "You're jesting. The Bard's a basket case loony and I'm not washing Jade's dirty linen for him, sonofamare."

Taure missed a swig and covered his dusty face in wine. He spluttered, wiped his mouth on his sleeve.

But Syke was thinking.

"So," he said, "either the plains are being taken over by some politically motivated half stallion with a massive inferiority complex – or CityWarden Larred Jade's deposited this boy as bait so we do a recce for him – or the boy's brain got flash-fried by the open sun. I'm riding towards option three."

Taure was still coughing. "Not being funny – but what if there is something out there? Even a loose bweao…"

"I'm not responsible for the open Grasslands, whatever the damned CityWardens may think –"

"That kid didn't come from the CityWarden –"

In the rising brightness, the sky was clear and the horizon empty. Syke commented thoughtfully, "Old Roderick's right about one thing, though. I don't like anything about this."

Taure said, "So – you believe in monsters. With longbows. This is loco."

"Yep." Syke picked up the leather mug that had been sitting beside him, tilted it to inspect its contents and set it down again. "Taure, old man, I trust my instincts. Something about this is giving me the fireblasted crawlies."

"You want to move camp?"

"Not yet," Syke told him. "I still don't trust that CityWarden as far as I can spit an esphen." A grin grew across his face. "I got a better idea."

11: MONSTER OUTSIDE ROVIARATH

The horsewoman leaned low over the neck of her mare, laughing like a daemon. Beneath her, the horse raced like an arrow shot from the sun, smooth and swift, her shoulders churning fluidly with her speed. Her heels kicked at the grass as she ran, she was as glad as her rider of the freedom of the Varchinde.

Triq was sitting astride the wind. The mare's hooves barely seemed to touch the soil, her chest knifed through the grass and it rushed past them, swishing as they ran. The horse was sleek and strong, and her mane flew in the woman's face, making her laugh even more. Sunlight bathed their skin, but they moved so fast the air felt cold as it thrilled past.

Triqueta's yellow hair and the mare's tail were bright as flags in the midst of the empty plain. Behind them, they left a ripple of wake.

There!

She sat up. In one hand was a horseman's bow, short limbed beneath the grip and long limbed above. She had several arrows in the same hand, resting against the wood and parallel with the bowstring.

The other hand nocked a loose shaft. Without missing breath or hoofbeat, she tracked the rustle in the long grasses, drew the string back to her ear, and let it go.

The arrow thunked into a squeak. The rustling stopped.

Gottim!

Grinning, she drew and nocked another – a reflex action. The mare, feeling the change in the pressure of the woman's thighs, made a slowing, inward spiral and came at last to a halt.

Somewhere behind her, voices. Ress and Jayr, laughing at her. Jayr's laughter was a rare sound and a joyous one – her past had scarred more than her flesh.

Triq hadn't asked – life was too short. However Jayr had come by her fighter's calluses and Kartian scarring, it didn't matter. Why not celebrate?

Showing off, she jumped up to her feet on the mare's back, balancing with no effort. She bowed like a theatre player, bow and arrows still in hands, then turned as if to do likewise to an audience behind her.

She stopped.

Against the bright eastern horizon, there was a black speck – no, two of them. They were too far away to see, they shimmered with heat-haze and pollen – but bweao ran alone, and they were far too fast for Range Patrol outriders.

They weren't on the trade-road.

Controlling a flash of nervousness, she paused, squinting against the bright sky. They were a long way out of bow range, but whatever they were, they were coming across the open grass and they were… By the *rhez*, they were fast!

Ress shouted, "What is it?"

"Don't know!" She dropped back into the saddle without struggle or thought. "Why don't you and Jayr keep moving – I'll run scout!"

None of them glanced at the clumsy, wheeled cart upon which the injured Feren lay dying.

* * *

Jayr the Infamous was being torn in half.

She was scratchy eyed from the sun, sneezing from the pollen. Their progress was agonisingly slow and she eyed the horizon almost eagerly, just waiting for some kind of contact. She had been raised to fight, trained to win from before she could walk. She needed and craved the adrenaline and the release that came with combat.

But in her own blunt way, she was worried about the boy.

Feren was getting worse. He called aloud to the empty sky, nonsense words and phrases, jagged fragments that tore at her memories and shredded her heart. He clung to his life only by the determination that had walked him, critically wounded, to tumble and fall at the edges of the Banned's awareness.

She knew that determination: only two returns ago, she had known it personally. How it felt to be young and alone, how it felt to fight through desperation and pain.

She needed to help him. As if reaching to her younger self, she listened to his fevered voice as it called out, a cascade of the broken pieces of his life and memory. Perhaps, if she helped him, she could purge herself of her own dark figments.

Yet she had no idea what to do.

As they prepared to move out, she watched Ress's calm logic, his gentleness – and his growing sense of despair – and she rode her big, bay gelding in another tight, angry circle round them. Daring everything.

Let them come – bweao, horse monsters! She wanted – needed – something to fight. She was burning beneath her skin with the rage of her own frustration.

Yes, you! Come finish what you started!

But they'd seen no predators, almost no wildlife other than winged.

Even the hunting had been scarce – while both Ress and Jayr

knew the basics of tracking and ambush in the open grasses, they'd found themselves reliant upon Triqueta's instincts and her lethal ranging eye.

With a tang of bitterness, Jayr nudged her animal with her heels.

The Infamous, Syke called her, jesting. Bare-knuckled, she could down a Range Patrol champion in under a minute and she'd won the Banned commander a great deal of wealth and favours. She was bloody infamous all right: she could do one thing well and, right now, she was infamously useless. As Triqueta raced her little mare out to the eastern horizon, Jayr rode to pick up the downed esphen from the long grass.

Behind her, Feren cried wordless anguish and hope.

Jayr swung down from the gelding's huge back, saw that their dinner was still alive. It quivered in fright, bright black eyes wide, blood matting its brown fur where the arrow had punctured its hindquarters. As she came close, it froze.

Neatly, she broke its neck.

Oddly, it made her feel better – a tiny taste of the adrenal rush she'd once been all too familiar with. Carefully removing the arrowhead from the pelvic bone, she drew a blade across the creature's throat and held it up to drain it.

Her horse flicked his ears at the flies, uninterested. He lowered his muzzle to graze at the full grass-heads.

"Jayr! Come on!" Ress sat in the front of the cart, spears by his side.

When the creature was at last bloodless, she shook it and slung it over her horse's withers, put a foot in the stirrup and settled herself on his back.

Almost there.

Feren cried out again as the cart began moving, rolling clumsily towards Roviarath and the advancing shadows of the Kartiah.

Jayr touched the gelding's flanks and he moved into an easy walk, the grasses swishing at his knees.

* * *

As the mare crested a long, rolling rise, Triqueta sat back, bringing the animal to an uneasy halt, her forehoof tamping restlessly at the soil. For a moment, Triqueta couldn't see where the specks had gone – then her gaze was drawn to a circle of birds, high and black against the afternoon sky.

Aperios. Carrion birds. Tracking something?

The mare shook her mane nervously.

She unslung the bow, strung it without thinking and checked her saddle-side quiver. She didn't nock, she had no target, but the birds moved lazily westwards, as if drawn by the Kartiah's darkness.

Seeking death.

She'd been showing off her horsewoman's skills before – now she stood up in earnest, swiftly, balancing easily, to look down over the long rise to the massive roll of empty plain beyond. Whatever those two black specks had been, she'd lay a bet the birds were following them.

Craning from the tips of her toes, she saw something strange.

Down there in the rippling grass sea, still a serious distance away, two young men, riders, long haired and bare chested, pushing their way forwards with an odd, deliberate gait. They walked in single file, leaving a long scar behind them. For a moment, she was puzzled. They were either closer than she thought, or they were bigger than Jayr in a lousy mood... Then the front one started at something by his feet.

Oh, you have to be jesting!

As Triqueta stared, bow forgotten, the young man spun sideways, lurched backwards – and grew suddenly, massively taller, high above the grass tops. His movements were wrong, incomprehensible... until she saw his dark smudge of hair was rooted all down his spine – and his spine ended in a back.

A horse back.

Monsters.

Dumbfounded, her mind refused to grasp what she was seeing. They were riders, surely…?

By the Gods – Feren's loco tale. It was all true.

Like any skittish Banned mount, the creature had spooked and reared – the familiarity of the motion was wrong, disturbing. His forehooves – claws? – danced in the sunlight before he plunged back down to the soil, tail twitching with agitation.

Then, like any Banned rider, he calmly turned to warn his companion.

Triqueta stared. Her returns had let her see some pretty unlikely stuff – even out here. But, half horse, half man – behaviour and body, action and reaction – it was loco. Crazed. As crazed as Roderick's doomsaying. As crazed as Feren's rantings.

For a second, she stood motionless, her hand white knuckled on her lop-ended bow, then she saw the second creature change angle, as if he was pointing right at her.

Alchemical impossibility.

Like a fireblasted novice, she'd sky-lined herself flawlessly against the afternoon sun, her shadow stretched way down the rise. She saw the two great creatures acquire their target, and then make straight for her, charging from a standstill to a flat-out gallop.

The birds set up a distant, gleeful cawing and the circle began to move more swiftly.

By the rhez…

Thinking fast now, tension in every muscle, she dropped back into the saddle, prepped arrows with swift fingers.

Feeling her urgency, the little mare needed no command – she, too, ran.

The rise defended them instantly. Bereft of a target, Triqueta lay her chest flat against the creature's neck and just let her race. She was fast, nimble – but whether she could outdistance those things...

She had to reach the cart. Feren. The horrors of what they'd do to the helpless wagon hit her like the pollen-headed flowers that exploded against the mare's chest and forelegs. Her heart hammered against the mare's hot skin...

...and they ran.

"Jayr!"

Alarm, command and sudden terror, Ress's bark made her jump.

She turned in the saddle – and swore in a hot rush of adrenaline.

Arrowing towards them, fast as the slender, racing arqueus of the southern plainland, Triqueta's little mare bolted flat-out loco, froth covering her muzzle and chest. On her back, Triqueta was low over the front of the saddle, her expression grim and her hair a crazed yellow cloud.

Blood hammering in her temples, Jayr slammed her heels into the gelding's ribs and he leapt forwards, neck arching. Raising his muzzle, he snorted snot and laid his ears straight back, baring his teeth like a stallion.

He charged forwards willingly and Jayr wondered what wrong reek he smelled.

Then she saw them – creatures that came out of the grasses, shimmering like a dream in the afternoon haze. These were the monsters that had shot poor Feren, the things Ress had refused to believe existed.

Ress had no such problems now. He stood by Feren in the cart, his hip braced against the side, and he smoothly fitted a heavy spear into the wood-and-leather thrower on his forearm. He had an almighty range with that thing. The first spear arced over Jayr's shoulder but fell short of the incoming beast.

Bleakly, he fitted another.

The beasts were not shooting back – as they came closer, Jayr saw they bore no weapons, or garments, of any kind. They were fast though, their forelegs and chests pushing through the grass, their huge claws crushed and tore at it. Even as Jayr reached her, Triqueta slowed her wild-eyed mare and, unspeaking, cross-drew her two wicked-looking serrated short-swords.

Jayr came up next to her. She was grinning, bright and hard as a polished metal blade. Her blood thundered, she could feel it in her belly and thighs and in the horse beneath her. Any minute now, her frustration was going to detonate.

The beasts came closer.

Now, Triqueta turned her mare in tight, agitated circles, trying to calm the animal down. Jayr's gelding tossed his head up and down, up and down. Big as he was, he was skittering, all four hooves tamping the soil like a crouching bweao – he wanted to fight as much as she did.

A second spear shot over them. This one crested its arc – then fell full-force into the horse chest of the lead creature.

"Ha!" Way behind them, Ress's shout was pure defiance.

The beast staggered, but was still running. Then he reached down to yank the thing bodily out of his flesh and snap it into jagged halves and flying kindling.

And he grinned.

Furious now, Jayr tightened her knees and her gelding sprang forwards, the grasses parting under the onslaught of horseflesh. Dismissing her bundle of javelins – she couldn't hit shit with them anyway – she unclipped her big, heavy-shafted spear.

The beasts were upon her. She held her horse in a thigh grip like a terhnwood pincer, and lifted the spear two-handed to aim it solid and point down.

The injured beast flashed past. A moment later, she heard Triqueta's high, ululating war cry; heard Ress's echo from further back. The other one came at her, chest first, wild haired, bare fleshed and screaming in anger and hate.

She snarled fury, leaned forwards, ready for her horse's move...

And the gelding stood straight up on his hind legs, his massive, cracked forehooves gleaming in the sinking sun. One caught the creature's human face, smashing his jaw sideways into a maddened, flopping gape. Blood and spit exploded over them both.

With all her weight and power behind it, Jayr rammed the spear downwards, past her mount's ear and into the muscled shoulder of the half-breed beast.

The point scored a red gouge in his flesh as he blocked the strike with fist and forearm. *Gods*, he was hugely strong. As the gelding plunged back to the ground, the creature reared in his turn, massive foreclaws extended and scrabbling.

A second spear rammed – *thunk* – into his horse ribs. He staggered, fell back to four claws, raking the soil into grooves of blood and fury.

What did it take to stop this thing?

One hand grabbed the spear and yanked it free. There was pain in his broken face now, rage in his eyes, righteousness where his jaw should be.

With the spear in his hands, mimicking Jayr's grip, he went to rear.

Anticipating her command, the gelding spun to slam him with both hind hooves.

Jayr knew he'd got it wrong when he buckled under her and screamed, shattering the daylight into tumbling shards of sound.

As the creature came at her, Triqueta sheathed one of her jagged blades.

She controlled the spooked mare with an effort. The animal danced broadside, her knees high and her eyes rolling white. Fresh froth dripped from her chin.

With one hand on the pommel, Triqueta came to a combat crouch, feet on the saddle. The beast seemed to think this was funny, it was grinning – the thing had incisors as long as belt-knives.

A little closer, you accursed alchemical half-breed, a little closer...

In moving, she'd lost her contact with the mare. As she leapt like a performer from one horse's back to the other, the mare gathered her legs and bolted – jarring Triqueta's take-off. Instead of landing on her feet on the creature's back, she landed and skidded, went splat on her belly, nearly going nose first over the far side.

The creature stank of sweat and flesh.

It shrieked, spat vicious defiance – his human body twisted this way and that as his hands tried to reach for her. Beneath her, his horse self plunged and kicked out, then went to rear.

Triqueta grabbed a handful of mane, pulled her body up and let one leg slide over his back. A moment later, he was tight between her knees.

And he went berserk.

Plunging, kicking, bucking, shouting wordless fury. His human torso leaned forwards, backwards. He twisted round, his hands scrabbled furiously to try and dislodge her. She was riding a whirlwind, a thunderstorm. His hair was everywhere, in her face, caught in her garments. She twisted one hand in his hair to the wrist; the other clung grimly to the serrated blade.

He fought like an unbroken wild thing, outraged and screaming. She gripped him with legs that had been riding a lifetime, rode the spasm and plunge and twist of his back. Dimly, she was aware of the gelding's sudden scream but her focus was sharp as a bodkin, honed to a fighting point and absolute.

For a moment, he stilled, quivering.

Calm as the eye of insanity, Triqueta brought her feet under her and rose into a half crouch.

Instantly, he started again – now racing forwards, tilting left and right trying to tip her from his back, then stopping dead to buck, and buck, and *buck* like an overexcited foal. She was riding him like a champion charioteer, knees absorbing his motion, hand and arm overtensed and shaking with the effort of hanging on. She was panting, sweating, the sun was making the pollen itch on her skin; her eyes were dazzled by the light. As the creature tore in a desperate circle, she clung – and her heart was hammering, hammering.

He stopped again. As if he knew what was coming, he bawled wordless aggression, turned his body round to seize her by the ankles.

But it was too late. With a scream that might've been pure insolence, she rammed the blade straight through his neck and rasped it free, ripping out his windpipe and the front of his throat as she did so.

His anger became a bubbling hiss, an explosion of air and gore. His hands scrabbled frantically as he tried to stem the gush, his chest and ribs strained as he tried to draw breath.

Die you bastard thing!

His great body staggered, righted itself, staggered again and crashed into the grass.

Hand and blade red with the creature's death, Triqueta jumped clear.

Her knees gave – but she was flushed, exhilarated. Head back, arms spread to the sky, she loosed the Banned's war cry again, a shriek of triumph.

Jayr's gelding screamed and sprang, leaping away from the creature he'd kicked at with his heels.

Jayr kept her seat – just – but the suddenness of the movement, the pitch of the horse's cry had her grabbing for his mane, barely clinging on to her spear. For a moment, she thought he'd bolt. She craned her neck to see what had happened to him.

And blanched.

Two lots of three massive gashes had carved a wicked, deep chevron in his rump. Raw flesh bulged visibly through ripped hide. Blood was streaming across his haunches and matting his tail, running in rivulets down his legs and staining the grass to scarlet red.

Strong as he was, the gelding was shaking. His back legs quivered and she felt him falter.

But he turned to face the creature anyway.

The beast stood wild and wounded, chest soaked in blood from his crazily hanging jaw, hair stuck to his skin, eyes glittering loco in the low rays of the afternoon sun.

Right, then.

She'd been waiting for this.

She took a hold of her anger and frustration, gripped them hard and strong and swung herself deliberately out of her saddle. She thumped the gelding on his shoulder, thumped him again when he didn't move.

When he cantered for Ress and the cart, she turned and faced the massive beast on foot.

Her heart rate was increasing now, a steady, rising thunder. She was completely aware of her body, poised on the knife-edge of motion and reaction. Above her, the monster was huge, elegantly muscled. This close, he smelled of blood and sweat and grass and pure, physical power. But Jayr burned now, her need to vent had found a focus. She pointed the spear up at him, a flagrant dare.

He raked the soil, shredding the grass. He shook his wild hair, twisted his broken face at her and made only noise.

She remained quiet, motionless. Her challenge grim and silent but for the whetted sense of rising eagerness in her chest and throat. She held the spear two-handed, close to the head to give her hard impact at short range.

Looking down at the ludicrous, puny human, he snorted through flared nostrils and snatched at her face with one extended claw.

It was almost too easy.

She ducked sideways, forwards, came up right between his two muscled forelegs. She slammed the spear straight into the socket joint.

And pushed. With every fibre of strength and determination she had.

He couldn't articulate a scream, he hissed and bubbled. Half shoved, he stood on his hind legs.

Letting the spear go up with him, she changed her grip and pitched her strength against his. Driving the spear point deeper and using it like a lever against his bulk, she intended to topple him sideways.

The point scraped bone, dug deep into the joint. He flailed with his good leg, claw flashing, clenching aimlessly. His back claws danced, trying to keep him upright.

Both hands white, spitting curses through clenched teeth, she slowly, slowly heaved him into overbalance. She felt him sway, and then totter. The spear head tore deeper into flesh and muscle and ligament.

He staggered and she screamed defiance at him. *"Go down you bastard thing, go down!"*

He lurched, staggered, tried to right himself – but he was too badly damaged.

He crashed to the ground like a rock, legs in spasm, eyes wild.

Cursing aloud, with no idea what she was saying, Jayr dragged the spear point free with a foot on his chest, then rammed it straight through the red hole where his mouth had been.

Her adrenaline crested in a scream.

And with a splutter, the beast died.

* * *

Smooth and grim, Ress fitted and threw a second spear.

The existence of the creatures had shocked his analytical mind, sent tremors through his confidence. As Triqueta and Jayr took the fight to close quarters, he was robbed of safe targets and he watched the monsters in disbelief, almost as if he expected them to dissolve in the summer's haze.

He fitted a third spear, awaiting an opportunity. Behind him, Feren groaned, stained with suffering.

What were they? Where had they come from?

These creatures were young. Had they been horses, they would have been the return- or two-returns-old, young males driven from the main herd by the stallion, yet still orbiting close to their dams. Add intellect, and that would make them...

Scouts.

It fitted, but it didn't answer the question. *How were they possible?*

Where the rhez had they come from?

His attention was caught by Jayr's gelding, cantering back towards him with an odd, shaky gait. Ress untangled himself from the spear thrower, jumped from the wagon and went to catch his mane, saw the savage gashes in his rear. As he grabbed for his precious supply of taer, he tried to strategise a solution.

And failed. He had *no* cursed idea...

The boy had to go to Roviarath. The audience with Larred Jade, demanded by the Bard, was now – by every God and his disbelief! – essential. The CityWarden must send force to answer this.

But that still didn't answer his basic incomprehension. Half a man and half a horse... it was loco.

How could such things even exist?

The Bard had raged about alchemy – about skills forgotten,

lost in times disregarded. What kind of learning was necessary to graft a man onto a horse's body? To keep it there? More than that – if these beasts were the two-return-olds, were they reproducing? Or being reproduced?

Was that what had happened to Feren's unfortunate teacher?

Alchemy or no, he knew how flesh worked. And this was madness.

In spite of the sun, he was chilled.

The taer covered the gelding's hide, soothing the terrible gashes in his rump and easing pain and bleeding. He blew through his lips and stood head down, buried to the ears in grass. Muscles in his shoulders twitched.

Agitated, Ress stroked the horse's sweated neck. Speculation was pointless – the monsters were real, they were *real*. He needed facts, and context, and he needed to extrapolate what the rhez this meant.

Was Roderick *right*? All this time, had he really known some vast and sinister truth? It was crazed. And yet...

...no more crazed than what he'd just seen.

The horse whuffled in pain, nosing the grass.

Across the plainland, the girls were returning. Triqueta was back astride her little mare, Jayr walked by her head and he could see them laughing, gesturing as they retold their separate fights. Watching them, the ageing apothecary smiled, a hint of paternal affection they would never see – somehow, their loco victory didn't surprise him.

But the questions were still coming.

His eyes tracked the descent of the aperios, the carrion birds, finally feasting on the creatures they'd followed for so long. Like a row of archers' targets, Ress set up what he knew, re-evaluated everything Feren had told him. The monster – the stallion – was real. It was a fanatic – crazed. Its agenda could be anything. He had to know where it had come from, how it was possible, what else may be coming in its wake...

The implications were terrifying. Ress's whole comprehension of reality had taken a sharp smack round the side of the head. What had Roderick said? *Just because you can't see it –*

Behind him, the boy said suddenly, "Thea!"

Startled, Ress turned – into a chill rush of shock when he saw Feren was sitting up. White faced in the sunlight, cold fever shining on his skin and his red hair a dark mat of sweat, he stared fixedly at the setting sun, the rising shadow of the Kartiah. His dry lips moved again, though the word was almost wistful, "Thea…"

"It's all right." Ress was back in the cart, rummaging hastily through packs and bags for something to ease his tension. "Rest easy, Feren, we'll find her."

He heard Triqueta laughing.

But the boy stared straight ahead, the dying sun reflecting red in his eyes. He was shivering, slim body wracked with desperation, his wasted hands clutched at his covers. "Don't leave me… with the monsters…"

Monsters.

The shadow of the Kartiah swelled as the sun touched the tops of the mountains. Like blood, red sunset light was flooding across the plain.

The girls came close, softening their elation to silence as they saw the cart.

"What happened to him?" Jayr threw the question at Ress as she went to check on her horse.

"I don't know." Ress smoothed oil across the boy's upper lip. Feren inhaled, inhaled more deeply. His eyes began to blink – at first confused, and then more heavily.

"Can't you see it…?" the boy said. Slumping now, Feren turned to look at the apothecary, struggled to focus. "The mountains… the shadow… I told her…"

Triqueta said, "Poor kid."

"Brave kid," Ress said grimly. He smoothed Feren's sweating

hair, gentle. "Rest now. You're on the edge of hope. We reach Roviarath before the dawn."

"We'd better," Triq said. "Whatever they are, soon they'll know that we know..."

The apothecary paused to look down at the boy, across at both women, then out towards the east, the Monument and the far distant sea. The Bard's madness was touching him, twisting around the questions in his head, an odd, creeping sensation: *Something isn't right.*

He said, "I don't like this."

Triqueta glanced at Ress. "You? Not got a rational explanation?"

He snorted. "First thing – make sure Feren's safe and cared for. Then, if Larred Jade hasn't got answers, I'm going downriver." He shook his head. "Light-alchemy, impossible monsters. Maybe the library has something."

"You're going to Amos?" Triq stared.

"He's hurt." Jayr was stroking her gelding's long nose with one gentle, callused hand – and almost pouting. "I want to *find* these things."

"He needs time and rest," Ress said. "And I'll need a guard for the trip. Triq'll take Jade's patrols to find this thing." He patted Jayr's shoulder.

"The Great Library's a ruin," Triqueta said. "Only thing you'll find in there is mulch."

"Not if you know where to look." He gave a brief grin. "Now, that esphen we were supposed to have for dinner – where'd it go? Don't know about you two – but I'm starved."

12: COURAGE THE WANDERER, AMOS

Deep in the tavern's cellars, high in the packed-tight shelving, Ecko had been acquiring *stuff*.

He'd clambered about like some strange four-limbed insect, scrabbling from stack to stack and shelf to shelf, exploring, learning, scavenging. One thing remained true wherever you were – you *always* needed a cache.

And this was a helluva place to get one.

Being down here was enclosed, familiar. It felt safe – even Kale the not-werewolf wouldn't find him in all of this. And anyhow, if these cellars didn't wind up in some underground tunnel system, then he was a monkey's uncle.

In the layers of shadow, no one could see him grin.

Craft tools – *tick*; vials of toxins and herbs – *tick*. The substances were unfamiliar, but the learning might be fun. Explosives – a little harder to come by. At some point, basic pomegranate grenades were a must – and he was *so* gonna be inventing gunpowder as soon as he got all the bits...

Stick *that* up the God of Evil's scaly ass and light the fuse.

He turned another corner, shelves and heaps and dust tails. There was a sliver of pale glitter over his head, moonlight on a tiny, cracked-mica pane. This was the most fun he'd had since he got here – with a little luck and a little chemistry, he'd have the Industrial Revolution in full fucking swing. Plus, there hadda be a giant-rat infestation down here *some*place...

The Bard's cellars, though, were rodent-free. Wines were stored in racks of ceramic and pottery – a multitude of shapes, colours and labels that looked like a collection of souvenirs. Wooden ale barrels were more familiar; spirits were stored in squat, dark bottles that might've been stitched leather. There was no glass, no metal and a distinct lack of dangerous chemical compounds.

Now that, Ecko figured, *just wasn't fucking fair.*

He kept looking.

Somewhere over his head, it was deep night. The Banned were still singing – he could hear them, raucous and off key, stamping out the time. The goldie girl had vanished maybe an hour or so before. He still had her dice – six-sided but the corners blunted and the symbols unfamiliar – now added to his growing stash of goodies.

Yeah, Eliza, Let's see what the pattern does with that decision, huh?

Ecko had made a den high in one of the racks. As he'd explored outwards, he'd found that the walls were brick, the mortar smooth. Under his feet, the flagstone floor was cold. Once, a flitting shape had made him start, but it was only the catlike thing he'd seen once before, lithe and warm to his heatseeker. It blinked at him and was gone.

Not a single secret passage had given itself up to his dextrous touch.

He'd passed through Kale's pantry, eyeing the bunches of greenery, the dried and pickled vegetables, the shelves of unfamiliar produce. Some of it he knew by name, but he wasn't convinced he trusted anything that didn't come in shrink-wrapped plastic. Food that looked like animal still kinda freaked him out – never mind the fact he had no fucking clue what the animals were. Little fat fuckers, bug eyed and skinless, hung upside-down by threading one ankle though a hole in the other…

From somewhere, a clattering made him start, a burst of laughter and boisterous comments. The noise made him curl back against the shelving, though it was a good distance away.

There was no one down here.

Yeah, this is my place now.

Ghost silent, he crept deeper.

As he moved onwards, he found it was harder to navigate. Tall shelves and sharp turns completely defeated his telescopics. Narrow corridors wound tight between overladen racks hung with soft streamers of dust. The floor left odd, uneven steps waiting to catch his cloak hem and make him stumble. This was Malice in Wonderland, some fucking loony trip, confused and chaotic and mazelike and thrilling… Maybe, if he went far enough, he'd uncover the prison, or the magical portal to the Major Bad Guy's front room. Maybe he'd find some skeleton from the Bard's closet – or a forgotten Questing Hero who'd died from boredom and bad beer.

Deeper.

Slowly, the light paled and grew thinner. The shadows climbed higher and wound round the stacks like smoke. The shelves were packed even tighter, here. It was a warren of nameless stuff, layers of wooden boxes that hadn't been moved in years. There were piles of junk in corners, lying in wait like creatures of the dark. Now, skitterings hinted at inhabiting critters – apparently the cat had a union. There were no cobwebs, but the dust was as thick as spider-silk armour and unfamiliar beetley things crawled over it.

Almost nothing had a label.

Jeez, it's like Christmas in here!

Chrissakes, did they even know what half this shit was?

Karine must have a full database in her fucking head. Nothing had numbers – was this what she recorded with her endless tally marks?

A sudden, rhythmic stomping shook the shelves and made him grin blackly in the almost-dark...

...and then he wondered just how far away that sound had actually been.

Shit.

Aw c'mon already, I was kidding...

The Wanderer's cellars were larger than the floor of the tavern, a helluva lot larger. Surely there *had* to be more than booze and shopkeeper basics down here. Where were the rings and the gems and all that crap? Where was the cache of weapons and armour? Where was the monster and the big ol' chest with the poisonous lock?

His grin grew, black and wicked in the half-light.

Where was the secret fucking door?

In fact – sod that – where was the thing that made the tavern work? The control room? The magical whosit? He'd give his carbon-black eyeteeth to know how to drive this thing.

Deeper.

Creeping in silence and wordless hope – there was so gonna be treasure down here somewhere.

What Ecko found, before he'd gone much further, was a wall.

Flat and cold and absolute, it cut his progress dead.

So much for White Rabbits.

Now what was he gonna do?

It wasn't just bricks: the wall had been covered – painted? – with something and it was filthy, stained with browns and greens and streaks of rot. In places, it was cracked and crumbling. A hefty whack with a sledgehammer would knock the bricks loose like teeth.

He wondered what the hell was on the other side – which bit

moved with the sunrise, which bit didn't. What would happen if something was half in and half out?

Cursing the absence of heavy-duty steel – a crowbar'd be good about now – Ecko flicked his oculars to scan for an alternative.

And he noticed something weird.

He was crouched at the edge of a small open area that seemed to face the wall itself as there was a slight downward dip in the floor. The only other thing down here was a single monster barrel that he could've used to boat up the Thames.

Hell, what'd he been saying about dynamite? Or was the Bard just ageing one motherlode of killer whisky?

The barrel was unlabelled, and covered in crap.

Great.

Around him, the shadows fell in layers of grey, like phantoms. The air was chill and old and smelled only of rot. It was quiet, motionless, even the crawlies had packed their little crawly bags and fled. He shuddered, carefully scanning the tottering piles of shelving.

No crowbar.

No monster.

He crept out to the centre of the dip, the middle of the wall. The shelves rose round him like an audience.

Yeah? Well watch this.

With a grin of defiance to the silent fears that lurked taunting in the darkness, *his* darkness, he spun hard and slammed one foot sideways into the mouldering paint.

Don't ever use a spin-kick in combat... but they're great for kicking shit down.

The impact was tremendous: it rippled almost tangibly through the air. The wall cracked, flaked, dust trickled to the floor. He exposed brick like bruised flesh.

Vulnerable.

His grin set, a black slash of pure, elated fury. *Now what?*

Huh? What happens if I make a damned hole *in your reality? Does it let through monsters from another dimension? Hey, like Lugan?*

He caught the thought, and swore at himself.

A second, savage slam sent a spiderweb of lines through the paintwork; a third made the wall judder, a river of dust trickling to the floor.

Or maybe I'm the monster, already here?

A fourth kick, a fifth. The paint was cracking now – broken flakes drifting to the floor like paper...

One of them had letters on.

Huh?

Ecko slammed the anchors on, his heart suddenly thundering in his chest. He recoiled, his targeters recalibrating, and he crouched down among the fragmented ruins, almost cowering.

The shelves rose, looming, round him.

He picked the flake up.

It was thin, cold. It crumbled even as he touched it, like some fucking forgotten relic, but his telescopics were enough. Upon it was a spider scrawl – barely a word, faint and faded.

It said, "...ien".

What the...

His momentum had been interrupted. His adrenaline was shifting, changing from confrontation and gleeful fury to a skin-crawling prickle that crept up into his shoulders and the back of his neck. Barely daring to breathe, he crouched by the damage he'd made, extended a fingertip.

And he realised what he'd just done.

Fuck me ragged...

The paint – stucco? – was a collage of colour. It wasn't mould he'd been kicking down – well not all of it – it was some sort of mural. As he backed up, looked up and around him, he realised that it was fucking huge. It covered the whole wall from one side of the dip to the other.

His scalp crawled.

He made a grab for the nearest rocklight, sent the shadows gibbering round him. Then he crouched again and, carefully, took a corner of his cloak, brushed where he'd cracked the artwork through to the bricks.

There, the tiny faded lettering said, "Tus…".

Tusien.

He shivered. His flake fit one edge of the hole perfectly.

What'd the Bard said?

The high days of Tusien.

Trembling now, he picked up other fragments, turned them over to study them, but they were dust, their wisdom lost.

Shit…

Angered, excited, frustrated, fighting to hold his adrenaline, he carefully, carefully, uncovered a little more, blinking at it like some fucking ageing Tech. After a moment, his oculars made out the remains of a tiny image – some sort of earthwork, stylised ruins.

It said, "The Barrow at Tusien".

Holy.

Fucking.

Shitweasel.

The wall was a *map*.

Shaking now, he brushed more dirt aside, and more. Getting his mitts on proper cartography had been pretty high on his list of wants – and he'd found nada. Now the whole world was laid out in front of him…

Or would be, as soon as he'd called in the cleaners.

He propped the rocklight on the barrel, cleared more of the dirt. Slowly, the colours and the imagery became easier to see. There was a distinct lack of scale – artists' rendition might've been more to the point – but it did the job, all right.

Chrissakes, where's a camera when I fucking need one?

There was Roviarath, lynchpin city. There was Amos at the

mouth of some huge mofo river, and further north there was Fhaveon, the Lord City the Bard had mentioned, on some kind of rock promontory, and watching a big old island across a surprisingly narrow straight. There was all the green shit – the hills and forests and mountains and lakes and the empty acres of grass... the faded colours made it seem brownish, rotten.

With a scrabble, he was stood on the barrel-top, holding up the rocklight to find the blip that'd tell him where the tavern was, the X he'd been waiting for. But apparently it wasn't gonna be quite that easy.

Great. The one thing I needed to find...

Scowling, he dropped back into his cowled crouch, steadying himself with the tips of his fingers, and covering his skin against the light.

He had to remember this, burn it into his forebrain somehow. If he was ever gonna to go any-sodding-where, he had to learn this stuff.

Some fucking joke, to put a map where he couldn't move it. What he wouldn't give for Lugan's monosharp pocket knife, then he could *peel* the damn thing off the wall.

Yeah, no chance of that. They didn't even have steel. Iron. Coinage. Everything that should've been metal...

Metal.

Oh. Jesus Harry Christ on a fucking motor scooter...

...two and two, you asshole. Usually make four.

The rocklight shimmered faintly as if it agreed with him.

Still crouched there, riding the barrel like Bilbo sodding Bigshot, he rummaged through his pouch for the piece of the blade he'd snapped, and held it up like a talisman. It shone the same deep orange, almost bronze, just like the goldie girl's –

Never mind that.

Ecko stared at the fragment, turning it in the rocklight so its broken edges glittered.

C'mon, think...

Ecko was recon – he was smart as fuck, when he could be bothered. And right now, he had that shiver in his skin that meant he was onto something – that there was a mystery, right here, right now, that was just begging him to kick it open.

Like the night he'd taken out Bob Pilgrim, like his stealth-run on Grey's facility, this was what he fucking lived for.

And the fragment of resin gleamed.

This shit grew on the *coast*. His eyes tracked the map, the colours of the paint.

What'd the Bard said? Something about "ever-cycling trade" – about the flow of this stuff balancing the flow of wood and stone that came the other way, from the mountains. The roads followed the rivers, both ran west to east, that much was pretty damned straightforward.

But he was *missing* something.

The fragment glittered, teasing.

Ecko knew jack and shit about agriculture. But he did know when he was on to something – his adrenaline was sparking and he was down from the barrel and pacing, a small, tight figure of shadow and gloom and sharp, hard focus.

What was it he'd missed?

He spun, closed his hand round the tiny resin shard and felt its edges nip his fingers.

Think!

His brain was firing, ricocheting from one idea and theory to the next. The terhnwood grew at the three coastal cities – Annondor in the south, Amos and the capital city Fhaveon – there.

He tracked the map, the rivers, the roads.

Then it hit him, just as if the Lord of Motivation had planted a boot clean up his ass...

It was *empty*.

Vast, open plainland. Scattered habitation. No stars in the sky; no metal in the rock. No lore. A horizon that gave every fucking appearance of being *flat*.

How in the name of everything that was unholy did they *navigate*? Just by the sun?

The thought brought a rush of thrill in his skin.

Was that why they didn't, or couldn't, travel across the grass? It had to be more than just superstition.

Oh, now I've got you...

Could this possibly, possibly, be making some kind of sense? He was staring like a man demented, his hand still curled round the tiny piece of resin. What if they had no effective way to cross open distances? Then their entire culture was restricted to the trade-ways that it knew.

One part of his brain was laughing at him – jeering while he tried to apply reason to a world that had two opposing moons and a werewolf in the kitchen – but he smothered the fuck out of it and kept going.

He was still missing loads of stuff. If they struggled to navigate, who'd built the roads in the first place? If the society was peaceful and prosperous, then why was the population so fucking small? So hugely spread out? It wasn't like they were short of food.

Was there some other factor here, something he'd not seen yet? Threat issues? Beasties clawing down city walls and chewing up farmland? Insane weather systems tearing the plains to dust and shreds?

Or was the Big McNasty already on the move?

More than that though – maybe the Bard *himself* was restricted in the same way? What had he said about landing in populated places?

Was he, too, unable or unwilling to cross the open grass?

Was *that* why he was missing so much learning?

Oh yeah, I've fucking cracked this.

In the fading rocklight, Ecko's grin was like a curving slice of nightmare, the new glimmer of a pure black moon. He was shivering with something between adrenaline and anxiety – something that felt like cold anticipation.

There's something that fucker hasn't told me.

Something he's avoiding – something he's afraid of?

Well, whatever the fuck it was, Ecko was going back up there to kick it out of him, if that was what it took.

When Ecko came back up to the taproom, he found the Bard sitting alone.

It was utterly, swallowing dark; the only light came from the white feather that Roderick held in his fingers. He was spinning it, and its pale illumination played over his face like the teasing of a ghost.

In that faint light, he looked old. His eyes were shattered, sparking insane. The lines around them were carved into his flesh, the shadows beneath were as deep as the shadows that lurked like spectres round the room. His lips were moving as though he prayed.

As Ecko crept closer, he could hear the words.

"*...Searching almost a hundred returns – I have dug every ruin, I have found every treasure, I have told every tale, I have faced every foe. Wherever these creatures are coming from...*" The shadows scudded, this way and that, as the feather spun forwards and back.

"Just this time, please; just this time..." Roderick swallowed hard, almost as if he were choking. "If my will can infest this wood, this brick, this life – please give me the choice...!" His other hand was flat on the table as if it was scanning his fingerprints or something. "I need to understand. I *must* –"

"Jeez," Ecko said. "What crawled up your ass and died? You look like shit."

Roderick didn't even start. He looked up, listless, his face drawn and lined. He looked like he'd spent the night writing mournful poetry in something thoughtfully entitled "My Diary".

"I feel like it," he said.

A moment later, he straightened his shoulders and pinned his grin back in place, his wicked expression that made the lines both mischievous and youthful. The light returned to his eyes. Ecko had an uncanny feeling that the man's mask had slipped, just for a moment.

But the face he'd seen was gone.

"All right, asshole," Ecko said. "I reckon it's time you 'fessed up."

"What? What do you mean?" Roderick laid the feather on the table and his grin broadened, just as if he'd never been without it.

"Why a sudden need to drive?" Ecko grinned at him, cold. "Don't tell me you're gonna get off your ass an' make a decision."

"And what 'decision' would you suggest?" The Bard's eyes flickered with echoes, though he didn't voice them. "I've always trusted the world herself to move this building as she needs; trusted it to manifest itself in places of wisdom and necessity. The Wanderer is wiser than I." He picked up the feather and began, again, to turn it in his fingers. "But tonight... Ecko, I wish you had been here to bear witness. The Banned found an injured boy, and our every fear is manifest. This is bigger and more terrifying that I have words to even frame. Not just the nartuk, a true tale of monsters – crazed beasts crafted from human flesh and will..." His knuckles were white. "How can I give words to my fear? I feel the gathering of the Count of Time. The vision I cannot remember pierces me as a sliver of ice and I feel figments like wings at my back. The Banned must rouse Larred Jade at Roviarath, and I... I have to take this to Fhaveon."

"What? You're not gonna go look for the monsters?" Ecko had a satchel on his shoulder – a one-armed rucksack thing that had been among his scavenged haul. His webbing was likewise stuffed with stolen goodies. He said, "When're you gonna quit stalling and strap on your hero kit?" His grin was savage.

"I don't *understand* yet." For a moment, the Bard's expression was startled. "I must go to Fhaveon, to Rhan. I must know what these things are, where they came from, why they're –"

"Another fuckin' excuse. If you wanna know about monsters, why don't you go out an' catch one?"

"The Council has to know!" Roderick brandished his feather like some sort of evidence. "If there are monsters loose, real ones, alchemical creations of flesh and horror – these things have not been witnessed since the days of Tusien itself! This isn't just a romp, Ecko! The cities must be warned – there are things happening here that are ancient and forgotten, yet new enough to be terrifying, and they involve the fate of the Grasslands entire. I'm no politician –"

"No shit."

"Yet I *must* – !"

"You *must* what? Sometimes I reckon you've been waiting for the bad guys so long that you've gone batshit." He sneered. "You gotta *map* downstairs. You've had this building – what – forty years? Have you looked at it, plotted anything, worked anything out? You fucking coward."

The Bard recoiled as if he'd been struck. For a moment, he sought words and found nothing. Ecko waited for the comeback, then snorted pure scorn.

"You're telling me all merry hell has just broken loose on your doorstep – and the best you can do is sit here and *pray* that your fucking *pub* makes your next decision for you?"

He crossed his arms, waited for the comeback. *Come on then...*

"Ecko."

The word was flat, potent enough to rock him where he stood, his mottled skin and black eyes and black sneer all shaded by his cowl.

He snarled, "What?"

The Bard was on his feet, now, tall and dark.

"This isn't cowardice – this *is* the decision. Ress must rouse Larred Jade. We must go to Rhan and to the Council in Fhaveon."

"What? More delegation?"

"You say you're missing information." Roderick's smile was mirthless, the shattered gleam was back in his eyes. "There's so much you still don't know –"

"I fuckin' knew it."

"Rhan, Ecko. Let's start with Rhan." The Bard's voice rose, shivering the pre-dawn air. "You jest about facing some 'God of Evil', about how your purpose is to defeat them? What if I told you that you're wrong? What if I told you that the Godfather Samiel sent an envoy, a creature of white warfare, of pure elemental light, to be the guardian of this world, and to guard and guide her?"

Ecko thought, *Oh you hafta be kidding me...*

"We have our champion Ecko. Rhan *is* that creature, he *is* this world's true hero. He's our mentor and warden and he's lived in the Lord City four hundred returns. He stands at the right hand of the Lord Foundersson. He defends stone and soil and flesh and family." Roderick held up the feather. "I'm mortal, with a task to perform. My time is long, even for one of Tundran blood, but it is finite. Rhan is something else entirely. What did you think this was?"

"Actually I thought it was a *pen*." The comeback was quick, but Ecko's thoughts were a seethe of darkness. In the still, dim air of the taproom, the rising shadows jeered him.

There's so much you still don't know...

Roderick said, every word a barb, "You've made a short-sighted and frankly quite arrogant assumption, but perhaps your future is not that clear or simple?"

His words were cut short by a sharp judder, a shock that

rippled through the air like a concussion.

"Our 'God of Evil' already has his enemy," Roderick said softly. He was a figure of gloom and air and strength and now madness, the shadows of the taproom rose around him in billowing darkness, the light from the feather illuminated the lunacy in his gaze. "The world has brought you here for a purpose, certainly, but we have to understand how you *fit* with her vision. We can't just – !"

The floor shook, from one end to the other.

"You crazy-ass motherfucker! I'm not...? Then what the hell am I...?"

The floor shook again.

"The world's vision, Ecko! Her nightmare! There is something else, something greater, something vast and timeless and forgotten. And things have come to pass this evening – critical things. It all starts from here, Ecko – *your* foe, *your* fight. We *must* go to Fhaveon! Rhan *must* see us! He will help us understand!"

"*Batshit!*" Baffled, reeling with confusion, Ecko's words were reflex – he had no idea what to think. "You're a coward and a fucking liar!" This world *had* a champion? This world *had* a hero? He didn't understand, he didn't even want to – all he knew was that he was floundering. He was surfing the shaking floor over a sea of what-the-fuck and he no longer knew what the hell was going on. Every time he thought he understood...

...that fucking bitch Eliza threw him a curve ball.

If she'd built this world for *him* – why pre-program a ready-coded champion? An uber-hero superbeing just gagging to spank the Lord of Chaos's ass the second his alarm went off? Was she trying to make Ecko take second place, learn humility – give someone else the glory?

Become a "team player"?

Well, fuck *that*. If eating shit was his exit door? He'd burn this place to the fucking *ground* first.

You hear that you bitch? I'll burn it down*!*

In his head, clear as an aural upload, he heard smoothly androgynous tones, *Success of scenario projected at 02.64%. Awaiting further parameters.*

Collator.

His anger froze into fear, and shattered.

The voice had been so clear in his mind that he fought the urge to spin round, to turn his oculars on every corner of the taproom, on the tables, the bar top, the fireplace, the door… his adrenals were kicked, he was shaking with the stress of his restraint.

Move and countermove. He could never win. This was in his *head*. He was hearing *voices* for fuck's sake. His grip on this reality was slipping like his grip on Grey's fucking wall – he half expected the whole scene to dissolve to greenscreen any second. He had no control over his own mind – Eliza could replace his memories, make him hear and see things, jump him round like a circus freak hit with an electroprod… and now, quite literally, he'd lost the fucking plot. If Rhan was the ready-programmed hero…

The air was starting to twist.

…then why the hell was he here?

The tavern juddered again. Like a bad trip, any second now…

Roderick's grin spread wider than his face. He loomed with power and the light from his eyes glittered in shards of splintered amethyst. Any moment now, he was going to laugh – and that laugh would echo across the grass and the tavern would ride it, twisting out of reality only to fall into existence far, far away from where the Banned girl had gone…

The world slewed around the edge of the plughole, and it started to scream.

But Ecko made his decision, and the pattern be damned. Faster than the light, faster than the darkness, he was gone.

PART 3: WAVES

13: RHAN FHAVEON

Rhan Elensiel, Lord Seneschal of Fhaevon, Foundersson's Champion, Gift of the Godfather and First Voice of the Council of Nine, was having trouble waking up.

The clear night air had congealed into a milky early morning. His mouth tasted like an esphen's backside and some motherless bastard had stuffed his head with grass. The wisdom of four hundred returns had taught Rhan many things – among them, the ability to know when he'd overdone it.

Dear Gods. You'd think I'd've learned by now.

With an effort, he sat up, rubbed a hand through his dishevelled white hair and ground his gaze into focus.

Samiel's *bollocks.*

He'd passed out in his front room again, apparently not able to make it as far as the door. Across the tall windows, his shutters were closed and the lingering smoke coiled through stripes of early sunlight. Around the room was a scatter of debris: carafes and goblets, empty food platters, long-stemmed pipes tumbled free from their stands. There were also various recumbent friends, in various stages of nakedness, each snoring gently in the aftermath of the previous night's revelry.

Oh, all right. The thought was sarcastic, it'd been a very long time since he'd actually given a shit. *I've really overdone it this time.*

But remind me why it matters?

With a faint, sardonic chuckle, Rhan sat up, creaking his heavy, pale shoulders to ease the knots in his back. His neck cracked. Immortality, for the Gods' sakes – frankly, it was overrated.

He reached for the nearest goblet, took a swig of the remaining wine and, still creaking, unfolded to his feet.

So. What threats does the world have for me today? Petty squabbling among the journeying merchants? Piracy? A shortage of roast esphen for the Foundersson's dinner?

Or perhaps the Halls of Above have reopened and allowed the stars back into the sky...

Protector of the World, indeed.

He took another swig of lukewarm red.

There were times down through the returns when Rhan had wondered if he shouldn't've been the inevitably ageing greybeard after all: the twinkly-eyed, wise-and-hale old man with the sinister presence and power to spare and the origin lost in mystery. He'd had the choice – he could've been anything.

But he'd figured that immortality was at least supposed to be fun.

Rhan had forgone storyteller-vagabond, chosen instead a form of height and breadth and strength. He was a carven statue, pale skinned and powerful, classic in feature and form. As carefully crafted as the very city herself, he was a warrior, Fhaveon's guardian and defender.

Hero. Or something like that.

Yet, down through the city's long returns, his titles had become hollow, jests bereft of anything but taunt – his dark foe had never come back. Instead of righteous fighter, Rhan had been a petty politician for four hundred returns – and *that* was cursed purgatory.

Who said the Gods didn't have a sense of humour?

The brief, acid chuckle came again. However he may physically appear, his immortality was its own blight – even the parties had palled in the end. There were many times he'd wondered if his damned brother had not been the lucky one. He, at least, must still have his passion.

Take me home, Samiel, Godsfather. I've paid for my misdeed. Enough now.

But the father of the Gods, as ever, wasn't listening.

Rhan had another slug of wine and rubbed the drowsiness out of his eyes.

Around him, his scattering of companions remained motionless. They were a ramshackle assortment, with one thing in common – they were his friends, and he cared little for age or status. He'd watched some of them grow from youngsters, known their parents and their families for generations gone. They were mortal, bright, fragile, and their time was so short – yet they gave him hope. While their lives and vibrancy could still touch him, he could still find the light in his heart.

Though there were times when he had to employ some interesting methods to remember where he'd left it.

Carefully, Rhan picked his way across the room, retrieving goblets and platters. He leaned down to pick up a pipe, tapped the ash into a bowl. By the Gods, if any of Mostak's overzealous grunts were to aim a heavy boot at his front door, he'd have a whole lot of explaining to do. The city's soldiery would take a completely different view of his habits – and *then* it would matter a great deal.

Humourless thugs – they were all about the rules. No damned respect for age or seniority.

What was that old jest about soldiers looking younger every return?

He picked up the ash bucket to dispose of the evidence. Four hundred returns or not, it was probably wise to be careful.

Four hundred returns, name of the Gods, the number was ludicrous. He'd no idea where that time had even gone.

The city had been in her infancy when Rhan had first come here. Still torn and bleeding, broken in body and in soul, he'd washed up at Fhaveon a shattered thing, uncomprehending of the punishment and responsibility that the God Samiel had decreed for him.

The price of his transgression – and the duty he'd carried ever since.

Garland House, at almost her highest point, had been the gift of the First Lord Tekisarri, eldest child of Saluvarith the Founder, and, at that time, barely more than a youth.

Teki himself, his daughter the GreatHeart Rakanne who'd gifted terhnwood to the Varchinde, her son Adward the Consolidator who'd then brought that gift back under Fhaveon's hegemony and designed the trade-rotations of the plains – from his very arrival, Rhan had stood by House Valiembor, parent and child, lord and leader. The God Samiel had decreed it, and so it must be. Each child of the city's Lord, each newborn Foundersson or Daughter, had been placed in his white hands as a babe, and he'd held them against his chest – so tiny, so wondrous and inexplicable! – and sworn his limitless life in their defence.

And he'd upheld that oath. Always.

But as the returns had bled by, his very oath had become empty – what could challenge him? The city was secure, the plains at peace, the scufflings of the Council essentially trivial. The terhnwood grew, its circulation was sure; the grass was harvested. He had everything he could want and he was *bored*.

He drained the wine, grimaced, looked for another.

But was halted by a quiet, smart and familiar rap at the door. *By the Gods! At this time of the morning?*

"My Lord." Scythe was tall, slim, young, despicably efficient, and smart enough to keep his judgements to himself. He also entered rooms without waiting to be asked. "I have no wish to... wake you," he said, "but there is something you should know."

Something in his voice chased the faintest flicker of tension between Rhan's shoulders. He put bucket and goblet down, straightened up, creaked again.

"What's the problem?"

Scythe, pointedly ignoring the tangle of bodies at his feet, held something up to the light.

"There has been another attack, my Lord, another fire."

The shock spread like opening wings – like the first breath of wind that warned of a storm to come. Something in the Powerflux; something that tinged the very edge of his elemental awareness...

"Scythe?" His voice was low, soft. "Where?"

Mutters stirred at his feet.

"From the farmlands north of Ikira, my Lord. The outermost edge of the terhnwood crop."

The terhnwood crop.

For a moment, he said nothing. Scythe's expression was absolutely blank.

"How long? Was anything found?"

"Evening yesterday, my Lord, and nothing has been found. The farmer sent her runner straight here."

Less than two days.

Implications rose out of the smoky morning, gibbering fears and threats. Plains fires in the summer were a known hazard, but there had been several of them reported, one after another, and something about them was striking him to his heart. A problem with the terhnwood crop, at this time of the return, would be beyond disastrous. If the harvest was in any way threatened...

Fhaveon, more than any other city in the Varchinde, was dependent upon her farmlands – not only for the tithe of food that fed her in return for her protection, but for the growth of the terhnwood that perpetuated the cycle of the Grasslands' trade. Fhaveon's crop was twice that of Amos and four times that of the southern city of Annondor – put simply, she was the Grasslands' single biggest supplier. Without terhnwood, the political and social circulation of the Varchinde would be undone – and the disaster would spread.

But beneath this, there was a greater and more fundamental fear.

Am I tested, Samiel? Is this where I must fight for real?

Somewhere deep in Rhan's immortal soul, there came a flicker of white flame, a flare of long, long forgotten anticipation. He rubbed a hand over his face, flexed his back.

"Scythe. I need runners."

"Already done, my Lord." He blinked cold eyes briefly in the rising sun. "The Council is convened at your command. You should also know the Bard is here. The rumours are all through the city."

"Roderick?" The flicker became a grin. "Bastard has impeccable timing. Get him too." He studied Scythe's expression, thinking. "Actually, never mind. I'll get him myself."

The Seneschal breathed his hangover out into the morning, could almost see it lifted away from him, dissipating like the smoke from his lungs.

"Damned mad prophet – he needs to be here for this one."

It was over in a moment, a flash of heart-lurch and disbelief, an extending hand, a cry, a jump of the floor and a crazed tumble through the substance of the world...

Ecko had gone.

Scathing and oblivious, Ecko had turned his black-toothed sneer on everything the Bard had tried to tell him. He'd fled into the grey light of the pre-dawn chill and the tavern was moving as if glad to be rid of him. Reality twisted around

Roderick, picked him up and tore him to pieces and spun him to somewhere new.

Ecko had gone.

Yet even as the world changed, so the Bard was on his feet, shouting, crying denial, riding the movement of the building like a Banned acrobat – but as the sickness and the darkness slowly spiralled to a stop, he staggered and caught himself on the edge of a table...

The taproom was empty, new light was chinking through the shutters.

Ecko had gone.

Instinctively, irrationally, Roderick was on the doorstep anyway, needing to find him, to call him back, to explain. *Don't do this! You don't understand!* Yet with the loss of one miracle had come the manifestation of another.

He stumbled into the crisp, sea-scented air of the tavern's foregarden, the old sign creaking above his head, and he found that his pointless cry had caught in a throat choked by another realisation entirely.

With no warning, there were tears in his eyes – a glitter of hope.

Before him rose Fhaveon, the Lord City of Saluvarith the Founder, the home of Rhan and the might of the Varchinde.

Ecko had gone – but Roderick was *here.*

He could not know if the tavern had heard him, responded to his desperation, but he was here, and Rhan would have answers – he would have direction and insight. The Council would help him. Please the Gods, he would no longer be carrying the burden of his vision alone. The alchemy of Tusien was manifest – it had been seen and witnessed. Now, at last – *at last* – the city could not deny him, the Lord Foundersson would rally his forces and offer his help.

He had to.

Didn't he?

Ress's warning haunted him: *"They'll lock you up."*

Sometimes, the weight of his forgotten vision was too much to bear alone.

Above him, the birds cried mournful in the morning air. Fhaveon was a cliffside city – she stood against the paling shine of the sky, the sun behind her shoulder and the rising tessellation of her streets and buildings all in soft shadow, shining with strings of lanterns and rocklights. Unlike almost every other coastal habitation, Fhaveon's face was turned away from the water – she looked inland and the streets climbed in glistening zigzags all the way to the silhouetted shapes of the cathedral and Foundersson's palace, high above. In the grey dawn, the city was alive with light – she had roadways and gardens of fantastical beauty, carven pillars and tumbling waterways and stone art and crystal-leaved trees that reflected the rocklights to a dancing gleam.

She was a jewel, built by the Founder Saluvarith from a vision of his own – she ruled the Grasslands with a detailed knowledge of trade and terhnwood, a merciless intelligence and the only real military might that the plains could muster.

The Bard wished that Ecko could see her – wished that he could have found one thing to make him realise that he needed to care...

I'm s'posed to think this shit is real?

I'm supposed to think it's not?

How could Ecko care, if he didn't believe in any of them?

For a moment, Roderick cursed his own stupidity – he closed his eyes against a complex rise of hope and dread and bitter irony. The Gods, as Rhan had told him many times, enjoyed their games of spite and childishness.

And without Ecko, without any kind of physical evidence, rallying the Council was going to be that much harder.

They'll lock you...

His fear rose again and he swallowed it, opening his eyes to look more closely around him.

As if this would help him judge how much of a task he really faced.

The Wanderer had manifest at the very outside of Fhaveon's skirting, in one of the many peculiarly empty patches that decorated her hem.

Many returns before, when Adward the Consolidator had brought the Varchinde's trade under the city's leadership, so the culture of the Grasslands had undergone a subtle shift. As the craftsmanship, transport and dealing of terhnwood itself had become the Grasslands' lifeblood, so many of the population had become perpetually mobile.

From this beginning had grown the ribbon-towns and caravanserai that lined the trade-roads – from this beginning also had come the founding of Roviarath as a formal city, rather than as the huge and ever-swelling sprawl of the Fayre. The old saying went – if Fhaveon was the Grasslands' head, then Roviarath was its heart.

With the swelling, mobile population of the trade-roads, the static population in the cities had lessened. In Fhaveon, the people had drifted almost instinctively towards her hubs – the harbours at the coast and riverside and the inner marketplaces. Out here, at the city's very limits, there were wide, rugged patches that had simply been abandoned. The buildings were not ruined – the homes and garrisons and outposts and tithehalls were built of the same perfectly pale, striated stone. Even here, they'd been constructed far too well to be tumbledown.

Yet, over returns of abandonment, the city's gardens had spread and the Varchinde had crept inwards, taking back its own. In many places the buildings were overgrown – the grass could be seen through the windows, growing up inside the very walls. Many creatures lived here: birds nested in rooftops and scavengers prowled the weed-grown streets.

Out there, The Wanderer was oddly isolated, a spark of life in a city deserted. The emptiness was eerie, beautiful and sad, a no-man's-land caught between the vast, coloured shimmer of the northern plains on one side, and the rising, rocky promontory that was the city herself, her strength uplifted to the sky.

But the morning was cool and quiet, edged in shadow and soft green.

Behind him, he could hear wakening voices, the creaking of floors. As if it had absolutely no regard for the momentous events of the previous night, the momentous events to come, the tavern began anew with each dawn – and there was work that needed to be done.

A flurry of birds rose suddenly, crying as if they were laughing at him. There was movement in the emptiness, but he did not see it clearly – sometimes, people did live down here, out of reach of the city's hands and fists.

The Bard stood in the tavern's foregarden, watching as the birds circled, then settled.

Whatever had disturbed them had gone.

Though he couldn't see it from here, he knew that Fhaveon was deceptive – an elegant face upon a body of stone. Her northern side, facing the Swathe River, was a slash of gorge, almost as though the hand of Samiel himself had cut the world, his wife, to her heart. Here, there were the wide wharves of inland harbour, loading terhnwood and salt, unloading stone from the Khohan Mountains, wood from Darash, food and ale from the Triangle Cities – Foriath, Narvakh and The Hayne.

There were bridges at the head of the gorge and a scatter of buildings that stretched down its far side, leading towards Ikira and Teale, and the city's outposts and tithed farmlands.

The final side of the city, facing the water, was the great Break Wall that ran sheer and mighty all the way down to the sea.

From the plains Fhaveon may look soft and wealthy, but Saluvarith had built her as a fortress – as a fortress against the water. The city had been made to stand and face her foe – and that foe was not the gentle grass that now crept softly over her hemline.

So many things, forgotten.

Rammouthe Island, barely a league across the strait, was beautiful – a haven for creatures and birds, for rare grasses and trees that grew colossal and unhindered. The city had been built to defend against a foe long forgotten; her people cared no more.

Only Rhan, defender and champion of the city and of the plainland entire – he, too, awaited the foe that the Council no longer acknowledged.

Above the Bard's head, a single bird hovered, watching the life below.

Roderick sighed, stretched, and went back to the building.

"There you are, you bastard." Rhan's sardonic bass was unmistakeable. In the warm, dusty dimness he seemed almost to carry his own light. "I hope you're awake, because we've got a sod of a problem."

"Samiel's teeth." Sat at the bar, an empty goblet in front of him, Rhan turned an arched white eyebrow on the Bard. "Guardian of the Ryll, you can't find your arse with a signpost. I've got a real crisis on my hands, here – what in the name of Vahl Zaxaar's bloodied batwings are you prattling about?"

"I'm not jesting." To Rhan's eyes, Roderick looked like he'd spent the night wrestling for his masculine virtue and losing. "This is all –"

"It's all a game. I've been telling you that for returns." Rhan clapped the Bard's shoulder, his grin affectionate. Roderick was half crazed, but his heart was true and his insight considerable. And for a mortal, he'd lived a sod of a long time – probably why he was slightly unhinged. "And find me the cellen, will you, I don't know what this stuff is but I'm pretty sure it's been drunk once already."

For a moment, Roderick blinked at him, his gaze fragmenting with frustration. "By the Gods, Rhan, have you heard as much as a word? Everything is in motion, the Count of Time gathers pace. Can't you *feel* – ?"

"Enough drama, you'll strain something." The Seneschal's voice gentled, but he gestured with the goblet. "This 'Ecko' character of yours –"

"He's loose, uncontrolled. Perhaps he went after the girl."

"He wouldn't be the first one to make that mistake."

"Or after the Banned."

"They'll carry his bollocks as a battle standard." The Seneschal thought about this for a moment, then he flickered a frown. "Let me get this straight. Your Ryll-born vision is telling you – what? This missing girl, this injured kid, these monsters, what in Samiel's name do they have to do with fires in the terhnwood crop?"

Roderick met his gaze, said faintly acidly, "Have you not felt it, Master of Elemental Light?"

"That wasn't the question."

Roderick's smile was bleak, weary. "The boy's tale – the creatures he described – they have sent ripples through my being as though I should know what they are. As though I should *remember*. This is alchemy of legend, it has not been seen since Tusienic times. The rumours are scattered but they grow – I have to bring this to the Council –"

"Sadly, Ress was right about that much – you can't take 'legends' to the Council, they'll laugh you out of the hall." Rhan's perpetually wry, slightly self-deprecating tone took the sting from the comment. "Again." He grinned. "Look. We've got a problem that's actually going to make them sit up – unexplained fires are real, tangible threats." He grinned. "Trust me. I'll make them hear you."

Roderick rummaged behind the bar, found a decorated

carafe and a goblet. Nodding his thanks, Rhan picked up the wine and chugged it straight. The cellen was quality stuff – he could feel his energy levels rising.

"By the Gods." The Bard shook his head. "You have no manners at all."

"I've got them exactly when and where I need them." Rhan passed the carafe over. "Go on, it won't hurt you."

Roderick put it down, said, "The world's fear is coming close – close enough to feel, to touch – !"

"This is the *Council*. They want terhnwood and power, more tithes from the farmlands, more incoming trade. They don't want saga stuff – ruined cities, half man, half horse, dark champions from other worlds – and, frankly, you don't want to look any damned crazier than you are."

"You're not hearing me."

"I hear you fine." Rhan sounded exasperated. "This is the Council of Nine – the rulers of the Varchinde." He dropped his voice. "It has other concerns – the Lord Foundersson Demisarr is not a well man, and I must watch the Merchant Master Phylos like a hunting bweao. And this morning, the fires are *spreading*." Rhan took another hefty chug from the carafe. "I don't need to tell you what would happen to Fhaveon – to the Varchinde entire – if we have a problem with the harvest."

Roderick picked up the goblet. The sunlight from the windows caught his hair making it glow almost purple – the rich, dark colour of his Tundran blood. "This is all connected, somehow, somewhere. Dear Gods, Rhan…"

"Of course it's connected, I'm not damned blind. I've called the Council to meet at the death of the sun. Before that, I want to see the evidence for myself – and I want you to come with me. Bear witness, if you like. With a little wit and some – ah – vocal dexterity –" he grinned "– I think we can make this work for both of us. Kill two daemons with one holy object, as it were – what the rhez was that?"

A sudden commotion had come from outside – from the deserted, grass-grown streets of the skirting. There was a cough of dust, and a loud rumble of crumbling stonework.

Rhan was at the door, his skin suddenly pricking and his elemental awareness shivering the sounds in his ears.

There, in the corner of two walls, at the base of a pillar, something stirred.

The building was a tithehall, a long, low shadow – it hadn't been used in returns. Once, it would have been one of many nodes upon the city's outskirts, the central storage points for the incoming farmlands' grain and meat and crafting. Once, there would have been a foodhall here, a gathering point, a fiveday bazaar, a centre for the complex filaments of distribution that spread the tithed goods throughout this local part of the city. There would have been soldiers, traders, travellers, and clerks. Pirates. Poachers. Opportunists.

Now, there was nothing. Only the cold store, lined in stone, and a shocked concussion that was rippling outwards through the morning air, the grass. A straying scavenger snarled and fled.

And there was something over there, something that stank of decaying air.

Behind Rhan, Roderick was on his feet, hand instinctively going for a weapon he hadn't carried in returns. A shock of real fear ricocheted through Rhan's form.

And a lightning shock of exhilaration.

Then there was the chilling scraping of stone on stone, the sound of something heavy being dragged.

There was *groaning* – a deep grumble of pain.

Rhan could *feel* the noise, like an avalanche or tree falling, a rumbling through his belly and the soles of his feet.

The Bard had moved for the window. Through the doorway, Rhan could see something, something low to the ground as if it had fallen.

It was trying to move.

Samiel's...

The thing was huge, but only half complete: head and torso and arms, sprawled on cracking tiles. Each hand was blunt like a shovel but more powerful than an earthquake. It dug them – *slam* – into the ground and tried to drag itself forwards, a handspan at a time. It was terrifying, somehow tragic. It had no expression on its stone face. From the grim slit of a mouth came the rumbling throb of pain that carried through the city's stonework. The noise was in the bones behind Rhan's ears; he could taste it in his throat.

It dragged itself a little further, piteous despite its size. Behind where it struggled, two huge stones had exploded, apparently spewing this thing out of the wall. The stones below had different markings – if this thing'd ever had legs, they'd been spat out somewhere else.

Everything was covered in stone dust and rubble.

Slam! It dug one hand downwards, splitting the tiles end to end. *Slam!* Fighting for every centimetre of ground, it dragged itself to the front of The Wanderer, looked up.

Rhan didn't need his elemental vision to see the tiles splintering beneath its weight. It was pure stone, a wall carving come to life. And it reached one hand up towards the window where Roderick stood silent.

The Bard stared, bereft of speech and breath.

"Wait!" Rhan was tense, almost shaking. He came forwards, slowly, his elemental awareness screaming alarm.

But he laid one white hand on the creature's head.

"I'm here," he said softly. "This is Fhaveon and I will never leave her. Your time is long gone. Rest."

The thing paused, struggled to lift its torso so it could look at him out of an eyeless stone face. Gently, Rhan stroked its head.

"Rest," he repeated.

It made a last, huge effort, held its hand out to him.

Then it collapsed into sand with a sigh that might've been relief.

Back in the taproom, Roderick flicked his violet gaze at the Seneschal.

"Rhan," he said softly. The tone of his voice sent shudders down the Seneschal's back. "What the rhez is going on?"

14: MERCHANT THE GREAT FAYRE AND THE HALLS OF LARRED JADE, ROVIARATH

Triqueta hated the rain.

But in the aftermath of the fighting, it suited her comedown. It hammered relentless, gusting across the plains wind. It soaked through her garments and made her skin sting with chill. Her overhood was flapping in her eyes and hair was smeared to her face in itchy strands. If she lowered her head, water dripped from the front of her cowl onto her saddle pommel, running down the darkening leather.

She had no bridle – she was lifelong Banned and had no need of one. Her hands clutched her cloak in a vain attempt to keep sheltered.

Stupid Grassland weather. You don't get this in the desert.

There were just occasions when Triq forgot that, desert blooded she may be, but she'd actually never crossed the Yevar Mountains and seen the Red Sands for herself.

Under her, her little mare was equally dejected, her head down and her mane sodden. As the wind caught it, it fluttered hopeless like a palomino-coloured rag.

The monsters seemed like a dream, a lifetime ago. Triq's energy had been soaked through and was running down the mare's legs to be lost in the soaking grass that rippled like a great grey ocean.

She peered at the darkening evening sky and muttered curses.

Throughout the day, the clouds had risen before them like great wings, mantling vast and grey over the mountains. Squalls of drizzle had harried them like harbingers. They'd pushed their pace as fast as they dared, confronted by breaths of cold that worried at hems and hoods.

Loosed across the massive emptiness of the open Varchinde, a storm could be a terrifying thing.

We'll stay off the trade-road, Ress had said, *Run parallel. Less trouble.*

He was right – this close to the Great Fayre, piracy was rife and the ribbon-towns notoriously opportunistic. And if Roderick's theory was right, no other predators would come anywhere near where the monsters had been.

So they were still in the grass.

The main roadway ran by the river to the south. If the air had been brighter she could've seen it – a line of grubby, brown shanties that grew slowly more sturdy as they came closer to the city itself. But already, it was darkening. Somewhere behind the clouds, the sun was sinking to a swollen red death upon the distant peaks of the Kartiah and the sky was deepening to a rich, dark indigo that swelled like a bruise.

Yep, Triq was in a really lousy mood.

As they came to the city, to the filthy patchwork sprawl of the Great Fayre, the rain rallied and attacked anew. It hissed with fury, sharp and fierce. Hunching even further, Triq swore, lowered her head and grabbed her cloak. Over them, the rocklight shine of the Lighthouse Tower became a smear of grey.

On his cart, Feren loosed fevered pain.

Life still fluttered in his heart; in his head, there were figments tormenting him.

The rain squalled and battered at them all.

"Go left!" Ress bawled. The cart chearl had lowered his head, blowing snot and water.

Yowling in the gaps in the walls, the wind swung sharply round to the north and the grass tops surrendered, shimmering flat to the soil.

Triq shouted above the noise, "What? Why?"

The voice of the river was rising.

Ress pointed. "Flag on the gatehouse!" he said. "City's on Watch!"

Feren called aloud, unintelligible syllables.

"I see it!" Triqueta spat water and blinked it out of her eyes. "Go, we're with you! Jayr?"

"Yes!" Beside her, disdaining cloak or overhood and soaked to her skin, Jayr stroked the injured gelding's nose and he nudged her with his shoulder, nearly pushing her over. In spite of his hurt, he paced forwards, ears up, as if he knew that help lay ahead. Jayr said softly, barely heard, "We'll get you some help, we will."

"More likely we'll get him boiled down for glue." The blackening wind snatched Triq's sceptical comment and threw it skyward, unheard.

Grown like a fungus round two thirds of Roviarath's walls, the Great Fayre was the trade hub of the Varchinde, focus of the plainlands' perpetually transient population – and there was a rhez of a lot of it.

Triqueta knew the Fayre well: she'd worked here, loitered and plotted and diced her way through its staff and its stalls, earned its respect. Here, you could barter for your home or your soul, trade your life or your time or your skin; here, you'd find wine, company, thievery and every manner of scheming. Teeming with the urgency that lurked outside the city walls, the Fayre had swollen into a cheerfully dilapidated mess that welcomed traders from all across the world.

It thrived, even under the savagely driving rain.

Scholar or no, Ress was unbothered by the filth and the chaos – his returns had taught him a thing or two about markets. Jayr, however, eyed it like some sprawling predator, her scars bright with water and tension. Triq hoped she wouldn't do anything loco.

They moved through it slowly, watching.

The noise was incredible.

Around them, the Fayre was a melting pot of hope and ambition and poverty and decadence. Desperation and opportunism followed them – beggars and panhandlers, wide-mouthed children and despairing, discarded humanity. Under the rain, hands were held out from all sides, pleas for help and attention. Several times, Ress had to forcibly repel a grip from the cart.

They slowed to a crawl, swamped by bustle and motion and racket.

"Padeshian dyes, lady? The finest in the central plainland!"

Between the stalls, Triq caught a glimpse of flame – guttering under the weather. A flamboyant woman in bright scarlet carried fire on her open hand, breathed it from her lips. She'd gathered a small crowd – mostly children, tugging at their parents' hands. Jayr gaped for a moment, but Triq chuckled – genuine elemental attunement was even less likely than...

...than monsters.

The children laughed and clapped and Triqueta turned away.

Her mare was jumpy, hooves precarious amid squealing vermin and squawking wildlife, the occasional fallen drunk. Haggling was common, it was vicious and occasionally violent – Larred Jade's soldiery did not patrol the Fayre and bursts of roughhousing were frequent.

A male voice called to Jayr to join him in an unlikely physical exploration. Jayr coloured, but ignored him. Triq snickered.

As they moved closer to the city, so the stalls became sturdier and more wealthy – their wares better quality and their garbage and chaos significantly less. Here, the city's defences rose above the morass and Jade's archers prowled warily, their eyes open.

Ress glanced back at Feren, and they picked up the pace.

Around them now, shouts offered rare and wondrous metals from the blind craftsmen of the Kartiah; stone from the mountains; wood from the forests that blanketed their feet. From the north, there was food and ale; salt from Fhaveon; spices from Amos; rich fabrics from Padesh and the cities of the far south. Wines flowed from Annondor; from Idrak came the prized hides of the racing arqueus. And everywhere, there was terhnwood, fibre and resin and fragment, the critical life of the Varchinde plains.

Fhaveon had might and Amos wisdom – but traditionally, Roviarath was the Varchinde's hub. She stood strong at the centre of the Grasslands' motion and wealth.

Sod that, Triqueta figured, eyeing the mucky mass of stalls. Right now she stood strong at the centre of the Grasslands' mud. It was everywhere, a sea of it, churned with grass and filth and rubbish.

By morning, the Fayre would be rotting garbage and liquid shit.

Triq's mare blew water and shook her soaked mane. The wheels of Feren's cart lurched and splashed.

"Not far!" Ress called.

Jayr grunted and cursed – she was almost wading, the mud caked on her boots. Her scalplock hung heavy, like a horse's tail, and the rain seemed to run along the lines of her scars.

Triq shivered.

As they came towards the rampart and the gates, rocklights were beginning to flicker, defying the rising dark. In there somewhere, among the pens and the pickets and the flapping stall roofs, there was music, drums and laughter. She could hear the traders calling banter and wares. Here, there were artists and storytellers, sheltering in the lee of the city.

One of them called out as they came past, "Look! Banned! They've come to deal with the monsters!"

"Tell the CityWarden!" called another. "There are fires in the farmlands and monsters loose in the plains! Our tithes are failing because our harvest burns!"

"Gods," Triqueta muttered, spitting water. "It's everywhere."

"Yep." Jayr slipped as her horse buffeted her again. "Will you stop that?"

Strapped in the cart, Feren called at the glowering sky. A frisson shivered through Triq's hunched and sopping form.

Monsters.

Roviarath's gatehouse was built of wood, once mighty but now split and cracked with age and weather. There was no archway, no rampart – the building sat snug between soil battlements that offered a sheltered walkway around their top. In better weather, you could tour the Fayre from above.

Now, though, the walkway contained only archers, dejected in the downpour.

As Triqueta and the others came closer, thumping to a stop with the rain now driving into their backs, they could see the watch-flag, hanging sodden and fluttering occasionally like a dying bird.

Triq shook her hood, wiped her face. She called into the hammering weather, "Triqueta of the Banned! I bear injured!"

"Picked your night for it!" The archers' commander, their tan, grinned down at her. "Gate's open, go on in. Did you find your dice?"

"Don't yank my rope, Cohn." Triq gave the guardsman a rude hand gesture. "If you know who took them – !"

"No, Triq, I don't. But I do know I wouldn't be letting you in city limits if you still had them on you." His comment was greeted by guffaws from further back.

"Why the watch-flag?" Ress called from the cart. "You got pirate problems?"

"Nah." The commander took a tiny block of wax from a pouch and rubbed it carefully down his bowstring. "The wild herds're on the move – they're much closer to the walls. And it's not only them – Deep Patrols say bigger beasties have shifted territory, they shot a lone bweao not half a day from the waterside." He grinned. "Don't tell me you lot haven't noticed?"

"Bweao?" Ress chuckled. "They kill it?"

"Fat chance!" The guard commander rolled his eyes, still grinning. "It was a young one, I think – they scared it off."

Triq spat water. "Storyteller said something about fires?"

"Not in this weather!" The tan laughed at her.

Triq groaned, and then, quite clearly, Feren cried out, "We see all but nothing!"

She turned, but Ress was already moving the cart forwards.

"Kid needs help. Must get to the hospice!"

"No problem!" The commander drew a shaft from the quiver at his belt and notched it, though he didn't draw the string. He nodded affably as they passed between decaying wooden jaws. "We'll send a runner up to old man Jade. Hope your lad's all right, there. And stay out of trouble!"

If he heard Triqueta's answering chuckle, he made no sign.

Larred Jade, CityWarden of Roviarath, was a tall man, lean and curved and canny, eyes as blue and clear as the summer sky. In spite of the rain that beat on the windows of the rocklit hospice, his skin was tinged with sunlight. Dark hair was caught in a gleaming metal band at the nape of his neck. White strands glittered through it, like the bright edges of his awareness.

Warden Jade was as sharp as a good blade and a fireblasted hard man to fool. Standing a head taller than his frowning apothecary, he was watching the dying boy that now lay, blood black and parchment white, upon the cool haven of the pallet.

He said, "Monsters."

Wet garments still stuck to her, dripping rainwater from her hem stitching, Triqueta turned to face him. Her hair was stuck to her like molten metal and the stones in her cheeks flashed, a warning – or a plea.

She said, "I know how it sounds –"

"It's crazed." He was tapping long fingers against his thigh – artisan's fingers, fingers for weaving success. The CityWarden was a merchant, and a very successful one; his knowledge of his craft was absolute.

"I know." She caught his eye, shrugged at him with deceptive innocence, then her expression sobered. "I saw them, Larred, we all did. I've never had anything like that under me. It was like riding a… riding a storm."

The words were inadequate to the thrill that sang in her blood.

"Address me as Warden Jade." It was reflex, his tone was both thoughtful and wary. He said, "Half human, half horse, lurking at the borders of the city."

Watched by a fidgeting Ress, the apothecary was carefully soaking Feren's bandaging away from the boy's wounds.

"Too long in the open grass, Triqueta of the Banned, plays games with your sight and memory – and that's without all the ale," the Warden said.

"Maybe," she told him archly, "but it's not a game when you tear out its cursed throat, feel its blood run down your arm. When you've got it under you and you're fighting for life, for control." Her hand tensed with the memory – the adrenaline, the fury, the savage and primal release of strength. Her voice alight she said, "I don't know what they were, Larred, but they're *out* there. And the bweao know it – why d'you think that flag's on your gatehouse?"

Jade's gaze flicked from Feren's wounds, to Triq's closed fist, to the empty rings at her belt – she carried no weapons in his presence. Water dripped from her as though she was melting, black puddles seeped across the stone.

"They're real, Warden." Ress's hands twitched, as if he ached to treat the boy himself. "Not a day's ride from here – though it's taken us a little longer."

Larred Jade did not turn to look at him. "What evidence did you bring?"

"For Gods' sakes…!" Triqueta curbed a flash of temper. Being out of the rain and the wind and the wet, she was welcoming the desert flame back to her heart, the passion of her people in her blood. "I had it between my *thighs*, Larred, a thing of muscle and fury and death. I didn't stop for mementoes."

"We've brought evidence," Ress said calmly. "Your people will tell you – look at the boy's wounds and tell me you know what made that hole."

The apothecary nodded, though he was intent on his work and didn't speak.

Rain scattered on the window. Somewhere deeper in the stone walls of the building, the wind had found a crack and now it keened like a lost thing.

The draught stole across Triq's wet shoulders and raised the hackles on her forearms.

Know what made that hole.

Monsters.

She was still shivering.

Jade spun on his heel and faced Ress full-on, his expression as cool and dark as the stone of his walls.

"You're known as a rational man, Ress of the Banned. You're telling me this tale is true?"

Ress shrugged. "Didn't believe it either – not 'til I was defending the boy."

"So what would you have me do?"

"Name of the Gods!" Triqueta wanted to grab him, shake

him, pull the images from her mind and force him to see them, rip him open, make him feel what she had felt. "Muster! Your cavalry should – !"

"My cavalry's going nowhere, Triqueta. Your scarred friend took her injured horse down to the stables –"

"You said you wanted evidence." Triq's tone was tart.

"*Don't* interrupt me again." Jade was getting angry. "Lots of things have claws, and lots of things make *holes*. The boy's hurt's serious and I'll tend it, of course, but we're on *Watch*."

"Why the rhez d'you *think* the herds have moved?" Triq's exasperation rang from the stone. "There's a new predator carving out territory, it doesn't take a member of the Banned to tell you that. There's also someone still being held, a Xenotian teacher, and we can't just –"

"Harvest time is almost upon us, Triq! The autumn is coming and the grass is changing colour. In only a few halfcycles the little death will be upon us. The grass will all die and the soil will be bare until the spring. I need every spare man, woman and child I've got to ensure the survival of my livestock, my farmlands, my people and my city – I don't have the forces to spare! The pirates –"

"Larred, don't be a –"

"Enough!" The Warden's loss of patience clanged loud and sudden, it caused Feren to mutter, his eyelids fluttering. "This is *my* city, Triq, my love and hope since Varya died. I've got no children – Roviarath is everything to me." The wind keened under his tone. "I'm the heart of the Varchinde, and what you're telling me is *crazed*."

Something in his voice was helpless, frustrated, caught. Triq said softly, "If this is the love of your life, Larred, then defend it."

The apothecary coughed, said softly. "The boy's infection is critical, Warden. I'll need to open the wound."

His face troubled now, shadows of the rain on the window speckling his skin with doubt, Jade nodded.

Ress said, "Warden Jade, you're facing predators and piracy with inadequate defences – I understand. But against the things we've fought?" He gestured at the grotesque, blackening swelling of Feren's hip. "They'll rip everything in their path to bloody pieces. We have no idea where they've come from or the size of their force – no idea what they want. They're not just animals. You should find them, before they find you."

Triqueta noted that Ress said nothing of the Bard's nightmare fears – this was hard enough.

Jade shook his head as if to dismiss the idiocy of it all. "You're suggesting these – things – have some sort of plan?"

Feren gasped and spasmed as the blade lanced the wound. Blood and pus soaked the apothecary's fingers, the boy's skin, the soft sheets of the pallet. A sharp, metal smell cut through the air.

Gore began to drip onto the floor.

Triq swallowed a mouthful of bile.

Jade was agitated, pacing. "Ress. I'm no warrior – and I'm no fireblasted gambler. If we don't gather enough grass, we all die. The pirates know this too – their attacks redouble at this time of the return. And the bweao..." He tailed off, his gaze seeing through and past the troubled, sweating apothecary. "This isn't Fhaveon. I can send a bretir for more force, but even assuming the Lord Foundersson heeds the message, it'll be five days before I have a response and a full cycle – twenty days at least – before any help reaches me. I need the warriors I have."

"So – what?" Triq spat at him. "You'll do nothing? Abandon the girl and hope it all goes away?"

He smiled, mirthless. "I'll make you a trade, Triqueta – you bring me information, and I'll mobilise. I want numbers, forces, deployment, tactics. I want to know what they are, what they want and how they plan to get it. I want to know where they are and where they came from – exactly the threat that they're offering." He watched the sheets under Feren deepening to a black smear. "My forces are limited – but I can risk one strike. If I know exactly where to hit and how hard. I'm going to play a game, I need to know the rules."

"For Gods' sakes, Larred – !"

"In return –" Jade held up a long finger "– I'll despatch the bretir to Fhaveon and brief my patrols to observe – but not engage. I'll look for information on the girl, and I'll heal the boy. If I can."

Ress said, "Thank you, Warden."

"Thank you, my horse's arse." Triqueta was barely clinging to her temper. "You want to know what Feren saw – !"

"I want to hear the account from him, yes."

"Is that your *payment*? Information? You soulless mercantile bastard."

Jade's face set white – for a moment, he was lost for words.

"Warden?" In the silence, the apothecary's tense question fell like a pebble and rolled across the water-stained floor. Ress turned.

Jade stood like a carven statue, watching Triqueta. After a moment, he said, "So in your world of reckless gambling, Triq, tell me." His voice was as tight as a rope. "What would you do?"

"I'd send out every mounted fighter I had, find the leader of the herd and pull its fireblasted guts out." A trickle of rainwater ran down her cheek, circling the opal stone. "Slowly. Along with some critical questions about its *mates*. The Fayre's like a willing virgin, Larred, her thighs wide open. Grass harvest or no, you could find yourself..." She paused. "What?"

"Isn't that just like the Banned? Act first, think afterwards?" There was a ghost of a smile on Jade's lips, humourless and angry. "Did Roderick take any action, frothing idealist that he is? Did he ride after the missing girl himself? Perhaps Syke's sending a war-Banned?" His grin was sharp edged; he didn't wait for an answer. "Or did he send you here to make me do it for him?"

Her anger skidded to a halt.

A cursed hard man to fool.

The truth clamped like a hand over her mouth, she couldn't move, couldn't think of a thing to say. The accuracy of his shot had knocked the passion straight out of her and now she was gasping, casting about her for anything with which to hit him back. "The scouts attacked us on the way, Syke doesn't..."

But Jade was nodding, smiling to himself.

She tried again, almost childish. "We're twice the fighters you are!" But she realised even as she said them that the words had been a mistake.

"Yes," he said, "you are. I make no effort to deny it."

Feren's thin scream made Triq shudder, she gave a half-panicked glance to see that both the city apothecary and Ress were now fighting to staunch the bloodflow from the boy's hip. A tide of thick scarlet soaked cloths and skin, flecked faces with dots like fragments of horror.

She could smell the blood. The wind still keened and rain scattered against the window, as if it sought entry.

The boy was going to die.

One last try. "Please Larred! Don't let them do this to anyone else!"

Jade faltered, faced by the same view, the same blood tide. He raised a hand. Upon his little finger, the wrought terhnwood-fibre ring of the City caught the rocklight and glittered. He said, "Do you really think that I'd do nothing?"

What? "I don't understand..."

"I'm a soulless mercantile bastard, Triqueta. I won't spare the forces of my city to chase down a figment. But what will I do?"

"It's not a figment...!"

Ress's voice said, "We're losing him." There was an edge of fury in his tone, and Triqueta wondered, slightly stupidly, if the city apothecary had cut an artery or something.

Jade said, "No one else needs to suffer like that. Tell me, Triq, what am I going to do?"

Soulless mercantile bastard.

I'm a merchant, not a warrior and not a fireblasted gambler. Roviarath is everything to me – I'm the heart of the Varchinde.

What will I do?

The realisation congealed and dripped like the rainwater from her hood, like the blood from Feren's wound.

"You're going to hire me – us – to scout for you."

"You, yes. I trust your passion. But your scarred companion lacks a Banned-trained mount and Ress, forgive me, is no warrior."

Triqueta said, "Hey, I'm no coward, but I'm not riding out alone."

"You won't have to." Larred was grinning like a Varchinde predator. "Ah, Triq – have you not realised the one thing that tips the scales here, the thing your monster hasn't bargained for?"

What?

Her bafflement must have shown, because Larred was starting to laugh. "If you could pick any one mercenary warrior, in the entire Varchinde, to hunt this beast of yours down... who would it be?"

She blinked, baffled.

Feren was fading now, his arms lolling from the pallet, his expression slackening lax. Blood soaked the pallet under him, the apothecary's hands to the wrists. Ress was fighting, still fighting, for his patient's life.

But the boy's face...

His crazed orange hair, his growth of beard.

Oh, by the fireblasted Gods...

For a moment, an older face, harder and battle scarred, overlaid her view of the boy's dying expression. Her blood sang his name, even as the memories flooded through her mind and body, sparking to a thrum between her thighs.

Feren gasped, an inhalation of hope.

Triqueta said softly, "Redlock."

Ress was sweating, shaking his head in denial – he'd carried the boy to safety, just for him to lose his battle in the clean, cool air of the hospice.

Hope.

Jade watched the boy's final moments, and his expression was troubled. "Faral ton Gattana, Redlock. Arguably the only warrior in the entire Varchinde who's cursed hard enough to face this thing. Not to mention avenging the death of his kin."

Triq said, again, "Redlock."

"He's here – came into the city yesterday morning. You might want to go have a word." Jade grinned. "Scout for me, Triqueta – tell me what I'm facing. Give me time to gather the harvest and expect reinforcements from Fhaveon. And *then* I'll call muster."

Damned canny bastard.

Ress swore again, his voice catching as though on the verge of tears. The apothecary was slicked with gore across his chest, his chin.

Feren gasped, his hands fluttered as if he heard his cousin's name and reached out to grab it. His last word was "please..." before the Count of Time came and took him away.

And the air in the hospice was still.

15: THE COUNCIL FHAVEON

Roderick sat silent. His hands twitched in his lap like reluctant strangers.

At his right shoulder, a pincer-faced military escort. Below him, the descending white tiers of the Theatre of Nine. At their base, a long carved table, flanked by eight cloaked figures, four down either side. The ninth figure, at the table's head, was the direct descendant of Saluvarith the Founder, Demisarr Valiembor himself, Lord of Fhaveon and Master of the Varchinde.

The Council had convened, and the Bard's presence was requested.

Demanded.

Below Roderick, the nine figures were hooded, their faces concealed. Above them, haloing both the table and the tiers of seats, the wall was carved into a great stone mural – the tale of Fhaveon's construction, and of her battles for survival.

The Theatre of Nine was astonishingly beautiful.

Once before, he had come here – some forty returns ago when he had faced the Lord Foundersson Nikhamos with a plea to take a tan of soldiers to Rammouthe Island, to search for answers there.

But his search had failed, his escort had been savagely slain, he himself had survived the magharta only because of Rhan's immortal, elemental friendship. The Bard did not feel welcome here. The rocklights were cold, the quartz fragments dull. Eyeless sockets no longer reflected the glory of the city's completion – they held the deaths of the soldiers who'd died to protect him.

Died screaming.

Standing in here made those screams seem suddenly very recent.

His hands knotted at the echoes. Beside him, his escort twitched. No, whatever beauty may lay outside the white amphitheatre of the Council; in here the Grasslands' blood flowed cold. This was not a room of celebration, it was a room of business – its sanctity tinged with fear.

Aside from the Bard and his escort, the rings of tiered seats were empty.

Roderick's nervousness was rising, he willed his hands to stillness. From Ecko to monsters to unexplained fires to the stone creature that had fallen from the wall – there were too many fears, too many implications, now lurking behind his presence here. They were overwhelming. However cold it may be, the theatre was where the decisions of the Varchinde were made, and he had one chance, one voice, one hope of making himself understood...

They'll lock you up!

Was he crazed? Really? Down through all the long returns of his search, there were times when he had asked himself if the world's fear had been only a nightmare, if the thing that he ever sought was only in his mind.

Maybe Ecko was right, and none of this was real.

Maybe they had to fight anyway.

There were monsters out there, and the wall of the city had come to life. A part of the past had crumbled to dust at The

Wanderer's very doors. And though Ecko was missing, the Bard would not give up his hope.

To doubt – *to doubt now* – would indeed be madness.

Pressure flickering through his skin, he sat quiet.

Waiting.

And the voices floated up through the cold like mist.

"It seems we've got a rather... serious piece of business, my friends." The Lord Demisarr had a slight hunch, his head twitched, birdlike. As he put his hood back, Roderick saw the early grey that threaded his tied-back blonde hair. "A threat to the very lifeblood of the city, it seems. Ah, Rhan?"

At the head of his side of the table and at the Foundersson's right hand, Rhan's power and presence were a relief – he was the only thing that brought life and light to this chill room. Above Rhan's head, a carved creature plummeted, burning, through the sky and then rose and fought for the city's survival.

"I've been out as far as Ikira and Teale," he said. "The fires are scattered, spontaneous and unexplained. Enough of them, and they will threaten the harvest. Runners have been sent to the closest farmlands."

Roderick had seen the damage for himself – craters and black ash, the soil hard baked, cracked as though from some colossal impact. The fires were completely random – there was no pattern or purpose that he could understand.

After a pause, Rhan said, "I believe the fires to have an elemental cause."

His words caused a ripple of shock about the table.

"Love of the Gods, Seneschal!" At the Foundersson's immediate left sat a small, taut man, his cloak marked with the pennon-on-spear soldier's insignia – this was Mostak, Demisarr's younger brother and military commander of both the city and the Varchinde itself. He was similar in features, yet a clear gaze and a solid jaw had replaced the flicker of his brother's nervousness. "At this time of the return, fires are commonplace. Their cause is pure idleness. I will send a man to each manor to ensure that the farmers watch their crops, and that we are secure against any failure of tithe."

"A necessary contingency." Beside Rhan sat a man of massive height and breadth, typically Archipelagan. His hair was the colour of metal and his features were haughty and strong enough to be cruel. The force of his presence made him appear to sit at the table's centre. This was one of the single most powerful figures in the Grasslands – Phylos, Merchant Master, lead voice of the Terhnwood Harvesters' Cartel and the ultimate controller of the Varchinde's cycling trade. Rhan had spoken of him many times – and always with distrust.

"These things can be controlled," Phylos said, "before they escalate into idiocy." The last word was a thrown weapon. Phylos's gaze flicked sideways to where Rhan sat. Dismissed him. "The Cartel will send runners to each manor to accompany the soldiery and carry news of increased city tithes. We must be secure."

Something about Phylos's look to Rhan sparked Roderick's nervousness to real fear. Already, Rhan's carefully structured plan was being diverted by selfishness, by a tangle of old tensions and conflicting priorities, by personal differences and political strivings, by desires so far from his own... He was beginning to understand why the Council couldn't help him.

But he had no choice. He *had* to speak and he *had* to make them understand. If only he had something he could show them...

Again, he cursed inwardly that he did not have Ecko with him. Ecko, for all his scorn, would have made them take notice.

That thought was enough to raise a brief, wry smile.

But the expression was short-lived.

"That will have consequences, Phylos." Next to the Merchant Master sat the Justicar Halydd, elderly and spear straight, correct and merciless in her mandate. She'd been a soldier all her life and saw the world around her in very severe terms. Her cloak bore the image of the executioner's sword. "If we demand greater tithes, the farmlands will become restive."

"Then we're agreed." Phylos's gesture indicated the matter was closed. "From now, each central manor brings their own farms' foods or terhnwood straight into the relevant tithehall. We will secure our surplus and the Varchinde will continue to trade."

In one speech, he had assumed control.

But.

Secure our surplus? Roderick's finger-tapping increased. *But the fires are genuine – and if you tithe the manors more harshly...*

"I don't think – !" Demisarr started.

Phylos was still speaking. "Mostak, the city's soldiery may be needed to secure and defend the stockpile."

"I don't think – !" The Foundersson tried again.

But Mostak was answering, "Additional forces can be deployed as necessary."

"Then the matter is closed," Phylos said calmly. "All in favour?"

"I don't think – !"

"That's *enough*!" The bellow came from a woman, square faced and strong shouldered, dark of skin and hair, standing at the foot of the table. The Council silenced as she spoke – Roderick realised she was Valicia, Demisarr's wife. "Pray *silence*, for the Lord Foundersson."

Rhan grinned at her. Mostak nodded stern acquiescence. Phylos shot the woman a look that could have scoured flesh from bone. She flicked an eyebrow back at him, almost daring. Roderick leaned forward, and his escort loomed over him.

"Tell me," the Bard said softly. "Will the farmers resist?"

His escort said only, "Not for long."

Not for long.

With a tremor of fear, the Bard realised that his crisis and Rhan's had already been lost completely – that no one in this room cared for Ecko, for fires or Elementalism, for alchemical monsters or dying boys, for stone creatures that fell from the wall… They cared only for the terhnwood.

And Phylos had turned this into some form of power play.

Not for long.

If this was how these people thought, this their game – if they cared only for the wealth beneath their noses – how was he to gain their understanding? Rhan's warning mocked him, *They'll laugh you out of the hall…*

Roderick was belatedly realising that he was utterly out of his depth.

But he had to make them see!

Panic began to close round his throat.

"I really don't think –" Demisarr stood to speak "– we can force the farmlands to suffer the armoured fist of cruelty from our Lordship. Feeding our people is our priority. Rhan, tell me of these fires."

Phylos coughed as though he covered scorn. There was an open ripple of amusement, apparently at the Lord's naïveté.

Roderick held his horror silent.

But Rhan was on his feet. "My Lord, they are not the result of carelessness, though perhaps a military watch would be a welcome thing." He threw his words across the table like rocks, the stress on the word "watch" was palpable. "We can ration stores and redistribute the crop if necessary. But for now, I would rather understand the cause of these fires and then remove it. Mostak, you'll assign a force to each and every manor, ensure that each manor's farms will be patrolled. We need to know what's doing this."

The Bard's tapping was growing frenzied. With one move, Rhan had effectively narrowed the field of the game to two factions – Phylos and himself. And he would defend the son of the Founder with the last drop of light in his blood.

Uphold his Gods-given oath.

Now, the Bard leaned on the back of the seat in front of him, trying to understand the subtle shiftings of power that were playing out below. Phylos and Rhan fought for control – but it was Mostak, the soldier, who held the strength that would enable one of them to win or lose.

Or was it?

With a grim smile, Phylos flicked an infinitesimal gesture.

And another member of the Nine spoke.

"With respect, I think not – my Lord."

At the table's foot stood a small, dark man, lean faced and empty eyed. There was no symbol on his cloak, no decor at its hem. His hair was the same almost-blue black as the Bard's and his whisper of Tundran blood betrayed him – this was Adyle, Master of the Institute, the Council's eyes and ears. He ignored Rhan and addressed the Foundersson directly. "There's another issue here."

Roderick saw Rhan's expression congeal, saw the figment of dread and dismay as it gathered under his skin.

Adyle was smiling like a man with well-weighted dice. "It seems," he said, "that the Seneschal's ears are closed to warnings. Despite the policy of this city, a policy that's been in place since the days of Tekisarri himself, Rhan has been importing eoritu from Amos –" he threw a small packet across the table "– and I have every reason to suspect the Bard is his distributor."

What?

The accusation was so sudden, so utterly unexpected… Roderick's blood thundered in his ears. His panic manifest. He couldn't breathe, he couldn't swallow. As if from some huge, roaring distance, he heard every word, every breath, every shock, every sigh.

"You *dare*?" Rhan's flare of white anger was unexpected – he was furious enough to cover any fear. "You dare go through my *house*?"

Horrified, the Bard realised that with this one stroke he had lost the Council, lost their attention and support and sympathy. He would never get the chance to speak his beliefs, to make them understand what he'd felt and seen, never enlist their help for what he now faced.

And the accusation itself...!

Without quite realising it, he was on his feet, shrugging off the escort's attempt to push him back down. "What is this game you play? You know I did not do this!" His blood screamed at him, screamed desperation. Leaving the soldier behind, shouting startled orders, he started to jump down over the seat tiers. Mostak turned, his hand going for the weapon he had left at the door.

"Gods-damned *sehvrak*!" Rhan spat venom.

But the Justicar Halydd was louder. "I knew it! My Lord Seneschal, this time I'll take you your *head*! You and that Gods-damned crazed storyteller!"

"The Bard's got nothing to do with it," Rhan shot back, "this filthy little *sehv* is playing *games*. What do you want, Phylos? Why have your lackeys gone through my house?"

"Deny it," Phylos said. Arms crossed over his huge chest, he was chin up, his expression severe. "Deny the eoritu's yours."

The game had indeed been reduced to two sides, and now one of them was winning.

The Lord Foundersson Demisarr was on his feet, hands helpless, mouth wordless.

Swearing, the soldier Mostak left his seat to intercept Roderick.

"Yes, the packet is mine," Rhan said. "But..." He stopped at the look the Foundersson gave him, a hurt child, uncomprehending. "My Lord... Demisarr..." He deflated like a windless sail. "I..."

"You've just *admitted* it." Grinning like a bweao, Phylos snatched the packet, opened it, sniffed it, threw it at Halydd.

The Justicar went purple, shaking with outrage. She shrieked, "*I will not have this substance in the city!*"

"Oh, *get over it*!" Rhan rounded on Halydd, his sudden snarl echoed from the walls. "It's mine – alone. I don't trade it, Roderick's never been near it. Take my head if you can – if your sword arm's still strong enough!"

Roderick vaulted the last of the empty stone seats and stumbled to a halt at the foot of the table. Before him, chaos – the Council of Nine, the rulers of the Grasslands, squabbling like children, jealous, vicious, greedy.

He had Ecko. There were monsters in the grass. He had witnessed a piece of the past come to life. The very elements stirred beneath their feet. Their harvest burned around them and they used it only for political gain...

He found himself angry. For the first time in returns beyond count, his hope and his fear were real, and close.

The world herself screamed in his blood.

This is a decision!

And to help her, he had to face down this theatre of fools.

"For *SHAME!*"

The acoustics in the theatre were flawless – the force of Roderick's cry robbed the Council of breath, of motion. He stood at the foot of the table like an avenging black-clad figment, stood as though it were his to command. His gaze met that of the Foundersson.

"This is the Theatre of Nine, the leadership of the Varchinde, raised by the hand of Samiel and the vision of Saluvarith himself. This is no place for games!"

Shocked into silence, they stared.

"You hold the might of the Grasslands in your unready hands, fire spreads through the very thing that brings you life – and yet you sentence your people to perish? Are you so bored?

So consumed by greed?" He looked around at each Council member. "How can you face the memory of the Founder with behaviour such as this? How can you sit in this place of your forefathers, and not be shamed?"

Phylos tapped his index fingers together, his eyes narrow and burning.

"Remember, as you struggle for power, that the world does not turn around the voices of this chamber; cares not for your *politics*. I have looked in the falling waters of the Ryll – and for all you plot and grapple and scheme, the thoughts of the world heed you not. If you do not look beyond yourselves, my Lords, your people will starve and perish – and hoarding their wealth will only delay the inevitable. The farmlands will burn, Merchant Master, they will be torn apart by creatures of nightmare, and you will live just long enough to *watch*."

He had them now – Rhan shone, Demisarr held back tears. Phylos eyed him with a calculating smirk.

"I am here –" with a bound, he was on top of the table, standing there as if he could call fire from the very sky "– to plead with you, my Lords, to throw myself upon your justice and mercy as I have done once before. The elements awaken: alchemical creatures are loose in the grass and the stone of your city has life. I see harbingers of the very peril the world has long feared – the peril I have brought to this Council once before. The Count of Time threatens us all, my Lords – we cannot be turning, one upon another, hurling accusations, sacrificing the innocent for a mere moment of power, a false dawn."

He walked, his cloak a billow of black in the cold, white room, crushing the herb and its accusation beneath his boots.

He stopped before the Foundersson.

"We must trust, remember what Fhaveon herself was built for. This is a city of power and strength – and I have come to give her new direction. If you wish to challenge the blight in your crops, then you must heed me. You must help me find the greater threat and thus bring the cure and new life to the Varchinde entire!"

Echoes of passion tumbled across the silence. The Council was still.

Then the Foundersson stood, looked up at the Bard with a gleam of hope in his pale blue eyes.

For just a moment, Roderick thought he had won – that he had brought the world's fear to the notice of the Council of Nine.

For just a moment.

Then Demisarr spoke.

"You are a visionary, Sir Roderick, a crusader for a truth so ancient we've lost its meaning..." He paused, shook his head, looked to Rhan... Then his eyes were pulled back to the packet, contents spilled on the tabletop, and he seemed to fold in upon himself, weighted once again by the white cloak upon his shoulders. "Your ardour touches my heart, touches all of us, but you're asking the impossible. As you say, I'm the son of my forefathers, bound by their law. The elements you speak of are but remnants of children's superstitions, alchemy is a tale of Tusien." He picked the packet up, spilled its contents onto the table at the Bard's booted feet. "Such things have no place in here. I am the Lord of Fhaveon. I must do as the mandate of my family bids. I must care for my people."

"That's not..." The words passed the Bard's lips before he could bite down upon them. "The world wakens, my Lord." It was a whisper, but it carried to the very roof. "You must heed me, acknowledge my request..."

"Like my father did last time?" Demisarr smiled, almost sadly. He crumpled the packet, let it drop. "Roderick, there is no great enemy upon Rammouthe Island, no lore you have missed. Every soldier that followed you died." He stood up, met the Bard's gaze. "Get off my table."

Mostak laid a cold hand on Roderick's arm. "Stand down," he said softly, "or I will break both your legs."

Shaking, unable to find a word or a thought to formulate

his failure, Roderick did as requested. Dry leaf matter scattered onto the floor.

Demisarr picked a fragment up, crushed it between thumb and forefinger. "Roderick of Avesyr, members of the Council of Nine – I'm appalled. This accusation is against my mentor, my teacher, my oldest friend. It eviscerates me like a blade.

"My word is this.

"Adyle, this one packet isn't proof – you could've brought it from Amos yourself." The Justicar snorted. "We reconvene in one halfcycle – ten days. You've got that time to prove the guilt of the Lord Seneschal and Roderick of Avesyr."

Rhan's expression was as cold as the marble wall, cold as his own carving. Roderick's blood was pounding in his ears like the feet of an army.

Ecko had abandoned him. The Council had not heard his voice.

Mostak's hand was like cold stone upon his arm.

The Count of Time was closing his grey cloak about Roderick's senses. He found tears at the backs of his eyes – it had all been so close, so nearly within his reach...!

"Rhan, you are under arrest – your title is foregone until your innocence is proven. You are no longer... no longer Lord Seneschal of Fhaveon." Demisarr's voice cracked, he took a breath and carried on. "And I don't need to mention what'll occur if you fail to attend the next Council." The Foundersson glanced at the Bard. "Either of you. Roderick, you also. You will join him. Neither you nor your tavern are permitted to depart the city."

"I have no way to control The Wanderer," Roderick said. "You –"

"Then it'll move without you," Demisarr said. "You'll stay. Mostak?"

The soldier Mostak commented softly, "Pull a stunt like that again and I'll gut you myself."

"This is madness!" The Bard's words were a rush. "This is all connected – this is just the beginning. You'll see. You'll realise – !"

"Enough!" Mostak said. "This is Fhaveon – and your crazed arse is mine. Your distraction tactic didn't work – and your demented preachings end here. No more scaremongering, Bard, or I'll throw you into the gorge myself."

In the cold white light, Phylos was smiling like a sated bweao.

"What a mess," Rhan said. "One halfcycle – damn those conniving bastards for going through my *house*." Rhan was pacing a small, plain square of a room, three steps one way, three steps the other. The walls were smooth and dry and pale grey. The door was bolted from the outside. "We're up to our ears in tumultuous world-ending horseshit – and Phylos chooses *now* to challenge my office? Opportunistic bastard – I wonder how long he'd had that packet of herb?"

Roderick was quiet, sat on the floor in the corner with his knees drawn up to his chest, like some errant, black-cloaked child. To be so impassioned and desperate – and to have been unable to touch them... The false accusation bothered him less than his own failure.

He was lost. He had staked so much hope on this meeting – and his need had fallen to the floor in ashes. Ecko was gone; the Council had refused to hear him. He could not return to The Wanderer.

Perhaps the greatest test of his life was upon him – and he had failed before he had even begun.

"Phylos seeks power." His response was reflex, empty. "If he owned the remaining crop, he could surely hold the city – possibly the Varchinde – to ransom. He could have anything he wanted."

"But why?" Rhan spun on his heel. "World domination?

Power for its own sake? I don't think so. Those fires were like nothing I've seen in four hundred returns – the ground still ached with the damage inflicted and I could feel the elemental might within. But how does this tangle with your monsters, the resurgence of alchemy, your champion, your 'Echo'?" He spun again. "I realise it's all connected – but I'm more damned curious about where it's going."

Roderick looked up, the rocklight reflected broken from his gaze.

"You're enjoying this."

"Ha!" The ex-Seneschal grinned. "I built these rooms – had them built. When Rakanne's son Adward expanded his hold over the Varchinde, there was resistance. Not war exactly, more… unrest." He patted the wall as though he were punching it. "Never thought I'd be the one in here. Or that you'd be damned stupid enough to be in here with me."

"I've never sold –"

"They know that. Whatever that bastard's up to, he wants us both out of his way. There's a pattern growing. It's just a question of what."

"Ecko talked about patterns," Roderick replied bleakly.

Rhan turned, jabbed a finger at the Bard. "Snap out of it, Loremaster, this is no time to feel sorry for yourself. You've been waiting for this moment all your life and I can *feel* pure light in my skin. We are *here* to face this, exactly this! Perhaps my old enemy wakens at last. We'd better arm up and get *nasty*."

Unable to bear Rhan's words and their challenge and exhilaration, unable to bear his own loss, Roderick found himself on his feet and turning away, standing by the bolted-shut door. Figments lurked unseen on its far side. He felt a cry welling up in his throat that was desperate for utterance. He strangled an urge to hammer the wood until his skin broke and bled.

"I wish Ecko were here. He'd –"

"He's not." Rhan started pacing again, restless, almost eager. "But we're not without options."

"We're under arrest." *We've failed.*

"Arrest, for the Gods' sakes." Rhan chuckled. "Do you think I'd be fool enough to build a gaol that could actually hold me?"

"You...?" The Bard gaped.

"Roderick of Avesyr, Guardian of the Ryll, bless you and your naïveté." Rhan's tone was almost gentle. "Have you forgotten? Whoever this fire-flinger is, they're not the only Elementalist – I have light in my heart and my soul, in my skin and in my very existence." He grinned. "I, too, awaken. Should I wish to, I could raze this city to smoking fragments, I could call lightning from the very sky and split the world asunder. Well, probably." His grin spread.

Bereft of words, Roderick stared.

"I can also *move* – out of here and without being detected or missed. And I have sources of information that may surprise you. Perhaps I can find some answers."

"And then what?" The question was slightly sharper than Roderick had intended. "There are too many questions. I feel I am chasing my tail like a sun-crazed –"

"Roderick, my oldest friend." Rhan clapped his shoulder, held it for a moment. "You were never meant to witness the nightmare that you saw. You hold the thoughts of the world in your mortal mind and your beating heart – and they overwhelm you. I know the fear that lives in your soul, that it eats you by the day and haunts you in the darkness. The world needs you, you idiot, and she'll protect you – as will I." As he spoke, the faint sardonic edge had faded from his voice. "Trust me, trust yourself. If this fails – and it might – then we go to the one place that can answer every question. Probably the one place that you should have damned-well gone to start with."

Realisation crystallised and shattered. "The Ryll. They will not welcome me."

"They'll welcome me." Rhan's gaze was peridot and white fire. "And if we have no other way to find answers, then what else remains?" His grin was like the first edge of the sunrise. "We ask Mother."

16: ASH THE VARCHINDE

It was dusk as Ecko sighted the ruin.

The evening was silent, any birds or creatures had fled the devastation and, for the first time since leaving The Wanderer, the trade-road below him was utterly deserted. A cool wind blew ripples of ash across the wide shine of the river.

"What happened?" Pareus asked. The tan commander had joined him in the grass, peering through the stalks at the wreckage. "What do you see?"

What the fuck do you think I see? Ignoring the wary mutterings of Pareus' patrol, Ecko spun his telescopics.

He saw destruction.

Seared grass, blasted soil. This had been a township that had swollen from the back of the trade-road like an abscess – now it was wreckage. Charred skeletons of trees stood witness to its ruin, buildings torched and crumbled, corpses twisted and blackened or crushed by fallen rubble.

"Someone blew the shit out of it."

Spars of charcoaled timber still stood upright, stark against the glitter of the water – the fire had been vicious, fast and hot. Hell, whoever'd been inside there hadn't had a fucking prayer.

At the heart of the little village the buildings were shattered, the ground melted and hollow – *like this place had taken some kinda missile.*

And that just wasn't *fair*!

Since when did this program do old-school flash-bang magic? Or was there something else the fuck out here that he'd not seen yet?

Jump this way...

He crawled forwards for a better view. Hell, no bastard round here had the right to blow shit up but him. And he was still working on it!

Beside him, the twenty-something wet-behind-the-ears corporal stayed in the grass, watching, and smart enough to be quiet.

Pareus. Corporal Teen. Squad commander. Now military escort.

Hell, you had to laugh.

Yeah, or you'd lose the fucking plot.

Ecko had fled The Wanderer a seething knot of questions and resentment – his sense of purpose had packed its bags and fucked off on vacation and he'd got no clue where he fit any more. This Rhan character had just put him out of a job and, frankly, he was *pissed*.

By the time he'd calmed the fuck down, the Bard was long gone and he was well and truly lost.

In *grass*.

More sodding grass than Lugan on downtime. Grass this way, grass that way, grass the other. Ecko was neither hippie nor cowboy – and limitless prairie was not his idea of fun. His telescopics had picked up some sort of tower, still faintly gleaming in the dawn – chrissakes, whatever it was, it'd have to do. Once he reached habitation, he could work out what the fuck he was supposed to do next.

He'd got a bagful of nicked gear and the kit he stood up in.

On the street, he could've survived indefinitely – but out here? Yeah, saving the world should be a fucking *doddle*.

Y'hear me, Eliza? I don't need help! This Rhan can kiss my mottled ass!

Chances of success: 26.75% and falling...

Bitch.

It had taken him until that relentlessly hot midday to realise that his rations were pitifully fucking inadequate – already rotting to overheated sludge. The local wildlife found him inedible, but it still buzzed round his face, driving him batshit. He had been stumbling, thirsty, cursing Eliza, Roderick, Lugan, and anyone-the-fuck else he could think of when he'd spotted a cadre of local goons, their weapons cast aside, apparently stopped for a nice little picnic.

No such thing as a free lunch?

Well whaddaya know, think I scored a bonus.

As he'd got closer, though, he'd realised they were kids. They were sunning themselves and laughing – these weren't squaddies, for chrissakes, they were more like a comedy road trip. If their vehicles'd had tyres, rather than a leg at each corner, Ecko could've been in and out smoother than a gossip journo in a whorehouse.

But, teens or no, these guys'd got something he didn't.

Orientation.

In short, they knew where the fuck they were.

He'd crouched in the grass, all itch and heat and dust and beasties, and watched.

When he'd accosted them, ghosting out of the sward like some sort of twisted dryad, they'd challenged him – they'd never seen anything like him before. He'd explained he was an ambassador of the Bard – it was as good a line as any – and wanted to go to the nearest habitation of any size. They'd been ribald, mocking, abusively friendly. They'd be going back to Roviarath when they'd finished their patrol, they said. Would he like a ride?

A *ride?*

Sure, if it had tyres and a *tank*.

Chrissakes, the thing wasn't even a horse, it was an ugly slope-shouldered monster that looked like the offspring of a horse and a camel. He was dealing with enough – the agoraphobia, the sudden onslaught of self-doubt – and he had to sit on some critter that was a half a ton of muscle with a brain the size of a –

Pareus nudged him, nodded. "Ecko." Distantly, black specks were circling in the sky. Ecko yanked his thoughts back to the smoking ruin ahead of him.

"What d'you mean," the commander said, "'blew the shit out of it'?"

Motioning his squad to silence, Pareus had belly-crawled to where Ecko lay. They watched the distant, smouldering town.

"Fucker did a helluva job." Ecko's black gaze made the kid shiver, though he tried to hide it. He was young, way too young. "You wanna tell me how? And with *what*?"

And where I get some?

Pareus flickered a frown. "I don't understand."

"Place exploded. Boom. Like the powder store went up or some wack-job chemist screwed up with the Greek fire. You gettin' me?" He grinned. "Ker-blooey."

"Anything left alive?"

"Only us." His oculars picked up shattered roof slates hanging from eyeless, half-collapsed houses, floors sliding into ruin. Charred bodies, adults and children, flash-burned as they sat in their homes. In many places, their stuff was still visible – broken ceramics, torn flutters of fabric, melted and glistening terhnwood-resin.

Ecko caught himself thinking: *Poor fuckers.*

They didn't even have a chance.

His focus spun back and forth as he scanned the ground. Charred animal remains, shattered fragments of lives. Here and there, tiny pockets of flame still sought fuel and oxygen, twists of smoke climbed from still-smouldering wood. Nothing else moved.

"Flash-fry job. Nothing livin' down there."

He spun his focus back to the grass in his face.

"We'll picket the chearl inside the rise," Pareus said, and his fingers flashed orders at his patrol. He checked his blade and bow. The kid was pale, but not afraid to make the decisions – vacation time was done. "Ecko, you'll take point. If there's anything left alive in there I want it found. Questioned." He took a long breath, then let it out. "We'll follow you. Tarvi!"

Ecko bared his black teeth in a grin, lifted his cowl further over his face. *The kid's got 'em when he needs 'em*, he thought, *maybe this won't be a rerun of* Aliens *after all.*

"See?" Ecko rasped a chuckle. "It ain't so hard. Get your goons in line, kiddo, let's party."

The vastness of the open Varchinde.

Ecko had only ever seen this stuff in movies – it was an agoraphobic's worst nightmare, emptiness more than anyone could fucking stand. It was more sky and wind and grass than he could get his head round, and, frankly, it was freaking him out.

It made him feel so fucking *small*.

He knew he was holding them back, there was way too much to deal with.

His first problem was called a "chearl" – it had a bad attitude and a sloping back and a Mohawk mane and a tail like a bog brush. Sitting on it nearly sawed him in half, but he was determined not to quit.

How hard could riding the damn thing really be, for chrissakes? It wasn't like it had an engine.

His second problem was the *dust*. The road was busy – heaving, compared to the population of the city – and dust from feet and hooves and wheels devil-danced like chaff across the roadways. Oddly, though it coated his lips and teeth, it lessened his feeling of exposure. It was soft, it diffused the sun and sheltered him from the godalmighty space that lurked, endless and featureless, behind the roadside buildings. As he rode the blade-line that cut the prairie in half, it billowed in his wake.

His third problem? His butt hurt.

But he kept his trap shut and rode on.

To one side of them, the bizarre ribbon of township rose and fell, in and out of the plainland – a thin, poor stretch of deadwood offering inns, pubs and whorehouses, general stores and rickety stalls. The further they rode, the poorer it became – sun bleached and tumbledown. He could hear voices, calling to the mass of travellers, asking them to stop and trade.

Ecko watched, kinda hoping for goblins. Some of these places *so* looked like there'd be an ambush – please? He flicked his oculars, mode to mode, twitched his fingers restlessly...

...but the goblins had packed their little green goblin bags, only the hobos and the winos remained.

Eventually, the township thinned, spotted and finally dissolved altogether, melted by the heat and trickling into the cracked and dusty roadside.

The neck of Ecko's beast was decorated with intricate whorls of stink, he didn't need his heatseeker to see the shimmer that came off its hide. As the pain in his spine and thighs increased, he became steadily more unfocused. He didn't sweat and his poreless skin struggled with the ceaseless beating of the sun, the open air, the endless wind, the changes in food and sleep. He'd've sold his fucking *soul* for a can of chilled fizz. Slowly, the pain, the heat, the motion of the chearl, the rippling grass, drifted one into another, and all into a blur.

* * *

At the edge of the ruin, Ecko crouched still. His skin was ash and charcoal, his cloak loosed like a live thing, folds flickered like shadows in the evening breeze.

Behind him, Pareus and the ten members of his patrol. Most bore bows and short spears, a couple had small, round shields buckled to their forearms. They were fast on their feet, lightly armed skirmishers – and they were suddenly taking this the fuck seriously.

Playtime's over.

They watched the township, and Pareus for orders. Ecko remained still for a long moment, oculars scanning every burned-out building, every crumbling wall, every broken cart and corpse – then he raced forwards, sharp and swift, barely stirring the ash as he went.

One dead corporate, two dead corporate…

He counted twenty-two before they came after him. Small units, archers and shieldmen together, the spears working in threes. They were noisy on their feet, but they were well trained and sheer, cold terror was making them focus. Not one of them spoke.

As Pareus directed them, they scuttled nervously outwards into charred remnants of buildings, ruined streets. They took cover where they could and occasionally shuddered as they passed something familiar, death curled on blasted soil.

Those kids were getting one helluva wake-up call.

Ahead of them, barely a wisp of darkness, Ecko was unarmed – he didn't need that shit anyhow. His targeters cross-hatched empty windows, likely cover, possible threat – he moved from stealth-crouch to stealth-crouch with accomplished ease.

He may be cussing the absence of wrecked cars, but this shit? He knew backwards.

He paused at the base of a cracked and roofless wall, kicked a charred skull from under his feet, shreds of skin still clinging to the jawline. He listened to the hiss of superheated air, the creaking of damaged timbers.

As the colours in his skin shifted with the sky, the stone, he watched.

Pareus was good, tightly focused like he was too terrified to fuck up. He was blade in hand, low and alert, watching the units of his patrol and the ground ahead of him. His second, Tarvi, was wide-eyed at the devastation. There was a smudge of tears and dirt down the side of her face, but her focus echoed his – she held her terror in rigid check.

The Bard's preaching Ragnarök – and this is our fucking army? He addressed the silent sky, bright and blue as though it didn't give a shit. *Jeez, Eliza, we're screwed.*

Eliza made no response.

As Tarvi came past him, spearman to each side of her, Ecko slipped out to follow.

Water. Dripping, annoying, cold.

His hand lashed out. There was a feminine squeak and a bark of laughter.

Spitting, he sat up.

He was crumpled at the base of a grassy bank – the air was cooling, there was fire-warmth to one side. Crouched by him was one of the grunts, a small, dark-haired woman with a sunburned nose. His first thought: *she's cute*. His second: what the hell was he doing down here?

For no apparent reason, his head was full of fire. Chrissakes, had he been dreaming, already?

A couple of the goons stood over them, grinning. One of them shoved a wooden bowl of glop at him. When he tried to move, every muscle shrieked protest and he sat back with a stifled groan.

The girl smiled. "You're sun-touched. You've stopped sweating. Here." She passed him a waterskin. "There's salt in the food – you'll need it."

His mind was struggling with the concept of dreaming – a dream within the program, that was fucked up. He shook his head, flicked through ocular modes, squinted skywards to see threads of cloud through the gathering dusk. He felt like shit.

"How the hell do you know what I need?"

She blinked, withdrew. "I'm Tarvi, I look after the health of these idiots. Pareus, our tan, you know, the rest of them –"

"Don't bother." He sat up this time, took three mouthfuls of lukewarm water and started on the glop with a grimace.

Determined to be friendly, she smiled at him. Her voice sparkled. "We'll head back to the city at the end of our patrol, take you to Larred Jade."

Round a mouthful of food, he said, "Great."

"Don't you want to know what we're doing?" She was bugging him, completely unfazed by his skin, his eyes, his teeth. Her hair shone with red highlights in the setting sun.

And he had *no* fucking clue why he'd just noticed that. He scalded his lips on another tasteless mouthful and turned away.

Around him was a small, flat campsite, defended by a low bank. The squad had put up a lean-to and a scatter of tents, though most of them were gathered with the critters at one corner. As Ecko glanced, one of them threw a bucket of slop water over his mate.

"We're making good time," Tarvi said. Greatly daring, she brushed her fingertips over the back of his hand. "Doesn't that hurt?" His skin shone at her touch.

He snarled at her. "Yeah, I'm a freakshow."

Not waiting for her hurt expression, he stretched, heard his joints pop and crackle. He felt like he'd been kicked round Wembley fucking Stadium. Picking up glop and waterskin, he shambled over to the fire.

Fire. He'd been dreaming about fire. Detonation. Power…

"You'll need this, mate!" Another goon threw a heavy, fabric roll across to him – a bedroll of some sort. He caught it without thinking. "Get your basher up, it's gonna piss. And tomorrow? You do your own damned chearl!"

Do what with it? Ecko finished the glop, feeling the firelight warm on his face – then, rebelliously, pushed the bowl into the flames. For a moment, it lay there as they worried at it, bubbling, blackening – then it suddenly caught, roaring into fierce life. Bright flame shot skywards, heat slammed into him. The fire was his friend, his security – he understood it and he welcomed it. In London, he'd made his name with it, beaten Pilgrim with it, made them remember that they didn't own the city...

For a second, a fragment of the dream came back to him – the last run he'd done, the one that'd gotten him the info on Grey. How it felt to be that powerful, to have that much skill at his fingertips...

Not like now, stuck out here weaponless and eating mulch, without even a fucking sleeping bag that he actually understood...

He watched the flames, trying to reach for more images, a fragment of home, something familiar. He almost felt like London was waning, getting less real as the plainland around him got more so.

Over him, the sky faded to grey, to deep blue, and at last to silver-accented night. Tarvi was still beside him.

The air became cold. He unrolled the strange bedding, pulled it round his shoulders. He missed London, Lugan; he missed the Bard. Hell, right now, he missed his fucking mom.

Both of them.

Over him, the moons shone insanity – one, silver body swollen, far too low and far too big, lit the plainland to alien freakishness. The other was a crescent, a golden fingernail. Above them, the black sky was completely devoid of stars.

The night noises were all-the-fuck wrong.

"What the hell am I doing out here?" He didn't even realise he'd said it aloud until Tarvi turned to look at him, face warmed by the fire.

"Huh?"

He didn't meet her gaze. "Out here. It's all fucking wrong. Why don't'cha have any stars?"

"They were cast down by Samiel, Godsfather." In the night's stillness, Tarvi's voice was perfectly serious. "All except one."

"How fucking literary." He chuckled. "That's right up there with your moons being gods, for chrissakes."

"Of course the moons are Gods." She laughed at him. "They're brother and sister. The sagas say they committed a... ah... terrible indiscretion and they gaze in yearning upon one another, only to know it can never be, and so they turn away."

Faced with her sincerity, her soft skin in the firelight, he lost the ability to be scathing.

"Impossible – and incestuous," he said. Something about it made him grin. He glanced sideways at her, head tilted. "How'd you know that?"

"I read?" She shrugged. "The yellow moon is named for Samiel's daughter Calarinde, she who not only tempted her brother, but also lay with the last of the stars – causing him, too, to be cast down. Yet because his crime was one of love, he was condemned only to loneliness – he was sent here, as our guardian and champion. Tales say he walks the mortal world to this day."

He walks the mortal world...

"Yeah." Ecko tucked the bedroll closer round his shoulders. "That guy. I gotta bone to pick with him."

The fire was warm on his face and it left its colours in his skin. He didn't speak again.

Ecko watched Tarvi watching the ruin.

She was small, round faced and round figured, though her fitness pressed tight muscle against the fabric of her garments. Her days on the trade-road had sunburned her nose, she scratched at loose skin at its edges.

Her hair was haphazardly tied back, though wisps escaped the leather band and drifted constantly into her face. She blew at them, stirring ash. Ecko stifled a sudden urge to push them back.

You can't go there and you know it!

Flanking her, the two spearmen were sharp-eyed, covering her back and each other's.

They ducked beside a wall. Tarvi slipped along its length to peer out...

...and stopped dead, hands gesturing.

Low to the ground, he raced rodent swift to stand almost behind her, crouched upon a fallen crossbeam.

Before them was a small and blasted square, flagstones cracked, buildings seared and crumbling to every side. It was close to the heart of the explosion and even the stone had melted. The ground was still hot, colours spiralled lazily into the darkening air.

Who could do this – what the hell had this kind of power?

On the far side of the square, there was motion.

On a crumbling upper floor, inside a black-edged window.

Tarvi held her spear and waited. Ecko hugged what remained of the building sides, slipping round the edges of the destruction.

His telescopics spun, found nothing, spun again. Whatever it was, it was below the level of the windowledge. Blinking, he flicked back to his heatseeker but the thermals of the square defeated him.

He reached the base of the building.

Behind him, Tarvi hadn't moved. She and the spearmen were crouched in the partial cover of the wall. She was flicking gestures at Pareus. Ecko saw the commander call the patrol to his side. Keeping to cover, they moved to the edge of the square.

Ecko touched his fingertips to the wall.

It was shaking – just enough for his sensitive touch to detect. Its foundations fucked, it was coming down – and whatever was up there was coming down with it.

Hell, he'd take that chance. He'd have to watch his ass – the wall was covered in ash and shit and if he failed to grip, he could bring it down on top of himself...

...but it would be so fucking cool – and she was *right there*.

With the ubiquitous prayer to the Bogeyman, he went up the wall.

Pareus skidded to a crouch beside where Tarvi waited.

"Movement," she said. "Second window from the left. Whatever it was, I haven't seen it again."

"You're sure?"

"There's something up there."

"Where's Ecko?"

Her eloquent shrug made him snort – whatever that Ecko creature was, it was a royal pain in the arse. Skilled, doubtless, but he'd seen Banned with more discipline. Why the rhez he'd been landed with this...

Not the time.

His guys were young, but they knew the drill – they spread out to watch the area.

Pareus crouched with Tarvi, sword bared.

Then, shocking across the burned-out silence, he heard a sky-ripping, high-pitched shriek – a crumble of damaged stonework, a skittering of many claws...

...and a full-throated male scream.

He turned in time to see Rift go down under a mass of slither, a dull gleam of sunset from scales, a grey puff of ash cloud, a shredding of claws and teeth. The spearman scrabbled for a hopeless second – trying to fight a seething mass of them off him – then he tumbled, screaming, thrashing, to the broken stone floor, the flesh literally being stripped from his bones. Charcoaled wood shattered, dark fluid exploded up the wall as he simply vanished, ripped into pieces, flesh from bone.

Tarvi was on her feet, hands over her mouth. Her face white to the lips.

And the ripple of death came onwards.

Magharta. A whole nest of them.

"To me!" he called. They needed no urging, the nine remaining members of his tan were already moving, scrambling over obstacles to where he stood. They reached him in a jostle, wild-eyed and ash blackened – they stank of fear.

But they held shoulder to shoulder, facing out.

The magharta had momentarily paused. Each one was barely the size of his hand, but there was a teeming mass of them, all snarling and tearing at Rift's shredded remains. Bones rattled against the stonework. Now they came on, undulating like water, flowing over the intervening debris.

They were claws, scrabbling at broken timbers. They were teeth, bared and stained with the flesh of the spearman.

Tarvi was whispering, "Oh my Gods oh my Gods oh my Gods..."

Pareus slapped her in the face.

She blinked at him for a second, staring almost straight through him, then began to breathe again, heavily as if she were about to throw up.

Pareus snapped sharply at her, "Don't lose it now!"

The magharta came on, swift and implacable. They grinned eyeless like figments, their faces were knife-toothed grins.

Edge shot one shaft, two. He pinned the lead creature, and its companions immediately turned on it, gleefully tearing into its flesh. As they paused, he shot another, and a fourth.

He was starting to panic.

Pareus watched, horrified, as frenzy ensued. The creatures became a roiling knot of scales and sinew and teeth and claws. They screamed as they tore into each other, sky-splitting shrieks that set teeth on edge and made the patrol want to cower, block their ears.

"Shit, shit, shit, shit!" Edge muttered. He was loosing so fast his shafts were going wide, clattering among the wreckage.

"Enough." Pareus stopped him, hand on his arm. "You're wasting them – you'll never make a difference."

"What do we do?" Edge's voice was high with terror. "Rift didn't even *see* them! We should run – !"

"We'd never make it – not over this ground."

"Wait," Tarvi said. She was white faced; her hands shook. "Cover me."

Pareus gave a sharp nod.

Whatever she was doing – it'd better be fast.

Ecko heard the inhuman screech, heard the ripping death of the spearman.

Halfway up the wall, hung there like a fucking ornament, he craned back over his own cloaked shoulder to see a running carpet of fang-toothed beasties converging on the terrified patrol.

Behind them, they left the shredded and scattered remains of the poor fucker they'd hit. Some of them were still eating him.

Scrabbling haphazardly down the wall-side, he felt the masonry judder as he moved his weight, but he wasn't going to hang the fuck about. His feet hit the floor and he was running across the square, stealth-cloak flapping gracelessly behind him.

He heard the wall groan.

And he ran.

It collapsed with a rumble. There was a wash of ash, an exhalation of dust; the ground shook as the wall fell. Ecko kept his feet and didn't look back.

He saw the archer – loosing hopeless, panicked shots into the midst of a spiralling ouroboros of tearing, ripping creatures, saw him hold his fire as if they stood on the Thin Red fucking Line.

He saw the critters uncurl themselves; turn back to the patrol.

Then he realised what the wall had been hiding...

...as another almighty seethe of them came out the building, and over the crashed masonry at his heels.

They had time.

Under Pareus's sharp, steady command, the tan held together. As the magharta feasted on each other, the patrol threw together a barricade – bricks, beams, anything heavy they could drag.

Crouched behind the makeshift, flame-blackened wall, Tarvi threw bags and vials out of her apothecary's kit.

"I don't have much," she said, "but it's pretty savage." As the wall grew higher, she scattered drops of liquid over the top – liquid that crystallised on contact with the air.

When the pouch was empty, she drew her belt-blade with a rasp and came to stand by Pareus.

"Ecko'll come back," she said. "He will."

"Of course he will." Pareus slapped her shoulder.

They both knew he was lying.

"Holy fucking shit!"

They were fast, flowing over remnants of shattered masonry. Ecko cursed the Bogeyman's luck for not ensuring the wall had fallen *after* the fuckers had started running, but didn't waste breath. His adrenals were fully kicked, the flood of heat and strength and elation slashed a grin across his face, made him turn. He picked up a sizeable lump of stone, flashed his targeters and turned the lead critter into a pink smear.

Its closest buddies paused. Their mistake – a hailstorm of savagely accurate, hard-thrown wreckage and the wave disintegrated into shrieking, boiling cannibalism.

He heard Tarvi, her shout loud across the plaza.

"Ecko! Ecko!"

As he turned, he saw the wave of critters hit the base of the patrol's shambolic defence wall. Some went through, claws tearing holes in burned timber. He saw the spearmen, clumsy at close range, trying to jab down at the beasties as they flowed up the outside of the debris.

The first one crested the wall, parted its needle teeth and shrieked.

Ecko was still running. He saw the critter begin to sizzle, steam rising into the dust from supercooking flesh. He heard its shriek redouble, saw its scales crisp and flake, its skin slough from its sides. It was steaming from the eye sockets, still shrieking.

Then it shuddered and collapsed, tumbled sideways into the eager fangs of its mates.

Another crested the wall, another. They, too, flash-fried like Lugan's fucking breakfast... Spearmen jabbed at them, shoving them away even as they burned.

One critter swarmed through a hole, dropped to the ground, another followed it. Another. Ecko watched as a spearman screamed and fell, hands beating at something ripping the calf muscle clean from the back of his leg. The other was in his face, ravening into his eye, its body curling in glee as its teeth tore. He was trying to scream, beat the thing off him, but it carved straight through the bone and into his skull, claws shredding the skin.

For a moment, his heels hammered the ground.

Then he was still.

Round where he'd fallen, there was chaos.

A heaving storm of the creatures fought to reach the downed patrolman, and turned on each other.

Pareus was yelling, his blade was fast, flicking the things from the wall top back into the oncoming slither.

The patrolman shot his last shaft into a creature that tumbled from the top of the wall – but one had got round behind him.

It sank its foreclaws into his leg and its teeth into the back of his knee. He stumbled, fell hard onto the bow and it shattered, splinters hitting his face and hands. The critter was still shredding. The fucking things were like piranhas, all teeth and ravenous, ripping hunger.

Piranhas.

"My tan perished round me. I escaped only because Rhan bore me home."

Jesus.

With a sudden, flash memory of Roderick's scar, Ecko went over the barricade.

His targeters flashed, his foot moved. The beast on the archer's leg was sent smash into the wall behind them – but there were two more, three, four.

They were all over the last patrolman, claws raking huge gashes, teeth pulling chunks of flesh from his face and chest and arms. He flailed, got his hands on one and tried to yank it free but it was claws embedded and ripping out his throat and ear, his blood-matted hair was tangling round its legs.

He was trying to scream – but one was over his mouth, eating its way into his jaw.

Ecko took one long breath.

And exhaled.

The creatures roasted, shrieking, blackened and cracking, crisping scales. Beneath them, the archer gave one, shocked gasp. He inhaled flame and his face was just gone, the flesh of his shoulders cooked under charred wisps of fabric.

Ecko had been dreaming – he remembered...

Tarvi was staring at him, open-mouthed.

But Pareus gave a rallying cry, defiant and enraged. He was bleeding from gashes in his sword arm. As Ecko glanced, he slammed his boot down on another beast, smashing it against the broken stone.

There were too many of them.

Ecko saw another of the patrol go down, screaming, under a welter of sinew and scale. More and more of them were breaching the barricade. His targeters were half blinding him, tracking movement too fast to follow. A spearwoman fell and they were all over her. She struggled to sit up but they flowed up her back and into her hair. He heard her skull crack under the pressure of needle-sharp teeth.

The critters' shrieks rose to a crescendo. Frenzied, they tore at each other in an effort to reach the prize.

"To me!" Pareus called again, but his patrol had been torn to pieces round him – there was almost no one left to hear his courage.

Ecko slammed a foot down on one, kicked another off the top of the wall – but they were still coming.

If he exhaled again, he'd empty the tanks – his little flamer was never meant to be used...

Fuck!

He snatched a lump of stone from the floor and slammed it down on the wall top, crushing the beasts to a smear.

In answer to Pareus's cry, one of the shieldmen fell back, came to stand beside the commander, defend them both. Pareus's flicker-fast blade was clearing the wall before him – between he and Ecko they were holding their side of the defence.

The other remaining shieldman unbuckled his shield and threw it from him, unable to bear the weight of the creatures upon it, claws fastened in the wood. He tried to rally, but they dragged him down, their ecstatic shrieks ripping the sky.

They flowed over him like a scaled death shroud, flashing with teeth and claws.

This is game-the-fuck over, Ecko suddenly realised. Himself, Pareus, Tarvi, the white-faced shieldman... *We're not getting out of this.*

For just an instant, he was tempted to let it go. *Yeah, so I fucked up, so what? It's not like it matters. Reboot, let's go again...*

...then one of the critters swarmed under Pareus's foot and closed on Tarvi; shreds of flesh still caught between its teeth.

She screamed, shrill and furious, as it ran up the front of her leg. Its teeth were bared, it grinned up at her.

Instinctively, the shieldman turned.

And they were on him.

Pareus cried horrified denial as if he'd never been so scared in his life. As his shout rose into the darkening air, the shieldman's turn spiralled into a delicate slump, down onto the stone.

The creatures had torn out his lower legs. They flowed upwards as he fell, raking his flesh, tearing muscle from bone, worrying at him like street dogs. Blood slashed the fire-damaged stone.

The shield hit the ground, spun for a moment, and lay still, Fhaveonic device glinting in the setting sun.

Holy shit.

Ecko had one shot at this.

"Get behind me," he said. "*MOVE!*"

Tarvi moved. Pareus was a split second too slow.

As the commander turned from the wall top, one threw itself at him, claws hooked in his cheek. Its weight dragged it downwards, slicing through soft skin, opening a second mouth in the side of the commander's face. Dropping his sword, Pareus made a grab for it, but it hooked round him like a pet and ravened its teeth into his cheekbone.

His face splintered under the force of its jaws.

His eyes burning with pain, fury, outrage, he grabbed the thing and yanked it off him, taking half of his own face off with it. Bone shone white through a mask of gore.

There was another one on his feet, and another.

"Go," he said. The word was barely recognisable. Astoundingly, he leaned down to pick up the sword and another one was on his wrist, his forearm. "Run! Now!"

Tarvi was over the gore-smattered wall where Ecko had cleared the route.

Ecko was going after her.

As soon as he'd done one last thing.

With a silent farewell to the commander, he exhaled his final breath of fire.

17: REDLOCK ROVIARATH

The man came out of the tavern to see three of them waiting for him.

It was raining, rattling on the mica and soaking into worn wooden walls, rivulets of dirt ran down the roadway.

He looked from face to face and said quietly, "Walk away."

"Never happen." The biggest of the three grinned. "You owe him – and you know it."

The rain was warm on the man's face. He rested his hands on the axeheads, shafts slung through twin rings at his belt.

"I owe him shit," he said. "Now walk. Away."

They went to grab him, force him up against the door.

With a thumb flick and a double rasp, both axes were free. The heads were real white-metal, glistening grey in the rain. One swift sidestep buried them in the ribcage of the first. The second hit the dirt when a tight, laced-up boot slammed into his groin.

The third, barely more than a lad, backed up, white faced, hands spread wide. The axeman planted his foot on the remnant of his attacker's chest and yanked both axeheads free, dragging ribs and lungs out into the dirt. The man coughed, spluttered gore and died, his final gasp lost in the rain.

The roadway was turning to mud.

The second man lay on his side, knees up and hands clamped between his thighs. He was white to his lips, unable to stand.

"Next time," the axeman said. "Walk away when I tell you."

"Sure," the lad mumbled. Carefully not looking at the corpse, not looking at it, he picked up his stricken mate, and the pair of them splashed away.

"Idiots." Redlock wiped both axes on the dead guy's breeches, kicked him clear of the tavern door, and went back to his goblet.

Three doorways down, Triqueta of the Banned watched everything.

Redlock had bootsteps that sent echoes through the grass – wherever he went, the Varchinde rippled at his presence. A curse of his reputation: he was an easy man to find.

The scrabbling sprawl of the Great Fayre spread around two thirds of Roviarath's city wall. The other third, facing south and west, stood over the riverside – watching the point where the three tributaries of the Great Cemothen River met and merged. Here, the water was white and wild, but a skilled barge commander would know the route about the banks to reach the city's huge stretch of wharf.

Many of the cargoes dropped here never made the city proper – they simply bled from the harbour's edges straight into the Fayre, swelling it more with every return. Harsher than the marketplace, the harbour was savage and opportunistic; cruelty grew like salt whorls on the wood. Rumour muttered that the slave trade had also grown here – that those with no one to miss them would find themselves in the hands of the Kartian craftmasters, and that they would never see the light of day again.

But surely that was only rumour.

The Kartiah Mountains themselves seemed very close, here, huge and jagged dark. Rising harsh over the rattling planks of the harbourside, their great heads were too high to see, lost in the rain clouds. To the north and south, they folded gently into forested foothills, woven with a myriad streams. Here, they were like the wall that ended the world, fragmented into towering grey wind carvings. They were timeless, colossal and impossible stone creatures that stood silent guard over the plain.

Only the seedy stretch of the harbour's tumbledown buildings defended the city from their dark might.

That – and Redlock.

In the returns since Triqueta had seen him, he hadn't changed – his garments were loose, battered and patched, his distinctive hair tied in a warriors' knot. He bore no wealth, no evidence of his birth-rank – just the axeheads, acid etched and wickedly hooked. The story went he'd taken them from some road-pirate lord.

He was still unarmoured, shockingly fast and hard hitting. Twin axes were an odd weapon choice – almost no defensive capability – but his brutal combat aggression was still as savage. He must be – what – forty-five returns? And there was no sign of his body slackening.

Skidding past her down the road, his two assailants were speaking in tones of awe.

"...Roken'll do his nut!"

"Roken!" The younger of the two was still shaking. "I'm more scared of the Mad Axeman!"

His companion said darkly, "Looked pretty sane to me..."

Still muttering, they tucked themselves under the buildings' overhang, grimaced at the weather, and continued onwards through the ribbon-town.

Triq waited until she could only hear the rain, then ducked out of the doorway and took a deep breath.

Told herself sternly she wasn't nervous. Nope. Not at all.

Twisted in the muddy road, the corpse was already being picked over. The scavengers scuttled, hunched and dripping, out of her way.

She bounced up the step, shook her wet hair, creaked open the door. Waited for her desert eyes to adjust to the poor light.

Definitely not nervous.

Before her, the room was worn: trade-road dust permeated every corner, stirring lazily with the draught. As the door closed, it drifted to settle on knife-scored tables and benches, on scattered, silent drinkers and a dirty, spit-stained floor.

Redlock didn't look up. He was alone, sat by the empty fireplace, bloodied and filthy boots on the table and cracked terhnwood goblet in hand. The sight of him sent a shock through her blood. She told herself sternly to ignore it. As her vision adjusted, she realised he looked older – more white lines at the corners of his eyes, more white threads through the knot of his hair.

But he was still Redlock, solid, practical, square shouldered; road-worn skin creased by boyish humour. The sight of him thrilled and buoyed her.

The lurker behind the bar grunted warily, eyeing her Banned leathers.

"Came too late to help, then?"

In the quiet room, the sentence was bright, brittle.

She defied embarrassment with a chuckle.

"Not that you needed any."

"Triq?" For a moment, he stared as if she were about to vanish – a Varchinde vision, a shimmer of sun. Then he dumped the goblet and grabbed her wrist, stood up to cover her in a huge hug and pound on her shoulder. "Gods' *teeth*, what're you doing in this dump?" He stood back, gripping her arms. "Let me look at you, mad wench. You don't look any different. And those rocks are still damned ugly!"

"I'll kick your arse." She shoved him affectionately, touched the gemstones in her cheeks. "I'm here looking for you – stuff you need to know." She had no idea where to begin. "Sit yourself down, Red, you'll need more wine."

The barkeep scuttled out with a faded skin. Redlock filled his goblet for her, took a swig from its neck.

"Ack. Stuff tastes like piss."

"Probably is." Triq grinned at him. "Pull up a bench, you oversized grunt – this is going to take a while."

It took a while.

As Triq told, at last, how they'd brought Feren to Roviarath and what Larred Jade's response had been, Redlock was elbows on the table, hand on his forehead shielding his eyes.

It was dark when she was finally done. Tallow candles gave grey smoke and bad light, two empty wineskins lay shrivelled on the tabletop.

Triq laid a slender, sunshine hand on his muscled forearm. "You okay?"

"Thinking." For a moment, Redlock didn't move. Then he looked up at her from under his brows, his expression stone sober, his mouth a dangerous line. "Feren died?"

"Jade tried everything."

"Then we go straight for the Monument." His decision was absolute. "We'll scout the ground and locate the creature – whatever the rhez it is."

"What, now?" Triq chuckled at him. "I only just got here!"

"First light." He wasn't laughing. "The horse I've got's solid, he'll run. If you look after him and we don't stop, we'll do the Monument in – what – two days?"

"He's not a Banned horse, Red, you'll run him into the ground." Triq snorted. "This monster –"

"Is history." His expression was grim, brown eyes glittering in the candlelight. "You offed two of them, how much bigger's this one? We can take him, no worries. The mares'll scatter – you *know* that – shouldn't be too hard for the soldiers to mop them up." He flicked an eyebrow and grinned, sharp as an axe-edge. "And I guess we'd better find Feren's teacher while we're at it."

"You're crazed." No, he hadn't changed. He was resolute, forthright – a man with no concept of "impossible". She grinned at him, shaking her head. Candlelight reflected from the stones in her cheeks. "You and I?" she asked. "By ourselves?"

"You're damned right 'by ourselves' – don't want your noisy lot messing it up." He laid his callused hand along her jaw, gently turned her to look at him. "I've known Feren since he was a knee-biter. When he was five, I made him an axe with a soft leather head – he and my daughter Raevan used to play 'road-pirates' round the orchards." The touch was gentle, but his insistence fierce. "Jade's a smart bastard."

"I'm coming with you, bet your life on it," she told him. "That monster's huge. Feren said it was *terrifying*."

He flickered a smile, and his thumb stroked her cheek. "So am I."

For a moment, they were eyes on eyes, breathless, waiting.

Heart suddenly thumping, she turned into his hand, kissing the skin of his palm. When he didn't move, she slipped her mouth around the tip of his thumb and ran her lips and tongue over him, her eyes catching his with a mischievous gleam.

"So are you, it seems." He watched her with a half smile. "You're not a girl any more." She bit him, taking mock offence and he laughed. He came round beside her on the bench, watched her expression for a moment, then gathered her into his lap, turning to kiss her with a strength and sensuality she remembered – *Oh Gods* – all too well.

She kissed him in return, wrapped her arms round his neck. Felt him harden like a promise under her buttock.

"Good to see you again," she said, grinning.

"You're a madwoman," he told her. "Why didn't Larred Jade muster?"

"Why do you think?"

He chuckled, kissed her again, briefly. "He's a mercenary bastard and we both know he's using me. Us."

"Red..." Self-conscious now, she pulled away from him. "Feren was your blood..."

"And I'll fight for him willingly – and Larred Jade damned well knows it." He grinned. "That monster's going to be horse steak by the time I've finished with it. Then I'll be having a little *word* with the Roviarath CityWarden."

She moved in his lap, relieved. "I don't doubt it."

"You shouldn't," he said softly. "After all, the old sod knew what he was doing when he sent you to find me." His lips brushed her cheek. "Like I could say no to you."

"Let's face it, who can?" Chuckling impishly, she pulled him closer, kissed him again, felt the gentle growl of appreciation through his skin, his mouth. He buried his hands in her hair and kissed her back – hard, eager.

Anticipation thrilled sparks in her blood – she remembered how good he felt, over her, under her. She'd once ridden him so hard he'd begged, laughing, for mercy... then he'd slid his hands beneath her buttocks and pushed upwards into her, not stopping until she'd come, and come, abandoned and wild, head back, hands in her hair...

For a moment, he pulled back, the lines round his eyes crinkled in a grin.

"So," he said softly, "you're staying here tonight?"

"Uh-huh." She shifted her weight until she was astride him, facing him, pressed hard down and into him, her agile fingers teasing out the warriors' knot in his hair. "Unless you had other plans?" Her raised eyebrow said it all.

"Hardly." He pulled her closer, murmuring again at the pliancy of her body, the strength in the grip of her thighs. His thumbs brushed her nipples, hard against the inside of her garments.

She shivered, her back arched, her hips pressed forwards in a motion that made him catch his breath.

He kissed her again, his loose hair tangling round her fingers. Expectation smouldered – spiced by long returns of waiting. *Gods*, he felt good.

The barkeep, standing over them, coughed pointedly and held out a drop-key.

Redlock grinned. Triq was off his lap and key in hand, beaming shamelessly at a red-faced taproom, all eyeing their boots. Stopping long enough to pick up another skin of wine, they headed for his room, laughing like a pair of overgrown 'prentices.

The sun rose over the plainland, light slowly flowing eastwards from the grey and glittering sea.

Somewhere beneath the grass, perhaps in the very grass itself, the Elemental Powerflux of the world was awakening. Fire had roared from sky, burned grass and terhnwood and flesh. And where there was flame, so ash and death had followed.

But in this place, the grass was green, heads of windflowers bright scatterings of colour. The sun lit the dark hides of two chearl, standing picketed by a single basher, tiny under the blowing clouds of the dawn.

The creatures slept standing up, the campsite around them quiet. They flicked their ears, their great chests rumbled at their dreams.

Ecko awoke to rain, pattering gently on the stretched-taut fabric over his head.

Beside him, a curled female shape was quietly shaking. It took him a moment to focus, then he understood. Her hands over her face, Tarvi was curled around her horror, turned away from him and twisted in pain under her bedroll.

Crying for Pareus, for her patrol perished to the last man and woman.

They'd been no more than kids, for chrissakes.

They'd been so much code, mathematically generated from his previous decisions.

They'd died with courage, and screaming.

Pareus...

Jesus fucking shit.

Unsure – almost embarrassed – Ecko turned onto his back, watched the rain running down the tent sides. Pareus's death was haunting him, and he had no fucking idea what he was supposed to do about any of it... When his sisters had turned on the waterworks, it was because they'd *wanted* something – attention, influence...

But the image of the tan commander, picking up his sword with half his fucking face hanging off... it was burned into Ecko's forebrain like a brand.

Real or not, the boy's death mattered.

It *hurt*, like the loss of a friend.

Carefully, he untangled the bedrolls, curled himself about Tarvi's back. He didn't speak – had no idea what he'd say – but his arm went over her and he brought her against his steelwire chest, his bare skin mottled the dark brown-grey of the tent fabric.

Now, she was really crying. Horror held in tight control was flooding out of her: gulping, wracking grief. She shook against him, her body soft and warm. She'd stripped down to her shift; he could feel her breast against his arm, her hair in his face, her buttocks soft in his lap.

Sternly, he asked himself what the hell he thought he was doing.

His reaction to her closeness was inevitable. His embarrassment redoubled, he tried to control it, held tight to panic... This was outside his experience, it'd been too long: he wasn't the same person, physically, chemically, as the

Tamarlaine Benjamin Gabriel who'd had the faintest fucking *clue* what to do with a woman...

With her this close, he was fifteen years old, for chrissakes, elated and guilty and wondering where exactly he was supposed to put his hands.

She nestled back against him, her sobs subsiding. Her softness in his lap was just too good – he knew he had to pull away but he couldn't move, couldn't speak. Somewhere in the back of his head, his own savage cynicism lashed at him – *You want affirmation? Wanna feel alive? Yeah, well feel this!* – but he barely dared breathe in case she moved.

Her hand reached backwards, stroked his hip, pulled him closer. His mottle-skin shivered at the touch, its colours now blending with hers. He was pushed right between her buttocks and straining at the light fabric of his pants.

Disbelief bounced somewhere between his head and his groin. This *so* couldn't be happening...

She found the waistband, pushed them down, lifted the light fabric of her shift... and she was there, naked, warm, soft, wanting. He was so hard against her skin and finally, finally daring to move his hand to cup the breast so teasingly close.

She caught her breath, held his hand in place with her own.

As she turned her shoulders, he could see her profile, outlined against the lightening tent. Her mouth was open, her breathing becoming shallow. With a deft, easy twitch, she moved herself against him and rested the head of his cock against her outer lips.

Oh. Fucking. Hell.

Warning sirens screamed through Ecko's head. He couldn't do this, he so couldn't do this – he'd given it up willingly when Mom'd remade him, he'd no fucking idea what that kind of adrenaline would do to his system...

But, for the life of him, he couldn't have moved. Like a nervous virgin, he buried his face in her hair, her shoulder.

She moved her hand, parted herself for him, slipped down

onto him – dear fucking God – a millimetre at a time, opening and moistening slowly as she slipped herself over him. She was tight, gripping him in smooth, sliding warmth and now he was the one shaking, his breath catching in his throat, against his black, assassin's teeth.

She didn't speak, whimpered in pleasure as she finally ground all the way back, taking him completely, his tightening balls resting, tickling, against her skin.

Then, with a shudder of breath, she started to fuck him in earnest.

As Redlock and Triqueta curled at last into sleep, so dawn stole westwards across the Varchinde.

Slowly, the sky paled to navy, to blue, to grey. The light crept up the trade-road towards the mountains, warmed the buildings of the ribbon-towns and the stone streets of Roviarath.

It lit the poorly fitting shutters of a cheap harbourside tavern.

Triqueta turned over, turned over again, and wondered where the rhez that headache had come from. She sat up to blink at a fully dressed Redlock, grinning over two steaming herbal mugs.

It was still raining; she could hear it on the window. She was tangled in a mess of cheap, itchy sheets. Her head hurt. As she downed the drink and got up to fumble for clothing, she wondered how he managed to look that capable on that little sleep. She splashed her face from the water jug and he chuckled at her torment.

They headed out into the morning, grimacing at the grey sky, sunk low over the mountaintops.

She was *never* drinking again. Really, this time.

Unaware of her rider's pain, the little mare whuffled as Triq threw her saddle over her back – she was eager to run.

Triq sunk deeper into her cloak, wishing it would stop raining. Or hurting. Or both.

Slowly, as the morning swelled into noontide and the sun struggled to shine between the massed ranks of cloud, she began to emerge from the tensed head throb of morning-after pain.

And she found herself eyeing the grass.

They were taking a loop, not crossing through the city. They were closer to the mountains here, and on the meeting point of three rivers, the soil was rich and deep. The grasses should be lush – she should be dragging the mare's head out of the grass with every fifth step.

But the plant life was tinged with black, like the edge of a nightmare.

Triq put her hood back, let the misting drops fall cool on her skin.

But she could feel a prickle of dread beneath their kiss.

In maybe a cycle, the grass would start to transform. From the Kartiah, all the way across to the sea, from the Khavan Circle in the north all the way to the far-distant Yevar, it would wash over with autumnal shades – reds, oranges, yellows, a hundred hues of umber and ochre. Its beauty was astonishing, as though the land burned with glory. This was the natural cycle of the world: this was how it should be and the cities and farms knew these rhythms intimately.

The grass harvest was a time of rural celebration. They gathered their crops and they paid their tithes to the cities, and their protection for the return was assured.

Finally, as the cycles rolled towards winter, the grass would wither and die completely. It would leave the vastness of the Varchinde naked under the cold sky.

Lifeless.

Then the predators would come; the desperate and the hungry and the foolish. The glory of the summer plainland would be lost in a world of struggle and death.

With the spring, the grass would grow once more, green shoots across the emptiness – and life would return to the

Varchinde. It was the cycle of seasons, air and soil; it was the way things should be.

But something was blackening the tips of the grass, closing the bright eyes of the wildflowers.

The rain soaked Triq's hair.

The grass was wrong, somehow. Its colour was wrong, it seemed infected, struggling – fighting a silent war against something she couldn't see.

Redlock joined her. "I know," he said softly. "I saw it in Vanksraat, like the very beginning of some sort of rot…"

"Do they know – Fhaveon, the CityWardens…?"

"Vanksraat sent a bretir to Fhaveon." In the sunlight, he looked older, worn down with age and combat. "They don't know what it is any more than we do."

Somewhere under the soft kiss of the rain, she heard Feren screaming.

For a moment she sat there, feeling the water on her face, watching the tiny, black tinge of death…

…then she turned the horse away and went back to the road.

They had a job to do.

Suddenly Tarvi said, "Wait!"

With a clunky effort, Ecko reined his beast into a lurching half turn. He lifted the front of his cowl. His butt hurt like he'd received the biggest S&M spanking ever known to man.

"What?"

"I think we're lost." Her voice was full of fear and resignation. "Oh dear Gods…" She rode her beast close to him, her gaze searching the grass.

He flinched back from the closeness, couldn't be this near to her, not any more.

They hadn't mentioned it. It stalked through his head continually, a tumble of images and sensations that he couldn't scrub from his memory. Contact and warmth and pleasure and reaffirmation and intensity. Her skin in the soft dawn light, the rain on the tent sides, her voice gasping his name, her hands pulling him to her, her body shaking with orgasm...

She made a grab for his rein and he let her take it – shied away from the touch of her skin on his own.

She scared him. He scared himself.

"Ecko? Can those black eyes see where we are?"

Pulling his cowl back down, he turned away, unable to bear it. With an effort, he slashed his black sneer back over his face, hid behind it.

He couldn't tell her, couldn't admit to himself, how good that had been.

Good enough to kick his adrenals sky-fucking-high as he'd let himself go, good enough to send him into fucking *orbit*.

Good enough for him to lose control of his targeters, his flamethrower.

If the tanks had not already been emptied, he knew he would've burned her to death.

It was in the midst of that thought that his telescopics picked up on motion, slightly to the north. A stone ruin, alight with a nacre of its own; figures moving at its base.

One of them was familiar.

Seeing her, Ecko realised something about fractals that he'd forgotten...

That, whichever direction you chose, whatever ripples you generated, the fucking patterns repeated themselves.

And the implications of *that* were too scary to contemplate.

Across the vastness of the Grasslands, the sun was setting.

It glared red, light spilling from under heavy cloud to coat the Varchinde in blood. The rain had finally ceased – but the heavy, bulbous sky had a metallic light that foretold the rising storm.

The air was warm and close, sweat ran down Triq's spine. Her mare was jittery: she could feel the elemental imbalance and she danced sideways, throwing her head and rolling her eyes. The wet grass swished at her chest. Redlock's gelding was calm – but exhausted. He'd run a long road, his legs quivered and his head hung low.

But they were almost there.

The Monument.

After the speed of her ride, Triq was tired, sodden, filthy and thinking lusty thoughts about inn beds and clean sheets. There were times, she thought, that even the Banned had their limits.

In the distance, the first rumble of thunder – soft and menacing. The rain began again, a ceaseless beating of grey.

They rode on.

She was getting nervous now – as they approached the Monument just as Feren and Amethea had done, a halfcycle before. The air was tight and breathless. The monster, the half-horse stallion, was here somewhere.

Waiting.

Slowly, the mountains' twilight swallowed them. Ahead, a nacreous, yellowish glow swelled upon the horizon. The thunder rumbled again, louder and closer – reddish light flashed behind the clouds. As the sun died on the spiked peaks of the Kartiah, she drew both blades, jumping at every swish in the grass.

"Triq." Redlock reined his beast and pointed. "Look."

Before them, the ground swelled upwards at last, lifting a jumble of massive, fallen stones to the swollen grey sky. In the gathering darkness, they gleamed like the mother of all rocklights, a powerful crepuscular glow, eerie and shivering Triq's skin. Around them, the rain sparkled as it fell and the grass was all stark light and black shadow.

The surrounding bank was high and dark – lifeless.

She had never been this close. All Feren's fears clamoured to be heard and she rode slowly upwards into that strange light, compelled and awed and silent.

The lightning sheeted again, blood red behind the glowering clouds.

Even fallen, the stones were immense. She'd no idea how they could've been brought here, built – allowed to crumble.

Forgotten.

Halting beside her, Redlock asked, "Can you feel it?"

"Feren said..." Triq was drowned out by thunder. She swallowed and tried again. "Feren said he heard it sing, said it was sad, deep and lonely."

"Doesn't sound lonely to me." Redlock chuckled irreverently and his laughter made her smile. "You ask me? It sounds mighty pissed off."

She was about to laugh with him when movement caught her eye: something big, running in the rain. Her heart hammered with certainty, but her voice was steady as she told him, "Talking of pissed off..."

There they were, three of them, huge and hair flying, highlighted into monstrousness by the Monument's illumination. The thunder rumbled as they came in. They were fast – *fast* – racing hard up the far side of the rise.

Dear Gods, they were *huge*. Bigger than the scouts had been, far, far bigger.

Triq's mare lifted her head, flared her nostrils and shook her mane, blowing rainwater. She was lifting her knees high, dancing on the spot like a Padeshian street girl. Triq let out her breath, let out the fear.

"They're coming."

"I see them." Rock steady, Redlock slid to the ground, axes in hands glittering with cold assurance. "Distract it."

She mustered a laugh. "You're *loco*." For a second, she stared at him, trying to make him meet her gaze – but he was watching the shapes, the light gleaming cold from their skin as they came closer. "Red–"

"Later," he said. "We've got guests."

In the moment between one heartbeat and the next, between the flash of lightning and the rumble of thunder, the stallion was there. He was huge, far heavier and broader than the scouts had been. His horse body was twice the mass of her little mare, his human torso massively muscled and sparkling with water.

He was beautiful.

And, Feren had been right, he was *terrifying*.

His thick mane of hair was plastered to him, clinging to the lines of his chest and shoulders. His eyes were terrible, more than human and less than animal – he was utterly crazed and he *celebrated* it.

He screamed at her, his incisors too long, like a bweao's. His claws rent the wet soil. Around him, the thunder crashed again.

Was this what Feren had seen?

Triq was aware that Redlock had moved, she didn't look at him. Instead, she stood in her stirrups and screamed straight back at the monster – shrill and utterly insolent.

And the stallion laughed at her.

"Little lady," he said. "Lady of the Banned. You who slew my scouts, my sons. Little creature thinks she can fight?"

Like his horse body, his human chest, his voice was perfect – powerful, sensual. It was deep, a throb she felt in her blood. It robbed her of words, and, for a moment, she was overpowered by his presence. Her mouth moved, but no sound emerged.

"And you, warrior, you smell like the other one. You seek to punish me? Little human – you're creature-born, forced to live with whatever your sire and dam could spare you. I? Am so much more!"

In the rain, the two flanking shapes had flashed past, trapping them. Triq kept them in her awareness, but her attention was on the stallion.

She found her voice and shouted, "There was a girl, an

apothecary. What did you do with her?"

"She was needed. To heal *flesh*." The word was a hiss, spat between his predator's teeth. "She belongs to us now."

"What did you *do* with her?"

"We gave her a home. A family. Purpose. There will be none of this for you."

The thing was crazed, the light reflected broken from its eyes.

Triq shrieked at it, "I don't know what the rhez you are or why you were made – but you're *wrong*. Half creature, life all twisted! The grass has no place for you!"

With a fluid motion, the great beast raised his longbow, nocked a flightless shaft like a spear, drew back the string.

"This place is *mine*! I was charged to come here; to guard the cathedral, the centre, the work that happens here. You, creature-born – your time is *done*." The broadhead was pointed straight at Triqueta's throat. "He knows you are coming."

"He?"

The stallion laughed, the thunder crashing through his mockery, the sparkling rain soaking his mane to darkness and shadow.

"Enough," he said. "You want to challenge me, little lady?"

He put the final pressure on the bowstring, released the shaft.

Triq threw herself sideways, hanging half out of her saddle. It skimmed past her so close the broadhead sliced a red line in the side of her neck. Her mare stood straight up, raindrops shattering on her forehooves – tiny against the almighty chest of the beast...

But the stallion stopped dead, staring at something behind her. *What the rhez?*

She twisted in her saddle, blades gripped in her hands. The mare plunged back to the soil, ears flat back and hooves tamping.

There was something else out here?

Beside her, there was movement, down in the grass.

Something dark, shadowed; something Triq couldn't see.

Something that threw two broken halves of arrow shaft straight up into the monster's face, daring it.

"Y'know, for a centaur, you're a lousy fuckin' shot." The voice was harsh, oddly accented, a rasp that tore into her ears. "Whoever made you? Shoulda had better blueprints." In the grass, in the rain, two red lights blinked up at Triqueta. "Hey," the voice said. "Good to see ya. I think you lost some dice."

What?

"Whatever the rhez you are." Redlock's voice. "Identify yourself."

"We're your three'n'fourpence," it said. "Looks like we're gonna dance."

18: FOUNDERSDAUGHTER TEALE, FHAVEON

Penya Esamy laughed and salt wind tickled strands of her tied-back grey hair. Beside her scuttled a slender young man with pale skin, dark eyes and the slightly haunted look of one who sought her services a little too regularly.

But Rhan's guise didn't fool her and he knew it. She'd known him far too long.

The day was overcast, the sky fluffed layers of grey. To one side of them, scattered buildings rose in zigzags to forested hills above the town – to the other, trade-boats hunkered down in rows upon the water, covered in sun-faded fabric and awaiting summer rain. The great city of Fhaveon had no sea harbour – and this little town of Teale, further north and on a gentler coastline, was lifeline to both fisherfolk and incoming coastal trade.

Flanked by a tall lighthouse and a blurred, grey-sombre statue, the harbour mouth was currently quiet.

Down through long returns, Rhan had grown fond of Teale. He'd been instrumental in the town's construction – generations ago, when Adward had been a young man, inheritor of his great-grandfather's zeal and fire. High on the hillside, they'd built the Hollow Theatre together, the celebration of the trade cycle that had brought peace and communication to the Varchinde. It stood there, as Rhan remembered, like a promise – a promise that the Grasslands would thrive.

Thrive. The dead lord's image was as clear as the daylight. He'd aged into a bitter man, thin as a spear handle, and smiling like its thrust. *Samiel's teeth, I'd like to take the old sod up there and show him what we're becoming.*

Teale was shabby now, more ribbon-town than trading post. A population once comfortable with a tithe of the incoming cargo had been suitably squeezed by Phylos's tight fist. The theatre shone bright as the sun slanted through the clouds. On the waterfront, many businesses were shuttered and hard-eyed predators loitered in gaggles in their doorways.

Watching.

Rhan could feel their gazes as they passed, he didn't look up. Beside him, Penya walked swiftly.

In the harbour, there were two of the great, square-sailed Archipelagan boats, their prow-sculpted maidens blank eyed and huge breasted above the wharf, smiling emptily at the rising town. These triremes would bring spiceweed, parchment and wrought-fibre gems – cargo then carried by cart and caravan south over the hills to Fhaveon herself, to the fiveday markets and the meticulous records of the Cartel.

They would return laden with terhnwood of their own.

The breeze filled Rhan's senses with salt, with weed and wrack, with a tumble of images never forgotten – he breathed them deep. The world may have no memory – but these, these were *his*, bought with his own endless time.

"You shouldn't be here, you great lunk." Penya spoke softly and with a long affection. She jabbed him with a conspiratorial elbow. "How the rhez did you get yourself arrested?"

"Carelessness." He shrugged. "I needed to tell you to your face, Pen. You've been a good friend, never betrayed me – I don't want to see this madness infect you. That – and I need to ask you something."

She chuckled. The slant of sunlight was obscured by the grey and the theatre's glow vanished back into the hillside.

"You didn't come for a last fix, then?"

"I came to say goodbye, you daft old *whytche*."

"Now there's a word you don't hear any more." Wheeling seabirds cried raucous laughter. "Facing the cold embrace of withdrawal, are we? I can make it easier for you, if that'd help."

The first splatters of rain began to hit his cheek.

"For the Gods' sakes, Pen, I know what I look like but comedown? The least of my problems." The harbour wind was sharp, it blew the rain into his face. He lowered his voice to a rumble. "Elemental fires, roving monsters, and that's only the beginning. You should... retire for a while. Things are about to get nasty."

"I can take care of myself. You taught me how, as I remember." Penya eyed a scattering of bored local toughs, loitering in a chipped stone doorway. Litter blew round their feet. Their eyes raked her like broken-off blades, but her hand rested pointedly on the long knife at her belt and they shuffled back. She shot him a look round the side of her cheek. "You took a chance coming here."

"They'll never notice me." Rhan grinned, took a minute approximation of a bow. "Trick of the light."

She chuckled, threw him a brief smile. Next to her grey hair and assured walk, he was slight and twitchy, hollow eyed and sallow skinned – carefully unremarkable. If Phylos's eyes were here, they'd pass straight over him.

"Walk with me," she said. "Round here, walls have bigger ears than you'd think."

The wind cut harsh as they turned from the waterfront and began to move out along the grey-stone harbour wall, blinking at rain and spray. Hands had built this, bare hands. Sweat and effort had carried these stones and piled them high from the water… Now, algae and shellfish grew in their cracks.

The tide pulled at them, hissing.

The elements awaken. Remembering Roderick's passionate speech, the cut of the chill brought Rhan a shiver of insight. Ten generations of Fhaveon's Lords, the might and vision of Saluvarith, now distilled down to Demisarr's weakness. Demi was a good man, and a true-hearted one, but Phylos would rip out his belly, garnish it, and serve it up at a Cartel party.

"It got away from me, Pen. I wasn't paying enough damned attention and now I have to fix it. All of it. The Bard's heart holds a fear that's crazing him – and this time his madness is catching." Anger flickered like light under his skin. "You're the finest herbalist I know – and I need you to do something for me." He looked back up at the hills that cupped the town, almost as if he expected to see flames spreading through the green. "Call it a suspicion, a feeling. I need to know if there's anything wrong with the grass."

"The moons on two sticks." Penya snorted. Below them, a boatman stood in the bottom of a small, local craft, picking spindly-legged crustaceans from a woven cage. He held them up, shook them, dropped the bigger ones into a basket, threw the smaller ones back into the harbour. "Y'know," she said, pausing to watch, "some of those creatures are hundreds of returns old. Hundreds." The boatman dropped another one. "They end their lives in that tar-stinky little boat – and we *eat* them."

Rhan stopped beside her, skin prickling, rain in his eyes. The clouds were sinking lower overhead. *Hundreds.* "Pen?"

"Why are you here, Rhan? Really?" She rounded on him, punched him to hide an odd note in her voice. "You've been arrested! I should throw you in the harbour!"

"Maybe he'll pick me up and put me in his basket. Penya –" now he turned her to look at him, searching her face "– what's the matter?"

"Nothing." With a flicker of more usual, impish humour, she took his jaw in her hands and kissed him on the mouth. "Come on, you – bet I can still beat you." She broke into a run, turned to grin at him, jogging backwards with strands of her hair blowing. She was still slender, a woman he'd watched grow from a fearful girl, into a lover, into a friend. "Come on, you timeless bastard, see if you can keep up!"

He chuckled, broke into a shambling run suited to his wasted appearance.

She taunted him. "Come *on*!"

He shambled faster.

Under his roughly sandalled feet, the wall ran to a long, embracing curve, protecting the harbour and ending in its tall, stone guardian, a statue with features long since blunted by coastal weather. He stood faceless, twin to the lighthouse, sombre and dark, the other side of the harbour mouth.

Defended by the guardian's plinth was a square cot, built like the wall out of shaped and carried rocks. Once, boats not wishing or needing to moor in the harbour had done trade here.

Now it was half tumbledown. No one had used it in returns.

Her laughter was snatched by the wind, thrown in his face.

Hundreds.

And the realisation hit him like a clothyard shaft.

Oh, Pen, you didn't...

The thought was sharp and sudden, hurting – but his certainty was absolute. Rhan lurched to a stop, his heart slowly crushing in a fist of pure, cold betrayal.

Hundreds.

"Pen?" It was a whisper, a plea of denial.

"Come *on*!" She was still laughing at him, her hair now coming loose from its tail. He hadn't really noticed how grey she'd gone – the death of her husband had hit her harder than she'd said. She was always so damned *capable*...

"Penya?"

Loss twined its way round denial, round helplessness and then round rising, righteous anger. Almost answering him, the sun broke momentarily through the clouds and lit the harbour to a brilliant blue sparkle, though the rain still scattered in his face. Shards of rainbow danced in the air.

Hundreds.

Warmth touched his skin. He raised his jaw, his determination. His rage.

Friends were rare to an immortal, to be betrayed by one was beyond belief.

Focus!

He knew they were coming and he let the light flood him, find the core of his anger, his certainty, and fuse with it, fuel it. Bright illumination saturated his being, burned like sheet lightning beneath his skin. He opened his heart, his mind, his soul. Around him, the very Powerflux invaded his form, wove itself into his breath, his being, and he was more than flesh, more than mortal. He was pure bloody quintessence – and, by the Gods, he was *angry.*

Rhan started to laugh; release, rising exultation. Defiance.

Come on then, you bloody bastards. Ambush me, would you?

With a massive effort of self-control, he contained the force, held the light beneath his skin and clung to his sunken-eyed image – but he wouldn't keep it for long. The illusion was burning from a hole in its centre – as though the sunlight had hit it, focused through a real glass lens.

His laugh sought utterance, gleeful and dangerous. It had been too, too long.

Come on then, show yourselves. I'll crush your skulls with my bare hands.

He forced his body to move, closer to the wall's end. He was still lurching, though it was no longer an act. Controlling his body was awkward – he wanted to blaze, to explode into the sky like a rising star.

Penya was still laughing as he came after her, shambling faster now. Behind her, the great, blunt-featured statue stared out over the water.

Tekisarri. Saluvarith's son, Rakanne's father. The boy who found me when I was washed up and broken at the base of the cliff...

...Damn you, Phylos, I'll tear out your spine for this!

And there they were, racing from either side of the cot, from its darkened doorway. There were over a dozen of them, dressed in the ramshackle woollens of fishermen but with the strong shoulders and raised chins that marked them instantly as military.

Mostak! You betray your brother? Your family?

The politics bothered him for only a moment. The scattering of guised soldiers spread into a loose line, armed with an unpleasant assortment of hooks, axes and gutting blades.

It started to rain harder. The shaft of sunlight was gone.

Penya shrieked, startled, skidded to a stop. "Oh my Gods!"

He snarled at her, "Get behind me!" Had she betrayed him? He'd no idea. The burning was too strong for reason, too powerful. But these bastards had made a *mistake*.

He was still on the wall – they couldn't come at him all at once. At best, they'd be three at a time. His grin was breaking free now, cracking through his sallow-skinned guise. His *bweao* laugh was audible, thrown high into the air by the chill sea wind.

Foundersson's Champion. Master of Light. Then. Still. Always.

He challenged them straight. "Come on, then! Rip those hooks into my flesh, damn you! Put my balls on a spear and take them back to the Council!"

But Penya shrieked again, pointing wildly.

On the lighthouse balcony, two archers, shafts nocked and ready to loose. And behind him, the three toughs from the doorway were ranging themselves across the wall top, slouching and smirking. Their knives were dirty.

"Nice ambush." His words were as sharp as a blade across the throat.

With a yell, they rushed him.

As he detonated, the rain sheeted across the harbour.

He came to with a start, his body jolting as though it had been in freefall. Somewhere in the back of his head, there were echoes of screaming.

Whose?

The air was deep cold, it stank of stone and salt and loss. And there was a pain in his back – a dull pain, a dark pain. A leftover ache like an embedded fragment of betrayal.

Penya.

He was hazy. Figments taunted the corners of his thoughts – flitting shadows he couldn't quite see. His light was extinguished, exhausted; his connection to the Powerflux broken. He hurt, mind and body.

He was alone.

With an effort of will that nearly tore him flesh from bone, he got his hands under his shoulders and pushed his chin up.

He blinked, grinding his sight into focus.

Glory and exultation. Dazzling light refracting through pelting rain. Arrows sparking into ash before they reached him. Warriors falling, hands over their faces to shield their eyes. Laughter thrown into the sky as he knew they couldn't touch him…

Dark stone walls, slick with green. A heavy wooden door cracked at the base and letting a chink of light point along the rock floor to the backs of his fingers.

…The tiny bite at his back, the spreading numbness. The shock; the denial. The fading, struggling, reaching. Rainbows

cracking, scattered across the stone like broken crystal. Falling, falling away.

Then nothing – "Kazyen".

He blinked for a moment, puzzled, figments still dancing, mocking him. Then he felt a shiver of fear as he realised...

...screaming...

...that wasn't everything. Somewhere between that falling and the jolt that'd awoken him, there had been a nightmare. A body, thrown through a shutter; a woman, pounding his chest with furious fists.

What?

He shivered, a frisson through his skin. The figments taunted him, flickering just too far away to reach.

A white face. A last, startled expression as it plummeted into darkness. And then the screaming, all the way down.

The frisson became fear – real, tangible fear. The figments laughed more loudly and his skin crawled with sudden dread.

Dear Gods, Samiel, Father. What did I do?

He needed to move.

Struggling to muster his concentration, he blinked at where he was – yes, sealed in Fhaveon's rock-walled gaol, the *oubliette* beneath her perfect stone. With a flash of bitterly ironic clarity, he realised this was another thing he'd built.

And this one he couldn't get out of.

He tried to stand, failed. His feet slipped on slick, cold weed; his skull boomed dully like the drums of the High Cathedral tower. His body felt like water, no cohesion. It took three attempts to even sit, elbows on his knees, head in his hands.

His face was scratched, four neat nail rakes down one cheek.

"Rhan, you cursed bastard, you filthy, faithless sehvrak!*"* *Fury and helplessness.* *"You owe him your oath, your..."*

For a moment, he'd caught a fragment of the nightmare and he froze, staring at it in horror. Valicia, Demisarr's wife, her shoulders and breasts bared, her hand clawing at his cheek...

the *hate* on her face... *No... that was beyond crazed...*

Then it was gone, and he was sitting there, hand pressed to drying scabs, to four bloodied weals of loathing.

Valicia? What happened?

Fear was congealing into truth – to be down here, he'd done a lot damned worse than a packet of illegal herbs.

He had to get out...

But he had built this one to be impregnable.

There was a voice outside his cell.

It echoed oddly from the rock, barking instructions in a harsh, merciless snap. It was too far away to hear clearly. Like a ribbon-town beggar, he dragged himself across the floor, placed an ear to a crack between the door planks.

Footsteps – hollow in the tunnel. A long, powerful stride, a billow of fabric, other feet scurrying to keep up.

He pulled back against the far corner of the weed-slick wall and sank into his hands, not needing to feign the despair.

The stern footsteps came close, closer. There was the fumble of a drop-key, the door creaked and the light opened fanlike across the stone. The shadow within it was unmistakeable.

"Rhan." The word was pure victory, as hard as a fist.

Phylos.

"Merchant Master." Rhan didn't bother looking up. His sardonic bass was muted, almost a growl. He was bruised, he'd realised, bones cracked, he could feel them – somewhere, he'd been savagely beaten. "I'll rip out your lungs and *feed* them to you."

The merchant snorted, glowered at whatever had been scuttling behind him, and snapped the door shut. He crouched before Rhan in a crumple of fabric, took Rhan's chin in a hand decorous with wrought terhnwood-fibre rings.

"How much do you remember," he said softly, "my Lord Seneschal?"

Screaming. All the way down. Filthy and faithless.

"What did you do to Penya, you bastard?" He looked up, gaze burning from under his brows. He didn't have enough energy to light a damned candle, but the anger – the anger was helping. He snarled in Phylos's face, "What did you *do*?"

Phylos laughed, a boom like an oarsmens' drum.

"I knew where you'd go – you're as guileless as a child. And I have her son." His shoulders gave an amused half shrug. "People are easy to shift, with the right lever."

Rhan surged into movement, a graceless half lurch.

"I'll tear off your sk–"

Slam! He was back against the wall, ringed hand hard on his shoulder, Archipelagan strength behind it.

"You're in no position to be making threats." The Merchant Master radiated smug savagery: it danced in his voice, flickered across his face. "You're finished, you bastard, you've hobbled this city long enough. Without you, Fhaveon ushers in a new age – an age where our terhnwood will rule everything we are, everything we want and need. I can wipe out the pirates once and for all –"

"By burning the crops?" Pinned by his shoulder, Rhan turned his face into Phylos's like an angry lover. "You *stupid* – !"

"I didn't burn anything, you herb-addled throwback. Believe me or not as you wish – I'm as... curious... about that as you must be." He grinned like a hunting bweao. "Though I can turn it to my advantage."

"Oh?" Rhan dared him, taunting. "And how would that be?"

"Love of the Gods!" Phylos spat a laugh straight back, though the pressure of his hand didn't ease. The rock was cold, and it hurt. "You'll be facing death for your crimes, Rhan. You may not have a future, but I'm not about to crouch here in the stink and tell you my plans." Now, he eased the pressure, rested his hand on Rhan's shoulder, mocking. "You'll go to your trial, your execution and your grave knowing that you gave this city, her rulers, into my hands. And without you holding me back, I can build Fhaveon to a glory never seen."

"'Trial, execution and grave'? You think you can execute me for a packet of illegal herb? Whatever your grand plan may be, Phylos, the Foundersson –"

"The Foundersson is dead, you damned fool." Phylos inhaled momentarily, as though the next sentence were one to savour. "You killed him."

What?

The memory was stark, cold and shocking, suddenly ice-water clear.

Screaming. All the way down.

He whispered like a breath of pain, as though he'd been punched in the belly. "Dear Gods...!"

"You'll be facing trial for the murder of the Lord Foundersson Demisarr Valiembor and the subsequent –" another savour "– *rape* of his ladywife, Valicia." Phylos's expression was sharp, metal cold – as though it hid glee beyond measure. "The Lady has a high heart and much courage – she'll bring a witness testimony that will *end your life*."

Hands. Beating at his chest. The body under him, spasming and furious – biting, fighting, struggling...

The memory made him shudder in shock horror – like a spear had been driven through his body. *Samiel! I couldn't have done this!*

As if it was his last, strangled air, he said, "No..."

But he knew it was true. Somehow, in that nightmare, he'd been in the bedchamber of the Foundersson. Had he been begging help, or sanctuary, or for the Lord to show courage against Phylos's rising power? He had no idea. But he *remembered*...

The struggling form of the man in his hands. "Rhan, what are you doing? Put me down, I'm not a babe any more!" Shutters shattering as the Lord went through them, the last clutch of his hand on the windowledge. Screaming. The long fall down into the gorge, into the night.

What had he done?

He was shaking, broken, hands quivering like an addict's. His belly roiled as if he'd throw up. His mind could manage nothing but pointless, empty, looping denial. *Nonononono…*

I held Demi as a tiny baby. Watched him grow. Swore my life to his defence. Stood with him as he married his wife…

…his wife! The white-flare release of an orgasm stolen.

"Get up, Rhan Elensiel." Phylos rammed his shoulder again against the rock. Shards of pain shot through his bruised spine. The Merchant glanced back as something blocked the light chinks, moved away. "Get up, and face your own execution. Like a man. If that's what you are."

Rhan stared, lost in disbelief. Impossibility raged at him, a towering mockery that clamoured on all sides – how had Fhaveon been this undermined, this quickly? How long had Phylos and the Institute been laying groundwork? And how in the names of the *Gods* had he not *noticed*?

Samiel's *teeth* – had he been asleep?

But he could answer that himself. *No, just bored. Inattentive. Drinking, smoking, entertaining his friends and varied personages of exotic tastes…*

Like herbalist Penya Esamy.

He wanted to rail at himself for being such a fool – but that time was past. The initial shock, the horror, was solidifying, now sending after-echoes through his thoughts – without Demisarr, his daughter Selana would lead the Council. She was young, easily controlled. If she named her mother Seneschal, perhaps there would be hope for the city.

But if she named *Phylos…*

It was an old, old story. Mainly because it damned-well worked.

By the Gods, this was crazed!

He shifted under Phylos's hand, strove to stand. His vision darkened, cleared. Pain skittered through his back, his chest *ground* as he moved – he wondered, bizarrely curious, just how badly he'd been thrashed. How badly he'd deserved it.

His mouth tasted of salt, blood and sand.

He reached a panting crouch and managed, "I don't know what you've done to me – what you've made me do – but it's a *lie*."

The Merchant laughed, unfolded to his feet with a warrior's ease. He stood over Rhan, blood-robes saturated to his knees.

Rhan said, "You touch Selana and I'll –"

"The way you touched her mother?" The Merchant Master turned to the door, threw the words back over his shoulder. "You're *done*. Today, Fhaveon begins her new life."

The Theatre of Nine still rang with echoes of the tumult.

Small beneath her father's white cloak, The Lord Foundersdaughter Selana Valiembor was wide-eyed, struggling to master reactionary shivering. She'd faced them, all of them, from the head of that table and she'd done her damned best.

Watching her, Phylos threw his own cloak across her chair – a splash of blue in this cold, white building. They were alone.

"You did well, my Lord," he told her gently. "Even without the grief and the outrage, the Council is a hard thing to control."

"'Control', Phylos?" Her voice was clear, remarkably steady. "I thought my role was to guide?"

"Of course." The blood-clad Merchant Master gave a slight bow, changed tack. "My Lord, perhaps now the meeting is over, there's a matter we can discuss privately?"

"The naming of my Seneschal –"

"No, my Lord." He smiled affectionately at her, as if the issue were farthest from his mind. "I speak of the burning – and the harvest."

Pain flickered a line between her brows. She put back the voluminous white hood as if she set her title aside, relaxed.

"I wish I knew," she said. "If this continues…"

"I've despatched runners, my Lord, following Roderick's hysteria. The Bard may be crazed, but there's no fault in caution."

The girl nodded. She wandered around the table, trailing her fingertips across its cold surface, looking up at the great mural carved into the circular wall.

"Do you mean what you say to me, Phylos? That this is a new beginning?" Cold quartz lay dead in the stone. "That Fhaveon will know new life?"

"Assuredly, my Lord. Enough of saga and history and forgotten woes." He smiled up at Rhan's plummeting stone likeness, a sharp edge of anticipation. "It's time we take responsibility, make our destiny our own."

"History." She was still looking at the great saga around her, the city's history, her construction by Saluvarith and Tekisarri, the gift of the GreatHeart Rakanne. "Meaning Roderick's vision – ?"

"Meaning the terhnwood, my Lord. Where is our life manifest if not in the grass, in the harvest, in the life of the Varchinde? Rhan murdered your father, hurt your mother and he will pay. It is your time now."

She turned, pale face and white cloak, the might of her forefathers graven in the stone behind her.

"Your vision is compelling, Phylos. I want to make decisions, to remember the strength of the Valiembor House." She extended her hand to him. "You'll help me?"

"My lord, your mother –"

"My mother is broken –"

"Your mother is *livid*." He met her eyes, took her slim hand in his own, ran his thumb softly across her skin. "But you're right, she's lost her objectivity – at least for the moment."

"Then you'll stand with me, Phylos? Help me steer the city through the chaos to come?"

"I will, my Lord." In a billow of scarlet, the Merchant Master sank to his knees, bent over the girl's hand. "As the Gods are my... No." He looked up at her, sincerity in every line of his face and being. "As *you* are my witness, Selana, Lord and daughter of Lords, I give you my life and swear that I will stand by you, defend and protect you; that I will guard this city as though she were my lover –" his hand tightened on hers, eyes searched her face "– and carry her to a future of glory and strength."

She was staring at him, transfixed.

He came to his feet in a rush, a paean of hope. "*We* will save the Grasslands, Selana, you and I!"

And she was in his arms, slight and soft and pliant, her breath as sweet as summer sunrise.

19: SENTINEL THE MONUMENT

There was a red and jagged flash, a wound in the sky that split the grey clouds right down to the plain. There was an instant – the stallion on his hind legs, his huge body black against the Monument's radiance. There was wet grass, shouts snatched away by the wind – and then everything screamed into motion.

His starlites flooded by the flash, Ecko kicked his heatseeker – the stallion was chill skinned in the rain but its body heat was a furnace. It was red hearted, red souled. Behind it, the Monument glowed like a kiln, a crucible of potential.

As the adrenaline jumped, everything swam, slowed. He shot forward, the grass buffeting him. He watched the colours that were the centaur's legs, its claws, but his targeters crossed its weakest point.

One foot in the bollocks and this thing was going *down*.

On the creature's other side, the heat signature of the axeman was slow in comparison – but as inevitable as a well-thrown rock. Both axes went for the fetlock on its rear leg. The bones were delicate; even on this monster, they'd splinter like dry wood. Hack the fucker off at the ankles – Ecko liked this guy's style.

In front of the beast, still spitting fury, the goldie girl Triqueta was outmatched and overwhelmed by the monster, a hot glow of anger against the cold mass of sky. She had no bridle – how the hell she controlled that critter, he'd no fucking clue – but she surged the horse out of range as blue-cold claws grasped at the air.

Her horse was freaked, dancing like she'd electro-jabbed it.

He spared a moment to hope that Tarvi and the chearl had gained the cover of the inside of the bank...

And his cross hairs targeted. Damn thing had balls the size of –

But the stallion was too smart.

From the colossal, upright rear, it went over – one staggeringly powerful jump that took it away from feet and axes, past where Triqueta timed her turn. For just an instant, its belly was cold blue against the sky, one side highlighted red by the stones' glow, then it landed in the thick, wet grass and its rear claws smashed out at anything following.

It lurched, spun round, teeth bared and foreclaws ripping the grass into a mangled mess of mud and fury. Its too-human eyes were demented with reflected light.

The rain glittered as if the air was broken.

"You *presume*?" It sounded amused. "Creature-created I am, you have no skills to match me."

"Sure I do." Ecko shrugged. Rain soaked his skin. "You wanna find out?"

The two mares closed, now, to flank him. They were smaller, high breasted and heavy shouldered with the same core glow and cold skin. Both bore curved bows and disdainful expressions – water ran in streams from their hide.

The sky flashed again, red as blood, red as the 'bot's target-scan, the thunder was low overhead. In the open plain, the rain was hammering merciless, it slashed into them like blade fragments.

Ecko kicked out his heatseeker to check weapons.

In one fluid move, all three creatures nocked, drew and loosed.

In elegant slo-mo, three featherless shafts ripped through the wet air, flexing with the force of the shot.

At the axeman.

Their strength was deadly, their aim impeccable. Ecko spared a second to wonder what the hell the draw was on those fucking things...

No idiot, the axeman was moving, perfectly practised, rolling sideways below the level of the grass tops.

Adrenaline hot, Ecko started to grin.

As the stallion screamed fury and denial, there was a shadow, red eyed, darting more swiftly than the shafts themselves. His targeters blipped – once, twice, three times – plotted the arc. One arm swept, wet cloak flowing behind it – and the missiles were knocked wide. Lost in the grass.

And he was was gone again – a phantom in the darkness.

The axeman got as far as "What – ?" before Ecko's harsh rasp shouted over the downpour, "So, 'creature-created'. What else you got?"

The second volley came straight for him.

He cackled... and he was simply no longer there. After a world of nerve-contacted firearms, a bow and arrow just didn't have a fucking prayer.

"Nice try, Sagittarius – you might wanna invest in some *sights*."

The beast bellowed rebellion.

Down in the mass of the grass, the axeman shot out, "What the rhez *are* you?"

"Toldja – reinforcements." Ecko's eyes flashed red. "Deal with the big fucker, I'm going after his harem." With a grin, he ducked sideways out of the axeman's vision.

And cursed himself, for the fucking hundredth time, for dropping Salva's rifle.

* * *

Triqueta's mare was terrified. She wasn't bolting – not yet – but she was whinnying through her teeth, her ears were back and she was shaking her wet mane against her neck.

Behind her, Redlock was advancing, combat-crouch, both axes spinning – one forwards, one back. He was soaked, hair and garments plastered to him, two thirds the height of the monster, but grim faced, utterly fearless. His confidence was palpable. Triq'd lay odds on his victory – an axe in the belly was going to slow that beast right down.

But it would get another shot before he closed.

Red lightning flashed.

In that instant, one of the mares squealed, rocked sideways and shot down suddenly at something beside it.

The other raised its recurve and loosed the shaft at Triqueta.

It hit her horse in the shoulder, skidded off bone and buried itself in the saddle-side.

The mare screamed, instinctually turned to bite.

The beast was nocking another, hands almost as fast as Triq's could be.

Shit!

Thunder threatened, it rolled low round her ears. Wind and rain tore at her clothing, her skin. One chance.

As the mare gathered her legs to flee, Triq knotted one hand in her mane, swung her head sharply round. The horse hesitated – that was all her rider needed. She sat back in the saddle, down and hard.

The creature stopped, fidgeting madly.

With burning fury, Triq turned her towards the abomination. The rain hit them both, full in face. Triq blinked and spat water, it ran from her skin like blood.

That damn thing wasn't getting off another shot.

* * *

Lost in the dark grass, grinning like a fiend, Ecko eyed the massive flank – ribs and muscles and hide – of the beast in front of him. He was still boosted, quivering with sustained adrenaline – soaked to the skin and waiting... poised...

Even with his speed, he was gonna have to be fast.

Then there it was – the jab of lightning, the IR-sight flash that exploded everything into split-second red light.

He put all his strength into it, every trick Mom had built for him, every fragment of his focus and adrenaline – and he lashed one perfectly placed kick at the side of the thing's knee.

As it turned, it saw a dark shape, red eyes...

...then the light flash was gone.

The leg splintered and the creature buckled, squealing in pain and fury. But it shifted its weight to the other legs and shot back at the shadows in the grass.

It missed him. As the thunder rumbled, Ecko had vanished.

One down, he thought to himself. *Three more to go.*

Redlock faced the stallion.

In the back of his mind – Feren, child and laughing, running through the citrus orchards of his Idrakian home. His daughter, red hair in the sun; his wife, the embroidery on the front of her gown.

The memory twisted. *Get out, Far! Take your ideals and your ambitions and see if they'll build you a home! See if you can eat them, sleep with them, love them –*

Her bitter, eviscerating voice echoed down through returns.

And with it came *anger*.

The flood of fury, the heat in his blood, the elation, the tight, narrow-focus precision. Around him, everything else had gone – the grass, the rain, the light, the storm, the sky. His world was honed, sharp as an axe-edge, his attention pure and absolute.

It freed him – he *lived* for moments like these.

The beast loosed its shot. It was close – too close – he twitched his hips and belly sideways.

It was past him and gone.

It wasn't going to nock another. He was racing forwards, low down through the grass, both weapons spinning into place with his full force behind them. A hard double feint, high at its chest – it turned the huge bow to block – but the axeman dropped sharply and the cuts came under, vicious and exact. He hit both lower forelegs, slashing flesh, splintering bone.

The stallion snarled, staggered.

His expression set, Redlock smashed it again, one side then other – then he dove sideways, out of its range.

This time, it shrieked, lurched forwards. One claw slashed at him, the heel of the bow slammed hard into his shoulder. It caught his roll and drove him sideways, almost to his knees.

The pain was sharp, the nock tore through fabric and skin – his blood surged, roaring in his ears. As he came back up, he threw his bodyweight into the beast, slammed the struck shoulder up under its raised leg. The opposite axe uppercut, hacked into ribs with a vicious impact. He heard them crack, splinters of broken bone visible through hide and flesh.

Hissing fury through gritted teeth, he tried to force the beast to fall.

He failed.

The creature's weight was too much for him; it was grinding him down into the grass. He wasn't strong enough to hold this colossal, soaking, stinking, struggling creature. He slammed his axe into its ribs again, and again; they shattered like dry firewood. He could hear the rumblings of its belly, the grunts of pain with each broken bone.

Then, suddenly, the creature's weight was gone. He staggered, nearly fell, his shoulder pounding. It stood on its hind legs,

claws flashing about his face, blocking the wind, the rain, the
light, like a wall. Its ribs were grinding, blood streamed down
its belly and legs.

Right, you bastard.

The thing has made its mistake.

Triq leapt her little mare straight at the monster.

The creature was big – the femininity of breasts and face
somehow more disturbing than the stallion's insanity. Shrieking
fury into the dark sky, she barged the mare broadside into the
beast's lower chest, haunches shoving at it like a cavalry mount.
Snarling, it dropped the bow and made a grab for Triq's wet
hair. She dipped sideways, one blade opening a triangular tear
across its ribs.

Foreclaws useless, the creature closed to shove back. It kneed
the mare repeatedly in the belly, making her snort and bare her
teeth to bite. It was close, too close, over her. She could smell
the horse-stink of skin and hide and anger, the sweat, the fury.
She could see where it had sunburn, the worn, wet leather of
the halter top it wore, the white scar that crossed one shoulder.
Its coarse, rain-soaked mane was hitting her in the face.

Spitting, shaking herself free of itch and water, Triq shoved
back, but her little mare was too small. Savagely snarling,
wordless and furious, the creature was gaining ground. Its
hands grappled for her wrists.

It said, *"Sister."*

The word sent a chill through Triq's flesh – as though some
daemon figment had called her by name. It was a hiss, an
accusation.

"Don't bet on it, sunshine." Barging, barging repeatedly, Triq
fought to push it back. Its claws pulled chunks out of the soil,
raking at the mare's delicate legs. Triq's shortsword tore open
another ragged gash, and another. Blood seeped into the rain on

its skin. "You know what this weapon is?" Slash, jab. "Do you know?" Barge, slash. "It's the one that killed your *foal*."

The beast's expression twisted, it bared predator's teeth. Its dark eyes – so human, so animal – met hers. Just for a second, there was sanity, realisation.

Motherhood.

Then one huge fist smashed her in the face.

Triq wasn't fast enough. She snatched her head sideways, but the blow caught her ear, slamming pain through her skull and making her reel in her saddle. Thunder rolled – she wasn't sure if it was inside her clanging head.

The beast was brutal – not fast, but powerful. It reached a hand for Triq's neck and brought the fist back to slam again.

She was dizzied, sparks exploding in her vision. Pain blinded her; rain battered her shoulders. She held on to both blades – just – kept the mare under her with a grip that was pure reflex.

The creature was laughing. In and out of focus, it swam in the grey air.

The hand caught her by the throat. Squeezed, crushed. She coughed, gasped, struggled to breathe. With half-panicked determination, she hacked one serrated blade viciously at the creature's inner wrist. Fighting to inhale, she dragged it through flesh, into bone.

It ripped, rasped, tore chunks from skin and muscle.

Then it shattered, terhnwood splinters stinging at the creature's arm – and at her own.

The beast spat ferocity, threw Triq back against her saddle; clamped the injured arm in its hand. Blood pumped through its fingers. It gave ground. Her head hammering with pain, rain streaming from her skin, Triq threw herself forwards and rammed the remaining blade, point first, into the pool of stark shadow under its arm.

This time, she made it scream.

* * *

For a moment, Redlock stood silent, the huge beast reared over him.

Then he moved, hard, fast, focused. He lunged forwards, slammed both axes into its soft belly.

And slashed them downwards.

The impact jarred his elbows, he felt them hack – cutting deep, flesh parting before steel. The beast juddered, screamed. As he heaved the blades free, he was up to his elbows in gore.

Intestines spilled from twin wounds, hitting his shoulders, sliding down his chest, staining him with the creature's death.

As it crashed back to the ground, he dove sideways and heard one foreleg crack.

It buckled, but still didn't fall. Its claws were catching its own sliding guts, they dragged, filth covered, through the muddy grass.

Yet it laughed, manically, vicious humour across the downpour.

"You want to stop me, warrior? You think you can?"

With a grim twist to his mouth, Redlock hit a low crouch and slammed one axe into its rear leg, just above the dewclaw. The second axe followed it, this one into the slender bones below its knee.

Its leg shattered. It faltered, staggered.

It plunged away from him, reeling, trying to turn. It was slipping on grass soaked in blood, tangling itself in its own viscera.

What the rhez did it take to kill this thing?

A second, vicious double blow, ribs breaking under the impact.

Another.

It was faltering, now, trying to get away from his relentless onslaught. Its hide was matted with rain and blood and fluid, its intestines were spilling from it like uncoiling rope. Its eyes were wild, terrible; its breath ragged. It half turned, raised the bow as if to strike...

And it started to shake.

The muscles in its legs were quivering. It staggered, just for a second, righted itself.

But Redlock was still moving.

Holding hard to his lunch, he ducked sideways through the wall of grass and came up before it with both axes gripped centre-shaft – ready.

He heard the scream that came from the creature Triqueta was fighting...

...but the stallion was still going.

A final, desperate effort.

It rode him down.

Ecko's boosting was running out.

He was coming down, shivering with aftershock. His belly was twisting round that familiar, hollow sense of loss.

The beast was searching for him. It was lurching painfully, claws raking, hands reaching into the grass. Its face – how did it manage to look so fucking girlie? – was twisted round hurt and savagery and suspicion.

And without his supercharged strength and speed, he'd got nothing that'd touch it – no weapon, no flamer, fucking sod all. What was he supposed to do – bite it to death?

He wondered what'd happened to Tarvi – she still had her spear, her bow. Unable to come up with anything any more creative, he loosed his Bogeyman breathing: wet, dank, rotting. And he kinda hoped the beast had read the comic books.

It turned, its shattered knee twisting, but it was sharp as a hunter, seeking the sound through the rain.

"I can hear you," it said. "Kartian creature – like us, created. Better than born!"

"Make that 'upgraded'." His voice came from behind it. As it spun, he was off through the grass, heading low and swift for the lifeless black wall of the bank.

Weapons. He needed weapons. He'd sell his fucking soul right now for a carbon-fibre blade and a couple of spools of monowire...

"You think?" The creature whirled, straining to see. "Better than we?"

"You betcha ass –" The taunt ended in a clumsy exclamation as his stealth-cloak caught in the grass, a sudden line of tension across his throat.

Fuck!

The creature wasn't as dumb as it looked – it homed in on the sound instantly. A hefty yank didn't free him – the fucking Bogeyman's luck was deserting him. It was too strong to tear, too complicated to unfasten. He tugged at it again.

Harder.

Nothing.

"Now, I see you, shadow-creature!"

It was behind him, right over him, its claws gouging angry chunks out of the soil.

He heard the other one scream as the horsewoman's blade slammed home; he saw the rising rear of the wounded stallion, saw the axeman fighting, weapons in hand. Saw him go down, churned beneath the beast's claws.

Holy shit...

Then the horizon exploded.

What the *rhez*...?

Triqueta saw the light from the Monument rise, saw it burn with yellow nacre as the stones caught alight, blazing into the clouded sky. The clouds returned the glare, their underbellies burned with furious shades of flame.

The air grew tight; she couldn't breathe.

The injured beast was grappling for her, trying to seize her wrists, her hair – anything to drag her out of the saddle. She ripped her serrated blade free of its flesh and slashed, barged, driving it back.

It was weakening, starting to falter.

The light swelled, dancing into the sky in great, leaping waves of colour that played over and above the swollen grey clouds. Where they parted, the air was burning. It wasn't fire – it had no heat – it was pure, raw elemental power, leaping from the broken Monument into the covering storm.

As her own foe fell, she saw Redlock go down under the claws of the stallion.

He didn't understand how the beast could still be fighting.

It was on him, a blur of legs and claws and trailing guts that tumbled him into cold soil and thick grass.

Horses wouldn't trample – unless they were trained, or had no choice. This thing was different: those damned claws were huge and it was going to shred him meat from bone.

He tried to break sideways, get out from underneath it – but the claws were everywhere, slamming down beside him. One came down on his booted foot and he snarled, slashed the axe clean through the leg muscle.

He tasted blood as it sprayed his lips. He rolled clear.

Just as Triqueta and the mare crashed into the beast's flank, then spun and thumped it with both horse heels. It staggered, caught its claw in a reel of spilling intestine and staggered again.

With one almighty sweep, shouting wordless into the storm, Redlock smashed its other foreleg.

Tangled in its own spewing life, it fell.

And the sky above it was burning.

* * *

Ecko saw the centaur stallion crash to the ground, heard the injured mare scream denial. He saw the horizon aflame, saw the *Borealis* screaming through clouds, lighting their darkness to fantastical colour. Memories of dreams, memories of memories – fire raining from the sky.

But there was still one of these bastard things right over him, her face twisted with hate, her hands reaching through the grass, one huge claw raised to snatch his head straight off his cloak-caught shoulders.

His boosting was down: he was exhausted, nauseous. His targeters tracked the assault even as they plotted the trajectory to roll away. His muscles fired, spasmed – his tank was fucking empty, he had nothing left.

Through the rain, he thought he heard Tarvi calling him as she had once before.

"Ecko! Ecko!"

That fucking claw was *huge.*

Then a blinding concussion knocked him backwards, a sizzling flare that seared his skin. He caught the reek of burned meat as he fell, twisted awkwardly by the caught cloak. His anti-daz iris-flickered, he could still see...

...see the black and smoking shell of the centaur mare, legs twisted, cracking sticks, the ground around it blasted. At the edges of the strike, the grass burned under the rain.

And the *sky...!*

The clouds were alight, pulsing waves of colour played under and through them. The Monument blazed like a burning building, waves of fire leapt between sky and stone. The injured mare was racing away, dodging side to side as the clouds roiled with fury.

The stallion was struggling to right itself, but the axeman was right in its fucking face.

"You move, you'll get one of these up each nostril. You hear me?"

The grass was burning in patches, tiny bonfires, rising smoke.

"Ecko!" Uncaring of the majesty, the destruction overhead, uncaring of the fires under her feet, Tarvi raced down the bank. She was warm, she was scared and awed and she was in his arms. She kissed him so hard she drew blood from his lip.

His pulse screamed frenzy at her closeness – suddenly his adrenals were back in play.

He held her, kissed her, felt her shake, watched the wonder over her shoulder. The world was burning, and he stood at its very edge.

He had dreamed this. He had no breath. It was incredible.

"What the rhez is going on?" The horsewoman was ducking as though the sky would harm her. "The world's gone loco!"

"Not a fucking – !"

But even as Ecko called back, the firestorm was fading, the dancing lights failing. The clouds lost their angry pulse, the rain fell normally, solid and cool. Around them, grassfires steamed and hissed.

Gone.

Only the Monument, still glowing, nacreous and nicotine yellow – damn thing was radioactive. It stood in defiance of the stormy darkness, the wind and rain seeming suddenly, oddly calm.

Tarvi was shaking. Hell, he was shaking too. Ecko had no idea what he'd just witnessed but it sure as hell beat the laser shows of the South fucking Bank.

"Not a fucking clue," he repeated. The clouds were empty, the rain just rain. His arms did not let Tarvi go.

On its belly, the broken centaur stallion was still massive, eyes crazed in the yellow light.

Its shoulders were broader than Lugan's – it looked like

some sort of fucking giant, crouched in the grass. It was pale, rain sheeting down its skin. Its hands supported its weight and it was weakening, struggling not to fall forwards.

But it still hadn't quit.

"I'm Redlock, Faral ton Gattana," the axeman said. One axe was back through its belt-ring, he held the other casually over his shoulder. "There was a boy rode out this way, 'prentice to a Xenotian healer. His name was Feren. He was my *cousin*."

"I remember. He was weak and injured." There was no surrender in the beast's tone. It was dying, but it was challenging them to the last. *"Expendable."*

"Injured, yes – but stronger than you realised." Redlock's axehead – was it actually *steel*? – glinted in the rain. Both hands were long gloves of gore, his hair and garments were covered in Christ-knew-what – he was one savage motherfucking fighter. "What happened to his teacher?"

"The healer's *mine*."

Ecko slid closer. The stallion's core temperature was dropping fast now – it was a corpse any second.

"He's pulled your fucking guts out, dobbin, you might wanna answer the guy."

The rain was slackening now, almost as if it realised the fighting was over. The thunder rumbled, far away towards the mountains.

Triq had gone after their horses. Tarvi to the Monument itself, her face a mask of wonder and bathed in its light.

"I'll die before I answer you." The beast seemed to find this funny. "One younger will be sent, the herd will live on."

"Not if I hunt down every last fireblasted one of you." Redlock rammed the top of the axe under the monster's chin, shoved its head back and stared it straight in the eyes. "Mares, foals, your entire damned family. Every single one of them will die. By my hand. Unless you tell me – where the rhez you've come from and where the *girl* is."

"And what the fuck just happened to the sky?" Ecko stood, arms crossed and casually curious. "Like whatever blew the shit outta the village we passed? What was that, fucking *target* practice?"

The stallion slumped bodily, mane falling over his face, pushed himself back up.

"Enough theatrics, asshole." Ecko wasn't buying that crap for a second. "What's with the fucking pyrotechnics?"

Redlock forced its head back further.

"What's the healer for? Why did you need her?"

His jaw pinned by the axe, the stallion looked down his nose at both of them.

"I am here to watch, guard – charged that all this is *mine*. You'll never get down there."

Redlock said, "You're starting to piss me off."

"Down *where*?" Ecko came forwards, his eyes red, his skin the blacks and greys of the plainland night, the yellow highlights of the Monument. As the beast looked, his eyes flickered through their scans. "Lemme guess. Mines? Dungeons? Secret passages? Fucking *dwarves*?" He grinned. "We got a healer here, too. She can keep you alive – for as long as this takes. So you cough the fuck up."

The rain was thinner now, wafting chill across the wind. Redlock was right in the beast's face. "What did you come from – and where's the *girl*?"

"The girl belongs to us. Maugrim needed a healer – he knows metal, not flesh. And they were dying. Without her, he was failing – and the world would rot and perish."

"*Who* were dying?" Redlock sounded confused, but Ecko spoke over him.

"Why do I know that name?" He paused to address the sky. "What're you playing at?"

The axeman spared him a raised eyebrow. Ecko didn't respond.

The centaur was still speaking. "The cathedral is *mine*. The Range Patrols –" the beast faltered, slumped, pushed itself back up "– don't understand. Maugrim is building – passion and fire – *helping*. Our crafter, our sire, our creator and guide and vision and strength sent us to him. Together, they will forge such sights! The Powerflux... the elements... all awake now." His head fell forwards, when he raised it again, his dark eyes were cracked with increasing pain. "Our sire... made us, he... The great stones, the grass, the work of Maugrim, the flower you creatures come seeking... he trusted them to *me*."

"He?" Redlock said, confused. "What 'sire'?" The stallion snorted derision, but Ecko had realised something.

"You're nothing, you're a fucking *guard* dog. Horse. You're a *minion*."

"He..." The beast struggled, swallowed. He rallied to spit back at them, fanatical to the last. "He... made us. He... gave the grass... to me. I guard... If you stop this, the world will *rot*."

"Listen to me, you fireblasted corruption." Triqueta was behind them, a travel sack over one shoulder. She stood over the axeman, arms folded, the stones in her cheeks catching the yellow light. "Feren told us... the girl – Amethea – said this was some great temple, some elemental stronghold, some passage grave to a forgotten hero. Is that where you were made? How do we get down there?"

The stallion said, "He must... be allowed... to finish. He told us... to guard... the future. Maugrim builds... the future..."

"You are making no fucking sense." Ecko grabbed a handful of the thing's mane. He was right in its face, wishing he still had his flamer. "Jesus, who programmed fanaticism, for chrissakes?"

Redlock said bleakly, "Who is this Maugrim?"

"Guessin' he's the boss man," Ecko said. "This place is some kinda power-node. He must be building something fucking huge – like particle accelerator huge. You gettin' me? Boom."

The stallion sneered. "He told us... you're all fools. The world stagnates round you, and you don't care. Maugrim –" he was gasping now, his eyes losing focus "– fights."

"Maugrim's going to get my boot up his arse," Redlock said. "Damn all this esoteric elemental shit – where's the *girl*?"

The stallion started to laugh, faint and cold. It dissolved into coughing, blood flecked. "He owns her, mind and body and soul. She won't even *know* you."

Tarvi was beside him, hand on his arm.

"There's no way down," she said. "But I found the taer."

"Creatures born." The stallion rallied, made a last desperate effort. His anger was gone now, even his madness. His last words were a plea. "We... were made... to be better!"

Then he faltered, his great body rolling sideways.

And he stared, empty eyed, at the sky.

20: TREASURE THE MONUMENT

They faced each other over the cooling corpse of the beast, its intestine slick with mud and rain.

"So. Was that fun or what?" Under cloud and darkness, through soaking grass and spreading gore, Ecko turned his maniacal black grin on the axeman. "You sure throw one helluva party." His skin flowed with the sick yellow light of the broken Monument.

"Where the rhez did you come from?" Redlock was blood to the elbows, saturated with violence. The wound in his shoulder was ragged and shallow, a bruised scrape against the bone. And he wasn't quitting yet.

Ecko grinned. "You'd never believe me."

Over them, the night sky was lifting. Between thinning, wind-blown cloud, glimpses of moons loosed strobes of light across the grass tops. Drizzle scattered, cold and cutting. The Monument's ghostly yellow nacre washed the plain with a sickly highlight.

A ruffle marked Triqueta's return.

The sight of her reminded Ecko of his flash of dread, of the inevitably repeating pattern. Of his fear that whatever choices he made, he would he end up, eventually and hopelessly, in the same fucking place.

That, in the long run, whatever decisions he made didn't actually matter.

His freedom was an illusion.

In the comedown, he shivered.

Chrissakes.

He held his hand out to her, something on his outstretched palm.

"Yours?"

"My dice!" The horsewoman was nearly as fast as he was – the dice were gone out of his hand. She brandished them at him. "Where in the name of the Gods...?"

"You will just leave this shit lying around."

Redlock said, "What happened to the – ?"

"Gone." Triq shrugged. Blood seeped from the narrow slice in her neck. "I took what I could from the panniers. The mare'll go home – she'll take the rest of them with her." She slipped the dice into a pouch. "We're stuck."

"See? I knew horses were bad idea," Ecko said.

One of Redlock's muscled hands clamped around the front of Ecko's cloak, lifted him almost clean off his feet. Ecko inhaled, cursed his empty flamethrower. His eyes flashed red and he bared his teeth.

"Gotta *problem*?"

Redlock snarled. "What. The rhez. *Are*. You?"

"Your unavoidable destiny. Now put me the *fuck* down before I break your face."

For a moment, confrontation clamoured loud.

"You were in The Wanderer," Triq said. She put a hand on Redlock's arm, a caution. "On the bar – I remember. You're a friend of the Bard?"

"I'm his..." The words caught as he said them, but he said them anyway – spitting them at the sky, at Triqueta, at Redlock, at Eliza. "I'm his Eternal Champion or some such shit – I'm here to save your ass. Now move your fucking *hand*."

Redlock let him go.

But Triqueta was staring at him, her jaw dropped, her dice forgotten.

"If the next words out of your mouth are about coming from another world…"

Ecko grinned. "Whaddaya know, he gave you my resumé."

"Don't be ridiculous." The axeman snorted scorn.

Ecko gave a jaunty, what-the-hell shrug and stood back, untangled his cloak, flickering his optical scans.

"Toldja you wouldn't believe me."

Redlock said, 'What are you, Kartian? Another alchemical monster?"

Ecko cackled. "The Bard's nightmare vision? The Bogeyman? You tell me."

"Enough!" And Tarvi was there in the moonlight, the Monument's nacreous glow making her shimmer. She looked oddly ethereal – the taste of her still tingled on his lips. Viciously, Ecko crushed the feeling, binned it with an addict's determination – she was a trained soldier for chrissakes, not some winsome heroine that needed a protector.

Fuck that noise. He wasn't going to babysit her, or any of these guys. He was just…

Just…

What *was* he doing?

His fingers were fidgeting with Lugan's lighter, clicking the lid open and shut, open and shut. Somewhere in the back of his head he could hear Eliza laughing.

Ah, Ecko. You know just what you're doing. Don't you.

Yeah, he did. He was proving that the Bard was wrong. Proving that he could do this. Proving that he *was* a champion. He wanted to be, *needed* to be, it was just…

On the heels of his admission came a realisation, an

understanding of something...

The fractal repeats itself! Of course it does! And that means this world is *mine – all of it, it was made for me.*

Why else would the goldie girl come back?

But that means...

For a moment, Ecko's thoughts were poised on the edge of explosion, torn between impossible, opposing poles. He wanted, needed to be a hero, a fighter, a champion. He needed the purpose, the validation. But at the same time, he likewise needed to be free, to achieve his success his own way, to escape with his mind intact.

But if the pattern repeated itself, then he had no freedom – every choice he made would just land him in the same place.

Was *that* the point? Was *that* the choice he had to make, the lesson he had to learn? His therapy? If he wanted to win, then he must toe the psychological line and be "normal"...?

His snarl was almost aloud: *I'm not playing your damned game!*

"We should go," Tarvi said. She was watching the horizon, all round them. "I don't like this – we should move away from the corpses."

"Wait," Redlock said. "We're not going anywhere until we get a name and –" he blinked "– explanation out of this character."

I said "another world". You want me to prove it?

The acerbic reaction never made it past his teeth.

"Down!" Tarvi's soft cry had them all flat in the grass.

"Where?" Instantly businesslike, Redlock was fast, axes in hands. He looked ready to hook the rest of that henge thing and drag it into the dirt, pyrotechnics and all.

Beside him, Triq was arrow nocked and silent, watching the rear. Her voice was low.

"I can't see –"

"I got 'em." Ecko's telescopics spun and locked. "Beasties.

Over a klick, south-west. Whatever they are, they're heading away. They've come out *behind* us, for chrissakes."

"They? What the rhez is a 'click'?"

"Easy, tiger – they're *there*." Ecko's mottle-dark arm pointed, and there were creatures, a dull red glow of motion, heading fast away from the Monument.

Great blurs of wildflower hampered his ability to focus. *For chrissakes!* He batted at them – then a rift in the clouds bathed the prairie in yellow-white madness and his tele-focus hit: they were right up close and personal. Ember-glow eyes, grey and broken faces, pitted stone muscle limned in fire. They were misshapen and twisted, worn like old rock...

"Jeez, they're on vacation from the local fuckin' cemetery."

"*Will* you be specific?" The only thing from the cemetery was Redlock's sense of humour. Ecko scowled him to silence and they watched.

He counted ten of them, twenty, more. They lurched unevenly as they ran in ranks, extended file. The grass flashed into ash and smoke tails as they passed.

He didn't need his heatseeker to tell him how hot they burned: steam flashed from their stone skin, the night air shimmered over them.

They were unaware of their audience, their surroundings, their attention was pointed straight forwards. One-track fucking program.

Triq said, without turning round, "South-west? They're heading for Roviarath." In her half crouch, she backed to where they'd gathered, heads low. Her voice was urgent. "I have to go back – Jade has to know."

"They're goin' like greased shit off a chrome shovel." Ecko borrowed one of Lugan's favourite phrases. "Too big for a recon force. Without backup, too small to hit a city... Fuck me."

"What?" Three voices spoke together.

Spinning his focus, he turned his black-slash grin on the rest of the little group, huddled in the grass shadow in fear of the Monument's light.

"They're leavin' a trail of fuckin' destruction a blind tourist could follow – with or without a guide-chip. Someone's gettin' *way* too cocky."

"Then they think they'll win?" Triqueta's urgency sounded like panic. "I *have* to go back!"

"They're fast and light – they're vanguard." The axeman watched their reddish gleam across the tops of the grass. The rip in his shoulder was leaking darkness, he paid it no attention. "I'm guessing they should've come out under storm cover... If they're leaving a trail, it's not by accident – something else is coming."

"We can find where it started, where they got out." Tarvi was biting her lower lip, her resolve set though she'd never been so scared in her life. "I'm not giving this up, not now."

Ecko's hand twitched towards her. He sternly told it to fuck off.

"You're not hearing me!" Triq's tone was fierce, but she didn't take her eyes off the rearguard. "The Fayre's defenceless –"

"But Roviarath isn't," Redlock said. "We'll never catch them on foot, they're too fast and there are too many of them – it's not like the city won't see them coming."

"The horses can't have got that far!"

"Triq will you focus! Larred Jade's a smart man, he's got time. The Fayre's population can shelter in the city – and Syke'll see them too." As the creatures loped away into the darkness, he stood up, gauging their speed. "I need you here."

"Why?" Triq spared him a look that shredded the skin on his face. "What the rhez are you going to do?"

"If he's gonna fuck your city," Ecko commented, "he'll blow it to charcoal spikes. We passed a township? It's like a crater."

"Maybe he doesn't have that kind of power," Tarvi told him. "Maybe he's still massing. We *have* to go down – !"

"Stop bickering, the lot of you." The axeman rounded on them, his face in shadow and his tousled hair lit to bright flame. "My guess? Whatever's coming is big enough to wipe Roviarath clean off the map." He slung his axes crosswise over his shoulders and grinned. "Let's hit it before it moves, shall we?"

"You're crazed," Triqueta said softly.

But Ecko was cackling like a fiend. Apparently, he was gonna be a hero after all.

From the top of the lifeless bank, the Monument's light twisting the colours of his back, Ecko tracked the devastation.

He was showing off, getting a kick out of his superior abilities. Yeah, he knew it – and he didn't care.

So it's fucking childish. You know what?

The grass was scorched, right down to its roots: the creatures' feet had left scars in the soil.

Their wake of destruction stretched like a runway towards the horizon. He watched the receding beasties, tracking their speed.

Fuck, they were fast.

He turned and caught sight of the centaur – both ribcages were ripped open and local critters were dining in style.

Scratch one McNasty.

He kept looking.

"There's a scarp, 'bout a klick from here, must be the exit point." He scrabbled down the bank. "Not guarded, but could be beasties under the drop. Now, who's got sixty feet of rope?"

Redlock said, "Let's go."

They moved, slipping through the grass like rats through garbage.

"...From Roviarath." Behind Ecko, Tarvi spoke softly. "When we found the blasted township... my tan..."

"I hear you." Redlock's tone was gentle. "I promise you this: the nightmares will pass. I know it doesn't seem like it now, but you'll be all right."

"We all die – and we all lose people we love," Triq said. "And the Count of Time heals all things. Live now, look forwards – life's short."

"I'm going to find whatever burned that town." Glancing back, Ecko saw Tarvi's profile, limned in the Monument's light as she turned to look at the axeman. The look, the memory, sent a shock through his adrenals – a shock that was unexpected and completely unfamiliar. *What the fuck…?* "And I'm going to –"

"Boo!" He wasn't even sure why he'd interrupted them.

"Shit!" Redlock's axe missed his nose by a nanometre. "You damned…! Don't do that again!"

Tarvi smothered a chuckle. Triq poked the axeman wickedly in the ribs.

Above them, a rift in the cloud bathed the grass in brilliant gold.

"You're funny," Redlock said. "But I've no idea who you are, have no reason to trust you – and advise against pulling shit like that again. Tarvi rides from Jade; she bears a pennon." Tarvi smiled at him. "You – better have damned good reason for being out here."

"I felt like a vacation." His grin was merciless. "Trust me or don't – that's your fucking problem." He blinked. "Let's get the hell on with this."

"We're in this together now, Ecko, all of us." Tarvi laid a hand on Redlock's arm. Again, the unfamiliar adrenaline spiked. "I've heard of you, Faral ton Gattana – who hasn't? We have to do this thing."

Redlock said, "I work alone. Triq's an old friend."

"Then stick ten paces behind me and, if anyone asks, we're goin' the same way." Ecko's black eyes were expressionless. "I'll save some bad guys for ya."

"Will you two pack it in?" Triqueta was watching the way the beasties had gone. "My family are out there," she said. "They're under threat – and I'm here with you idiots. Syke'll be in a lot deeper horseshit if we don't sort this now." She threw a glance over her shoulder. "Let's find this sonofamare."

"Well, whaddaya know," Ecko said, his black grin broadening. "The adventure that started in the tavern ends with the fuckin' underground maze. The big bad guy? He'll be right in the basement – along with the flatscreens and the white goods."

Triq said, "What the rhez are you talking about?"

"He does that," Tarvi told her. "You'll get used to it. Sometimes I think he's seen all of this before."

"No fucking shit." Keeping his cackle to himself, Ecko slipped back to the scarp.

"Abandon Hope, All Ye..."

The short climb was an easy one; the moons had fought through all but the thinnest cloud and handholds and outcrops were plentiful. With his cloak tucked back, Ecko reached the base in moments and peered into the rift. The air was blood warm, it tasted like all kinds of wrong.

His heatseeker picked out the breadcrumbs – touches of fading warmth still clung to the rock, char marks like handprints. They showed the passage of the departing beasties – and the route into the maze.

Easier to follow than a ball of fucking string.

Nothing else moved.

Faintly disappointed at the lack of door-guard grunts, Ecko loosed his cloak and went into the cave mouth.

Here, goblins. Heeeeeere, goblins, goblins.

The floor was uneven, the narrow walls had protrusions that caught his elbows. There was a tall space over his head, as if the triangular crack in the cliff face simply stretched backwards into the stone, but the passageway itself was tight.

Comfortingly so.

At last, the arch of sky was gone from over his head, the endless wind in his ears had ceased. In the sudden quiet, they were cold and they sang with imagined sounds. Ecko found himself breathing relief, his shoulders falling. He hadn't even been aware of the tension until he'd let it go.

Walls. Ceiling. Stone. It wasn't quite the old underground south of the river, but *fuck* was that better.

"What do you see?" Redlock was right behind him.

"Dark. Little patches of heat that say 'bad guys went this-a-way'. How come there's no beasties, no traps, no door?"

"No one comes out here," Tarvi said softly. "Why would they leave the trade-roads – they've got everything they want. They don't care about a load of broken rocks; they care about the grass harvest and the terhnwood flow, whether they can trade for a luxury this halfcycle. There's only the taer, and few remember that."

"Some things," Ecko commented, "just don't fucking change."

He flicked out his heatseeker.

And saw there was light.

It was so faint, he could almost have imagined it. It danced broken, refracted and reflected from something he couldn't see – something below the level of the steadily descending floor. If he looked up, minute echoes played in the crack over his head, stalactites – or were they the other ones? – had an edge of glitter, like amethyst chandeliers in some trippy-hippie bedroom. There were lichens on the wall, opening like a myriad mouths, as though they hungered for the taste.

They were kinda creepy.

Whatever this was, it was no fucking dungeon – no set of mines. This was more like fantastical potholing – never mind sixty feet of rope and a grapple pistol, he needed a hard hat and a flashlight.

The illumination was just enough for his starlites. As the harsh rock walls around him became a soft wash of grey-green, he crouched low to the coarse, pebbled floor and crept downwards.

The creatures' heat had left a trail of soot a blind cleaning 'bot could follow.

The others came after him, weapons in hand.

Slowly, the passageway began to open out.

Here, there were fragments of regular stonework in the natural stone walls, nonsensical oddments of order amid the rising rock ripples of an expanding cave. Ecko could hear the steady drip of water.

There was more space here. Above them, a crack in the ceiling had lifted and opened out into a wide and jagged layer of fangs, uneven and shining as the cracked light touched them.

The trail came from *there* – on the cave's far side, a wide, dark mouth full of dancing glimmer. The burns led that way like an unwound ball of string. If the goblins were guarding anything, he'd guess that'd be the door.

The girls were whispering, their voices carrying up into tiers of teeth.

And the small cave answered them.

A shattered crystalline sound, atonal and dissonant. It oscillated in uneven waves, an irregular rebroadcast from stalactites and walls.

Ecko shuddered. Redlock turned, but they'd quietened instantly.

The four of them paused in silence.

Water dripped, faintly, maddeningly regular.

Gesturing for the others to stay put, Ecko was off. He made

no sound; he left no trace. Following the beasties' trail, he ducked under the arced maw of spikes and raced, swift as a darting insect, across the openness to slam his back against the far wall.

He looked into the entranceway.

A target-length before him, the ceiling lowered to twin fangs, joined floor to ceiling as if the jaws were lodged half shut. Between them were the recently shattered remains of a forced stone door – behind it a throat that swallowed the light.

Before this entranceway, like a towering guard, was the biggest fucking wind chime he'd ever seen. Suspended from the ceiling, it was taller than he was – hell, it was taller than Lugan – it was more than an artwork, more than some fucked-up chiming-crystal mobile... The rocklight at its centre was trapped to loose crazed rave-party shafts of brilliance across the entranceway, out across the cave and deep into the darkness of whatever lay beyond.

He flicked out his starlites and stared, stunned.

Ecko had never been one for nightclubs – even before Pilgrim had gotten a hold of them. Now, though, he stood as if he were the last fucker left on the dance floor – alone amid a spangled kaleidoscope of reds, blues, purples. Dark lights surrounded him, like a promise – or a threat. The thing lit the walls to a hundred shades of insane goth.

As he looked, he could see that it was damaged – it was half hanging, crystals split and darkened, smeared in soot.

An ancient light show, shattered by the heat of the sortie?

Experimentally, he let out the faintest, audible breath.

And it answered him, a struggling discord of warning.

Echo, Ecko. It was a security system, for chrissakes, guarding the doorway. If the cave out there condensed noise, it must've been placed in exactly the right position to go off like an aural claymore the second someone coughed...

Fuck knows how long it had hung here, singing gently to

the *drip-drip-drip* of the water and waiting for something to set it off... Then the stone beasties had kicked the door down and thundered past it like Lugan's old Harley. *Whumph* – exit one doorbell.

So – this "Maugrim" not only left a "bad guy this way" trail for the city authorities to follow... but he disabled his own defences?

He was either a prize asshole or he knew something they didn't.

Maybe both.

Bollocks.

Telling himself he was only going to take a little look – who knows, maybe it had a switch? – he slipped over and past the broken remnants of the door.

Redlock was sweating.

The air was close and still. He was uneasy, dry mouthed, aware of the reek of dried blood and the itch of his now-stiffened garments. There was a stone in his boot.

Behind him, Tarvi twitched constantly, hands fidgeting with her neckline, her belt. He was perturbed by her inexperience, concerned about some explosive delayed reaction to the horrors she'd seen. Behind her, Triqueta twisted her ankle and cursed under her breath – she felt like rising tension. He trusted her combat instincts, her courage and reliability... but she didn't like enclosed spaces and he knew the rock was pressing down on her chest and throat. She wasn't one to scream – but she may well loose the Banned's battle cry purely to defy her own fear.

As for the other one...

Trust me or don't.

Redlock had been riding the trade-roads nearly twenty returns. He knew the Varchinde, its cities and markets, its trade and its predators. He trusted his instincts as much as his axes...

and this whole damned thing stank like last week's fish.

Despite Tarvi's assurances, he trusted that... thing... about as much as he trusted his one-time wife.

Damned crusaders and damned kids – he worked alone for a *reason*.

Whatever that "Ecko" thing was, when it turned, he'd be ready for it.

Past the busted door, Ecko slunk through a tight neck of stone and paused at the edge of a broad, flat-floored chamber. A scent teased his nostrils – something familiar – oh for chrissakes so familiar...

He stopped, breathed it in like a fragrance.

It was overwhelming, so good, so *missed*. A scent that breached walls, worlds and memories and brought his past into his forebrain with a crash.

This is the Bike Lodge, mate. We'll find some work for ya, gotta pull your weight round 'ere.

For a moment, he clung insanely to the hope that he was home. That he'd passed his fucking test, that she'd taken pity on him – that he'd stumbled through some fucking interdimensional *rift* – and he was there, waking up in his own sleeping bag. That it was all over; that tomorrow, the only thing that awaited him was a twist of solder and Lugan's battered old arc welder...

The scent caught in his throat, it made his breathing ragged, like a sob.

Please...!

Between one shaft of crystal light and the next, he tumbled down the crack between realities – and the closeness was too much, he couldn't bear it. He had no idea how much he'd missed it until it was shoved right in his face. His own denial shattered, standing in its fragments, he found himself almost in tears.

This hadn't happened to him!

Tell me this whole thing's a fucking dream, please! Grey plugged me in, didn't he? And you've found me? You finally fucking found me! Tell me this bullshit ride is over!

The smell was engine oil. Rich and dark, filling his senses with images of a home he may never have left. He could smell metal, the faint tang of fuel. He inhaled it, filled his lungs and his soul with it. He could picture the Bike Lodge in his head, Lugan's battered desk, the fridge for the endless beers, the frames and the tanks and the engines scattered across the floor...

...the rain, silver on black windows.

It was so real – *so real* – that if he held onto it hard enough everything else would be gone, a total-immersion game that was just playing on the headset in his hands. He could see it, that tiny screen – on it, distant now, grass and moons and air and cities of white and endless unrolling fucking roads...

He could drop it.

And he could stand on it. Feel it shatter. Gone.

But the maddened, broken searchlights of the crystal hanging were lurching through the chamber, passing over his skin and leaving tiny twists of colour in their wake.

In amongst the smells of his home, there was another scent, equally familiar, but not one that belonged in the ferrocrete walls of the Bike Lodge.

He could smell death – the sickly sweet stench of rotting flesh.

The real world cracked, crisped and was gone in a flash of flame, burned by the exiting critters, by the Monument's fire. The fiction rose to swallow him, back into the caverns of the Varchinde plains.

There was no escape from his own head.

You fucking wuss. Get a grip. Deal with it.

He dried his oculars on a corner of his cloak. Took Lugan's lighter out of a pouch and crushed it until his fingers *hurt*.

And he was angry: sick of being taunted, of being jerked around while she laughed at him. Of being led by the fucking nose. Of understanding one minute – and being at a total fucking loss the next. Of hearing voices, of having dreams. Of Tarvi's...

Don't think about it!

He was walking into a trap – she'd laid out a trail he couldn't help but follow... and everything he passed told him Maugrim was waiting for him. For them.

Yeah? Well bring it on.

Wherever she was, he made her a promise – a promise of what he'd fucking do to her when he got out of here.

"You hear me? ELI-ZAH! *You hear me?*"

And the crystal detonated.

"Shit!"

Triqueta was weapons on the floor, hands over her ears.

Around her, the cave exploded in a single, terrible scream. The sound was impossible, multilayered, discordant and crystalline. It smashed into her like shards of broken stone. It was the death shriek of a thousand thin, wild voices that slammed back from every rockface, lashed from every leering tooth.

Redlock's boots spat dirt as he broke into a run.

Tarvi was after him, calling Ecko's name.

Retrieving her bow – and relieved that Syke hadn't seen that lapse – Triq moved more slowly, watching the cave around them.

The sound ended in a single, Gods-almighty smash.

Disharmonic echoes reverberated, jangling her teeth, but the scream had gone.

And the quiet was deafening.

Nothing moved. The crazed lights had died. The water drip-drip-dripped as though it hadn't even noticed.

She heard Redlock call her, his voice a crack of precision

through lingering layers of resonance. He didn't sound like he was fighting.

He sounded...

The last of the crash flowed back from the walls and was gone, a dying wave of sound.

In it, she could hear Ecko laughing.

Ecko said, "You mother*fucker*."

In her hands, Tarvi held the rocklight. It lit her face to ardour and wonder.

And it lit the chamber – rock walls more regular, a lower ceiling. This one looked like it'd been hewn, indiscriminately pickaxed out of the stone. In places, the semi-regular brickwork showed again – but that wasn't what Ecko was looking at.

Around him, an oil-stained stone floor, rags and old papers, scatters of nuts and washers, fuel cans, spray cans, demijohns. The tarp in one corner covered the bike – he hadn't yet gone that way. He was cackling like his mind had finally fucking snapped.

I broke your doorbell, Maugie. Come and get me why don'tcha?

Around him, the spiralling fairground lights had gone. Occasional, now-stilled refractions lit the walls, colours surreal. The smell was still there – the smell of home, the smell of death – but he was looking for something.

He unclamped his fingers. Lugan's lighter was still in his hand.

Fuel.

Refilling his tanks would be ten kinds of fucking awkward – but if he'd just woken up every major cave-dwelling nasty from here to the doors of Hell, well, he kinda needed a weapon.

He searched.

Behind him, Redlock was picking up washers like they

were the gold coins of some fucking dragonhorde… letting the steel tumble through his fingers, jingle as it hit the floor. His expression was wary. He kept one axe in his hand and one eye on the entranceway.

Tarvi held the light high and looked wider. She picked things up and stared at them as if they would hiss into steam and be gone. She moved gracefully, light on her feet and her hair…

Stop it.

Triqueta appeared in the doorway, patches of light on her skin, her mouth gaped round speechless shock. Chuckling, Redlock threw a handful of washers at her and she caught a couple, opened her hand to stare at them.

"White-metal? How…?"

"How much luxury d'you want?" He laughed at her. She stopped to pick up another handful, stared at them – then lunged to stuff them down the front of his shirt. While he swore, laughing, she ran for it, feet skidding on rusting metal. Grinning, he picked up a random gear and spun it at her like a discus. It didn't fly very well.

Kinda freaked that'd found the treasure before they'd actually mashed the bad guy, Ecko picked up another can, shaking it to hear the sloshing of –

Tarvi screamed.

His boosting lurched – now, which was verging on annoying. It spluttered, coughed into life like an old engine, carried him to her side even as he wondered where the bad guy was at.

He couldn't keep fucking doing this – his endocrine system wasn't getting time to reboot for chrissakes. Was she *trying* to wear him out?

But she was backing out of a corner of the chamber, clinging to the rocklight as if to draw its warmth.

She said something, cleared her throat and said it again, "I know this man."

Redlock had stopped fooling. He stood by the chamber

wall – by the soot marks that told where the beasties had blundered through. Stuffing a handful of washers in a pouch, Triq crouched by the entrance to the broken crystal, the light glittering from the stone in her cheek.

Tarvi backed into Ecko, small, soft frame, hair – *again* – in his nose. He half expected her to turn round, bury her face in his shoulder – was wanting it and dreading it and working out how he could push her away – but she was staring, transfixed, at the source of the reek.

Ecko said softly, "Fuck." He'd found where the death smell was coming from.

Three corpses, twisted and broken. He'd seen such things before.

But they were *metal.*

A plated hide, an exquisitely fine insect carapace, covered each one – eyelids, fingertips, genitals. Like one of his Tech's, Mom's, more fucked up experiments...

...trusst me, Tamarlaine. I can make you the besst. Hold your faith in me, my little one, my child, my obssession and creation. You wissh ssuperpowerss? I can make your dreamss come true...

...they'd been enhanced, a botch-job that'd gone terrifyingly off the rails – and he *knew* how it felt to have your skin delicately peeled back, your flesh exposed, the naked and intimate secrets of muscle and fibre and joint, all bared to eyes unseen in the darkness. He knew the screaming and the savagery of the pain, knew the terror of being that utterly helpless and vulnerable. He knew the hope, the struggle to retain self and sanity as you were remade, transformed into something more than human...

He'd survived. Through trial by blood and terror and nightmare and painstaking reconstruction, he'd survived. He'd survived by sheer motherfucking will.

And he was unbreakable. Nothing could ever torture him like that again.

These fuckers hadn't been so lucky.

He found he was shaking, nausea in his throat from too much adrenaline. Against him, Tarvi was steady and warm.

"Ecko?"

His hand was on her shoulder, a grip like steel, but she didn't wince or pull away. Her hand went over his, pale skin against the mottle his Mom had given him.

An anchor.

He said, "Maugrim did this?"

"That one – there – he trained with me. I didn't know him well, but –" her voice shook "– name of the Gods, what *happened* to him?"

Anger, fear, outrage, heat in his face indicating a rising need to throw up.

"Seems someone likes to play." His rasp was like a broken saw, as rusted as the steel that was scattered across the floor. Steel that this bastard had been using to create some fucking superbeing. "And got it wrong."

The rocklight shone from the tiny plates, each one crafted with an expert touch that even Ecko couldn't match. Beneath them, the flesh was beginning to decompose, to swell, blackening, through the cracks. Their eyes were open, death masks twisted with the kind of exquisite agony he fucking understood.

He *understood*.

There were marks on the stone where the cave-critters had come, but they'd turned away, empty bellied. The guy Tarvi knew had a plate across his mouth, carved with a ghastly impression of a smile.

Someone had not only done this, they'd enjoyed it. Found humour in it.

Ecko retched, controlled himself. His mouth tasted of bile. Jesus, looking at this, he was beginning to think it was Eliza who needed the fucking shrink already...

In the back of his mind, he heard his conversation with the Bard.

I'm s'posed to think this is real?

I'm supposed to think it's not?

Kale, talking about pain. Pareus, burning to death...

Tarvi turned round, wrapped herself in his arms.

Looking over her shoulder, Ecko found his rage blazing uncontainable, his own pity and helplessness and snarling frustration mocking him. *Dance, Ecko, daaaaaaance!* To be that close to home – and then to face his own most terrible and most elating memory...

Eliza was taunting him, making him *feel*.

And, even against his will and better judgement, he knew that those feelings were growing stronger.

21: CRAZED THE GREAT LIBRARY, AMOS

The air was thick and shadowed, soft with age and decay.

In the gloom, Jayr the Infamous shivered uneasily, absently rubbing her scarred arms. Chill breaths of draught exhaled rot and damp stone. Her boots sank in softness, a carpet of age across a broken floor. In places, curious creeper had forced itself through the wall and then died from the lack of light.

At one end of the long hallway, the Great Library had crumbled into collapse and pale sunlight slanted through the dust, touching delicate fingers to the rubble below. She could see the faded corners of books protruding, as if they still sought rescue.

She shuddered.

Over her, rising ringed balconies led up to a once-bright, real-glass dome, now dark with bird droppings and age. One pane was cracked, others missing, and the balcony edges beneath were fallen away with returns of invading weather. Their remnants covered the central mosaic in rubble and fragments of once-carved woodwork.

If she held up her rocklight, she could see only shadows. They hung in the dust between bookshelf and wall, balcony and branch and empty doorway, they lurked as though they were *waiting*.

Jayr could take a Range Patrol champion to pieces in shorter time than it took to tell it. And this place was giving her the *creeps*.

Ress sat cross-legged by a small scatter of books. He wore old pince-nez and he squinted at faded scribblings, words and pages that dissolved to nothing at his touch. Occasionally, he reached to scrawl something on a fresh page to his other side. He was frowning intently, rubbing his short beard and blinking in the poor light.

Jayr kicked out a clean place and sat by him, back to the wall, scarred shoulders crawling with tension. She reached to pick up a book – and the thing fell through her hands like sand.

Suppressing another shudder, she rubbed her palms on her breeches and picked up the next one.

"Careful." Ress's whisper was instinctive, the gloom swallowed it whole.

"Like one more dead thing's going to matter." Her callused fingers were covered in old webs, her lap was full of dust. She, too, was voice lowered, almost fearing what she'd disturb in this forgotten place. "This is loco. Five days on a downriver barge – why did I have to come? You know I should've –"

"Jayr." The apothecary grinned briefly. "Change of focus won't kill you."

"What're you even looking for?"

"Alchemy," Ress told her. "Half man, half horse. Monsters. Where they came from, who made them. Why." He crooked an eyebrow. "Seems the Bard isn't so crazed after all."

"We're the crazed ones." She was young, still prone to sulking. "Still don't know why you need me."

He chuckled, the sound oddly subdued.

"Your horse has got to heal. And you can read… feel… basic Kartian, which I can't. I need your strength." He glanced at her over the tops of the pince-nez. "This is Amos, and I could do worse for a bodyguard."

"Against what?" She eyed the shadows. "Is there something else in – ?"

"Not in here, Jayr, out there." He chuckled. "Any monsters in here are only in the books. Now, make yourself useful. Stuff on ancient, Tusienic discoveries – how they made bretir, and chearl. Whatever those things were, they came from the same –"

"They were no match for us, I'll tell you that." The memory of the fight made her grin, brief and tight. "I hope Triq's okay."

"You're both infamous, Infamous." He shoved his glasses higher up his nose. "Now work!"

Jayr grumbled, "Why'd you teach me to read Grasslander anyway – too many letters." After a final, uneasy survey of the dimness and the filth, though, she looked at the book in her hands. It was called *Reasonless Phemonenæ*, the words embossed into a battered leather cover. Something long dead had nibbled the corners. Glancing at Ress, she was tempted to put it back.

Then a word caught her eye.

Listed as part of the contents was "Memory".

On an obscure impulse, she let the pages fall open, and blew gently at an eternity of insect husk.

The writing had faded to deep blue, ink bled out into the page. She brought the rocklight close and began to read:

Thus it appeared to my eyes upon landing that the Strait has fooled us, and we had failed to disembark upon the much-beloved Substance of the Gods, yet had instead landed upon the cruel shores of a hostile world. The fabled and beauteous inhabitants of the Ilfead-Syr *were illustrated in old murals taller yet than a man, and more graceful than the most elegant of women, powerful of mind and body and voice. They bore skin between their fingers and between*

*their toes, and they were able to see in the turbulent waters
that surround the island.*

*We carried gifts to them – the strength of muara, the
power of cauxe, the beauty of ghyz, and we carried the
greetings of the mainland, not heard in a thousand returns
of the spring.*

*How could we have believed that the Substance of the Gods,
the Ilfead-Syr, the home of the Well of the World's Memory,
could be so utterly chilling to the souls of such as we?*

*The chill could be heard in the silence, felt in the air,
it leeched the warmth from our very feet. The weakest of
the crew broke and ran for the water to lose the sense of
nothingness in the turbulence of the waves.*

*How long we walked with the chill sinking into our bones,
I do not now remember, but we found at last the island's
inhabitants, their beauty no fable and seen even in their
deaths. Yet their faces were empty – their eyes held nothing
but nothing, telling us that nothing had been their deaths.*

Jayr paused and read that bit again. It didn't make any more
sense the second time.

*How better can my poor language explain what we have
seen? How long they have been dead I do not know, but
even now, they are still whole, as if only asleep, and there
are thousands of them here.*

*Aleché, God of Inspiration, grant me only that I may
portray the depth of horror witnessed by our eyes. The
farther we searched, the more dead we found, slumped in
their homes, or curled against walls where they had simply
fallen. All were made more terrible by their faces, faces
that held, not despair, and yet not relief or release, and yet
not even a sense of duty, guilt or fear. Their eyes reflected
nothing, they held emptiness, lethargy, apathy, as though a*

thriving and joyous population, the Guardians of the Ilfe, the Well of Memory, an entire race and culture, had died of simply giving up.

Jayr shivered and rubbed at the back of her neck where her hair was tickling. It was getting colder in here.

And the Ilfe *was gone! Gone as if it had never been! How is the World to live without her memory? My horror complete, I turned to my crew, seeking their support and friendship, only to find myself alone in the glade of the Well. Alone on this island of the dead, on an island where this empty death would still be stalking.*

My journey back to the ship has been as a nightmare to me. Fallen with the dead of the island are now the dead of my friends, their faces holding the same awful emptiness, even their weapons undrawn. What manner of enemy can cause such utter destruction? Why have I, and only I, been spared the fate of the crew?

So thus do I wait for this death to stalk me at last. I write what I have seen, and it shall be hidden in the hope that it will return to the mainland to be seen by other eyes than mine. All my horror and my grief do I pour into this text, and when it is gone, I feel that this death of nothing will come for me.

The fears of this island are founded in reality. Do not, I beg of you, ever return here. I pronounce this island as Ramm-Outhe – Accurséd of the Gods. We have lost the Ilfe. The World will die because she cannot remember.

Jayr put the book down and rubbed bone-deep cold from her arms and shoulders. Her scars crawled with tension.

"Ress...?"

"I said work!"

"Listen to this." She read him the tale, watching him, saw his eyes widen and his shoulders shiver as hers had done. His jaw lax, he took off the glasses and his expression washed with perplexity, then rising disbelief. As she finished, he mouthed the word "*Ramm-Outhe*", then said, "There's a tale that the Bard visited Rammouthe on some sort of mission, and came back scragged. Everyone that went with him died. There's a daemon, a beastie, meant to be incarcerated there?"

"And it cooked him, I take it?"

"He didn't find a beastie, he got munched by the wildlife. The tale of the daemon goes back further than that though, I'm trying to remember how it goes..."

"What? You lose your memory too?"

That made him blink, almost as if he sought to attach significance to what she'd said – as if the loss of the world's memory could somehow also affect their own. He unclipped his glasses, pointed them at her.

"Have you ever been to Fhaveon? It's an odd city – it's built backwards, like a fortress facing the water, facing Rammouthe Island across the Bava Strait. The tale goes that Fhaveon was built on the site of an older city, a city razed to dust and ashes by the very daemon that Roderick went seeking. When the daemon was defeated, and Saluvarith built Fhaveon, the God Samiel sent a creature of light and warfare to be a guardian, and to ensure that the daemon would never return."

"Come off it," Jayr said. "That's exactly the garbage they tell in the market –"

"Put the book down." The voice was cold, female. Both Ress and Jayr started. Jayr was on her feet, her stance instinctive and her breathing tense – but the woman stood a way back, cloaked in the library's shadows.

"Dear Gods." Ress scrabbled upright, almost dropping his pince-nez.

The woman was tall, gaunt, pale, she wore the gloom like a

gown. Caressed by darkness, one long slim leg was visible, one white shoulder, one side of a sharp-boned face.

"My Lord." As flustered as she'd ever seen him, Jayr watched Ress touch both hands to his sternum and bow, spreading his arms wide. It was an obscure and formal gesture the Banned rarely used. As he shot her a look, she awkwardly did the same, feeling oversized and clumsy. The book in her hand felt like it was made of stone.

"Ress of the Banned. Jayr the Infamous. What brings you to my library?"

"Knowledge, my Lord." Ress was almost stuttering. "I –"

"The centaurs." She gave a brief nod. "I understand why the Banned would be curious – half man, half horse, is that not your prerogative?"

Jayr said, "How do you – ?"

"Know?" The woman gave a soft, chill laugh. "This is Amos, and I am her Lord. Little happens in the Greater Varchinde that the grass does not bring to the walls of my city."

"You're *Nivrotar*?" The question was out before Jayr could stop it. "Ah... my Lord?"

"You take me for a custodian?" Nivrotar, Lord of Amos, probably the single most feared of the Grassland's City Wardens, unwrapped herself from the shadow. "There have not been custodians in the library for many returns."

As tall as Jayr, as lean as a knife blade, face angular and beautiful and cold, she carried herself as if the library was her courtroom. White skin and black hair, a black gown that left one long leg free, that bared her shoulders and whispered on her skin as she moved. The shadows seemed to follow her, a cloak of darkness she bore with long ease.

She wasn't Grasslander. Her colouring was Kartian, Tundran? Her features and poise Archipelagan? She was every realm of the world and more.

She was alone.

"Give me the book." Her outstretched hand was not a request. About her wrist there was a black tattoo, a design that curled like creeper up the inside of her arm.

"My Lord, we didn't mean to intrude." Ress tucked his pince-nez safely in a pouch. "The door wasn't guarded – wasn't locked..."

"Wasn't standing," Jayr muttered, innocently eyeing the roof.

"Knowledge is forgotten treasure." The Lord of Amos opened the book Jayr had been reading, carefully turned the pages. "Only I walk here still – when the strife of my city wearies me." She shut the book with a slam – and it burst into a cloud of dust and crumbling leather. Gone. "You know this, Ress of the Banned – the time of the scholar is passing, just as it did for you." She tilted her hand, let the dead book tumble to the floor. "And you, Jayr the Infamous." For a moment, she met Jayr's dark eyes and her smile was almost feminine. "This is an odd place for a Kartian slave."

"I'm not – !" Ress laid a hand on her arm and she made an effort to curb her temper. "I'm Banned now."

"Of course you are." She blew dust from her outstretched palm. "The Banned is the last refuge of the exile, and has assumed its place with pride and power." Jayr shot Ress a baffled look, but Nivrotar waved a long, white hand. "One day," she said, "you must tell me the tale of how you fled the... ah... entertainments of the Kartian PriestLords, and joined Syke's heretical ranks. One day, but not today." She smiled at both of them, but the expression was sharp, curious, careful. "Today, we speak of alchemy – and of the daemon you so carelessly mention."

Ress said, "The Bard –"

"Ah, the Bard." For a moment, Nivrotar frowned – a fragment of recollection, a figment crossing her face. Then she shivered and gathered the shadows about her. "The Bard has been here many times, seeking answers and direction, seeking

the very daemon you cannot name." Her smile was touched –
a flicker of sensuality. "I am the Lord of Amos, I have walked
here with him and the words have been our sanctuary. There
are words we have read and regretted, words we have read
and rejected. And there are some words we have dared not
read at all. Are you so wise, Ress of the Banned? Are you
wiser than we?"

"My Lord..." Ress gathered his breath. "You're answering
my questions with questions." He was narrow eyed, wary and
guarded. "The creatures that we fought, can you tell me what
they were?"

"Perhaps I have forgotten." She smiled. "Perhaps I, too,
have lost my memory, and what lore I once knew. Knowledge
is power, Ress of the Banned – and a wise foe will take that
power from you. Yet hear this."

She paused, ensuring that she had his full attention.

"You speak of the fall of Tusien and the fate of her lore. And
you speak of the founding of Fhaveon the fortress, the might
that guards the Varchinde against our foe. That foe, Ress of
the Banned, was the daemon Kas Vahl Zaxaar. It was he who
destroyed Tusien and her learning, he who made war upon the
Grasslands and destroyed the great city of Swathe."

There was something odd, almost ironic about her tone, as
though there was some private jest that she could not share.

"And then Saluvarith came, and Fhaveon came, and Rhan
came – and the daemon was defeated and he faded from
our ken. Perchance it is Vahl Zaxaar himself who holds the
alchemical formulae you seek, I know not." She smiled thinly
and brushed the last of the dust from her hands. "Sadly, neither
I nor my library retain the learning of Tusien, such things are
not held within these books. You are wasting your time." She
stepped back, and the shadows slid over her skin. "Should you
need me, call at my gates. The tan commander will grant you
escort. Farewell."

Another step, and she dissolved into the dust.

"What the *rhez*?" Jayr took two steps after her, saw no one. "Hey!" The word was gone in the shadows – there was no one to hear it. The Lord of Amos may as well have dispersed into the decaying air. *"Hey!"*

"Hush!" Ress was on his knees. He replaced the pince-nez, carefully sifted through the remnants of the book. "You can't shout in here – vibrations – you'll cause all kinds of trouble." As Jayr watched, he picked up a corner of leather, turned it over to reveal the paper peeling from the inside. "That was crazed – but she's right. There's power in knowledge." He was almost trembling. He picked up fragments of a page, pieced them together in a pattern on the mosaic. "'Kas' means daemon, and 'Vahl Zaxaar' – I know the name –"

"She's completely loco."

"She not, though." Another piece – and another. "There's something here – why else would she destroy the book? Our mention of Ramm-Outhe? Maybe there is something there? Maybe it was a warning?"

"If the Lord of Amos wanted to warn you, she'd put a crossbow bolt through your foot. Can we leave now? She's just told us there's nothing here."

"Why give us that name, though? Was she jesting? You're right, Vahl Zaxaar's a market tale, a figment –"

"Figments!" Jayr looked at the page, puzzled together on the floor. "She's loco, and she's just told us to leave. Come on, let's get out of here."

"I think she's hiding something." He slid a final piece into the page. "The alchemical formula must be –"

"She's not *hiding* anything. She said that Roderick's been through the library –"

"Doesn't mean it isn't here," he said. "Shut up and help me."

"All right. Just one more." Jayr tore at a nail, muttering, and gave a short, pointed sigh. Dust danced. "Then we get the rhez out of here." Sulkily she joined him, kneeling on the tiny, cold tiles.

He said, "Last one. Promise."

For a moment, she eyed the fragmented page, then she glanced at Ress's expression and groaned.

"You'd better mean that." She spat out the nail fragment.

The fine writing was outlined with sigils, all now so faded she could barely see them. They hurt her eyes.

"What can you see?" he asked.

"Looks like someone's used this as a cleaning rag." She studied it for a moment, trying to piece together letters and sigils into some form of narrative. "*'Time when Substance of the Gods, In grip...'* Then something about flame. There's mention of a 'Promise', and a 'Master of Light'." She looked up. "This is crazed."

"Maybe," Ress said softly. "But this has been crazed since poor Feren fled those monsters. Let's get on."

"For Gods' sakes," she told him. "It's the damned great prophecy that foretells the end of the world. I mean, I can't even make half of it out. '*...When the Final Guardian, is broken at the...'* Past?" She blinked, words swimming on the fragmented page. "Huge chunks of this are missing. I can see something about a *'darker jest...'* blank, *'...fear manifest'*."

Inexplicably, the hairs on the back of her neck were standing up.

He looked at her. "Do you understand any more of it?"

She held the rocklight close. "*'Time the Flux begins to...'*" She shrugged. "That bit's gone. Then, *'Nothing is more powerful, at last than...'* The rest's too rotted to see."

Her chill was growing.

"Right at the end," he told her.

She was almost nose on parchment. "*'When love of life is distant...'* then *'Time the World becomes...'* The last word of both lines is missing."

With an odd relief, she pulled her attention away from the mess, rubbed a hand over her hurting forehead, rubbed the prickle from her forearms.

"Okay," she said, half defiant. "So we've got half-eaten verses of poetry."

But Ress was thinking now, restless and intense.

"'The Substance of the Gods' – is Rammouthe, we've just learned that. The 'Final Guardian' – Roderick is or was a Guardian of the Ryll. The 'Master of Light' – at the founding of Fhaveon, Samiel sent a creature of light to defend the city. Nivrotar's just told us that much."

Ress was staring at the shadows, unseeing. In his glasses, he looked like a crazed prophet about to disturb the soft air with a rant about the Final War.

"The 'Flux' – the Elemental Powerflux that's supposed to connect their souls, light and darkness, ice and fire. Roderick was right – he was *right* – this is all somehow connected."

"You'll be telling me he's got a champion from another world next." Jayr resisted the temptation to scatter the fragments into the dirt. "I don't know why this even matters!"

Ress began to chew his lip, eyes losing their focus.

"You wouldn't believe how much it matters! I need to think."

"You think yourself in circles." She sat back, crossed her arms and watched him.

"...I think there's something else here, Jayr. Something more than just the big daemon beastie..."

"What?" Jayr had lost him already. "Why?"

He stood up sharply and began to pace to and fro upon the shattered mosaic.

"The book Nivrotar broke, the loss of the world's memory. The island's inhabitants died of emptiness, of apathy. Surely a daemon would be all fire and lightning and torture and hooks?" He turned, his eyes focused and oddly bright. "I think there's something *else*."

Jayr snorted. "Something we've forgotten?"

"Yes. Exactly!" He picked up his parchment, leaned on the wall, scribbled frantically for a moment, then held out the paper to her. He was grinning like the birth of the sun. "The daemon's a normal part of our culture and mythology – every tale's got one. He's in our legends and we remember him. Just about. But there's something we've forgotten –"

"What are you – ?"

"It's a puzzle, Jayr." He was almost dancing a jig, bursting with eagerness and energy. "Gods, it can't be this simple – this loco. All this time – and the Bard's been *right*. The world had a nightmare – a nightmare that Roderick witnessed. And if the *Ilfe,* her memory, was on Rammouthe Island and it was lost – then no one can recall what that nightmare was. Your book said, 'The dead carpet the Island of the Accurséd!'"

He broke into laughter that edged on hysterical and Jayr backed up – his expression was demented, fixated.

"Whatever killed them, whatever destroyed the world's memory, that's what the world fears, *that's* what the nightmare was about. All this time –" he was alight, afire with understanding "– and I've found it. I've found what the Bard's been looking for. He's right, the world really *does* have a forgotten fear."

"What the rhez are you on about?"

He leaned down to grab her shoulders, feverish, his eyes glittering.

"It's so simple. Yes, there's Kas Vahl Zaxaar, we know about him, we can face him. Maybe our defender, the master of light, will come back and fight him. But there's something *else,* don't you see..."

"No I *don't* see." Flesh crawling, she threw him off her, scrabbled to her feet. "This isn't some intellectual joke for your scholar brain! You're analysing too much, reasoning yourself into seeing stuff that... You're just making stuff up! Nivrotar is loco – and so are you!"

Ress was laughing, wild, crazed.

"But I'm right," he said to her. "This transcends *everything*."

"Have you been at Syke's pipe?"

He started chewing his lip again.

"An entire *race* just fell down and died. Of emptiness. Good Gods…"

Jayr flopped back into her spot on the floor, baffled. Without thinking, she crumpled Ress's notes into a pouch. His eyes were distant, he was paying no attention to anything but his thoughts.

"They died of giving up."

The energy faded out of him as he realised the scale of what he'd uncovered. He sat down, touched the fragmented puzzle with awed fingers.

"Can apathy be sentient? Perceptive? Jayr, this is too big to comprehend."

"Then stop," Jayr muttered, half in answer, half to herself. "Can we please get the rhez out of here? I need the sun."

Ress's gaze focused on her and he stared, bemused, blinking.

With a sudden chill, she realised how empty he looked.

Empty.

"Ress?"

Inexplicable fear dumped tension through blood and muscle. She jumped up, frost icing across her back. That was enough – she was taking Ress out of this fireblasted building. Like, now.

"But I'm not afraid," he said, smiling at her. "I find this… fascinating." The way he said the word made her reach for his arm, drag him to his feet.

Fascinating.

"That's it," she declared, "we're going to find ale. And a bar fight. And you some company. The cheaper the better."

He was a dead weight, slumped in her grip, his gaze fixed on nothing.

"I was reading something…" He leaned down and she let

him go. He stumbled to his hands and knees, began to gather the broken papers to him, pieces dissolving into ashes even as he touched them. He seemed to have no awareness of what he was doing. "I need them…"

"Ress…" Jayr reached for his arms, held him easily. "Don't…"

He started to laugh, high-pitched and humourless. His gaze bifurcated, then focused on her again – but with an effort.

"Jayr. What are you…?" He struggled against her grip but wasn't strong enough to break free. Beneath them, the puzzle scattered. "What's happening to me? I can't see, I can't think… oh, Gods, my *head*…!"

He fell forwards against her shoulder, shaking. The last time Jayr'd seen someone like this, Taure had overdone the pipeweed and seen figments in the grass for days. She wondered if he was going to throw up and leaned him back to sit on his heels. She held up his chin, searched his face for sanity.

But his head lolled. His glasses fell from his nose, shattering as they hit the floor. Pieces of precious glass mingled with the pieces of the poem he'd been reading.

Fascinating.

"Ress?" Not knowing how to help, she shook his shoulders, shook him harder. He shuddered violently, and slumped forwards. She caught him like a child, a dead weight against her body.

"Ress!"

Then his head came back up. He looked up at her, his neck at a crazed angle. His eyes were blank and he stared straight through her, straight through the rotting cavern of the library, through the shadows and the slanting sun. He was transfixed by something eternal, something she had no way to see.

He was white to the lips, his pupils huge.

And he was frightening her.

"RESS!" Right in his face.

"I *understand...*" he said, fervently. He clawed at her garments. She brushed his hands away, fighting to control the shudder. "I see the water, but her thoughts are transitory." He knelt up, but his gaze seared a line across her skin. He was leagues away, ardent and crazed. "The grass cries out to be heard. Do you hear the *stone*?"

Stone?

Jayr watched him, horrified, found a sob catching in her throat.

"What the rhez is the matter? What stone?" She stood up, heaved him upright, her boot shattering the last of the puzzle as she did so – she barely even noticed. "Ress, please... *Ress!*"

For a moment, it seemed he looked at her. His face was lit with a wondrous smile, vacant and ecstatic.

"Jayr..." he said. His breathing was short, his weight hung limp. "We did it. The world... shows me... her fear. Like the Bard, I can *see...!*"

"You can't see *shit*!" She shook him again, shouted in his face – but she may as well have tried to reach the fireblasted moons. Tears twisted her mouth, she had no idea what to do, no idea what'd happened –

Her hand slipped. In a slow, graceful motion, Ress tumbled backwards to the floor. Ancient paper scattered, puffed into dust.

Lain in its midst, he started to thrash, mouth working, hands clenched white into claws. A thin keening spilled from him. For a moment, he almost seemed to be trying to fight, trying with all the might of his scholar's mind to banish some figment that assailed him.

Froth trickled from the corner of his mouth, his back arched and his heels drummed.

"Nnnnnn...!"

His poem was gone.

Jayr threw herself over him, legs over his thighs, hands on his wrists to prevent him hurting himself against the stone. His neck corded, his head turned from side to side as if he tried to avoid a kiss.

"Nnnn...!"

She screamed his name in his face, sobs uncontrolled.

For a moment, he tried – his frenzy paused and he seemed to struggle to focus, to look at her... Then he screamed like a chearl and his body spasmed, shuddered, and collapsed.

His eyes were open, staring up at the broken balconies, the cracked glass.

The dust.

Barely daring, she choked, "Ress?"

He blinked, his jaw moved.

"Ress?" She sat back, wiping tears.

He broke into sobs, hands clawing at his face, his hair.

"Not strong enough!" His nails left red lines in his skin. "Rain and wind and metal – a city of glass and stone and vast, soul emptiness..."

Jayr grabbed his wrists as though he were a child. "Ress!" She was terrified – had no idea what was happening to him, what creature had come out of the book to assault his mind...

"He sees... wakes, needs power and powerlessness. They're all sleeping. There are needles in his arms."

He tried to free his hands. When Jayr released him, he buried his scratched face in them and started to cry.

"Mother... I listen. I hear the *grass*!"

"Ress..." The word was despair, disbelief. "I don't understand."

Gods, it can't be this simple – the Bard's been right all along!

Had he? Had he found some terrible, ancient truth? Or, like Feren's conspiracy, had his stupid brain just made something out of...

Something out of Nothing.

It was so ludicrous it almost made her laugh.

Through sobs, he said, "It's all so beautiful." He was staring up at the crumbling balconies, the filthy, broken skylight. At least he was calm. "Older than we are, layers of buildings for a thousand returns…"

What is? She wanted to ask him, *What can you see?*

But he fell quiet, laying on his back on the broken mosaic – a sacrifice to the forgotten knowledge of the library.

For a moment, Jayr stared at him, panic clamouring at her, crying for release.

But she had no time for that now.

She was going to go to the palace.

She was going to understand the figments that tormented her friend.

And if the Lord of Amos didn't help, Jayr was going to pull her city down round her ears.

PART 4: TORNADO

22: VISION The Palace of Lord Nivrotar, Amos

It was approaching the birth of the sun in the grubby sprawl of the Amos city state. Mist seeped out of bleak walls, lay in wait on cobbled streets, lent the dark city a pale shroud of fear.

In places, patches of disease across her shadowed face, there were battered stretches of sagging buildings, their roofs rotting and their windows cracked. And among these buildings dwelled the city's scavengers, the derelicts, the poorest of the poor. They swarmed like rodents after every scrap of food or information.

And then fought like bweao for what they found.

There was no council in Amos, no institute, no Fhaveon-trained military, no private forces of mercantile security. In Amos, there was only Nivrotar.

Her word was law, her whim death.

And now, she faced a madman.

Ress of the Banned lay broken, a twisted figure upon the cold stone floor of the Varchinde's most ancient building. He didn't see the great, vaulted ceiling, the elegant figures that turned stone faces towards the Lord's seat, or the carved, black-winged aperios that stood silent watch. He didn't see Jayr, crouched beside his pallet, anger etched into each white scar on her skin.

In stark contrast to the artists and poets, the philosophers and performers that waited upon Lord Nivrotar's every breath, neither Banned member paid her any attention. Ress stared into nothing as though answers taunted him. Jayr stroked his sweating forehead, frustrated and helpless.

"Ress of the Banned." Lord Nivrotar had cast aside her gown and now wore blackened mail of real metal, a sword at her hip upon a tooled-leather baldric. Her hair was loose waves, making her complexion white and her eyes as dark as bruises. "You are a fool. And yet..." She stood to descend the steps.

Jayr watched her, resentment smouldering. She chewed on a fingernail, spat out a fragment.

As the Lord moved, the court stood with a rustle of fabric. Several people offered her a hand, but she ignored them. She paused at the foot of the pallet to stare into Ress's thin white face.

"What do you see?"

"How the rhez can he tell you?" Jayr's insolence caused a gasp, a susurration of muttering. "He's loco."

Nivrotar glanced around her courtiers, silencing them. Her gaze settled upon one elderly philosopher.

"Can you comprehend his visions?"

The philosopher bowed, cleared his throat. "He babbles, my Lord, cries aloud, speaks to things we can't see. He has witnessed something that has overpowered his mind."

Nivrotar dismissed him, turned to the apothecary.

"His health is damaged?"

"He's Banned, my Lord, strong, even with his age." A wary glance at Jayr. "His suffering is only in his imagination."

With a faint chink of mail, the Lord of Amos sank to one knee beside Ress.

In unison, her court sank with her.

"What do you see?" Nivrotar watched Ress's face with a fascination torn between pity and awe.

Ress's eyes flicked back and forth, his mouth worked as if to speak. He sprang suddenly taut, and his eyes flashed, inhuman, with a terrifying discharge of colour and energy. Then he collapsed into despair and curled up like a baby.

Baffled and helpless, Jayr was fighting to control a choking knot of emotions – she wanted to sob, or scream, or hit something until it bled. She had no idea how to help him.

"You're the scholar!" Her mouth shook and the next words were a sob. "Help him!"

The court rustled in shock.

Ress was pale, rocking slightly, back and forth. Words still fell from him like pebbles, but they shattered as they hit the floor and were broken before sense could be made of them.

"Bring him food," Nivrotar said. "Now!" Echoes of her order rang from the pillars. In a flurry of feet, a door opened and banged shut.

Slowly, Ress turned his head to look at them, and Jayr almost screamed.

His eyes were unfocused, both pupils huge but one larger than the other, his irises dark as blood. Shadows moved beneath his skin.

He blinked several times before he said, "I saw the Ryll, the water. Roderick... all this time." A line of spittle trailed from one corner of his mouth and lost itself in his beard. He leaned forwards to confide in her. "We should have listened."

Jayr shivered, tried again. "Ress? Don't you know me?" Her voice caught on pleading with him. "Ress? Please... Say that you know me, you know who I am!"

But his face crumpled. "Mother, I hear you. How can I help?"

With a short exhalation of annoyance, Lord Nivrotar unfolded to her feet.

Jayr's mood changed like the twitch of a curtain – seeing the Lord's movement as dismissal, her grief caught light and burned. As Nivrotar turned away, Jayr pounced.

"What did we find? What was in that book?"

Nivrotar tapped pale fingers upon the hilt of her sword.

"My Lord."

Jayr crossed her arms over her chest. She was unused to facing anyone at her own height – but the Lord was slender, fragile by comparison. Jayr tensed powerful muscles beneath scar-carved skin.

"Answer the damned question."

The court cringed.

Nivrotar's tapping fingers gained speed. She gave a short sigh, but Jayr spoke across her.

"He did find something? Didn't he? Did find something you've missed? What're you going to do, torture it out of him? Torture it out of *me*?"

"If I deem it necessary." Nivrotar measured Jayr with eyes as deep and dark as an underground lake. "Find me the healer Jemara"

"Yes, Lord." A messenger scuttled.

Ress said, "The world screams."

With a soft, metal chinking, the Lord knelt beside the mad ex-scholar, her court echoing her movements.

Her hands touched his face, gently wiping the spittle from the sides of his mouth.

"I fear for you," she said gently. "If you have somehow shared Roderick's vision, if you have tried to see the world's nightmare... You are not a Guardian, have no way to encompass what you have witnessed. I fear it has riven your mind."

He smiled blankly at her.

"Yes," he said. Then he clamped his hands over his ears and began to rock back and forth relentlessly, repeating, "He knows, he knows, he knows, he knows, he knows, he *knows*...!"

"Who knows?"

"He saw, the only true vision." He stopped, shouted in her face. "But he cannot *remember*!"

Helplessly, the Lord returned to her feet, hands knotted at her sides. Jayr didn't move as she spoke to the apothecary. "Take him into your care. Jemara will sit with him at all times and scribe everything he says."

"Yes, Lord."

"Each morning, you'll bring those writings to me."

"Yes, Lord."

"And you." She turned to Jayr. "You were appointed his bodyguard and so you remain, you will stay by his side. When his pain makes sense to you, you will tell me."

"I'm not leaving him." She glowered at the servitors as they picked Ress's pallet up. "Anything happens to him, *anything*, Syke'll be down here. And he can make a right mess when he tries."

"I do not doubt it," Nivrotar said wryly. "Now go – I have work that must be done."

As they carried Ress from the audience hall, he cried again, "You must hear me!"

Jayr was silent as she followed him out.

Jayr had fallen asleep in her chair when Ress's screaming woke her, shattering the night's stillness into sharp-edged fragments of sound. He sat upright, suddenly as a shock, hands wrapped over his head.

Wordless, inarticulate, expressions of fear, grief, anger – she didn't know. They ripped through the small chamber with a soul-deep pain that made her flesh crawl.

She tried to soothe him, but the noise wore on her thinning patience and soon she was shaking his shoulder, shouting, "Ress! *Ress*! Ress, for the Gods' *sakes*!"

But he didn't hear her. He was next to her, and he was in another world.

"*RESS!*"

With no warning, he was silent, hugging his body in anguish, his face contorted.

Rocking back and forth, he began to mutter, "No, no, no, no-no-no..."

Jayr clenched her fists in an effort to stay calm.

"Ress, *please...*"

She was reaching the end of her tolerance. She'd been all night with minimal sleep, unwilling to leave his side. Nivrotar's entourage of alchemists, philosophers, healers and apothecaries were all damned useless. Any idiot could tell that Ress was loco, but they couldn't do horseshit about it. And the longer he was trapped, the worse his torment became.

Singing calmed him. When he heard a voice, high and sweet or deep and powerful, he would strain with every fibre of his being to listen; then collapse as if it was not what he wanted. After that, he would shriek, or sob, or talk frenziedly earnest gibberish. Once, he'd howled for mercy from the tortures of an unseen hand.

And she'd watched it all, helpless, unable to face the enemy Ress fought – just like she'd been unable to face Feren's infection. If she'd been able to touch it, she would've torn it apart.

Ress had dissolved into terrible sobbing, a pitiful sound. If he could have seen himself, he would have perished from humiliation. The loss of his mind had one sole blessing – he didn't know what had happened to him. Trying to muster serenity, Jayr laid his head on her shoulder. He was unaware of her presence.

"Shhhh." Her voice was gentle. "Trust me, I won't leave you."

Slowly, his weeping softened. And it was quiet.

Outside, far below, the wide waters of the Great Cemothen

River crawled past to the sea and the vast, dark sprawl of Amos slept on uncaring. Trapped in the height of Nivrotar's dark castle like some feeble damned maiden, Jayr had found herself hating the city for surrounding her, for its smells and moods, and most of all for its ability to swallow suffering.

Just like the Kartiah.

Her past was too close; it haunted her.

Where was Syke? Where was Triqueta?

What had *been* in that fireblasted poem? "*Time the Substance of the Gods...*"

"Please," she muttered, "give his madness to me. If he has great vision, then let him go."

But the Gods, as ever, were not listening.

A knock at the door made her start.

"Yes?"

It swung open to reveal Nivrotar herself, the healer Jemara hovering uncertainly behind her.

Jayr stood upright.

"What?"

"I dislike his screaming." Nivrotar swept into the room. She was wrapped in a cloak the colour of dried blood. As the plump, cheery-faced Jemara hesitated awkwardly, the Lord stopped by Ress's bed. "We must take control."

"Control?" Jayr said.

"Jemara." Nivrotar gestured for the woman to speak.

"It goes like this," Jemara said, shrugging round shoulders. "There's a way I can unlock his mind – but it's dangerous. Some people ply these substances for recreation, some believe that their visions bring them great truth. Others –"

"Jem," Nivrotar said warningly.

Jumping nervously, the healer said, "There are various narcotics, hallucinogenics..." she tailed off, watching Jayr's expression.

Jayr snapped, "He's not touching your – !"

"Think about it," Nivrotar said. "If he can open his mind, we may understand him."

"The problem is," Jemara said, "that Ress has strength and experience – we'll need more than a little. Eoritu's euphoric – it can be addictive, and it could make him worse. Once it's in his body, we'll have to lead his visions where we want them to go. Do you understand what I'm asking?"

Jayr looked down at where Ress lay. He slept peaceably now, his face lined and sunken.

"Will it hurt him?"

Jemara shook her head.

Nivrotar said, "Not his physical health."

Where was Syke? Where was anyone that could take the weight of this decision from her shoulders? *Ress, what did they do to you?*

"Do it," Jayr said.

Heat.

Tight, sweating passageways lined with smoothed rocks and a sheen of panic. Ceilings low and dark, close and choking air.

The slash of a stone blade into flesh. Spilled blood spirals inwards towards a heart of fiery, crystalline awareness. Then a rising sense of hunger and an eagerness for release.

Elemental. Sical, *creature of fire. Such a thing has not been seen upon the world in a lifetime of returns.*

Here in the passageways, the twisted corpse of a Kartian craftsman, shattered by huge strength. His insides have exploded from his mouth, blood covers his face and chest – he'd thrashed for a long time as he'd been slowly crushed to death.

Here, a creature created of alchemy – a crazed cross-breed of man and horse. It stands in deepening night, the Monument its backdrop, a storm raging over it... It's colossal – and its death crouches in the grass.

Here, a man on his knees, a slim, fair-skinned woman before him, abandoned in pleasure and passion. The man is grinning like a predator, ringed fingers twisting in the soft flesh of her buttocks. She has incredibly long black hair, thrown wildly down her back and shoulders. She cries aloud, snarls pleasure through clenched teeth...

...and the stone grows into her flesh. Even as the man withdraws, the creeping calcification reaches her throat, her face, and she is left there – head back, lips parted, frozen forever in stone orgasm.

With her final cry, the image changes.

In that rise of passion and release, the stirring Monument awakens completely: it blazes with new, raw power.

The man's strength is complete. His rings glinting, he stands before a brazier, a broken and twisted pillar. About him is a vast, dark chamber and within it, rank upon rank, stand blunt and misshapen creatures of rock, dark silhouettes against the light. They are ancient, creatures forgotten and now wakened from long rest. There are embers in their eyes and a terrible, grinding power in their movements. The man can feel the steady pulse of the Powerflux. He can pull its might towards the centre, towards himself.

And it is glorious.

But then he realises –

A cascade of water overwhelms the vision, what the man realises is lost. Ress hears her voice again, crying denial. Her waterfall blinds him, deafens him – he knows she was trying to show him something, but she's too powerful and the images drown him. He tries to shout, but water fills his eyes, his mouth.

There!

The grass, the vast carpet of the Varchinde, all bowing towards the Monument, paying homage to the man's potency as he pulls the World's energy inwards, building, building his stone army...

What was she...?

Oh, my Goddess. Mother...

At its edges, at the feet of the Kartiah, the Khohan, the Khavan Circle... at the eastern shoreline, where the great terhnwood crops grew... to the far south, the forests at Gasharta, Naskala...

...death is beginning in the grass. As the energy of the Powerflux is sucked inwards by the Monument, so the edges of the Varchinde begin to perish. Rot, devastation, a wave of lifelessness sweeping inwards: the terhnwood plantations crumble and the trees are twisting in pain.

The World will die.

The waters of the Ryll bathe him in horror.

And he screams. And screams. And screams.

"Silence him!"

The Lord Nivrotar was on her feet. Jemara shaking and white faced.

Ress's appalling shrieking rang from the ceiling, ricocheted from cold, stone walls.

Jayr held his shoulders, shouted in his face.

"Ress! Stop it! Ress!"

Then the noise fell away, collapsed into desperate, panting breaths, a hunted animal. He rasped, "This... is just... the beginning. There is no *time*!"

His eyes were open, stark and wide and staring. His back was arched, his hands worked aimlessly, reaching for something – or pushing something away.

No time.

"Oh, you're so fireblasted clever." The Banned girl challenged the Lord of Amos and the castle healer. "What the rhez did *that* achieve? Look at him!"

Jemara's cheery face held fear, her hands twitched helplessly by her sides.

"I don't know. We gave him clarity, but what he *saw*..."

Nivrotar stood still, her silk-gloved forearms crossed and the fingers of one hand rapping a silent and restless tattoo.

"He was clearer – stone and flame and sex and power. Great elation and great fear. Will he stand another dose?"

Jayr glowered. "No way."

Jemara agreed with a reluctant shrug.

"Then we can't reach him. How do we help him free himself?"

"My Lord." The healer was still shaking. "His mind is beyond my strength – whatever he can hear has might beyond anything I comprehend. Benign might – but such *fear* –"

"We must know what he sees."

Frustrated by her helplessness, her hands itching to fight, to rip his madness out of him by the damned *roots* if she had to, Jayr moved to the window, to look out at the pinpoint rocklights and flambeaux of Amos stretched below. The slow roll of the river ran to either side of the palace's island, black strips of bridges sliced its broad shine into cold squares of metal.

Above her, the air was cool and clear, the sky arced over her here as it did in the desolation of the wide Varchinde. Somewhere out there, the same moonlight shone upon Syke and the Banned, upon Triqueta racing to avenge Feren. She leaned far out of the unshuttered window, muscled belly flat against the stone sill, and allowed the breeze to touch her skin.

She didn't *understand*. Her hands tightened on the windowledge. She wanted to wrest this thing from his mind and throw it to the floor and tear it to pieces. She wanted to *fight* –

Behind her, healer and Lord contemplated the now quietly muttering Ress. She could hear them talking, the Lord of Amos demanding answers, the healer having none to give. If only Ress was awake, he would be smarter than both of them.

If only Ress was awake.

If only –

Shit!

All three of them were caught off guard by his sudden movement.

Writhing, he had both hands clamped over his ears in an effort to shut out a sound only he could hear. His face was pale, sweat had sprung out on his skin and the blankets stuck to him as he twisted his body this way and that, trying to find release. He was gagging, perhaps trying to speak but choked with horror at what was tormenting him.

As Nivrotar turned to grasp both of his wrists and hold him down with unexpected, metal-wire strength, he forced out his cry for help, gasping for breath as he spoke...

"Rhan... no, this cannot be!"

"Jayr!"

Jumping to help, Jayr wrestled one of Ress's ankles motionless, then held it still while she grabbed the other. As she pinned him down, muscles flexing, she caught the eyes of Amos's Lord watching the ripple of power in her shoulders with a curious light flickering in their darkness. Only for a moment, then Ress began to struggle and howl and her attention turned back to the bed.

"Let me go! Let me go, let-me-go, let-me-*go!*" He was fighting them, really fighting them as if he knew they were there, but his sight was still turned inwards. *"Rhan, they've taken Rhan. I have to tell him!"*

"Who?" Nivrotar leaned right over him, her curtain of pitch-black hair touching his face. "Where is Rhan? Whom do you have to tell?"

For an instant, just for an instant, he seemed to focus upon her face. He was still, staring into her eyes as though she compelled him to motionlessness. For that instant, his mouth worked, he tried to say, "Nivr-otar. Deathless sleep, passionless, empty – the world's fear – comes. Rhan – you must... The Bard... I must... see –"

"Fhaveon's Council is not my concern." Nivrotar's voice

was soft through her curtain of hair. "To involve myself would be a declaration of –"

"No. I need..." Ress clawed one thin hand about her shoulder, pulling her close almost as if to embrace her. He was shaking with the effort needed to remain focused. "Roderick... must... know... what I've seen. All of it. This..." He was panting, sweating. "This is... what he's been *looking* for!" His voice rasped with the import of what he was trying to tell them. "The Bard... I hear him, see him. He must *understand*!"

Nivrotar stared into his face. "I can reach Roderick, if I must. What do I tell him?" For a moment, the dark eyes of the Lord of Amos searched the crazed veteran's face, his disfocused gaze. "Ress. A moment longer, stay with me. What do I tell him?"

"The world's fear comes. It is manifest." His voice was breaking now, his breathing becoming sobs. "She showed me *everything*!"

Jayr blinked, baffled and hurting.

Nivrotar said, "The world's fear." She sat back on her heels, considering. "I tried to protect you, Ress of the Banned. You have found the answer, but it has cost you your mind. Can you..." Her tone was gentle now, almost as if she were terrified to upset the delicate, desperate balance of his cling to sanity. One pale hand stroked his cheek. "Can you tell me... can you tell me what you can see?"

Her meaning was clear, though unspoken: *Without costing me mine?*

"My Lord, the drug is still in his blood. His sight is clear, but his words –"

"Ress." The Lord stroked his cheek again, her white fingers gentle. "What does the world fear?"

"Nothing! It's outside the Count of Time; it's Nothing! *Kazyen*!"

Jayr said, "What the rhez is – ?"

"The world's fear! Tell him!" Ress's mouth exploded in red

and he fell back, silent, his eyes staring empty at the Amos night. He was still breathing – but his mind was gone.

Nivrotar stood up.

Her voice was like a death knell as she said, "Send a bretir to my... emissary... in Fhaveon. Whether we understand them or not, Ress's words must reach the Bard.

"And we must pray that he understands."

Out of the darkness, images fell like drops of rain. They were infrequent at first and they delighted him. He turned his face upwards, blinking to see. Then they were more numerous, a downpour covering and soaking him – until they became a cascade like a waterfall, an onslaught, battering him down.

He tried to run from them; ran until he felt his chest would burst. Perhaps he was trying to outrun the water, to save himself from the assault; perhaps his running was just another image and he was tiny and tumbling, drowning under the deluge.

Somewhere, the voice called his name again, far distant, begging him to listen. It was female, desperate. He was a child, it was his mother; he was a man, it was his wife – her tones were coloured with hope and terror. Hear me, child. You must hear me. You are so close. *He tried, but the images were battering him, drowning him. They were coming too fast.*

Desperate, he reached out to hold on to something. And he saw...

The Ilfe, destroyed. The Well of the World's Memory – gone. A single fragment from the chaos that tumbled past him, one he clung to, a lifeline. With it came others – the broken Monument, the desolation of the Great Library, the chill white of the Theatre of Nine. All of these things, decaying, because the World could not remember. In the instant of this realisation, a vast time passed him, an aeon of understanding.

Child who sees, you must hear! Help me!

The voice was a cry of feminine grief, terrible enough to make him cringe. He raised his arms and tried to cry back to her, "How?"

But she did not answer him, and the waterfall had gone. He staggered at the sudden lack of pressure. Fell, panting, to the ground.

She had left him.

He opened his eyes.

Sealed in hopelessness, far below the surface of the great Lord City, Roderick stirred in a breathless, wordless panic.

His mind was tumbled by images and memories, splashing fragments of things he had once seen, the same images that had swirled at the back of his mind all of his life. They were bright, now, like sunlight on the water. He had to blink to see that the room around him was dark.

The Ryll. The water and the fear. The tumbling, nonsensical chaos of the world's nightmare – this, he knew.

But the vision was not his.

Then who…?

He sat up, understanding flooding him like a chill.

It brought him more awake. He found that he was shivering, almost as though he had been in cold water. Pieces of the images still floated at the edges of his mind. They were strong – there was a cry of pain still in his ears and fear in every layer of the darkness around him.

What had he seen?

For a moment, he was still, didn't move. As if more motion would disturb the last of the images, make them evaporate in the darkness, he sat poised – but they were fading even as he reached for them.

Was there flame – was there anger?

The shiver became a shudder, a tease across his skin. A

certainty, though he still wasn't sure what it was.

As a youth, the Guardians had welcomed him – the first of his kind to be born in the Ryll's home city of Avesyr in a hundred generations, hailed as the hope of his people. There were few of them left, even then, scattered watchers of a myth forgotten, adhering only to their own history and a mandate more ancient than they had words to recall.

They had taught him many things – to watch the water and to comprehend the tumble of the images within. They had taught him to fight and to run, to understand letters and music, to craft a story to entrance an audience.

They had also taught him to think.

In the darkness about him, the dream fragments were thinning to nothing. They left only isolated images, echoes that made no sense – but one thing remained as clear as Tundran ice...

He *knew* that that vision had not been his.

Someone *else* had seen the same thing; someone *else* had witnessed the thoughts of Ryll, the world's nightmare.

Someone else had seen the thing they'd called heresy, the blasphemy he had committed.

The thought brought him fully awake and he was on his feet in the darkness, thinking, thinking. He was still shivering, as though the cold had sunk into his bones. He needed Rhan, he needed Ecko, he needed The Wanderer, he needed...

He needed to understand what he'd seen. It was the closest he had come to the world's nightmare, the closest in more returns than he could recall – and the feeling that time was closing in upon him was suddenly exhilarating and dreadful and powerful.

But whose vision was it?

He placed his hands against the cool of Fhaveon's core-stone, and tried to remember.

I am a Guardian. I know how to do this.

...and he was standing upon a solitary rock tower. He was alone, utterly alone – as if he were the last mortal, or the first one...

...there were lines of energy woven within the grass, the power fluxing through them, soul to soul. This was natural: this was the way things should be...

...the magma lake that was the soul of fire; the vast, carved caverns that were ice; the hearts of the Kartian PriestLords that held the dark; the great sarsen monolith that had once been the OrSil, the soul of light. The Elemental Powerflux, awakening...

...but to what?

The Monument, reborn and alight with fire and blazing at the very sky...

And that blaze brought death.

His vision cleared, and Roderick knew – he knew where Ecko had gone.

He also knew something else, the thing that he had feared from the beginning.

Did I not tell him? Did I not try and explain?

Under the Bard's skin, horror crawled like panic. The knowledge was absolute, but he was completely helpless to do anything about it – he barely realised that he was hammering the wall until pain curled his hands into claws.

Everything was connected – and Ecko had left without the full information.

I tried to tell you...!

Ecko was wrong. His impulsive, chaotic nature had taken him too soon, and without the right information.

And he might just make everything worse.

23: AMETHEA THE MONUMENT

They had incoming.

From the chamber that Ecko'd named the "lock-up", the passageways had changed. As though the open caves were only the entrance hall, they'd become somehow more formal – tighter, twisted and narrow. A feeling of age and tension had grown here, it watched them pass, skulking behind the shoulder-to-shoulder stones that sternly walled them in. The air was breathlessly warm.

Redlock resisted the need to cough, dry mouthed, the urge to hunch his shoulders as though he were trespassing. He felt like this whole damned thing was so ancient it'd cave in at the touch of his boots.

Before him, Ecko was almost impossible to see – a figment that flickered from wall to wall, curve to corner to side passage, a grinning, black-eyed shade. He didn't trust it, had no idea what it – he – was capable of. He could feel Tarvi's nervousness, Triqueta's rising sense of panic – worrying about other people slowed him down.

But Triq was strong: he knew her bravery and was glad to have her at his back.

The fading rocklight still showed char marks, faint dustings of scattered soot that lured them onwards. Hanging roots were scorched and shrivelled, smaller stones cracked clean through, or fallen in pieces to the floor. At points, there were old carvings in the walls, softened by time, their meanings long-lost.

The axeman had the peculiar certainty they were going in a circle.

Too many damned tavern-sagas.

Ecko's eyes flashed as he turned. Instantly, the axeman was alert.

Ahead of them came the beat of heavy footsteps, swift and regular – distant, but quickly becoming louder. There was an almost-flicker of light.

Redlock whistled softly. The passageway was a long, narrow curve, silent stones walled them in.

Tarvi answered him, "Seems we've got a patrol."

"Then we stop them," he said. "We need to find a side turning. Whatever they are, they're not catching us with our breeches down."

"They'll come at us single file," Tarvi murmured. "If you can hold…"

"And if I can ambush the damned things, I won't have to." He gave her a brief grin, glad she was able to focus. "I don't know what they taught you in Roviarath, but never be afraid to fight dirty."

She chuckled wickedly, seemed to like his audacity.

He spared her an additional glance – she was cute, but the same age as his daughter – then noted Triqueta's expression and set his face to grim certainty.

"Let's go – we'll have to move quick."

With Ecko before them like a dark harbinger, they ran.

* * *

"You don't need to do this, please..."

In the flicker of the brazier's flame, she'd seen the image of the trade-road, the bustle of the little township. Dirty streets and wooden walls, traders and grifters, beggars and families – it was a swell of population on the water's edge, as though the unrolling ribbon-town had been dammed by the shoreline. Carts moved, making ruts in the mud, chearl plodded, tails flicking, children ran underfoot, chasing and wide mouthed.

But their laughter was silent – she heard only the soft crackle of the fire.

Maugrim was behind her, his heat at her neck, his hand forcing her to watch.

And before her was a hollow, a broken basin – a twisted, jagged stump of stalagmite like a cracked-off tooth. If he craned her head back, she could see its sibling, high above, also broken, as though a shattering hammer force had split the pillar asunder. Yet it yearned still – water and long returns of mouldering soil had renewed its growth, as if it writhed imperceptibly downwards, needing to be rejoined.

Now, flame-light teased it closer.

Maugrim's voice, soft as a growl in her ear.

"You showed me the key, little priestess – how to unlock the secret. I would've given you everything I had, anything you asked for. I can change the world, thanks to you... and you repay me by bloody cowardice? By trying to run away – like some rebellious street kid?"

"Whatever you've awoken –"

"You've awoken." She felt him grin, his breath warm. "We've awoken." He stretched his hand past her and the firelights flashed on his white-metal rings. "Never forget, sweetheart, you started this with me."

In the fire, wavering in the image, a tiny flame-angel with eyes white-hot. A Sical, he called it, an elemental, a creature of the Soul of Fire. It watched them, unblinking, the image of the township shimmering through its form as though through high-summer heat.

Hard against her back, Maugrim stretched his hand into the flame.

She expected his flesh to crisp and blacken, but he was unhurt, his rings glowing red and fierce blue heat playing at their edges. The Sical nuzzled him like a pet.

She heard it in her head. *Feed, I. Hun-ger.*

"Do you see it?" he asked her. "Watch."

The creature grew, hot against her face. It seemed to draw strength from his touch – somehow it was both in the fire and in the air over the trading post. It was a miniature sun, blazing with eagerness and fury.

She said, "No, Goddess, no…"

You did this with me.

As though the creature phased between one place and another, it drew the flame about itself.

Feed, I. Hun-ger.

She saw in the fire. She saw it through the fire, as though through an elemental window. She saw it rain death upon the town.

In silence, she watched the detonation, the ripple of heat and impact, tumbling buildings like charred parchment, wood exploding into fierce life and the blaze within reaching the sky. She saw the pouring forth of black smoke, the panic and the running and the dying and the terror.

She saw the Sical kill, lazily and perfectly, just because it could.

She covered her face with her hands.

"If you resist me again," Maugrim said to her softly, drawing his hand from the flame. "It'll dance on your burned remains." He placed his hand on her arm and the heat of his rings made her scream.

* * *

Never be afraid to fight dirty.

Ahead of them, the flicker was rising to a red glow – a sullen gleam that swelled against the stone. An edge of pressure came before it, making sweat stand out on skin. The relentless pound of heavy stone feet grew louder, closer – soil trickled from the roof, from between the slabs in the wall.

Ecko pushed himself faster, his telescopics spinning to pick up the telltale light difference that would mean –

There!

A sliver of darkness, a straight flicker of highlight – a turning. He gave the others a flash of his LEDs and he ran, low and fast, his soft shoes light over sand-dry soil.

He heard them come after him. Approaching, Redlock gestured for him to get out of the way.

"Not this time." Ecko grinned, black as a promise of death. In his hand was a small pottery container – a secret prize, something he'd liberated from Maugrim's lock-up. He was bouncing it in his palm – and well aware he was *way* too eager to see what it did. "You wanna fight dirty? I say we fight fire –" in his other hand was Lugan's lighter, now refilled "– with fire."

"What the rhez is that?"

"Progress."

Tarvi said, "Oh…" Her reaction brought warmth that had nothing to do with the incoming nasties.

Shut *up*! he told himself. The pottery impacted repeatedly against his fingers. In his other hand was the metal bite of home. He found them comforting, somehow bridging the gap between one reality and the other.

This is the Bike Lodge, mate…

The thumping stone feet came closer. A line of soil shivered down the wall.

"By the Gods…" Triqueta breathed softly, tailing into silence as the pounding was in their ears, in the rock about them. Past the square stones that limned the entranceway...

The creature was rock, a cloak and cowl of ancient, worn stone covering twisted, eroded grey muscle. It had hooves – solid like a horse's and impacting hard on the floor. Its gait was heavy enough to judder the walls.

More soil trickled. Ecko bounced the ceramic globe in his hand.

But its face...

Blunted, empty features, worn down like a graveyard statue. Its expression was hollow despite the flame in its eyes – its cheeks were sunken in stone-shadow.

Behind it came another, a second, a third – each one twisted, damaged, wrong.

"How did he get so strong, so quickly?" Tarvi said softly. "He's not –"

"How'd you know so much about this?" Triqueta's comment was only half humorous.

Redlock had thrown a scowl over his shoulder but the beasties were single focus, lumbering onwards in the charred trail of their mates. As the last one passed the end of the passageway, Ecko sparked the lighter and leaned round the edge of the stone.

Oh, this was just too perfect.

His targeters crossed, plotted, described the arc. The big crack in the stone, the gap between roof and floor... yeah, *that* one...

The pottery sphere left his hand and sailed, slo-mo...

He watched it lodge in the crack.

And the world exploded.

In her dreams, Amethea had heard the death of the crystal. A distant echo, a faint, discordant jangle.

She awoke with an image flickering at the corner of her

thoughts – a creature of darkness and shadow, eyes like black-on-black pits and laughing like insanity.

The harsh laugh and the jarring chime layered one upon another as she stirred into wakefulness and the choking tension of Maugrim's heat.

Remembered where she was.

Before her, he had turned from the huge brazier, his hand half raised and his rings glittering fierce. However much she hated him, he drew her eyes like a campfire on a cold night.

"They're early," he said. His grin was tight and wary.

Who...? Hope was a forgotten light: the rock of resentment in her soul was buried deep so the Sical would not find it – but she knew where it was. *Who're early?*

Around them, four naves in a vast, elemental cross, the ruin of the Great Cathedral was lit to a brilliant orange anger by the brazier's reconsecration. Behind the glowing, broken-topped walls, she could see hints of the cavern outside. Upon the walls, the half-seen shapes of the window frames flickered. And over it all, the vast arch of cavern roof glistened as though damp, and the lichens quested like open-mouthed sparks, lusting for the light.

In the brazier's heart the Sical danced, bright-eyed and fervent. It was tiny, it wavered with no real form – but the *eagerness* that radiated from it was palpable.

She could see he didn't trust it: he kept it trapped and hungry. Loosing it was easy – getting it back under control required strength.

Her voice carefully dull, she said, "Do you – we – have time?"

Maugrim laughed, his hand in the brazier and the Sical nuzzling him, pleading. Its eyes were sharp, glowing white-metal.

"They've got some stuff to be thinking about, sweetheart, a few distractions." He glanced at her, his predator's smile hot with hunger. "We've got time." Smiling at her – Goddess *why* did he still smile at her like that? – he spun on his heel to gesture expansively at his silent congregation.

Amethea had tried to ignore them, the endless ranks of silent figures, hunched and misshapen, stretching back into the dark.

Waiting.

They made her want to curl close to the fire.

They were worn, pitted, irregular. They filled the gloom with threat, with twisted, broken muscles of grey stone. Some of the pedestals were already shattered, crumbling, but they waited for his call, for the freed fury of the Sical to rain fire from the skies.

It was as though the destruction of the township had been merely a gesture made for her, an illustration of his strength.

A test.

To take Roviarath, he needed power.

And Amethea knew that for power – he needed her.

Detonation.

Tearing force and staggering concussion. A splitting crack, a thunderous rumble of falling stone. A rattle of rocks, a hiss of soil, a cloud of dust. Coughing and confusion. The passageway around them shuddered.

Redlock and Triqueta were shouting. Tarvi was on the floor in a jumble, her mouth hanging open.

Ecko grinned like a fiend.

"Boom," he said.

"What the rhez...?"

Leaving the axeman to his apoplexy, Ecko slipped through the settling debris, picked his way carefully over the pile – it groaned faintly, shifting and settling.

The passageway they'd come through was completely blocked.

Throwing the fucking thing had been a gamble – but the

Bogeyman's luck was with him and the rock had cracked clean through, split free from the wall. Over it, the entire ceiling had come down.

He could smell soil. From somewhere, there was cold air.

Beneath the fall, the four beasties were rubble, their shattered remnants scattered amid the heavy, broken slabs. Their light had gone out: their eyes only empty sockets in ancient, stone cadavers.

Rumbles echoed through the rocks, loose stones hissed in the distance.

Redlock was behind him, boot on the stone, axes in hands.

He said softly, "What did you do?"

"Hoisted that fucker Maugrim with his own petard." Ecko was crouched, watching the debris – he was half convinced the remains of the beasts would move by themselves. "He wants to play blowing shit up? I wrote the fucking rulebook."

The axeman gave a tight grin. "I don't think he's playing by any rules."

Ecko cackled.

"Can we get out of here?" Triq sounded almost plaintive, she was watching the ceiling. "I don't mean to piss on anyone's campfire – but I'm betting the rest of this is coming down. Any time now."

"There's a draught." Ecko gestured with a hand which was trying to turn the colours of the tumbling dust. At his ankles, the tips of his stealth-cloak were shifting, stirring imperceptibly. If he raised his palm, he could feel it: cool breath on his fingertips. "Can't go wrong with a secret door – even when you hafta make your own."

"That's not a door," Triqueta said. "That's a hole. You're not telling me you're going to dig...?" She made a noise that was half scorn, half fear. "You'll bring the whole damned Monument down on our heads!"

"We need to get off the marked route," Redlock said. "Good

thing there were only a few of those things – next time, we might not be so lucky. How many of that weapon have you got?"

"Not enough," Ecko told him, patting his webbing. "Not enough."

The boom was soft, but unmistakable. Somewhere above, the stone seemed to judder.

Maugrim stopped, tense and dead still. In a silence broken only by the crackle of the brazier, he listened.

Starve, I. Fuel, give. Now?

The Sical's plaintive, coaxing hunger was hot on his face. He ignored it.

He *knew* what'd made that explosion. What he didn't know was how Larred Jade's idiot patrols had gotten here so fast – or had been smart enough to identify the contents of his stash.

What the hell else had they picked up?

He glanced at Amethea. She watched him, dull eyed and lank haired. She was sunk within herself, too afraid to flee, too meek to strike back – the Sical terrified her. The savagery of the passion that had first stirred the site had bled from her like hope.

He was – almost – sorry. She'd been key and lock and conduit, both heart and catalyst.

But, like Vice, her usefulness was done.

Under his boots lay a huge stone slab, circular, the broken stalagmite at its centre. It was carved in a spiral with a language long-lost – elemental images, pictograms, tiny lines twisting steadily inwards. Once, it had split into quadrants, sarcophagi – now, each one was fused into place by the long Count of Time.

When he called her name, she obeyed without question, eyes on the fire.

One last time.

* * *

Axes struck soil, scraped on hard, broken-edged rock.

Hands shovelled roughly, dirt packing under nails.

Redlock was digging, spitting dirt and shaking it out of his hair.

Triqueta, further back, watched the tunnel – the broken pile of rubble, the roof. Sweat ran down her temple and trickled round the edges of the opal in her cheek. Her jaw jumped with tension.

Tarvi picked up rocks, threw them aside as the axeman broke through the wall.

The draught grew colder. Blind, squiggling things quested eyeless in the sudden air, the wash of it was almost fresh.

There were chinks of light coming through the soil, angled beams like tiny searchlights spread as the wall came down.

Ecko, unable to rid himself of the conviction that the beasties would reassemble and rumble upright, looking for revenge, paced the edge of the rockfall, nimbly jumping the stones that Tarvi threw at his feet.

She winked at him and his belly tightened. He thought about something else.

So – you still watching, Eliza? Extra points for creativity? For the shortcut?

"I'm through," Redlock said. He hooked another chunk of soil and ripped it down, roots hung pointless and pale. One more, and the hole was large enough for Ecko to get his shoulders through.

And large enough to flood the rockfall with light.

Yellow light, like nicotine, nacreous and familiar.

Tarvi said, "That looks –"

"No shit." Ecko didn't need to be told what it was. "I guess we've arrived. You lot stay the fuck put, willya? I'm gonna find the elevator."

"The what?" Redlock was ruefully examining the axe-edge, reaching in a pouch for a whetstone.

"In the words of the prophet – we're goin' down." Ecko's skin writhed with the colour of the light. "The big bad guy's always in the last place you look. So fuck that – we are *so* starting at the bottom."

Without waiting for their confusion, he pushed through the soil, chill and soft, damp against his skin. He spat it from between his lips, felt the roots tail softly over his face.

He heard Tarvi whisper, "Careful!", felt her hand almost touch him as he scrabbled to make the hole larger.

He knew what the light was – had an idea of what he'd...

Holy fucking mother of god.

His anti-daz flick-flashed.

Halfway in the wall like he was Malice through the Looking Glass, he stopped to stare.

Behind him, the others were forgotten. Maugrim, his stone beasties and his pomegranate grenades, his bike and his washers, forgotten. The Wanderer, forgotten. Eliza, Lugan, the Bike Lodge, the Virtual Rorschach, forgotten.

The light made his skin blanch to jaundice. He blinked his black eyes and he didn't care.

Pushing himself fully through the hole, he righted himself to stand, breathless, upon the edge of a void. A wide and plummeting shaft, a bottomless drop his telescopics could not penetrate: the very brink of nothing. In the walls, spasms of light flickered downwards, sparking electricity like faulty cables they deepened in hue as they were lost in the darkness.

It was a movie set, a tableau for an epic fight scene – impossible.

Before him, a wide balcony, ancient stone grown with pale creeper that snapped, dry, under his touch. The balcony ringed the wall – it threw jerky and random shadows. It didn't quite surprise him that three other entranceways were blocked with old rockfall and the open-mouthed, light-seeking lichens.

The light shaft was carved into an almighty and continuous

mural – prehistoric figures dancing or fucking in celebration or anguish, caressed by the current that ran through them. The creeper covered them, crawling with a dead lover's hands – they danced away, the light making them restlessly carouse until they were lost, down, down in the dark.

What's this now? The road to hell?

Compelled, he picked up a loose pebble.

Bring it on.

But before he let it go, he looked up.

And over him was the underside of the Monument.

A flat, stone ceiling, cracked as though under great impact. Upon it was engraved some sort of spiral, gradually winding outwards – but it was roughly, randomly penetrated by the undersides of the stones.

Thrust through the ceiling, splitting it in places to the edge, they were jags of rock, juts of stone, edges and corners.

And they *shone*.

And the light spiralled out to the walls.

And bled through the figures and down.

For chrissakes, Ecko thought, *this place is way too fucking creepy.*

Leaning on the balcony's edge, holding the pebble out over the massive drop – *oh you so know I have to!* – it occurred to him to wonder what the fucking hell was keeping that ceiling intact.

He let the pebble go.

And watched it, tracking it with his telescopics until he could see it only in the flashes of the wall light... until the darkness swallowed it whole.

Waited there for a moment, listening for the monsters, the drums in the deep.

When they didn't stir, he contemplated the rough stone stairway that turned about the shaft's wall, spiralling down into the very belly of the Powerflux.

So. Let's go wake 'em up.

* * *

When he kissed her, she tasted ashes.

The brazier was fierce at her back, his hands and lips were hot, but she was closed to him. The rock of her resentment was still in her heart. She wished she could hear the stone.

She remembered Feren: she remembered their ride, the Monument, the creature. She remembered the sunset, the rising shadow of the Kartiah. She remembered Vilsara, a world away, still safe behind Xenotian church walls. Had she ever wondered what had become of them?

Like Maugrim's touch, the stone blade in her belly was hot, it burned her soul. She gasped, a tiny sound of shock – he was kissing her still, letting her fold in his arms and lowering her to the stone spiral beneath his odd black boots.

"Sorry sweetheart," he said, his voice deep and soft in her ear. His fingers stroked her jaw. "Seems time's caught us up."

Thick fluid welled over hands she couldn't remember moving – she looked down at them, uncomprehending. Her own blood between her fingers, soaking her garments, seeping slowly, slowly, into the runnels of the carved-stone floor.

And inwards.

Vaguely, she thought there should be pain. Belly wounded, she should be screaming, but she only looked at him, confused.

She heard herself say, "Why?" and already knew the answer.

He said, "This world is rotting, dying from the inside. Complacent, lazy, self-absorbed – when I came here, he showed me how to fix it. How to burn it all down so it can begin again! He showed me *truth* – took me and taught me because I understood. And so did you, little lady, my priestess, my healer – at first, so did you." He smiled down at her. "It was good, wasn't it?"

She could see the brazier's light behind him and the bright eyes of the Sical, watching her, wanting...

He stroked her hair away from her face.

"I'm sorry – genuinely sorry, Amethea." On some level, he seemed to mean it. "I'd've taken you all the way with me. But betrayal, cowardice – they're low. You've hurt me – and I have to fight now. Roviarath is mine – and from there, we will grow…"

Over her, the almighty twists of the stalactite pillar flickered with the Sical's hunger. She could hear it, a voice like fire crystal, eager and coquettish and charming.

Feed, I!

She struggled to one elbow, blood pulsing from her belly. The blade was still in her flesh and the blood was slow – so slow. A part of her wanted to wrap one hand round the handle, yank it free, spend her last breath ramming it through his bearded throat, but he still compelled her, even after everything.

Instead she said, "Who's 'he'?"

He leaned forwards, pressed lips of fire to her forehead. She felt like she'd been branded.

"Who else?" he told her softly. "Kas Vahl Zaxaar, cast down by Samiel just like his brother Rhan. He sleeps – mostly – but there are those who understand his soul."

"Like you?"

"Vahl brings *passion*. There is no place in his world for the mundane."

In the darkness of the shattered naves, the eyes of the stone army started to glow.

24: FIGMENT THE MONUMENT

She was small, feminine curves carried confidently by tight, agile fitness. She had dark eyes, a turned-up nose, sunburn and a tension about her that spoke of great fear – and great bravery. She was smart, knew tales even the Bard hadn't told him. She had watched her patrol destroyed around her, had cried for them and lain in his arms, gasping and wanting, needing to remember to *live*. He couldn't begin to imagine what she'd –

For chrissakes will you stop that?

Ecko ripped down her image, screwed it the fuck up and threw it as far from him as he could, resignedly aware that it would bounce down the stairs and sit there, gleaming in the low throb of the light, until he picked it up again.

Beside him on the wall was the worn relief of a full-figured woman, dancing with Vegas abandon in the darkness. The light pulse flickered through her stone skin.

They were deep, down here, the air was damp and slimy stuff was growing in the walls. The light was as purple as bruising, now almost black. He didn't need his UV to see the phosphor glow of the lichens, of fingernails and eye sockets. He remained invisible – but with the stilled, chilled gyrations round him, he felt like he was nightmare enclosed, heading down and down into some forgotten well-hole.

Yet Tarvi was there, her eyes afire, her hands on her breasts like the woman in the –

Stop it!

He looked back, upwards at the others, clambering weary legged and precarious down the worn, winding rock staircase, yawning drop to one side, hands trailing over the damp. In the almost-dark, the light glimmered over their skin, glittered from the gemstones in Triqueta's cheeks. He had no idea how far down they were going. His telescopics were trashed: he couldn't see shit under his own feet.

Above him, Tarvi and Redlock were sharing a joke. She was laughing prettily, her teeth shone with sudden blue-white, a flash in the mist of shadow. Triqueta shoved the axeman with a boot to shut him up.

The sight of them sent a lightning shock through him. Ecko couldn't help it – his adrenals fired, his targeters reacted. *He would have burned her to death.* More new feelings – he was a fucking jealous kid, resentful and sullen like some overgrown street teen. He *wanted* to hate the axeman; he *wanted* to find reasons why, rationalise his emotional reaction...

For fuck's sake will you get a fucking grip already.

Unthinking, he stood on his cloak hem, overbalanced and rocked for a moment at the stair's outside, black fall yammering at him. As he regained his balance, his adrenals had triggered – his heart was in his mouth, his pulse rate screaming gunfire in his temples. Then he was slumped against the wall, against the bare, slime-slick breasts of the dancer.

Struggling to breathe like some fucking wheezing asthmatic.

Tarvi was there, a shape in the darkness, a hand on his forearm. Her nails glowed with a flicker of electro-varnish. He could imagine her touch sending heat ripples through the almost-black colours of his skin.

"Are you okay?" she asked.

"Get the fuck off me." His rasp was low. He drew back from her, dropped a step. Bruised light crossed her face, her expression was closed. She looked – *oh, for chrissakes* – she looked hurt.

"Oi," Redlock said. "If she wants to care for you, let her. Don't want you slowing us down."

He had no energy for fury.

"You wanna flying lesson?"

The axeman's grin became a laugh.

"Might be more of a diving lesson. Triq says –"

"Triq says, we're near the bottom," Triqueta said. "Can't you feel it?"

The air was cooler, almost cold. Their voices had changed: no longer echoing, lost into the distance.

Triqueta held out her hand, turned it over. Ecko's starlites showed him a plume of fine sand, sparkling as it tumbled slowly past. It made lazy whorls in the air.

"There's a draught," Redlock said.

Cursing silently, Ecko flicked options, kicked his UV.

Jesus Harry fucking Christ, you are so pulling my chain...

Mom had never made his oculars to deal with this shit, any of it. Every which way, his enhancements were failing, breaking.

Yeah, Eliza, I know what you're doing.

They'd found the bottom of the shaft.

Twenty metres or so below him was pure black light, a pool of it, a mirror of it, a still, flat shine of dark illumination.

Jump, it said. *Go on...*

Ecko was no sparky, but he totally got that the Monument stones were some kind of node – they were pulling energy, storing it. Zapping it down the walls. And feeding it here – this thing was some sort of capacitor.

But then what?

Ecko found that he wanted – needed – to blow his way through, to announce his presence with detonation and destruction. To rip the whole thing wide open and uncover what lay below.

He missed London. Life was so much easier with hardware.

"There's something else here," he muttered. "Where's the draught comin' from – Maugrim leave the door open?"

"I wonder what's on the other side?" Tarvi grinned wickedly at him, the deep lights playing upon the curves of her face. He loved the mischief in her expression. He wished he could show her, *really* show her what he could –

Fucking stop it, you asshole!

"Apparently so," Redlock said. "Ecko, I know she's cute, but keep your head in the game."

Ecko shot him an LED eye-flash, a sneer.

Head in the game. They were going down a dungeon, for chrissakes – the axeman had no fucking idea how funny that really was.

The stairway ended in a stone landing – a drop point the size of a virtual dance-pad. No balcony, no security – a tiny, solid square of safety suspended like a dock over the bottomless battery-stone-of-doom.

It was compelling. At the bottom of the stairs, Ecko crouched on the edge of the platform, shadow within shadow, contemplating the shine...

...and looking for something to throw. Y'know. Just in case.

In the wall was a single entranceway, a massive stone lintel, cracked with age, grown with green stuff, carved with phosphor-glitter eyes. It had an eerie, carnival appearance.

Tarvi came to stand beside him, her leg touching his shoulder.

Behind them, Redlock swore – he'd turned his ankle on the slippery step.

She was a pressure of warmth, her reflection a silhouette. In its darkness, her eyes gleamed white, shards of light were caught under her nails, making them almost clawlike. Somehow, her reflection looked monstrous, inhuman. Still, the nearness of her caught in his throat, his belly – the heat of the contact made his blood rage and his lip curl. He stood up, closing his cloak with a deliberate, concealing action.

As he did so, she turned to him – and something caught his attention.

Something about her reflection – something...

Wrong.

For a second, he was stone still as if hit by a basilisk. Then, flesh crystallising in certainty, he watched her reflection, her ghost shadow, disbelieving, *wanting* it to be fake...

She couldn't be... He couldn't've been *that* fucking stupid...

The query was pointless. The ghost was still there, over and above her. And he knew *exactly* what it was.

"Question," Redlock was saying. He'd moved to cover the doorway, axes in hands. "If this Maug-rim is expecting visitors... why haven't we been attacked? Right now, we're as vulnerable as a 'prentice with a cauldron for a helmet – where're the shock-troops? I'd have shot me right off the damned wall."

"You can't shoot for shit," Triq told him.

"True enough." Redlock chuckled and the sound rolled back from the slick, carved walls. "I'd've made you do it."

Ecko wasn't really listening. He was staring at Tarvi's silhouette, now side-on. Out there in the stone shine, or whatever-the-fuck it was, tiny spasms of light flickered like eels.

Some part of his mind shrieked at him, *You knew it, you fucking knew it! You've known it all along!*

You fucking asshole!

"We – Ecko – blew through the wall," Tarvi said, nudging him with her elbow. He recoiled from the contact, throat full of horror – fear that it was true, fear that it wasn't. Dismay at his own naïveté. "Maybe he's not expecting us this soon?"

"Smart girl." Redlock nodded. "You get out of this, I'll put in a good word to Roviarath for you. That old sod Jade owes me a favour or two." He winked.

"Really?" Her eyes were wide. "CityWarden Jade? You would do that?"

Blush.

Downcast expression and eyelids half lowered.

Oh, for chris*sakes,* suddenly it was all so fucking obvious. Ecko wanted to slam his forehead into the wall for being so dumb. She was shovelling it on with an entrenching tool – an Oscar-winning performance to a rapt male audience.

Yeah, so he was that stupid after all.

Suddenly, it was all making sense.

The magharta – at no point had she actually fought them. Her patrol had been shredded round her. *Just so he'd feel?* The stallion – the Monument raining fire and the fervour in her blood when she'd kissed him. The legends she knew – the information she had access to...

He'd *so* fallen for the oldest trick in the book – *Oh honey, you're so hot!* He berated himself, vicious, silent, scornful. *What were you thinking?*

All right, already. No prizes for gettin' the answer to that question right.

In the shine of the stone, her reflection was distorted. Not just the monstrous white eyes and claws, but the shadow that stood with and over her – her guardian spectre. Lush, wanton, terrible.

Irrefusable.

Every schoolboy's fantasy; the creature every comic-book teen had tacked to his bedroom wall. The ultimate, intimate vision, the dream made flesh...

Figment.

He heard Eliza laughing, heard Collator's cool tones – *Chances of discovery at checkpoint four-two-niner: 87.12%.* He heard his sisters giggling as they needled him, endlessly needled him... they'd grown into corporate sell-out bitches, every one of them.

Unaware of the congealing of Ecko's soul, Tarvi had thrown her arms about the axeman's neck, catching him in an awkward and impulsively charming embrace.

"Thank you!" she said, breathless and wide-eyed. "Thank you – I don't know what to say!"

Triqueta coughed. Redlock disentangled himself.

"Not a problem," he said. His voice was gruff, he seemed to be reaching for "paternal". He stepped back. "You've more than earned it."

For a second, Ecko was poised, trembling – indecisive. He knew what he should do, but for chrissakes, how *good* had she felt?

How *real*.

How much he wished it could be –

Fucking stop it! For the last fucking time. Mom told you – remember? – and you gave it up to be what you are. You gave it up!

"She's not earned shit," Ecko said. He threw the cloak back, crossed his arms over his chest. He'd been unable to fuel his flamer, his adrenals were precarious – for the moment, he left them untapped. "Unless she 'fesses up right the fuck now – what the hell is goin' on?"

"Ecko?" Redlock turned, Tarvi half shrank behind him.

"She's not human. And she's playing us all for a bunch of assholes." His eyes met hers. "Aren't ya?"

"What?" Tarvi was shocked, hurt, open mouthed. "What do you mean? Ecko...!"

"Play me for a mug, you bitch." Ecko eyed the axeman. "Get outta the way."

"This has to be a jest."

"Get outta the fucking way. She's a rat, a spy, a creature. A *figment*. All of this – fucking bullshit. Pareus died saving your life, you little whore – did you set those critters on him? Did you know they were there? Did you murder nine members of your own patrol so I'd feel *sorry* for you?" His anger was returning now. "Didja? *Huh?*"

"What...? How could you...?" Tarvi was white faced and broken, she sank sobbing into Redlock's torn shoulder. "Pareus... Oh Gods... Pareus was my *friend*...! Ecko, how could you even *think*...?"

Redlock's mouth was a grim line. From her vantage, Triq watched, narrow eyed over arrow nocked.

The axeman said, "You sick bastard. I should pull your damned spine out."

"The centaur mare – did you blow it up? Save my life? Why?"

He was in a low crouch, aware that his back was to the open edge of the tiny platform. His targeters tracked Redlock's axe, eyes, chest, Triq's bow.

"Who's pulling your strings?" he demanded.

"No one's pulling... that night after Pareus died... I was so afraid... and you..."

"Afraid my fucking ass. How dumb d'you think I am?" At Redlock. "Get outta the way."

The axeman dropped into a half crouch, weapons glittering.

"I don't know what the rhez you are – but I've run out of patience with your horseshit. Back off – now."

"This is loco," Triq said. "The first one of you two idiots that moves..."

"Bring it on." Ecko's adrenaline was kicked, he was already moving. He had one shot at this – if he didn't take the axeman down with the first strike, he was fucked – he'd be shish kebab.

Redlock was fast, his reactions were shit-hot. Even as Ecko's feet moved, the axe was dropping, down and around in a perfect, aggressive block.

But he wasn't fast enough.

The axeman was human; Ecko was not.

Targeters flashed. The foot snapped high, impacted hard against Redlock's sternum. Something cracked. The axeman fell into Tarvi and both of them sprawled into the wall.

He caught Triq's arrow shaft out of the corner of his eye, but he was already in front of it – it spanked from the stone, terhnwood head shattering.

Then he stopped, really sick now, quivering. The low lights of the tunnel were sparking in his vision. He mustn't black out... mustn't fucking black out...

The Bogeyman's luck was with him: he kept his feet – and his stomach.

Triq was shouting – what did they think they were doing? Tarvi was crying out at a sudden shock of pain in her back.

She'd hit the corner of the stone support, the axeman's weight on top of her. *Deal with that, you fucking...*

Redlock straightened up, fighting for breath. Ecko wondered what he'd broken. Not much. In the darkness, the white gleam of the axeman's eyes was utterly unholy.

"You traitorous little bastard. I knew I couldn't trust you. I'm going to –"

"*What?*" Ecko savaged back. He was shaking, trying to hide it, struggling to find his anger in the midst of his vision spinning like he'd been dropping monkeydust all night. "You'll do *what*? I'm faster than you, stronger than you, more than human, built to be a fucking *hero*. Mom made me like this because I *wanted* her to. I *asked* for the fucking pain." Was he telling himself or Redlock? Or was he telling Eliza? "You bring that axe near me, fuckwit, you're getting a steel enema."

"Try me." On foot, Redlock had killed the centaur stallion. He came forwards, the axes spun, edges dancing with the dark light.

Ecko thought, *Yah, fuck it.*

Kicked his boosting.

It failed.

No fucking way.

They were so intent on each other, on the edge of the

platform, that Triq's movement startled them. She was a swift gold streak, down two steps, past Redlock's back and lunging, swearing, through the lintel doorway.

"*Men!*" she said. One hand in her collar, she hauled the fleeing Tarvi back on to the platform. "And where do you think you're going, sunshine?"

Redlock started to cough. Sagging with relief, Ecko was almost on his knees.

"Fat lot of use you two are," Triq said. "All that macho posing. Look at you both!" She shook the captured Tarvi like a squealing esphen. "Spill it, girlie, or I'll show you what the Banned do to people who betray their *friends*. What are you?"

Redlock was trying to speak, but the cough was making him shudder. Blood flecked the inside of his palm. He grimaced, wiped it on his breeches.

"Is *everyone* damned crazed?" he said at last.

"No more than usual." Ecko watched him, wary. "You ready to listen now? Or d'you wanna play some mo– ?"

Tarvi raised her gaze, met his black-on-black oculars. *Help me, Ecko. She'll hurt me. Help me.*

Like electrodes to his temples, his brain exploded.

Images detonated, an expanding writhe of top-quality late-night porn. She was under him, over him, round him, on her knees before him – not just Tarvi, but her real self, her immortal and impossible self. *Figment*. No lover – be she flesh, fantasy, flatscreen creation, body sculpt or brainrig – no lover, even in his dreams, could fulfil him like this.

Let me, she said, her eyes still on his. *Let me show you.*

In the basher, after the death of Pareus and his patrol. Only this time, his breath was lethal – he exhaled and she *burned*.

Oh fucking hell.

She burned for him, with him. The ultimate forbidden fantasy, the fire lived in her flesh and he took her anyway. She loved him, saved him, wrapped herself around him and they burned together, the ultimate consummation and release.

They were consumed, a pyre. They burned away.

Ash, blowing forever across the decaying grass.

Let me show you.

Ecko found himself on his knees. The desire to take hold of her, to rip her from Triqueta's grasp and bury himself in her, was overwhelming. Black teeth clenched, he forced himself to stand.

Aren't there enough goddamn people in my head already? Damn suck-u-bitch, get out!

Dimly, he was aware of the axeman, still coughing. Redlock spat shards of his past through scarlet-flecked teeth.

"Shynane, please... You're not... my wife any more..." He was doubled over from the pain in his chest. His vision was his own, and he was locked within it.

Tormented. But fighting.

Tarvi's eyes narrowed.

Then she turned her hell-gaze on Triqueta.

Weapons forgotten, the horsewoman didn't hesitate. Her hands grabbed the front of Tarvi's shirt, pushed her back into the rock wall. Triq was desert blooded, she lived in the moment and had no thought of resistance – she kissed the creature with a passion that wrapped Tarvi's hands and thighs round her, embracing her eagerly in return.

Redlock hauled himself upright, cried, "Triq!"

For a moment, Ecko thought he was doing the schoolboy-fantasy thing, then he realised something horrifying.

Triqueta was *darkening*.

In the blackness, lit only by the deep-purple throb and spark of the wall, she was caught in the embrace of a monster – and she *shrivelled*.

For a moment, all of Ecko's ocular sensitivity couldn't explain what he saw – but as the axeman surged forwards, coughing still, he realised what the creature was taking.

Time.

The gemstones flickered and flared – but the skin around them shrank, became lined and weather-beaten. In the space of a heartbeat, a silent scream, Triq went from thirty to forty, forty to forty-five –

The back of Redlock's axe clipped Tarvi smartly round the side of the skull. She dropped the horsewoman to the platform, turned on him and hissed through her teeth. She was crouching now, her skin dark, her eyes as white as bone, her nails curved into hooks. Fingers splayed, seeking.

Triqueta hit the stone and lay like a dead thing.

Oh, fuck.

"Please," Tarvi said. Her voice was a throaty mockery of her earlier innocence. "You wouldn't *hurt* me, would you? Think what I can do."

"Yeah, right." Ecko laughed at her. "I got one more fantasy that's all yours."

"Oh don't I know it." She flicked her eyebrows at him, igniting fires in his belly.

"Why did Maugrim send you?" Even as they circled, shifting on the tiny platform, seeking advantage, Redlock was pure business.

She moved, trying to keep both of them in sight, keep their backs to the edge of the lake.

C'mon, Ecko told his endocrine system, *c'mon let's not wait 'til fucking Thanksgiving, shall we?*

The axeman lunged, double slash. But she moved like a dancer – fluid, impossibly graceful.

"Maugrim?" she said.

As he pressed the advantage, pure focused aggression, she opened his face with one lightning claw-slash.

She was laughing. Ecko hadn't even seen her move.

Holy shit. Okay, unholy shit.

"Fool boys, you have no idea." She teased them, sucked blood from her fingertip.

Ecko, targeters wavering, snapped his foot sideways, a strike to break her elbow.

He missed. By about half a klick. She seemed to evaporate, recoalesce.

"Why do you fight?" she said. She flicked her claws at him. He snatched his head sideways. "It's not Maugrim I'm answering to."

"That's helpful." Low and wary, Redlock spluttered a cough.

The axeman lunged again, one blade, two. The platform was too small for this shit. He was trying to drive her back into Ecko, but she spun from between them.

"Maugrim is detailed to take Roviarath. I'm here to make sure he does."

"I'm not playin' twenty fucking questions here." Ecko turned to keep her in sight. *Where were his adrenals?* A second kick, a snap of his foot at her shoulder – his targeters were off.

She blocked it, forearm as merciless as fucking scaff bar. Snatched it down and sideways, twisted her wrist to make a grab for his ankle, tried to tip him.

Fuck!

Her claws scored his reinforced skin. He snatched the foot back, kicked again, one, two, three, repeated piston-kicks at the side of her head – even unboosted he was fast as fuck. And now scared.

But she was faster.

She was simply gone, his foot contacted air and he almost staggered.

"Steady." Redlock seemed to be enjoying this.

Ecko spun back, savage now – hating being this in-fucking-adequate. He had his trickery for a reason, felt suddenly like she was some school fucking bully – picking on the little guy. He and the axeman found themselves shoulder to shoulder, their backs to the platform edge.

"Think about it," she told them. She came forwards, closing

softly, like hands about their throats. She had them now; the heat and scent of her were rising around them both. "The Bard is gone, Rhan is defeated. Jade and Valiembor will fall. Maugrim will take the heart of the Varchinde, just as another will take its head." She was smiling at them, warm curves and her claws receding. "And I want Khamsin."

Ecko blinked. "Come-what?"

Redlock coughed, doubled over, hacking like an old man.

He managed, "If you don't answer to Maugrim…?"

She shivered, delighted and anticipatory. "No, I am the eyes and ears and *touch* of another." She was close now, any closer, she could touch them. "He *feeds* me."

Ecko's heels were over the edge of the stone.

The Bard is gone. Rhan is defeated.

He feeds me.

He could see movement behind her, a shape rising to its feet, drawing a wicked, serrated blade. He didn't look at it – he kept his eyes on Tarvi's.

"What the hell're you talking about? Who feeds you?"

"You don't know." She seemed to find this hilarious, her laugh was full throated, bouncing back from the walls. "All those tales, and he missed telling you the one that actually mattered. Delicious."

Delicious.

Ecko snorted. "He kinda didn't have time. Did you blow up the village? How the hell did you do that?"

"You're sweet," she said. "But not too bright – that wasn't me. I think that was just… target practice." Her smile was needle-sharp. "The magharta – yes, I arranged the deaths of my patrol. It made you easier to control. Killing the centaur – I'm Kas, in my own way, both damned and powerful. I can take advantage of quintessential force."

"So take advantage of this, already. You gotta capacitor right here. Why don'tcha just blow us up?"

"There's enough force here to tear the both of you into pieces." She came closer still, ran a hand down each of their cheeks. Her touch was lightning, fire: impossible promise and pleasure. "But your lives are far more valuable – your time feeds me, belongs to me."

Behind her in the darkness, Triqueta was on her feet. She was older, leaner, grimmer, her expression lined with severity and an absolute lack of mercy.

"I don't think so." Her abrupt gesture was hard, final.

Tarvi shrieked as the serrated blade slammed into her back. For a moment, her hand reached to Ecko, for his time, for his help, he didn't know. Her dark eyes begged him, *Please*, she said, *help me*. A hundred images tumbled through his thoughts. *I love you.*

Triq said, "You betrayed your tan – your family." With a wrench, she yanked the blade free, watched as Tarvi crumpled. "You're not betraying mine."

Ecko watched her slump, his arms folded and his chin raised. His expression was flat, his oculars dry.

Please...

His foot connected hard with the side of her skull.

"Bitch."

She didn't move again.

25: TWICE FALLEN FHAVEON

They came for Rhan at last: the soldier Mostak and the old priest Gorinel.

Neither of them spoke, and they didn't meet his gaze.

Rhan was numb, broken, listing somewhere between hopelessness and denial. He made no effort to resist them, nor to plead for understanding as they blindfolded him and bound his wrists. The bonds were crafted of fabric and smelling of camphor, but they held him as if they were Kartian metal.

Their shame was bond enough.

Wearily, the old priest raised his spread hand to Rhan's chest and touched him with each finger in turn, pressing them home like marks – a gesture unseen in Fhaveon in hundreds of returns.

An odd and momentary thought: *Who had been the last person that the city had put to death?*

Rhan couldn't remember, and obscurely, this bothered him.

Gorinel's voice was a soft, barrel-chested rumble, almost regretful. "By your might, Samiel; by your mercy, Cedetine; by your justice, Dyarmenethe; by your wisdom, Cemothen; by your love, Calarinde…"

Rhan quelled a surge of misery – like the bonds, like the ritual itself, the names of the Gods were so long-unused that the church had no knowledge even of their meaning, of the identities they tried to invoke. For an instant, he allowed himself to plead to them, silently, to the very heavens themselves, *This cannot be!*

But the priest continued as if the Gods had not heard him. Gorinel pressed the palm of his hand against Rhan's chest, as if marking him with a brand.

"This man, Rhan of Fhaveon, has been found guilty of treason and regicide. He is sentenced to be outcast from the city..."

Under the darkness of his despair, Rhan remembered, *You have been found guilty of the crimes of pride and ambition, Elensiel. Your opinions are of no concern to me. You will Fall.*

"...that he may lay down his sin with his mortal body, and enter the Halls of the Gods..."

Did you not realise the cost of your temptation? You are Dæl, Star-born, you and your siblings are the most favoured form of life we created. We gave you all, and yet you desire to elevate yourself more. You know the laws, our halls are ever barred to you.

"...untainted by his actions..."

Do not fail in the duties we have charged you with, Elensiel. If you do, the mortal world will seem as sweet as my daughter's embrace compared to the fate that will befall you.

"...By the rule of Heal and Harm, we take life that life may be spared. In the name of the Gods..."

From this time forth, you are "rhan", homeless. You are charged with the care of the mortal world. If you fail me again, you will be nothing.

"...let justice be done."

Let justice be done.

Mostak, commander of the soldiery, responded to the old priest's final words, just as Dyarmenethe, brother of Samiel, had done, over four hundred returns before.

"Justice will be done."

And, just as the hands of Samiel and his brother had held Rhan out over chaos and let him fall, so now did these hands lead him out to face a fall from another height – to once again plummet into the cold waters of the eastern sea.

The fall would be less far, but this time, there was no Tekisarri to pull him free, and to give him purpose and new life.

He was condemned.

...You will be nothing.

For now, though, he had a moment – a fragment of time to cry his denial, to prove his own innocence or Phylos's guilt, to free himself and release the stranglehold that the Merchant Master closed about the city. A single opportunity to wrest back control and to uncover whatever real plans Phylos harboured. If he failed, and if his brother Kas Vahl Zaxaar ever returned, then the daemon would tear the Varchinde to screaming pieces.

My poor people. The thought was a thread of light in the darkness. *What will happen to you?*

And they marched him, stumbling in silent darkness through stone corridors, a solemn tramp of feet echoing from the walls.

The hands brought Rhan to the scene of his final ruin, and they gave him a push.

Blind, he stumbled through twin doors, heavy and cold. A rising roar of sound hit him like a tide. He knew where he was – in many ways, this room was more familiar to him than his own skin.

This was what Tekisarri had given him; this was what the Gods had charged him to care for. His life had been spent in this room.

As other hands took the blindfold from him, though, he almost quailed.

In four hundred returns of his guardianship, he had never

seen this many people in the Theatre of Nine.

The implications were sickening, but he could not find the thoughts to articulate them – he was overwhelmed by shouting, by the rising tiers of faces, by the mouths contorted in hate and loathing.

By the expressions of righteous fury.

He found himself lurching forwards. Unable to put his hands out to steady himself, he was almost on his knees.

For the first time in returns without measure, the great, cold theatre had life. It raged with energy, with anger and pride, with the burning-loyal soul of the Lord city. As Rhan's eyes traced upwards across the people, perhaps looking for an end, looking for a face of hope, a single expression of support – Scythe? Penya? Dear Gods, Roderick? – he could see that there were soldiers, spear bearing and silent, standing in the alcoves in the half circle of the back wall.

Over them, the carved story of Fhaveon's founding glittered, mocking, and he looked away.

At the table, eight of the Nine were gathered – the pale-faced Selana now in her father's chair, upright and tiny amid the chaos. Her Council were unchanged, only Rhan's seat was empty, his own carven likeness, ever plummeting, now seemed in outright scorn.

He took a pace towards it, purely out of reflex. It had been his seat for four hundred returns and he could not...

He had failed.

Failed Samiel, failed Tekisarri, failed the family Valiembor, failed his damned brother.

Will you miss me, Vahl, if I'm not here to fight?

But Vahl Zaxaar, it seemed, did not hear him.

Phylos rose to his feet in a billow of blood-fabric.

"There he is!"

Reaction spread from him like shock. The sea of shouting faces reddened with fervour, mouths wide, eyes flashing. A

chant began at the back of the crowd. *"Rhan! Rhan! Rhan!"*
Fists punched the air in unison.

For a moment, the shouts counterpointed the ghost memory
of Demisarr's final shriek, the feel of his wife's lithe and furious
body...

I did not do this!

His unheard cry was desperate with incomprehension.

Valicia herself stood like a wall, her arms folded and her
expression stone. She had the courage to meet his gaze and face
him down, and he knew that she would cast him from the city's
heights herself, if she could.

Then there were soldiers beside him. Hands on his arms
propelled him forwards.

As he came fully into the bottom of the theatre, the crowds'
frenzy redoubled, shrieking and chanting. They were a mob,
savage. The missiles started – fruit, spit, stones. There were
faces he knew, lovers and friends, and they were jeering hatred.

They believed.

He lifted his chin in challenge and defiance – not to the
people, but to his own despair.

I could not have done this!

A fruit pit struck his chest. He flinched. Another struck his
shoulder, his ear. He almost lost his footing, but forced himself
to stand. Briefly, he remembered the terrible plummet of his
Fall through chaos, and wondered if it really could have been
any worse than this.

*Rack up the tankards, my brother. Perhaps I will be joining
you after all.*

One figure surged out of the teeming people, his shouting
lost in the crowds' roar, but his intention clear as he tried to
hurl himself down onto the theatre's floor. A jolt like lightning
jarred through Rhan's body as he saw the loathing on the
young man's face. He stopped, transfixed, tried to meet the
man's gaze, defend himself, deny this insane accusation.

He said, "Scythe...!"

But Scythe was caught by a soldier's hand on his shoulder, efficient and ruthless. A moment later, the soldier had snatched the young man up and carted him away.

The crowd jeered and wailed.

Phylos held up his hands for silence.

Slowly, the tides of movement stilled. A child cried at the back and was hushed by a gentle murmur.

"This is Fhaveon," Phylos said, "the might of the Varchinde. Built by Saluvarith, ruled by the First Lord Foundersson Tekisarri and by his sons and daughters for four hundred returns. We are the Grasslands' Lord and guardian, the people of the plains look to us for hope, faith and terhnwood.

"And we cannot let them down."

The crowd was quiet now, watching the Merchant Master as if transfixed. Rhan could feel that the room was growing oddly warm.

Sweating.

He shifted, oddly uneasy.

What?

"There is a legend, people of Fhaveon," Phylos told them, "one we have all heard in the markets and bazaars. A tale that this city was built to face a daemon, that Saluvarith brought the white stone of the Archipelago here to the Varchinde and that he constructed a fortress, a great wall upon the water. He built a city of might to ensure that this daemon would never return.

"And the tale goes on. It tells that he was sent a champion, an immortal warrior to stand upon the city's wall and watch always for her foe.

"We ask ourselves, people of Fhaveon, if this legend is true."

The people were silent. The tale of Fhaveon's construction was well known, but few treated it as anything more than a tavern-saga. In this world of trade and terhnwood, the word "daemon" had a ring of the ludicrous.

Phylos was smiling like a benefactor. Rhan was watching him now, unsure where this gambit was going.

The air was growing warmer.

The Merchant Master was still talking. "Fhaveon has stood proud for four hundred returns, unthreatened for lifetime after lifetime. And we have seen no *daemon*." The word was scornful, with a tinge of threat.

Somewhere in Rhan's heart, a worm of fear was burrowing, beginning to curl. The air was making his breath catch in his throat.

Don't do this. Whatever you're going to do, don't do this...

The people were beginning to mutter, shifting in their seats. The Merchant's smile spread to a grin full of teeth.

"My people, we stand at the edge of new beginning – of a time when we can finish the work that Adward began, when our very command of the terhnwood cycle can take control of the Varchinde entire. And I say to you – that the daemon is no *legend*."

What? The air was close, humid. Under the brilliance of the white rocklights, people's skin was beginning to glisten.

Phylos held his hands higher. "Wait! Heed me and I will explain! I say to you that this 'daemon' is propaganda! It is a story perpetuated by this –" he indicated Rhan and the susurration of the crowd grew louder "– this *man* –" the word was spat "– so he can soak up our comforts and our time and our wealth and our work and do *nothing*."

The accusation was close enough to the truth to leave Rhan breathless. Something in him said, *No, it wasn't like that, I've always...* But it was there, like a fibre-pin jabbing in his skin. If he had been fulfilling his mandate, he would have seen this coming, returns ago.

Phylos did not stop. "He is a lodestone and a drain upon us, a figure of indolence and luxury. Who can know what takes place under the roofs of his home? I say, that if there is a daemon, it is the daemon *sloth*, it is the daemon *idleness*, it is the daemon that keeps us from our crafthalls and tithehalls and farmlands and markets! This – creature – has believed that he is above the laws of this city! He has traded in substances we abhor, he has corrupted our youth, he has –" and here he paused, arms raised completely and blazing with red fabric and rising heat "– murdered the loved Lord of this city and taken his wife by force –"

"I did *not* – !" The cry was torn like a sob from Rhan's throat – a cry of denial and horror. "I did not touch the Lord Demisarr, nor lay hands on his wife, I – !"

"You *lie*, daemon!" Savagely, Phylos rounded on him, his red robes vivid as gore. He used his voice like a goad, forcing the crowd into a frenzy. "You are an *infection*! You have controlled and manipulated the sons of Saluvarith all your life! You have sat in this very room and pulled our strings like puppets! You claim innocence, yet you have inflicted such harm…!" He turned to Selana, overpowering in his presence and strength. "If he is innocent, my Lord, it is time for him to tell us the truth behind his longevity. The truth behind the *bargains* he has made that have given him four hundred returns of life!"

Phylos turned back to Rhan with a curiosity that verged on avid.

Flattened by Phylos's demand, Selana, also, turned to look at him.

"The Merchant Master is right," she said. Her voice was small in the chaos, but the crowd quietened to hear her. "You are a blight upon the city – and a blight upon my family." The word was a painful crack and she stood up, quivering with tension. "You are a drain upon our resources and a stagnation to our growth. Your time is done."

For a moment, Rhan could only stare at her.

He said, his voice barely a growl, "Make no mistake, the daemon Vahl Zaxaar exists. And he will return."

But the words fell to the floor and he realised they sounded as ludicrous as Roderick's visions. The crowd were tittering, some calling for answers and others for blood.

His hands still bound, Rhan raised his voice to call over them.

"All my life, Merchant Master," he said, "I have guarded the children of Saluvarith, and I have watched the Grasslands flourish under Fhaveonic rule." In the sea of people, jeers began. "I swore my oath of allegiance to the First Lord Foundersson Tekisarri, who named me his Seneschal, and I have upheld that oath for four hundred returns. To whom have you sworn your allegiance, Phylos? To your own *greed*?"

For a second, he almost had it. There was a moment of quiet, the stillness in the eye of the storm – a moment when Selana turned startled eyes upon her mentor, where Valicia's gaze narrowed. Gorinel the priest studied Rhan intently. The soldier Mostak's forehead lined as he strained to think.

But Phylos laughed – astonished, disbelieving laughter that shattered the stillness like crystal.

"You choose now to spread dissent?" He guffawed, as if at a great jest. Then his laughter was shut off. "Answer the question, Rhan. To whom have you sold your soul? To what?"

Ignoring Phylos, ignoring the crowds' mockery, Rhan faced Selana, and paused.

The room was seething with heat.

He sank to one knee.

"I am Rhan, Lord Seneschal of Fhaveon," he said. "And I swear by my Gods-given mandate that I am Dæl Rhan Elensiel, Master of Light, keeper of Saluvarith's vision, and of this mortal world. I love and guard this city with everything I am. And when my damned brother returns... My Lord, heed me. Without me, you and everything you love will perish in flames and screaming."

The theatre was silent. Selana stared, stunned. Valicia's skin was white.

Then, somewhere in the crowd, Rhan could hear Scythe's voice, shrieking accusations.

Knowing he had only this one moment, the single chance to seize the situation, Rhan said, "You know your legends, my Lord. You know who and what I am, and why I have lived four hundred returns." He raised his voice to call out up through the Theatre, his voice filling the room with sound. "And you know that I did not, could not, have raised my hand against the Lord Demisarr – or against his wife."

Gathering her wits, Selana opened her mouth to speak.

But Phylos was frighteningly fast. "Would one of the Dæl import illegal drugs? Seduce the city's idle and take them from their work? Host parties that damage and distress our youth?"

Rhan stared.

"I say you are a plague – a blight. I say you are *arta ekanta,* a daemon figment that has taken on the form of the city's saviour!" Phylos moved around the edge of the table and raised his voice to an impassioned cry. "Perhaps you *are* Vahl Zaxaar! You are corruption in our *midst*!"

Horrified by the speed with which Phylos had overturned his plea, Rhan tried to stop him.

"No – !"

"And I say you must *die*!"

The soldiers stepped forwards to restrain him. About him, the crowd surged into outcry, demanding satisfaction. He looked for help, but there was no one to even meet his gaze.

His failure could not have been more complete.

There was no further assurance he could give, no way he could reclaim his place – the city belonged to Phylos and there was no move he could make.

He collapsed to his knees, the heat sobbing in his chest.

And they dragged him upright, and walked him from the theatre for the very last time.

* * *

Rammouthe Island.

By legend, the Island Accurséd. The home of the Ilfead-Syr, the world's lost memory. The last refuge of the sleeping Kas Vahl Zaxaar.

From this height, it was a grey line against the horizon, a hummock of darkness.

No ship had touched its shore since the Bard's disastrous reconnaissance, some forty returns previously. No foot had dared its soil. Stood upon the very top of the sheer white wall that ran down the eastern edge of the Fhaveon to the roiling sea, Rhan wondered, rather foolishly, if they would release his wrists – if he should swim the Bava Strait and reach the island safely.

And what would be waiting for him if he did.

If anything still lay there, the island had swallowed it long ago and refused to give it up.

The sky above Rhan's final moments was vast and distant, merciless. If the Gods were there, they did not look down to see him. Images assaulted him – plummeting through air and cold and pain, war and chaos, stormy skies and hammering seas, scourging the city's foes with light and with metal, Kas Vahl Zaxaar, closer than brother and powerful, terrible enemy...

...the tiny newborn that was the next Foundersson or daughter, holding each one in his white hands and promising them his loyalty until the end of the Count of Time...

Rhan lifted his face to the wind.

"A long wait, my estavah," he said to the horizon. "And this is how it ends? Wake up, damn you. You owe me breakfast."

But, like the Gods, his brother did not heed him.

It was Phylos who came to stand with him, red robes snapping in the cold wind. Further back, Valicia had come to watch and Selana, Lord Foundersdaughter, stood with her mother's hands on her shoulders. The warrior Mostak stood with them, looking for a moment like a sharper, colder version of his murdered brother. They were a family wronged, and he could see nothing in their faces that spoke of understanding.

I did not do this. You must know...

"Last words?" said Phylos softly.

Then something crawled into the edges of Rhan's awareness – something strange.

With a peculiar shock, Rhan realised that the curious, sweating heat he had felt in the theatre was coming from the Merchant Master himself. In Phylos's Archipelagan frame there burned eagerness, anticipation. Expectation. A whetted and savage hunger that was as familiar to Rhan as his own white light.

Knowledge crystallised in an instant and, as though his own light had shown him, he understood.

He *understood*.

And the weight of it drove him to his knees.

How could he have been so stupid? So phenomenally blind? How could he...?

"No." He wasn't even aware that he'd said it aloud. "You can't have..."

"Oh but I can." Phylos smiled at him like an old friend. "Rhan, your indolence has damned you as effectively as the words of Samiel himself. Your bonds hold you in honour – spiritually as well as physically – and in a moment, you will tumble from the top of this wall. When you do, the Varchinde loses her head." He watched the horizon, still smiling. "Think, Rhan Elensiel, as you're falling, so House Valiembor is falling with you. And it's not the only one." His warmth grew. "Your brother, your estavah – he stirs with might. And his time will *come*."

"Don't do this. Whatever he offered you –"

"Are those your last words?" Phylos laughed. "There will be no war, Rhan, why should there be? I hold the trade-life of the Varchinde in my hand. The city and the Grasslands belong to me. Why should there be returns of bloodshed, strife and fighting, back and forth, when these things can be so simple? The head –" he ran a finger across his throat "– and the heart."

Rhan said, "Roviarath. You damned bastard, what did you *do*?"

Phylos reached out a hand and snapped a tiny fragment of metal around Rhan's still-bound forearm. It burned – but Rhan didn't know what it was.

"Now," Phylos said, "will you jump – or do I have to push you?"

The metal bracelet itched. The Merchant Master leaned in, tapped it and said, "A little... security. I want to make sure you hit the water, and I want to watch you *drown*."

Rhan shook off Phylos's touch, walked to the very edge of the wall. Below him, there were carved faces of creatures in the stone, their teeth bared at the sea. To the north, the Swathe River roared from its gorge and the water seethed white and angry.

He turned his back on the drop and faced his accusers.

"My Lady," his voice was solid, even in the wind. "Upon Samiel's name, I did not take the life of the Lord Demisarr, nor inflict any harm upon yourself."

Valicia snapped back at him, "I bear your bruises on my *skin*."

"I will return when I can prove my words." He stepped backwards into the empty air. "Look for me."

And he fell.

Again.

The last thing he heard was Phylos's voice, "Now we finish this. Get me the Bard."

26: CATHEDRAL THE MONUMENT

An image danced enticing in the brazier's light…

Roviarath.

The Grasslands' most populous city, the hub of the Varchinde's ever-cycling trade. Maugrim had lived on her doorstep, he knew her strength: to the west, the waterways that brought wood and stone from Irahlau and Vanksraat, the exquisite craftsmanship of the Kartiah; to the east, the Great Cemothen River and the trade-route to the docks and spice markets of Amos, the triremes of the Archipelago.

About her fine and decorous stone skirts, the vast defenceless sprawl of the Great Fayre – now evacuated, abandoned and skeletal at the CityWarden's back.

CityWarden Larred Jade sat mounted, waiting.

About him, his militia. He'd sent the younger ones and the ones with families to warn the farmlands, and block the trade-roads. With him waited his veteran range patrols, nine tan in all, ninety warriors, thirty of them mounted. Upon the wall, another seventy archers.

A ludicrous and pitiful number. And Maugrim knew – not one of them had ever fought anything more dangerous than a road-pirate. They were the over-stuffed city's only defence.

And the Monument's creatures, fire and stone, were blazing through the grass towards them.

Come the dawn, the Fayre would burn like a Fawkes' Night fire.

And while Jade was dealing with the aftermath, the Sical would raze Roviarath to the ground – all but the walls.

And the heart of the plains would stop beating.

Triqueta paused on the edge of an impossible garden.

Deep under the Monument's glow, verdant, swarming and growing almost as she watched it, was a madness of crumbling stone and lushly tangled, fecund life. There were trees – insane that they should grow down here – stooped and arching under the weight of wild, strangling vines, pulling them down until their trunks splintered. There were archways leading from nowhere to nowhere, broken buildings, twisted staircases that ended in only air, their stone cracking under clawing fingers of creeper.

A spreading, thorny knot of wild bramble blanketed everything, entangling and burying it. In places, it flowered in delicate white; in others, it bore fruit that rotted uneaten. Down here, the very seasons were corrupt.

She was shaken to her core, weakened and uncomprehending. *What had Tarvi done?*

Her knees hurt, her back, the joints of her fingers. Her face felt strange, tight, the stones in her cheeks somehow loose. The skin on her arms and hands was spotted with age, no longer her own. Her *hair* felt wrong.

She had no way to see her own reflection. And she was afraid.

Yet they'd staggered, Redlock coughing blood like an old man, down a curve of ancient, clumsily hewn tunnel and found themselves on the edge of...

...this.

This was ornamental lunacy, the Goddess herself driven loco by an overspill of naked, elemental power. Light shone from the walls, veins of crystal and spreading lichen growth, it cast harsh, angled shadows and dazzled them after the darkness of the well.

She didn't like enclosed spaces. She liked this, this distortion of the natural wild, even less.

Her hand tightened on her bow, gripping it against a sliding sweat of nervousness.

Ecko's rasp was subdued. "Fuck. Your hydroponics guys went on a bender, huh."

In front of her, he was as dark as a nightmare, as sharp as a blade. As he moved, the harsh shadows of the crazed canopy slipped over his cloak and the colours in it stirred and shifted as though the leaves blew in an unfelt wind.

Triq missed the breeze, the open sky.

She listened, straining to hear – something, anything. The stillness disturbed her – there were no creatures, no birds or sunlight. She could hear only her own heartbeat, the pounding of her pulse in her ears.

Redlock coughed again, wiped blood from his lip. The claw slice in his cheek was swelling to an angry scarlet.

"I'm guessing we can pick up the char trail pretty quick. Ecko, what d'you see?"

"Green shit," Ecko told him. "More green shit than an Amsterdam biolab. Hang on…"

Flicking his cowl over his shifting mottle-skin, he tilted his head as though listening. Triq counted one, two, three – and he was gone, dissolved into the chaos. Not a leaf shook, she didn't hear him leave.

Summoning her courage, she touched a hand to Redlock's muscled shoulder.

"What happened to me?" The kiss haunted her.

The axeman turned to her, his face troubled.

"My fault," he said. "I trusted the wrong person – let familiarity govern judgement. Won't happen again." He dropped one axe through its belt-ring and ran callused fingers over her cheek. "You may not believe this," he smiled at her, "but I think it suits you."

"What suits me? No, don't mess me about, damn you. Just tell me. What did she do?"

His hand paused. "You're older, maybe... ten returns." His thumb brushed her lips. "And still beautiful. Perhaps more so."

Older.

She turned into his hand, kissed him as she had done in the ribbon-town tavern, a hundred returns ago.

"From anyone but you, that'd be the worst line..."

No, not a hundred. Ten.

That explained the aches, the stiffness, the thinness of her face and the length of her hair. Explained why the stones in her cheeks hurt – they were attuned to her skin, her bones and her growth, an old desert tradition whose truth was long forgotten – they hadn't had time to adjust.

And neither had she.

Redlock's hand hadn't moved. "It's only ten returns or so, Triq." He grinned. "I still have a couple on you."

She found she was biting her lip, trying to stop her face from crumpling. She swallowed twice before she could speak.

"You don't understand." Her voice was a whisper. "My sire – was desert-born. We grab at life because we don't have enough of it. My returns don't measure as yours do. I –"

"Enough." His mouth was on hers, gentle. She returned his embrace – wilfully banishing the yammering memory of Tarvi's death kiss, her heat and softness and hunger.

"Oh for chrissakes." Ecko's rasp made them jump apart like guilty 'prentices. "Good thing there are no beasties down here, you guys'd be dinner. Will you quit snogging already and come and look at this?"

* * *

Amethea was aware of the darkness.

It was over her, it was closing on her vision. It was writhing down from the sinuously twisting, sliding knot of stalactites above her. It was falling, droplets of black water that kissed her hot skin.

She was aware of the brazier, though dimly. She could hear the rising celebration of the Sical, its delight in her blood, its need to be free. She almost felt sorry for it – Maugrim had no business trapping it like that.

She was aware of Maugrim himself, his presence still stung her flesh. He was watching the descending writhe of the pillar, eager for the union that would fuse cathedral to Monument, belly to throat, and loose the elemental at last.

She couldn't stop him.

The thought was surreal: she was dying. After everything. Down here in this forgotten place – and no one would ever know what had happened.

Apothecary, heal yourself.

Then Maugrim was turning from the brazier's visions, his heavy tread ringing hard on the stone floor. She heard him, as if from a hollow distance.

He spat one word, shock, disbelief, a sudden arrowhead spiking the side of his scheming...

"Redlock."

And the word sank through the darkness in her head, sending ripples like waves of hope. *Redlock.* Feren's warrior cousin, beyond all ken, all reason.

He was *here.*

The Sical shrieked, flapped its wings like a trapped bird. Sparks flew. As she struggled onto her elbows, the blood ran anew from the wound in her belly – why was there still no pain? – and she realised the fire-creature was bigger.

A lot bigger.

Oh dear *Goddess*.

This was not some tiny, trapped being: this was the cathedral's corrupted heart, an Element manifest, the pure and naked wrath of the Soul of Fire. It was too hot, it shone brighter than the sun and it stood taller even as she watched it. It was rising above Maugrim, its light searing the walls.

It was Maugrim's heat and lust given form – and it was craving release.

Feed, I. Soon.

Maugrim was swearing, words harsh and unfamiliar.

"All I fucking need is some goddamned self-professed hero – arrived in the nick of time to rescue the bloody girl." He jabbed a ringed finger at Amethea. "Don't go away, little lady, seems you've got a friend wanting to join you."

She stared in a wonder of realisation – a comprehension of something amazing.

He was *afraid*.

Apothecary, heal yourself!

Feren had survived. How could she do any less? Breathing steadily against her suddenly rising heart rate, she lay back down, feigning the edge of unconsciousness. She had no intention of being a hostage.

But what could she do? Think!

The Sical screamed, hissed. As its wings flapped, it threw blasts of heat and sparks. *Feed, I! Now! Free!*

"Soon." Maugrim promised it. Amethea heard a heavy, metallic jangling. "You're mine – you'll do as you're told. If you wait –" she heard him shudder, anticipation, excitement "– if you wait, you'll have more fuel, better fuel. And you'll be free."

Loose, I! Its hiss dissolved into the crackle of the fire.

Barely daring to breathe, Amethea heard Maugrim's boots cross the cathedral floor.

* * *

The garden was as still as a corpse.

It was claustrophobic, stagnant, hot and heavy. The weight of it pressed down on Ecko's shoulders. Too much green stuff, too much *life* – it was freaking him right the fuck out.

He watched everywhere, oculars flicking through multiple channels. His adrenals were still down – his starter motor coughed, but wouldn't turn over.

Damn you, bitch! He wasn't sure if he meant Tarvi – the name stung like a ripped scab – or Eliza.

The axeman and the girl – girl no longer – were behind him, feet soft on the overgrown gravel path. Together, they crossed what must once have been a stream, now a rank, crusted gully, and came to the edge of the undergrowth.

Ecko pointed, shards of light on his mottle-dark skin.

They had reached the lair of the Big Bad Boss.

Over him, over the garden, the cathedral was a bombed ruin, a nightmare hollow of blackened stone. The huge window was shattered, fragments of coloured glass hanging twisted from the web-work frame. Walls stood headless, jagged and crumbling, as though the cavern's teeth had bitten them clean through and had spat back the bits to crash among the plant life. He didn't need his heatseeker to tell him what lurked within.

Okay, so I got here. Now what?

They faced a broken doorway, rotted wood hanging crazily from ancient hinges. Between them, a red-lighted throat like the fucking Gates of Hell.

How he would *love* to just bring this whole thing down. How easy it would be...

Overhead, he could see the underside of the shining black stone – the capacitor they'd come past – now shot through with energy like storm lightning. On either side of the doorway, a gargoyle crouched in an alcove.

Redlock crept past him, gesturing at them to keep pace. "Keep together," he mouthed. "Watch your backs."

No fucking shit.

Warily, they slipped from the protection of the crazed tree canopy. Ecko scanned the wall tops, aware of his vulnerability – he felt insect small, sniper fodder. A rat at the bottom of a fucking fractal maze.

Closer still – until the gargoyles could be seen clearly.

One was a stone figure, female, naked, her long hair streaming back from her carved face, holding her head to the wall. Her stone eyes looked straight out over the garden, unblinking.

Redlock's hand tightened to white-knuckled tension at the sight of her, but Triqueta was staring, narrow eyed, at the other figure.

Male, long hair intricately woven, elaborate scarring like some serious fucking body art. His face was narrow chinned, oddly triangular, one long, delicate hand was half outstretched.

"He's alive," Triq said softly. She moved to look up at him, peer into his face. Like the woman, his eyes stared at nothing and the stone had closed over his mouth and nose.

"No shit." Ecko had kicked his heatseeker – he could see the warm contours of colour, writhing manically beneath the blue stone exterior. Impossibly, the man was struggling, noiselessly, frantically. On some level beyond the physical, he was completely conscious and fighting to be free. "Happen to have a chisel on you? A road drill?"

"How does he do this?" Triq's voice was pale with horror. "Men onto horses, flesh into stone. Carved metal cara– Oh by the Gods."

The heat signature had fluctuated, flickered at the sound of her voice.

"He's Kartian," Triq said, almost a whisper. "The scarring shows his craft-rank and family."

"So...?"

Triq stepped back. "Kartians of rank are metalworkers, craftmasters." Her expression was set. She tipped a single washer into her hand. "Looks like you're staying there, sunshine. Give you some time to think. All the time in the world, in fact…"

Metalworkers. Carved-metal carapace.

"Best place for him," Redlock said.

"He's gonna get real fucking bored," Ecko said, grinning. "Shame."

The colours screamed at them – desperate, doomed. They were walking away from him and he knew it.

"All of this," Triq said, "is really starting to piss me off. Everything's twisted… forced, corrupted. Life, the cycles of the elements, the seasons – it's distorted, the air *stinks*." Ecko noticed the age lines that carved through her face, they gave her mouth a bitter downturn. "People fight, that's fine – but you can't live by abominating flesh – or by stealing *time*."

Redlock said, "Triq – easy. I know you've –"

"Stuff it, Red. Enough horseshit."

She moved swiftly, slamming the rotted door to the ground. She stared grimly into the cathedral, past rows of silent, stone figures to the blaze of power at the centre.

"Did you hear me?" It was a challenge. "Come out, you damned coward! I'm done gaming – come out!"

It rebounded from the walls like the Banned's war cry, like the harsh sound of the blade in Tarvi's back.

"Impulsive wench," Redlock muttered, chuckling. "Can't say I blame her. You with me, Ecko? Let's go mess this bastard up."

"I hear that."

Ecko wrapped a hand round the hard edges of Lugan's lighter and they entered the cathedral together.

A blazing pillar, a conduit of flame.

Even from as far away as the huge building's centre, it

seared his face like an incinerator, blinded his heatseeker to an almost-white magnesium flare. His anti-daz kicked, he checked, left and right. The ranks of rotted stone statues were all too familiar and he so *knew* they'd come lumbering to life. There was a faint, sullen glow to their eyes, to the lines of their grey stone – as if they drew strength from the fire ahead of them.

The bastard had an army, mustered in ranks and waiting for the call to action.

Great.

Odds of getting outta this alive? Right now, about 00.0-fucking-2%

"Was this the point?" Ecko's soft rasp was aimed at the flatscreen he couldn't see, his watchers, his judges.

Ahead of him, Triqueta was a shadow against the firelight.

"Face the Big Bad Boss with no kit, no weapons, no adrenaline? In London, I could take this out in three minutes flat. And you fucking know it!"

He raised his voice, added his challenge to hers.

"Show us whatcha got, Maugie. I'm the last person in the world you're gonna scare with *fireworks.*"

There was no response. The statues didn't move.

Ecko snorted. Ahead of him, the massive blaze seemed to shift with a life of its own. Its light danced from the walls.

And it was beautiful.

Fire raining from the sky.

His attention compelled, he found himself addressing his questions towards it.

"What're you teachin' me here – teamwork, humility, resource?" His voice scraped like a handful of pebbles. "Do I triumph over Evil with wit and sticky tape – ?"

"Who're you talking to?" Triq dropped back beside him.

"Keep moving." Redlock muffled a cough with the back of his hand.

They walked forwards, the blaze on their faces, the ranks of silent, stone soldiers to either side.

Triqueta muttered, "We're going to get jumped any second…"

But Ecko barely heard her. The pillar of flame was still growing – reaching almost to the cavern roof. This close, it was too hot to look at, yet it pulled his oculars as hard as it pulled the compass in his pouch.

He said, "Or do I find some truth in the Final Showdown – and go on to Save the World?"

There was a figure within it, indistinct, yet powerful and glorious.

Oh dear fucking God.

And it called him by name.

It sent sparks through his blood, illuminated his weakness, touched him, stroked his soul with impossible insight. Fire was domination and recognition, destruction and statement – but it was defender and protector, warmth and security, love – the family he'd shunned as a child, the acceptance he craved and scorned.

Worthy, you. Grant everything you wish.

Tamarlaine Benjamin Gabriel, the slender, pale no one who had surrendered his humanity to become a comic-book anti-hero – become the Ecko, the nightmare, the ghost in the darkness – and it shone upon his darkest heart, the desires he dared not form. It saw them, took them and offered them back to him.

Dream, you. Desire, you. Grant everything you wish.

Champion, more than human, phantom and legend and costumed icon – untouchable by pain, unreachable by love. The public knew him: they devoured his headlines and were amazed by his deeds… but they never reached him. He was enigma and mystery, in complete control of his own reputation.

Then why had he gone to Lugan on Fawkes' Night, why had he gone?

The creature answered him.

Hear your loneliness, I. Understand.

Fire, the Bard had once said, *was a God of Truth*.

Grant you the world, I. Burn or secure for you.

Eliza had taken away everything he'd acquired, everything that gave "Ecko" validation. In its place, she'd been peeling him back to Tamarlaine. She'd tempted him with physical love. Now she offered him – what – family?

Or was she tempting him – giving him the chance to burn it the fuck down, just as he'd wanted to at the beginning? Raze it all, prove he didn't care, prove he was no one's fucking toy?

Was this the exit he'd craved?

Turn back to page one.

Or was it fail and reboot?

She was *still* fucking with his head.

"You know what you can do?" His voice ricocheted from the walls, shattering into the harsh sounds of a real, snarling challenge. "You can just kiss my chameleon *ass*!"

And all hell broke loose about them.

Above him, a fragment of the stone wall tumbled to shatter upon the floor. Ecko jumped, half turned, but ahead of him came a rasping grind of stone – the floor was sliding, like tomb lids scraping from their places. His nostrils caught the scent of burned flesh.

He yowled at the shattered roof, "Yeah? Bring it the fuck on!"

But he was drowned out by a second crash of falling masonry. They had no cover, nowhere to run – they found themselves surrounded now by the hazy outlines of two dozen figures in flickering, fiery robes, surrounded by their rising chant. As if they sensed him looking, one raised its face to smile at him – its mouth was full of flame.

Tarvi's vision: he would have burned her to death.

The fire pillar was taking form as the sounds caressed it. In a moment, the strange chanting reached a crescendo and came to an abrupt, expectant stop. Hazy figures raised their hands in ecstatic worship as a coalescence began.

Ecko was transfixed. He hung on to Lugan's lighter like an anchor, but he could only stare.

Cloaked in heat and power and beauty, impossibly tall and crystalline in gracefulness, bewinged like an angel but blistering their skins with heat, the flame-creature rose incandescent, spreading arms and wings.

With an inarticulate cry, Ecko was on his knees as if his every dream had manifest for his fulfilment.

Redlock backed, wide-eyed and unsure, pushing Triqueta with him. The heat made them raise their arms to shield their faces.

Above them, the drifting figures began to chant again, softly. Slowly, they rose, their hair and robes had become sparks and flame.

Insanely, in the middle of the furnace, Ecko's oculars caught movement. A figure – pale, female, desperate – crawling behind the broken base of a statue. She was curled about her belly, watching the wavering heat of the Sical with an expression of terror – and a peculiar, savage sense of righteousness.

It spoke to them, in a soft, warm voice that crackled with power.

Promised fuel, you. Need, I.

"I… We…" Triqueta stumbled over words, staggered by this glorious fire-creature that crisped the hairs on their arms. "You're… You're trapped? Enslaved?" It was a brave shot. "Let us help you."

Its head angled towards her, its eyes the blazing white of melting metal. It had no features, just a body of flame.

Hunger, I.

The spinning figures turned faster, becoming a wheel of sparks all around them, their chant continuing to circle. The Sical paid them no attention.

Awakened, I. Give fuel, you.

With a shriek, the wheel of ghosts stopped turning, and the figures swooped like vultures, hands reaching and faces stretched with glee. Redlock slashed madly, but burning claws caressed Ecko's cheek, setting off explosions in his skull and making him crumble further to the floor. The fire breath of the spirits yammered in his face and his head started to spin up into the air with them.

"Cedetine!" Incredibly, the cry had come from the cowering girl – she was obviously hurt, but her sheer determination rang from the walls. Near her, there was a smaller brazier, a stone bowl set into the floor. As Ecko hauled himself back to his feet, the girl shoved her bare hand into it and hurled the contents at the manically swooping figures.

"Shit!" he shouted, and ducked.

Redlock and Triqueta fell back.

Bright sparks of fury struck the flaming, ghostly shape and it began to really burn, its mouth open in a shout of glee.

Or was it pain?

Or was it both?

For a moment, it raged incandescent, and Ecko watched with horrified fascination.

There was a deafening blast, and the light exploded. Beside it, another ignited, and another. Their crackling voices screeched to a climax of power – and they were taken by their own conflagration.

Aftershocks rocked the walls. More of them split and tumbled to shatter on the hard stone floor.

The Sical paused.

But the girl's voice rose amid the noise and the raging, a rallying cry – a cry of such pain – and such strength...

"To Cedetine, World Goddess and Mother, I seal this Chapel by Fire. To Cedetine, World Goddess and Mother, I seal this Chapel by Light. To Cedetine, World Goddess and

Mother, I seal this Chapel by –"

"By *blood*, little priestess. Yours."

In the sudden, shocking silence, the voice could only belong to Maugrim.

The fire spirits were white ash, drifting downwards like chaff. Above the softly crackling Sical, they rose once more, carried by its heat.

"By right of foresight – by right of doing what no one else can."

Triqueta had run to the girl.

Redlock's tension was palpable – he was itching to fight.

But Ecko stared, stunned.

The man's accent had been pure South London – and his *clothes...*

He was wild haired, bearded, his denim cut-down and oil-stained jeans more familiar to Ecko than anything he'd seen. They looked like the lock-up, like Lugan – like home. As Maugrim walked to meet them, firelight glittered from multiple silver rings.

Across his shoulders, he had six-plus feet of heavy steel chain.

The compulsion of the Sical was still tugging at his oculars, his nerves, his heart – temptation, validation, failure – he needed to know what it was.

Ecko wanted to speak to the greaser, its master, somehow reach him and ask him – for *chrissakes* – so many questions. *How are you here? What happened to you? Is this real or in my fucking head?* From the lock-up and familiar, oil-stained denim, he had a sense of aching kinship that held him silent – because he had no idea what to say.

By right of foresight – by right of doing what no one else can.

Everything seemed to have closed on this moment, on the silver rings on Maugrim's fingers, on the white eyes of the Sical.

But Ecko was silent a moment too long – and Eliza took the chance from him.

He saw Redlock advance with his axes gleaming in his hands. He saw Maugrim unloop the chain from his shoulders and began to spin it, fantastically dextrous figure-eights, flashing in the firelight.

The axeman would chop him into fish food, chain or no chain. For just a moment, his instinct screamed at him to go after Redlock.

He needed to know!

But his eyes were still drawn to the burning form of the Sical.

Hunger, I. Need, I.

Its flame-limned arms opened towards the writhe of the stalactite high above and it blazed with the promise of supremacy.

Around them, the stone army ground into life.

27: SICAL THE MONUMENT

The flame-angel burned, mighty as a Fawkes-night detonation, hurling its fire into the cavern like a shout. Sparks leapt from it, the wash of heat was incredible.

It was glorious, compelling and fascinating and destructive. Fed by the stone capacitor from above and by blood from below, it was the heart of the fractal pattern, the single image that would repeat itself endlessly, consuming, expanding.

Tarvi had shown him a taste of its glory.

Ecko's adrenals were awakening: he could feel the buzz in his kidneys, the thrill starting to sparkle in his blood. He was poised on a blade-edge of indecision – to take down the axeman, to free the creature and burn this whole fucking mockery to ash...

Turn back to page one!

But Lugan's lighter was cool in his hand. The elemental was fatal. It would make his program fall to pieces around him, code crashing on the screen he'd never seen...

Head games.

Everything his Tech had done to him, everything she'd put him through and given him – he'd asked her for all of it. Because Tamarlaine needed to be Ecko.

And Ecko *was* a fucking *hero*. Whatever.

Yeah, this world has one fucking champion, and that would be me! *Call my bluff, willya, bitch – I make my own fucking choices!*

In the centre of the conflagration, the white-hot eyes were still visible. A nebulous, fiery arm reached out to them. It held the fascination he'd known all his life. Like a person with vertigo feels that irrepressible urge to jump, so Ecko now understood. He let himself fall, he let the fire light him, he opened himself to his own power and passion.

Stop fucking fretting already, stop second-guessing yourself. You are Patient fucking Zero. Whatever power there is – control it. You are the damned fractal – the pattern spreads from you!

His adrenals screamed as they hit overdrive.

From behind where Ecko raged, Redlock came past him, dodged through the gaps left by the open sarcophagi, and lunged, double slash, for the figure of Maugrim.

The Elementalist's attention had been thrown high and wide – as though he, too, raged with the Sical's fire – but he was still quick enough to dodge the axe blades. The chain lashed in twin figure-eights, to his left and then right. He crossed the ends over as though they were as light as rope.

Redlock's brown eyes narrowed at this display of skill – they were close to the fire, and the huge brazier sprang sweat from his skin.

The Sical's life glistened from the chain, made the axeman's red hair blaze. As Redlock moved in for the second attack, first one end of the chain and then the other caught him across the ribs. He staggered in pain. Maugrim paced him, round the brazier's edge, still backing away from the range of the short-handled axes.

But in Redlock's ears raged the adrenaline of his battle lust.

The pain caused a surge of fury that made him grin, tight and eager. This was the feeling he knew with every nerve ending. He welcomed it to him and his anger uncurled, precise and targeted.

He knew how to fight two-handed, knew the tricks and how to avoid them. The impressive double whirl should gain the offensive, it was a tactic he understood. With fast feet, he went forwards. Both ends of the chain whipped past him, catching his hair as they crossed over. He spun the axes easily, hitting Maugrim in the belly and slashing deep. The Elementalist coughed blood, but did not pause. Bracing his weight, he surged forwards, and in one swift movement, wrapped the length of chain between his hands about Redlock's neck.

And fought to tighten it.

The chain-ends lost their coordination and clashed to a stop.

Redlock couldn't breathe. His lungs strained for air, he could feel the pressure in his face. The heat became anger. He'd not crossed weapons with this madman to die at his blood-blackened hands.

For Feren. For his damned *wife*, his daughter.

Grunting, he threw his weight forwards into the loop. Maugrim, surprised, crashed to the floor, Redlock's knee in his cut stomach. One axe whipped over the chain and upwards.

The Elementalist coughed blood; it streamed from his nose and mouth and matted his beard.

The axe blade was almost in his face. He let go of the chain with one hand, catching the shaft, trying to push the warrior's weight off him. Redlock tried to pull backwards, but Maugrim broke his nose with the other, chain-wrapped, fist. The axeman fell backwards, losing his grip on his axes and skidding to the floor. His head bounced off the stalagmite pillar and he shook himself, half stunned.

The Sical blazed above him.

Maugrim got his feet under him, kicked the axes behind him and grinned.

Weaponless, sharp needles of pain jabbing into his face, Redlock grabbed one end of the chain, and pulled.

But Maugrim held it firm. He swung the free end a couple of times to build momentum, then smashed Redlock across the shoulder as he pulled himself to his feet. Whipping it back, he struck again across the other shoulder, the chain slashing through the fire and spilling sparks. For a moment they played tug of war, but upright now – Redlock let go.

Maugrim staggered. Redlock skidded past him, scrabbled for a second, then spun back with axes in hands.

They stalked each other again. Redlock's nose splashed across his face. Maugrim's belly cut seeping, but not deep enough. The Elementalist's eyes reflected the fire of the Sical, but Redlock fought for Feren's death and with certainty born from long returns of winning. He would not back down.

Before Ecko, the statues were grinding into motion.

Rank upon rank of them, eyes of fire and stained grey stone graunching into life as if the Sical were their master. But Ecko was fighting now, his speed inhuman, his targeters flashing, crossing, homing – faster than a thought and flickering like a twist of darkness. His fear and doubt had been burned away in the decisiveness of motion.

He *was* a fucking hero.

One foot, a powered kick that sent the first shambling attacker staggering backwards, its chest cracked like the rotting stonework of the walls. His own shout echoed back to him. He crouched, his fists before his chest and face, switched feet and kicked again, his targeters leading him, plotting trajectory and weak point. His blood sang with oxygen. A second impact, a second stone critter halted in its tracks – and it simply crumbled, a rumble of rubble crashing to the floor.

With a spin, he took out a third, a lashing piston kick that dropped it, crashing backwards and shattering into pieces.

They came on, closing around him, almost closer than he could take out – but he was on fire. One foot struck under the chin of a fourth and took its stone head clean off its shoulders.

Their eyes glowed sullen, they were walling him in, reaching for him with pitted grey hands – they ground as they moved, stone zombies from a forgotten graveyard. A savage spin-kick took out a fifth, axed back for a sixth. The rubble was building round him.

You see me now, Eliza? Huh?

He had *so* been waiting for this.

At the cathedral's heart, still trapped by the brazier, the Sical raged livid – imprisoned and furious. It spoke now, crying out in its own liquid-and-crystal tongue, but it could not get free.

Beside it, Redlock and Maugrim fought back and forth, savage and desperate.

Amethea had denied the elemental the last of its fuel. She was weak, battered, burned and bloodless – but she was on her feet, and the stone resolution in her heart was at last set. No more fear.

Beside her, the Banned woman was arrow nocked, guarding her charge, but watching Redlock for an opening, watching the shadow thing – whatever it was – spinning like a daemon in the midst of the incoming shamblers.

Stone splintered and shattered as it struck. It had a grace and fighting style she'd never seen – its feet slammed like weapons and the shamblers exploded into dust.

She had dreamed about it – black eyed and fierce.

"Thank you," she said, belatedly. Stupid, unnecessary, inadequate. "Feren, did he – ?"

"He died – but he found us first. He was braver than I've ever seen. I'm Triqueta." She gave a weary grin. "I'm no apothecary, but I did nab this off the girl that was."

Died. Amethea was numb: there was an odd hollow where her grief should have been.

She stared at the pouch, scattering contents across the blood-spiral stone.

And in it, at last, after everything: the taer. The pollen they'd left Xenok to find.

Something in her heart found it funny, bitter, outrageous. She was laughing, hurting, crying – Feren was dead, but Redlock was here. The nightmare was over.

Relief choked her. It was so long unlooked for – and it fought like a daemon almost within her reach.

Triqueta thumped her shoulder gently, awkwardly affectionate. Amethea smiled, striving for control – but then her eyes were drawn to the dark length of the stalactite, slithering still towards the fire, striving to complete the conduit.

She had started this. Her inability to resist Maugrim's charm had ended in this madness, in this rising promise of destruction.

"We have to stop this," she said. Redlock and Maugrim were fighting, fighting. The Sical's blaze was roasting hot. "*I* have to stop it."

I started it.

Triqueta rubbed the stone in her cheek against her shoulder – easing an itch.

"Then you're going to need a really big bucket of water."

Maugrim danced his chain, battering Redlock backwards as the warrior tried to regain the control of the fight.

Keeping track of the chain-ends was pure instinct: he didn't see them, just reacted. Redlock was dodging, dancing and lunging, the call of his blood pounding in his ears, his focus as sharp as a knife. He was backing, aware of the hollows of the sarcophagi behind him, but making Maugrim move in the hope of tearing his wound. A dark stain spread down the Elementalist's odd garments.

Redlock saw his opportunity. He dropped the axes, dove between the chain-ends, seized its centre and pushed Maugrim backwards. A foot around the back of his ankle, and he fell, cracking his head on the stone.

Redlock was on top of him, the taut stretch of the chain across his throat. The warrior's shattered face was gruesome, his brown eyes held no mercy. He was as much stone as the cathedral's walls around him, as the stalagmite pillar that held the blaze of the Sical's prison.

Maugrim fought to breathe as his vision blackened. He fought to call aloud, to his mentor and protector, his teacher and rescuer.

Vahl! Vahl! Help me!

He had known all along that the daemon wouldn't tolerate failure.

Ecko was being swamped.

Stone hands tore at his cloak, his flesh, his face. They pressed into him, grabbing for his limbs, cadaverous stone faces and eyes of the Sical's fire. He dropped a circular, sweeping kick, took two of them off their feet, but the press came on, stamping the fallen into fragments and dust.

They were too close packed, he couldn't breakroll through them to change position. He lashed a low kick, broke the base of another and sent it toppling backwards – but the press behind it was too close, it didn't fall. It teetered, rocked, and then smashed downwards towards him.

He slammed himself sideways – it missed, crashed into pieces.

But he was too close now. Hands reached for his shoulders and gripped him, grinding into his reinforced skin, into his collarbone. Fingers wound round his upper arms, cutting off the bloodflow, crushing muscle painfully against bone.

He still had his feet – in front of him, the creatures broke like pottery, but there were too many of them.

And they were pulling him down.

Redlock pushed down on the chain with a strength born of anger and exhaustion, focus and fury, pushed until Maugrim stopped struggling, pushed until his face blackened, until his tongue swelled from his lips and his eyes bulged with horror. Then he let go and stood, the adrenaline still pounding, his chest heaving, his sight dazed and scarlet. There were tears of anger running down his face, sweat sheeting his body, but he did not care. He picked up the axes and the chain, and looked up at the huge might of the Sical.

It didn't care that Maugrim lay twisted. It was reaching for the cavern roof, for the twist of dark rock that stretched down towards it. Beside it, shadows against its flame, Triqueta defended the injured teacher. The elemental paid them no attention – perhaps they were all too small for it to notice.

He had no way to face that thing, no weapons to touch it.

Slinging both axes and spinning the chain for momentum, he ran the stone tightrope between the open sarcophagi and raced for the stone wall that was closing round Ecko.

They were clawing at him now, sharp stone fingers ripping his skin. Their silence was eerie. He kicked and thrashed, but he was held down like a scrawny street kid by a bunch of gangland bullies. He was yowling abuse, had no idea what he was saying – could Eliza see this? Was this how this fucking fiasco would end – shredded by a bunch of animate fucking *statues*?

Then there was a ripple of impact, a harsh ringing of metal on stone. He could hear Redlock swearing vengeance and warfare. Behind him, the claws slackened.

Again. They swayed at the blow, their attention turning from him.

With a twist and a shove, a furious flailing of feet, he was free. Shreds of his flesh clung to their fingers, blood slid over his skin.

Fuckers.

For a moment, he was on his back on the stone, doing the fucking dying fly, then he flipped himself to his feet and lashed a kick at the closest shambler.

The hard *jang* of metal rang again. The things staggered at the impact.

He heard the axeman shout, "Ecko!"

"Still breathing!" He spun back. One kick, another, repeated and savage, against the press of stone that separated him from Redlock's vicious, slamming, chain onslaught.

He saw the axeman spin the chain over his head – once, twice – then crash it into them full force.

They shattered like glass under the impact, pulverised, fucking *dust*.

There was a gap – his targeters didn't need to tell him. He was through it like a rat.

And they were still coming, ranks of them.

"I won't stop them all!" Redlock was shouting. "We have to get out of here!"

Amethea shouted back at him, "We have to stop the Sical!"

"With what?" Ecko was shaking now, the comedown was hitting him and he felt sick, weak. The shamblers were still coming, there seemed no end to their silent, stone determination.

"We stop them now," Triqueta said. "Or they'll tear Roviarath to the ground. Everything dies!"

Maugrim lay sprawled, eyes bulbous and grotesque. He stared sightless up at the Sical as though shocked by its power.

Feed, I!

"Oh my Goddess," Amethea said. "Look."

Blood had seeped, dark and slow, from the axe wound in Maugrim's belly.

Where the lids of sarcophagi had lifted, they'd left the very inside of the spiral intact – the closest point to the brazier, the platform upon which Redlock and Maugrim had been fighting.

Maugrim's blood had spilled upon it, it spiralled where Amethea's had done, mingling with hers.

And the Sical grew bigger.

For a moment, the horror of the mistake held them all completely still.

Around them, the shamblers advanced. Before them the elemental reached for the surface, for the air and the sky.

Its crystal celebration chimed in their heads – Roviarath would burn, and with it, the rest of the grass.

Fuck, Ecko thought. *Fuck, fuck, fuck!*

He was out of options. What the hell did he do, chuck a fucking blanket on it?

Chuck...

The pressure in his webbing-pouch gave him the answer.

And he started to laugh.

Amethea looked at the dark jester, chilled by the demented cackle of its humour. She was barely keeping her feet – Triqueta's taer had sealed the wound in her gut, but it was a patch, she could feel the blackness on the edges of her vision, just waiting to crowd in and close over her.

Maugrim was dead. Throttled, broken. She should feel relief, she should be celebrating, kicking his swollen-faced corpse and spitting on his memory.

But the creature he – they – had set in motion was rising like the sun.

She watched as the lean, dark-mottled figure unclipped something from a strange belt.

"Guys?" he said. "Remember this?"

"What...?"

The question was drowned out by Triqueta's "Oh *shit*...!"

And he threw the pouch on the fire.

The initial detonation tore through the building.

Walls rocked, masonry tumbled and smashed. The first ranks of the stone warriors were blasted backwards and shattered, scattering their followers with dust.

"With me," Redlock roared. "Run!"

The pomegranate grenades blasted open in every direction, one after another, each one filling the Sical's form with sparks and scattering pottery shards and hot coals to the bloodied, spiral floor.

But then the brazier started to rumble, the pillars of the stalagmite shook.

The floor quivered. The light in the cavern walls flickered and dimmed. From overhead, a loose stalactite smashed to the floor, then a second.

The writhing of the pillar stopped.

And the Sical shrieked, crystalline and furious – they heard it in the bones behind their ears, in their skin and in their thoughts.

"Yeah," Ecko shouted, "and fuck you, too!"

The walls about them trembled, dust billowed. The axeman was coughing, coughing, wiping his lips as he ran. Triqueta was half carrying the injured teacher. Ecko, running with them, turned back to see what was happening to the Sical.

It was screaming in his head, livid and shining, brighter, brighter.

Over it, stones were tumbling from the cavern roof. Water was starting to hiss through the gaps, spraying wide like an office failsafe.

"Run, dammit!" Redlock's hand closed around Ecko's ripped, skin-shredded arm and dragged him away from the spectacle. "The char path will take us out! That way!"

Ecko stumbled on his cloak hem, but kept moving.

Amethea said, "What did you do? What did you throw...?"

"I was tryin' to make gunpowder," he said. "Made a helluva bang."

The cavern roof juddered, rocks fell and smashed, stone shrapnel slashed outwards.

The great black capacitor stone cracked from end to end, its lightning shivered and faded.

And the elemental *screamed*.

Then the brazier under it collapsed.

The last thing they heard as they fled into the crazed garden was the piercing, mind-shredding shriek of its detonation.

Dust settled, drifting across a faint breeze.

Water dripped slowly from the cavern roof, a slow rainfall onto devastation – the destroyed remnants of the garden, the shell of the cathedral, now a scattering of low walls, mud and rubble.

The brazier had been drowned, destroyed, fallen stones cracking as they cooled. The Sical was gone.

In the quiet, Maugrim's first breath was a rip of noise – a rasp of harshness and debris on his ruined throat. His face hurt, his tongue was swollen against his teeth. He swallowed, rubbing a ringed hand over the bruise across his neck.

Then he began to cough, eyes watering, clearing himself of

pain and dust. He inhaled another rasping breath, tried to sit up.

"What a waste."

The voice was male, as familiar to him as his dreams. It was calm, almost scholarly, but the threat was naked and razor-sharp, its edge under his chin.

There was no point even pleading for mercy.

"Please..."

"Get up now."

Maugrim rubbed his throat again – strangled with his own chain, indeed – and clambered slowly to his feet.

He'd lost. Meddling kids.

Something was bugging him, needling at the back of his mind – when his head stopped spinning, he'd place the rasp, the stylised imagery. The accent was familiar... Had he used the word "program"?

The scholarly voice repeated, "I said, 'Get up'."

Beneath the slash in his t-shirt, the axe wound in his belly had gone, a scar in its place where he'd seared it closed, just as he'd once healed Amethea. Maugrim felt drained, looking out across the mess, the bloody bombsite they'd left behind them. He had no idea where to go.

Ash.

Then he felt his mentor's hand on his shoulder, soft, lethal.

"Finish this."

He could say only, "Yes."

There was nothing else left for him.

28: GUILT ROVIARATH, THE CENTRAL VARCHINDE

Evening. The shadows of the Kartiah stretched long across the sunset grass.

In the glowing, dusty air, a green-and-white banner flapped like a live thing, seeking to escape from CityWarden Larred Jade's spear tip.

The last of the sunlight glittered from the weapon's terhnwood point.

The creatures came fast, lumbering semi-mindless, stone and fire and destruction. Flame flickered about them, smoke and ash rose in their wake. They'd fanned out into a ragged line, an oncoming storm front for the swathe of devastation they brought: blasted soil, blackened grass.

Behind them, abandoned farm buildings guttered with flame – blossoming flowers of light in the fading evening.

Jade watched them, white-knuckled, fear in his merchant's throat.

I am no warrior.

I don't have a choice.

Around him, horses stamped. His foot patrols stood silent, dread coming from them in waves.

As the creatures came closer, he could see the red of their eyes, the heat that rose from their stone shoulders.

From the wall behind him, he heard the tan commander.

"Nock... draw... *loose!*"

The volley arced over his head, shafts slashing through the sky. Arrows fell with a hiss, shattered on stone, clattering into ash and failure.

"Second rank!"

Jade's hands tightened on his rein. His breathing was shallow, panic settled on his armoured shoulders, goading him.

A second arcing hiss of arrows shattered terhnwood heads on faceless rock.

And the creatures came on.

"Flat-fire!" called the archer commander. His voice was confident but faint, wind snatched – the deserted wooden expanse of the Great Fayre separated him from Jade's nervousness. "First rank! Eyes and joints! Nock... draw...!"

Their shots were random – the setting sun was behind them and they were shooting into the city's long shadow.

Tense, almost nauseous, Jade held his riders. The spear was unfamiliar in his hand, his resin-and-fibre armour uncomfortable, heavy. It chafed his neck. The horses were jumpy, the approaching smoke was spooking them. Beneath him, his own mare jittered, shaking her head, clattering the terhnwood fixtures of her bridle. To his left, he had six tan of spearmen, sixty fighters in all. They stood two-deep behind a wall of shiny-new shields. They were anxious, wary, anticipating the impact.

Jade's grasp of logistics was solid – the overnight evacuation of the market had been flawlessly smooth. His muster and deployment was as his tutors had once shown him, markers on a map. He knew the theory.

But out here, his clinical tactics were coming apart like rotted fabric.

They hadn't warned him about the *fear*. It was all around him, he could taste it.

This isn't strategy any more.

Another hiss of arrows came hard, downwards over his head, shafts slicing deadly through the air. The creatures took no notice.

They were almost upon them, their red eyes on the Fayre's deserted stalls. As one, at some unheard signal, their lumber became a run.

Here we go. Jade swallowed, let out a breath.

With a barked order, the shield wall snapped together smartly, spears bristling. Their training was flawless, but the creatures were too scattered, too widespread – as the wall stepped forwards and punched hard into the centre of the attackers' ragged line, they were already round its edges.

Some turned inwards to lash at the spearmen's flanks; others ran straight for the Fayre.

Arrows struck them, sprang back.

Jade had no idea what he should do.

The shield wall held, just. Spears clattering uselessly off stone shoulders. Terhnwood shattered – too fragile. Stone hands tore at shield rims, methodical, relentless, grey-cadaver faces chillingly motionless. Their assault was completely silent. He could hear the defiant shouts of the fighters, the archer's command to loose at will – but they weren't enough, weren't nearly enough.

The second rank of spearmen was turning, fearful, needing to see what was happening behind them. Orders were snapped, but they broke anyway, some of them running to save the bared wooden uprights of their livelihood.

Smoke billowed across the battlefield.

His heart screaming in his chest – *What are you doing?* – Jade saw his first warrior die.

He was flanked, torn down from the shield wall's edge, claws and ripped skin, a frantic scrabble for a belt blade that snapped like a stick. His cry carved a wound in the CityWarden's mind – a scar on his memory until the end of the Count of Time. *Failure. Guilt.* The stone creature was on the spearman, unassailable. It burned his flesh, buried its broken talons in his skin and tore him to pieces, shredding muscle from bone, bearing him down in grim, grey silence, trampling him into the churn of mud and gore underfoot.

Sickened, Jade could only watch.

And it didn't stop – red eyes brighter than the glow of the setting sun, it reached its claws for the next target, seized him as he turned, and tried to shove his spear crosswise over its chest and push it back. Heat reddened his face. Beside him, the rank was cringing away from a scorching, tearing death – they edged sideways, staggering, frightened, spear-points in every direction as the sides of the formation crumbled.

As the second man went down, Jade saw one of them throw up.

At the centre of the wall, the fighters rallied. Someone was shouting. They were stamping forwards, in hard time, one pace after another, shields slamming as they went. He saw one creature fall back, then another.

Hope sparked – but it was brief. Fire and smoke were rising into the dusk, visibility failing now. A shield rim caught alight. The fighter threw it from her, yelling in shock. Another scream, another man down.

The fallen man's hand stretched for a moment, begging for help, before he was trampled into the churn of mud below.

The creatures were tearing into the side of the unit, ripping their way towards the centre. Fighter after fighter saw the friend next to them shredded, ground down, burned and screaming. They were turning to defend themselves, their friends, tangling spear shafts. One punched his shield rim with a slam into a stone thing's face – it hesitated. He hit it again, and again, and again, screaming terror and defiance as it rocked, cracked, and crumbled.

He let out a ragged cheer, echoed by those round him.

Beside him, a horsewoman shouted, "Hit them in the back! Now!"

It was all happening so fast. Jade shook himself, raised the banner, waved the order. Beside him, his mounted drummer hammered out the rhythm, throbbing through the smoke.

It was like a tavern-saga, unreal.

As the horses moved, the foot-fighters were being seized, flesh blackening under burning hands, their bones broken and torn from their sockets like meat at a banqueting table. They were people he knew, people whose greetings and families were familiar to him.

Denial screamed loud in the CityWarden's head.

Ears back, his mare broke into an unsteady canter, then a run. Around her, a thunder of hooves, a rising of dust – a raw shout of defiance. The curve of Jade's kite shield bounced at his knee. The drummer continued to pound out the rhythm – it sounded like bravery. Spears were couched. He found his voice and added his cry to the roar. A courageous sound, a futile one.

But they raced for the creatures ripping into the shield wall.

He caught a glimpse of the beasts that had got round behind it. They were skirmishing now, harried by lone fighters, arrow shafts bouncing back from their grinding, shifting stone. Smoke rose round them like shadows. Their reactions were startlingly swift. One lone spearwoman jabbed inexpertly, saw her spear tip shatter – and the thing was on her, bearing her to the ground in pitted grey silence.

Jade saw it for only an instant: it raised a stone fist over her, she struggled to push it away, her hands crisping. She shrieked in fury, a sky-ripping, emasculating sound. The thing punched clean through the front of her skull.

Got up, looked for another kill.

And the wall of horsemen hit.

In the dust, in the heat, in the smoke, in the stench and noise of fear, he kept his seat by sheer reflex. The mare was barging, haunches into stone – he could smell the burning of her hide. His spearpoint was useless. He hung grimly onto his pommel and reins with one hand, used the other to keep the banner aloft, a beacon of green and white. One foot lashed out at a creature. He jarred his ankle and it turned to eye him balefully from skull sockets full of fire.

He heard himself shouting, "For Roviarath! For the Varchinde!"

Chaos swirled round him.

But several creatures had reached the edge of the Fayre.

Jade's hands were numb, his arms pricking with tension. Disbelief surged through him as the first uprights caught. *This couldn't happen to him, to his city, to his friends...*

The Fayre went up round them like matchwood, blazing fierce and immediate. Flames caught and danced with the dusk breeze, smoke poured upwards into the darkening sky. His archers fell back, coughing.

Through the thumping of hooves, drums and heart, he thought he could hear the commander shouting to rally, but the sound was desperate under the spreading, flaring bonfire that was Roviarath's wealth.

Then a voice, "My Lord! 'Ware!"

In the smoke, there was a creature suddenly right on top of him, stone claws reaching for his mare, gouging at the flesh of her neck. She whinnied like a scream, teeth bared, danced crosswise nearly costing him his seat. Around him, the thunder of hooves was interspersed with shouts, snorts, the sharp sounds of terhnwood shattering on stone, the cries and slams of the shield wall.

He heard another horse scream – really scream. He heard

the crash as it went over, the harsh clatter of its tack as it hit the ground. He heard it struggle, heard it grunt, repeatedly. He heard the rider bellowing swear words.

The spearmen fought on, shields slamming and feet stamping. Their commander was hoarse, his voice a rasp of coughing as he tried to hold the line together.

The drum thundered.

Before him, was the voiceless, faceless thing, the only awareness the vicious glow of red in its skull-socket eyes. Heat poured from its skin.

He had the oddest feeling it knew who he was.

Another horse went down. Somewhere in the smoke beside him, he saw the shape fold sideways. *Get up*, he willed it, *get up!* Through the wheeling, stamping chaos, he could see the woman who'd shouted, turning her mount in frantic circles. There were three of them round her – they'd had enough wit to separate her from her tan.

The beast in front of him paused, watching. Red eyes like twin flares of hate.

"You know me, don't you?" It was a whisper. "You know who I am."

Then he remembered something – something from his tutor, long ago.

And in a rush, he realised what he should do.

On the wall, the archer commander fell back, visibility almost nil.

The smoke whorled and eddied – he could see the fires, spreading through the Fayre, see the spearmen falling back from skirmishing as the heat overcame them. The handful of beasts that were loose in the bared woodwork of the market were wreaking devastation – and there was nothing to touch them.

Almost nothing.

Upon the wall were stockpiled water barrels – a contingency that'd made his troops groan with the necessity of pulley-hauling them, hand over hand, to lay them in rows on the top of the bank.

He could see Jade's green-and-white banner, fluttering, flashing, a flare of hope in the wreathing grey, the dancing sparks. He thought he heard the Lord shout, a bugle call of defiance.

He raised a shout of his own.

"Cohn, to me!"

The hefty shape of Cohn dropped his bow and lent his strength to the barrel. With a straining of muscle, a cording of tendons, an almighty heave that bit pain into their fingers, they hefted the thing onto the top of the defences.

And threw it as far out as they could.

"Yes, you know me!" Jade was shouting now, his idea bright in the front of his imagination. He could see the map old Master Atheus had laid out for him – the city, the docks, the walls, the Fayre – the three tributaries of the Great Cemothen River that fed into her vast, wide wash.

"Come on then! I'm Larred Jade, Lord of Roviarath. You want me? I'm here!"

The thing came forwards. From the corner of his eye he saw the horsewoman – he must learn her name – turn as the creatures surrounding her lumbered towards him. Several more sets of eyes burned through the smoke.

He raised the banner, waved it high and clear.

"I'm here, you stone bastards. You see me? Right here! You know who I am!"

They closed on him, smoke rising, the air shimmering, the heat making his mare sweat under him. He counted three, four, five of them – six – that was enough.

With a jab of his heels, he jumped the animal through the closest gap and ran her for the river.

And they came after him, needing to tear him down.

With a splintering crash, the barrel exploded, shattering like ribs upon the hard ground.

A wave of water hissed over burning uprights, wooden stalls, spread out through the packed-hard mud. Steam plumed into the air. One of the stone creatures was caught by the outwash. It paused, as though confused, rocked back and forth on the spot for a moment, then tried to come for them.

One step, two – and there were cracks in the stone. The red light limning its muscles had faded, steam poured from the joints – and the supercooling rock cracked, split.

A third step and it crumbled, shapeless grey stones lost in the blackened mud.

Whooping like an idiot, the archer commander ran for the next barrel.

They were *fast*!

Waving the banner like a madman, he was upright in his stirrups, shouting at them – daring them to chase him down and tear his city from his very flesh. And they came on, driven, the fight around them forgotten – they were fixated by him, and they were going to rip him apart.

He broke out of the smoke, suddenly he was blinking in the dusk light. Ahead of him, the river sparkled, it ran wide and swift, fed by waters from Irahlau, Vanskraat, Blinn, Aldarien, the very Kartiah themselves.

The map in his mind was so *clear*.

"Come on then," he said to himself. "Don't falter now."

The city walls flashed by to his side – amazingly, there were spectators standing there – pointing at him and nudging their companions. Were they damned insane? He didn't have time to think about it. Below the decorated stone, the empty skeleton of the Great Fayre tessellated slowly into the harbour – river boats bobbed, abandoned. Birds wheeled over them, crying mournfully at the smoke and the noise.

The scent of water filled the air – sweet, fresh.

Deep.

They were almost on him now – claws reaching for the mare's rump. She jumped, flicked her heels at them. He fell forwards sharply, winding himself on the saddle pommel.

Reminding himself he wasn't Banned, he sat back down.

"Come on then!" Waving the banner across the morning, back and forth, back and forth, he was shouting still. "I'm Larred Jade – and I'll damned well teach you to burn my city!"

And he ran the mare out onto the wharf.

Watching the CityWarden vanish into the smoke with six of the beasties after him, Rika wondered if the old sod had finally lost his mind.

Around her, all was wheeling, screaming turmoil. The cavalry had lost its formation almost instantly. She could see the remnant of the shield wall, still hanging together, though harried at both flanks. From somewhere in front of her came a second splintering wooden crash.

The creatures had scattered – they seemed to be everywhere. A flicker of red light, a flash of sullen eyes, a shout, a scream. Abandoning their useless terhnwood spears, many of the foot-fighters had resorted to shield bashing – haphazard and dangerous.

Even as she turned, trying to see what was round her, she saw a shield catch light, gutter and flare into angry life.

The fighter threw it from him, went for his belt-blade.

He was already dead.

Rika was impressed with her Lord's courage and wit – but less sure that six of the creatures had made that much of a difference.

As the fighter scuttled backwards, breaking the line and slashing at the incoming creature, she wondered, with crazed clarity, if the city would live to see the morning.

Jade halted the mare at the very foot of the L-shaped wharf, her hindquarters dipping as she skidded on wet wood.

As she turned, river behind her sparkling in the sunset, the stone creatures were still piling forward, hard and fast, eyes fixed. They left charred, hissing imprints where their club feet slammed, echoing, on the heavy planking.

He waved the banner at them, taunting.

"You kill me, the city's as good as yours. Come on, you bastards, I'm here."

Noiseless but for the rapid *thump-thump-thump* of their step, they came on – swift, eager, burning, claws reaching to rend.

The wharf was shaking beneath them, wood charring and splitting. The mare teetered over the water.

She skittered her hooves as he gathered her to leap.

As they came for her, eyes red, he held her until the very last moment... Then they sprang sideways, skidding out of reach.

The hairs of her tail were caught in the stone claws of the lead creature.

It ran straight over the wharf's edge into the sparkling morning water of the Great Cemothen River.

And sank without a trace.

With a crash, the shield wall gave, shattered, splintered wood, staggering fighters, shouts of fear and fury. No longer defended, each fighter was alone, spinning to see what was round him, coughing in the smoke.

One man fell back, clinging to his broken arm – shards of shield still hung crazily from the handle and strapping.

Through the gap, an arrowhead of creatures came tearing, ripping to left and right. Broken now, the foot-fighters scattered, falling back. Some rallied into groups, huddled into mini-defensive formations, spears bristling, daring the creatures to come near.

And they did, stamping the shields down, ripping them loose and tearing into the soft flesh beneath.

Rika had dropped her useless spear, hung her big, kite-shaped shield on her arm. One savage slam from the shield rim and the stone creature before her was down.

She had no idea where Jade had gone. Grabbing the attention of the wild-eyed drummer, she roared at him to sound the regroup.

Roviarath wasn't going down without a fight.

Tumbling, splashes. Two, three, four of them.

A hiss of angry steam.

He turned his mare in time to see the fifth creature hesitate – and the last one run slam into it, sending them both over the edge.

The waters parted, swallowed them whole. Steam billowed, a glow in the sunset.

And there was quiet.

Jade sat stunned, he thought he could hear cheering. Birds rose, crying, into the darkening sky.

For a moment that seemed endless, he wanted to cheer back. He waved the banner at them, could hear them, faintly, "Lar-red Jade! Lar-red Jade!" He found a lump in his throat – clenched his jaw, blinked.

But they were only six – the walls of his city were still beset, flame poured from the empty marketplace, smoke swirled thick through the air. He could still hear the screams and shouts of combat.

He touched his heels to the mare's flanks, and, banner streaming, raced back into the mêlée.

Rika was screaming through the stamping of hooves, the drum-pounding, the mayhem.

"To me! To *me*!"

The creatures were loosed, determined and silent, faceless and pitted and grey. She could see them through the smoke, red lines of heat, watch them as they slashed one way and then the other.

Their lack of expression was the most frightening thing of all.

The shield wall had disintegrated under their onslaught, the archers had stopped shooting. Scattered battles ranged round her – one on one, the fighters were no match for the stone claws of the monsters and they were being shredded, left to die in the mud. Jade had gone, they needed to rally.

"To *me*!"

Then she heard the drum cease as the lad was pulled, yowling, from his saddle. His horse fled in a clatter of stirrups.

Without a thought, she rode the creature down.

But the gelding under her baulked. He backed up, throwing his head and snorting, trying to drag the rein from her hand. As she fought to keep the bit out of his teeth, she felt a savage rip in her calf muscle.

The drummer was screaming like a young girl, high and terrified – then, abruptly, silent.

Biting back tears of frustration, sorrow, fury, she yanked her leg out of reach, tried to kick.

But it had her by the ankle, talons sinking into her flesh. Its other hand grabbed her thigh, crushing, claws penetrating the muscle and making her bite back a scream of her own.

She drew her belt-blade, slashed at its stone wrist, watched the blade crack and dangle uselessly from its central fibres. Spitting "No, no, no", she jammed the remnants into the thing's red eye socket.

Its claws dug harder. It was trying to drag her out of her seat, rending huge wounds, deep in the front of her thigh. The pain was savage, blood stained her breeches, blackness laughed at the edges of her vision.

The last thing she saw, as the smoke swirled and parted, was the glow of the sun, dying slowly upon the jagged peaks of the Kartiah Mountains.

Hooves thundering, Jade charged back into the smoke.

To ruin.

His defence was shattered, his Fayre in bright flame. Riderless horses cantered through the smoke and were gone. Spearmen, those that remained, huddled in groups, eyes streaming and terrified. Many had fled.

My Gods, Jade thought, *what have I done?*

His banner was dull in the smoky air, the grass around him was burning, the mud underfoot a churn of death and gore. He heard groans, whimpers of wordless pain that tore at his heart.

How had this happened? How had this...?

The dusk breeze plucked at the banner, tumbled the smoke about him. Through a momentary eddy, he saw a cluster of the creatures converge on the gatehouse – on the massive, wooden double gates, closed and bolted for the first time in his memory. Archers ran to the muster-call.

He had no doubt the gates would burn.

And after them, the city.

"Samiel!" The cry was crazed, but he had nothing else left. *"You can't do this!"*

And the Varchinde answered him.

He heard hooves: a thundering that shook the ground, flashed sparks from the grass-devouring flames. Through the wall of smoke and mist and horror, he could see shapes – hazy, mounted. And the *air*...

With a high, ululating war cry that echoed back from the city walls, they were there – exploding through the smoke, bridleless, savage, utterly disordered.

His black mare on her hind legs, bellowing defiance, Syke of the Banned wheeled his arm above his head and sent them as a flat-out run, slamming into the rear of the creatures assaulting the gates. They didn't bother with weapons – the mounts fought for themselves, forehooves slashing, back hooves shattering stone with hammer blows that exploded dust into the air.

He heard a ragged cheer from the archers on the wall.

Reining his mare to a halt, the Lord of Roviarath stared at the war-Banned, heard their yowls and catcalls, wondered at the sheer viciousness of the attack.

He had the oddest feeling they were enjoying themselves.

One hand on his monster recurved bow, Syke brought his snorting, prancing mare close by.

Jade looked at him, stunned. Said only, "Why?"

"Triq," the Banned commander replied. He gave the Lord a shrewd, narrow-eyed look, then turned to watch the ramshackle mess about him. "Her mare came back. I saw these bastards running, I figured she'd failed. She died – Ress and Jayr – because I didn't rally when I should've done." He let off an idle snap-shot at a lumbering stone creature, hitting it neatly in the eye socket. Its stone head turned to look at him. "Well, we're rallied now."

"You couldn't have come just a fragment earlier?" Jade was starting to laugh – at his reprieve, at the end of the grief and the horror. He laughed as though he were crying. "They're not dead, you fool – though your guilt's appreciated..." He stopped, choked by smoke and relief.

"Guilt, my arse." Syke's denial may as well have been a confession. Around them, the Banned were scattering the stone assailants into tumbling rubble. Spearmen were laughing, coughing, picking themselves up. He heard the cry to rally from close to the wall.

Jade managed a grin, though it struggled to reach his eyes – they'd seen too much.

"The scouts said the Monument's collapsing – the light's going out." He clapped the grey-eyed man on the shoulder – old friend, old adversary, familiar thorn in the CityWarden's side. "Be proud of Triqueta – she won."

"So did you, you daft old sod," Syke told him. "So did you."

29: LOREMASTER FHAVEON, THE MONUMENT

Roderick was woken by a stealthy *rap-rap-rap* on his door.

He lay still, taut in the darkness, listening.

He'd been dreaming – again. Dreaming of the Ryll, glory and tumble and sparkle and spray. Dreaming of the very mind of the Goddess – too much for mortal man to bear. The aged Guardians stood watch, but had they never touched the water.

Somehow, he had seen the waterfall with more clarity than he ever had. Yet the image had been split, broken – had he seen it through some cracked casement, some twisted reflection?

Rap-rap-rap.

This time, the noise brought him fully awake.

Like a child afraid of figments in the night, he held himself breathless and stock-still.

Rap-rap-rap!

The noise was hastier this time, almost nervous.

Pulse racing now, the Bard swung himself into a sitting position, put his bare feet on the cold stone floor. He rubbed his eyes, shoved his filthy mass of hair out of his face, and then got up and padded over to the door. He was stiff, his legs ached from lack of use.

He said, softly, "What?"

"Roderick! You're awake!"

The voice was unknown to him.

Puzzled, he replied, "Yes. Who is it? What do you want?"

"Hang on."

There was the sound of a drop-key being lifted. A moment later, a tiny crack of yellow rocklight touched his discarded black boot and then spread outwards in an arc across the floor.

Startled, he backed away. "Who are you? Who's there?"

The crack opened wider, and the light blinded him after days in the gloom. Raising an arm to shield his eyes, he saw that the incoming figure was a soldier, a young woman, pale and furtive.

And the last cold shock doused him.

They have come for me. No Ecko, no Rhan, no hope.

He found himself shrinking back against the wall, sudden fear robbing him of breath.

It was over.

The after-images of his dreaming broke loose, spilled free and made the hairs on his arms prickle. Faced by the soldier that had come to take him to his death, he was still shaking at fragments unnamed – something about a creature of crystal and fire?

The shattered-window image came again – through it, he could see the waters of the Ryll clearer than he had ever done, clearer than even the Guardians had ever witnessed. It was as though there was something in the way, some conduit or device, something that both enhanced and defended his flawed mortal vision –

A cold, hard object was being pressed into his hand.

Startled, he looked down.

The door had opened enough to let the soldier slide through and pull it almost-closed behind her. She was pressing a weapon into the Bard's anxious grip, a long, narrow poignard, real white-metal, with a nasty-looking point. For a moment,

Roderick blinked at it, baffled – was the city offering him another way out?

A way to end his own life with dignity?

Love of the *Gods*...

The first spark of rebellion ignited somewhere in his heart. He said, "No..."

But the soldier was speaking, low and urgent.

"They're coming for you. Any minute now." The woman looked back at the door and spoke quickly. "Everything's changed. Demisarr is dead, Rhan has been cast down. Phylos closes his fist around the city, and around the Varchinde." She was sweating. "I bear you a message, brought by bretir from the Lord Nivrotar in Amos. She says you must go to her. And she says to tell you, 'The world's fear comes'."

"*What?*"

Ice shivered through the Bard's skin. Demisarr, Rhan, Nivrotar. The world's fear. The Monument, blazing. Ecko. Death in the grass.

It was too much to take in.

But the soldier was panicking now.

"You have to get out of here! They're coming!"

"How do you know this?" Roderick gripped the woman's shoulder, striving for stability. "How do you...?"

"I don't. I'm just a message bearer. The Wanderer's still here. If you hurry..." The soldier glanced back again as other feet sounded further down the passageway.

"For the Gods' sakes, get out of here." The Bard gave her a shove. "I'll work it out as I go." His heart was really pounding now – fear and freedom and elation and questions and an almost-understanding that he would reach for as soon as he had a moment in which to think. "And – thank you!"

Thank you... for another chance.

The young woman nodded at him, slid out of the door, and was gone.

They're coming.

In his mind, perhaps a part of the dream, perhaps just a sharp stab of his own conscience, Roderick heard Ecko's voice. *You're a coward and a fucking liar!*

The Bard left his boots where they were. They were clumsy and noisy, and he needed to be quiet.

But his hand tightened around the cold metal grip of the poignard.

The great cliff upon which Fhaveon stood sentinel was a warren of tunnels. Smugglers' tunnels, miners' tunnels, tunnels of stealth and opportunity.

Stinking of cold rock and rimed salt and drying wrack, the tunnels' existence made the Lord city seem hollow, oddly unstable.

Roderick had been down here before, many returns ago, seeking rumours of Swathe – but, like the outcome of his hunt for Kas Vahl Zaxaar upon Rammouthe Island, he had found nothing.

If the legendary Swathe had ever existed, it had been obliterated utterly – down to the last seared and moulding fragments of its residents' bones.

Demisarr is dead. Rhan has been cast down.

Phylos closes his fist around the city, and around the Varchinde...

Mother of the Gods, Roderick thought. *What has happened to Fhaveon?*

From ahead of him, he could hear voices, a burst of coarse laughter. On chilled but silent feet, he pulled back into a side passage and waited.

He was trembling – cold, dread and anticipation.

Images still haunted him. Fighting and fire. The Great Fayre, burning. Demisarr Valiembor, Lord of Fhaveon, plummeting, screaming into the gorge. Phylos on the clifftop, and an unholy heat that blazed from his skin...

Roderick knew that heat.

The voices were coming closer.

Pulling back as far as he could, the Bard stopped, striving to reach for the memory – to piece it together from the scatter of images that he'd seen, this time so clearly, in the Ryll.

Demisarr's wife, Valicia, thrown down and struggling, that same heat savage and penetrating and unwelcome.

Dear *Gods*.

And the realisation was there – the understanding. Kas Vahl Zaxaar, once Dæl, cast down to the great halls of the Rhez below the world...

...and so, *so* like Rhan.

Vahl Zaxaar was *stirring*.

Even as the Bard was incorporating the thought, in the passageway outside, the voices were coming closer. They were soldiers' voices, relaxed and bantering. One voice broke into ribald laughter, and one of the sets of boots broke away.

The laughing voice said, "Don't get lost mate. We'll never find you!"

Never find you...

Oh.

Dear.

Gods.

Never find you!

And the understanding of what he'd seen crystallised, shone brilliant, and shattered with spectacular force.

Of course!

That was what he'd been missing! All this time, all these many returns of searching! He could still hear the terrible, screaming deaths of his tan upon the grassy hills of Rammouthe, feel the rip and shred of his own wounds and scars, the taint of his hopelessness...

But Vahl Zaxaar was *not there*, he was not *on* Rammouthe! *He never had been.*

Fhaveon was built to guard against a tale. A fiction, a saga, a legend so carefully spun to keep her attention from the real game...

To keep Rhan distracted, bored and inattentive...

While the real assault came in, slowly and stealthily, like soft boots in the night.

The boots of the soldier were coming closer.

In that one moment before the soldier was upon him, everything in Roderick's mind was snapping into place. His clarity was almost making him laugh with the shock of it. It *was* connected – it was *all* connected – by the Gods, he'd been right all along. Everything he'd seen and sought and found – the fires, the creatures, the alchemy, the Elementalism – it had all spun from the same source, it all came, ultimately, from the now-awakening Vahl.

And *Phylos*...!

Again, the image of the Merchant Master on the clifftop. Demisarr, screaming. Valicia, fighting. Rhan, hands bound and falling. The tumultuous splash with which the city's defender hit the surging white water...

Phylos was the avatar, the harbinger, and he'd insinuated Vahl into Fhaveon like a disease –

"Oi!"

Gods!

Roderick started like a novice – his hand tightening on the blade. The soldier was right there, hand halfway to the drawstring of his breeches as through about to go for a piss.

"You reek! What the rhez...?"

The poignard was very heavy, very cold, and very sharp.

He didn't have a choice.

The Bard's free hand went to the soldier's shoulder, spun him, staggering, into the wall. The other hand inserted the metal blade, cleanly and neatly, up and under the point of his chin.

Straight into his brain.

The man's eyes widened. They were blue, clear as the dawn sky.

His mouth opened, but he made no sound.

Leaving the poignard where it was, the Bard caught him as he fell and lowered him carefully to the floor.

It was all over in a second, and he felt sick.

But also oddly, strangely elated.

For a moment, Roderick stood there. He contemplated the body – the man was young, small and slight – then he bent to remove the blade and wipe it on the soldier's wet breeches.

The man had pissed himself as he'd died. Urine and gore seeped across the stone.

Roderick swallowed bile, and stood up.

Somehow, he felt stronger – as though he had defeated some nightmare figment, some lingering taunt of Ecko's accusation of cowardice...

I had no choice.

And I have no choice now.

Now, he needed to head downwards, west and quickly, away from the sea and towards the rear of the city's skirts – down to where The Wanderer had last been.

In his mind, he could still feel Vahl Zaxaar's heat.

Demisarr is dead. Rhan has been cast down.

As the faint flickers of rocklight moved like the monsters of his mind, more fragments were coming to the surface, more realisation and insight. He moved swiftly now, picking up his pace until he was almost running.

As a youth, Roderick had craved knowledge – and the staid rituals of the aged Guardians had bored him. He was restless: he wanted so much more than he was permitted to see.

And, in his adolescence and rebellion, he had done what mortal man was forbidden to do.

He had touched his human flesh to the waters of the Ryll.

In that moment, he had seen the mind of the Goddess, he had seen her fear, her ultimate nightmare, and it had burned a hole in his mind. He knew it was still there, but neither he, nor the world herself, could remember it.

Yet now, in that hole, there was light. There was a broken mirror, a cracked window. A reflection. There was a man, huddled on a floor with his hands wrapped around his head. He was screaming, thin and piteous and desperate.

Roderick knew who he was.

Ress.

The light flashed rainbow, sunshine through spray. And through the broken gaze of the madman, Roderick saw Rhan, pulled under by the raging of the eastern sea. He saw Ecko, fighting in firelight, and the Monument, shining with a ghastly nacre of stolen power. He saw a rising creature of flame and crystal. He saw the Great Fayre, abandoned and sweeping with flame. He saw Demisarr, falling, and he saw Larred Jade, fighting for the heart of the Varchinde.

And he saw the madman on the floor, writhing like a shattered thing, words forced from twisted lips. He was trying to communicate something imperative, trying to tell him...

Ress's eyes opened. They were disfocused, one pupil larger than the other, but they sought Roderick's own as if there was no distance, no time. For just a moment, across the Powerflux and the open grass of the Varchinde, there came a shock like a contact, a moment of absolute clarity.

The world's fear comes!

Roderick stopped, staring at the image even as it faded.

You! You are the mirror that shows me!

But the image was gone, and the hole in his mind contained only the darkness.

He shook his head to clear the after-echoes. Around him, there was sweet, clear air.

He'd come to the end of the tunnels.

And there, ahead of him, was The Wanderer, warm and home and welcome. It stood in silhouette against the sunset, but the lights in its windows glowed – and they outlined the shapes of the soldiery that stood around it.

The world's fear comes!

Ress of the Banned. Insane. Yet somehow in possession of the ultimate truth, the truth that the Bard had forgotten.

The world's fear comes!

Kas Vahl Zaxaar was rising, certainly – the blood-red robes of the Merchant Master heralded a new dawn for the Varchinde. But that was not what Ress meant. In his warning cry, Roderick could hear something more.

Her fear – her real fear – was not Vahl Zaxaar.

It was something else.

And it was that something else that Roderick needed to know.

The man with the vision has no power – and the man with the power has no vision.

As the sun sank towards its death on the tips of the far-distant Kartiah, as the shadows grew long and golden across the Varchinde and the last of the daylight made Fhaveon shine like a gem...

...so Roderick the Bard went to reclaim The Wanderer.

It all happened so quickly.

As he came out into the sun, his bare feet itching on the weed-grown road, so the door of the tavern opened.

As if they had been waiting for him.

Merciless and soundless, a swift, capable shape emerged and broke the neck of the nearest soldier. The body slumped sideways, hit the wall, slid broken to the ground. Behind Sera's chill efficiency, Karine took up a defensive stance. In her hand was the short wooden cosh that normally lived behind the bar, she was grinning like a hunting bweao.

The tan of soldiers never knew what hit them.

The Bard knew Sera's history, but had never seen him fight – he was tight, controlled and utterly brutal, his precision was as sharp and cold as the finest weapon. Fhaveon-trained skirmishers, three of the soldiers moved towards him, each one wielding a short, one-handed spear and a small buckler, embossed with the device of the city.

But he was ready for them.

His expression calm, Sera moved to anticipate their strike. Rather than let himself be surrounded, he took the fight to the first one – grabbing his spear and pulling him off balance, then bringing his other fist straight into the man's face. Swiftly reversing the spear, he turned on the second one, parried the first jab, then kicked the outside of the buckler, spinning it wide of the woman's body. She gasped as the spear-point went clean through her belly.

The third one was older, wilier. With the buckler strap still over his knuckles, he had both hands on his spear shaft and danced backwards, keeping Sera at its point. Sera glanced up once, caught the eyes of Karine in the doorway, and advanced, forcing the man to retreat.

The slam of the cosh made the soldier's eyes roll back and his knees fold.

For a moment, the doorman flickered a grim smile.

The other three had turned and come for the Bard, spreading into a loose line.

Sera took two running steps and launched his spear, javelinlike, at the sky.

It arced, spiralling lazily, terhnwood shaft glittering, then began to fall, gathering speed. It hit one of them clean in the back of the neck and flopped him forwards like a child's doll. The other two glanced, hesitated.

Sera reached for another spear.

But the poignard was metal in Roderick's hand and there was still blood at its hilt.

He'd killed one person already. He was stinking and tired and filthy and he *itched*.

He'd had about enough.

"What the rhez do you think you're doing?"

His voice was a challenge in the still evening air. Birds lifted, cawing alarm. Barefoot and uncaring, he strode across the broken roadways to where the two members of the tan now looked at each other and backed up, wary. Behind them, Sera had picked up a second spear but he was waiting, watching.

With the sunlit might of the Lord city rising behind him, and The Wanderer's lure in front, the Bard had a tangible authority – and he was at the outermost limits of his tolerance.

His voice resounded. "The man behind you can rip you into little pieces in less time than I can tell it. So I suggest that you pick up your weapons, and your comrades, and you get your backsides the rhez back into the city. And when you go, you tell the Merchant Master that Rhan may have fallen, but that I am still here. You tell Phylos that I know who he is, and I know what he's done, and I know *exactly* what he's sold his soul for.

"And you tell him there will be a *reckoning*!"

The two soldiers were retreating as the Bard strode forwards.

Behind them, there was a sudden scuffle in the tavern doorway and Karine rounded on something that the Bard couldn't see. She had fury and courage, was swearing with vicious, high-pitched anger. As Sera turned for the tavern door, she sprang at something and was gone from sight.

The Bard raised his voice. "Go! Or help me Gods I'll send that promise back with your *heads*!"

For a moment, he thought they'd say something, defy him, but they were backing away so fast they were almost stumbling and, when he twitched his hand and let the poignard catch the sunlight, they gathered their legs and their spears and they fled.

Roderick reached the doorway to see a body slumped across a broken table and Sera, with a doorman's long practice, closing his fist in the collar of another and spanging his lolling head repeatedly off the wall.

Karine was stood with her hands on her hips, indignant and uninjured, chastising him about the mess. Silfe's brown eyes peered wide from behind the bar.

Roderick the Bard was home.

"They will come for us," Sera said. "We do not have long."

There had been hugs and tears and questions and explanations – and there had been a cold and glorious moment with his head under the water pump in the back yard. Eight days had passed since the ill-fated Council meeting, eight days since Phylos had taken the Council.

Now, standing at the window with his hair still wet, looking at the sunset as it lit the plains to a huge, burning light, Roderick's righteous fury was evaporating into a more rational fear.

They were outcasts, criminals.

Murderers.

Behind him, Sera was turfing their unwelcome guests out of the doorway and Karine was picking up a scatter of plates and leather mugs from the long tables. Silfe sat quiet, an odd avian creature perched on her arm. It was a lean thing, hook beaked and featherless, its wingspan massive. Around one dew-clawed ankle, it had a terhnwood band that marked it as the property of the Lord Nivrotar.

Silfe stroked the bretir's ugly head and it burbled at her. They were smart things and affectionate, like both nartuk and chearl, alchemically bred by long ago Tusienic scholars.

Alchemy. Old skills, like old lore, like old might and Elementalism – all of it, now awakening.

He understood now. In the rousing of the sleeping

Monument, so the Powerflux itself stirred to life – and so other things stirred with it.

But the nartuk, the half-man, half-horse monsters, these had come before the Monument had risen. Somehow, somewhere, there was an alchemical scholar that was using ancient skills...

...was that scholar Vahl Zaxaar himself? Or was it something else?

The floor juddered again, sending prickles of unease down Roderick's spine.

Sera said, "There are lights moving towards us. Their formation suggests the Council has called a considerable force. I suspect they will not be lenient."

"You should leave," Roderick said, turning from the window. "This is on my head alone –"

"Oi." Karine's reprimand was stern. "This is my home and I'm not calling last orders 'til they drag me out of here by my hair –"

This time, the floor shook harder, rattling the pottery in the wine racks. The rumble was longer, they felt it through their boots and in their hearts.

There was no mistaking what it meant.

The Bard lifted his head, the faintest whisper of humour flickered through his blood, chasing the darkness of his mood out into the last of the sun. "Silfe," he said softly. "Send the bretir back to Amos with a message for Nivrotar. Tell her to keep Ress of the Banned safe and as well as she is able – I must see him."

The floor was shivering now, the movement making the weapons on the walls rattle against beams and brickwork.

Roderick said, "Where's Kale?"

Karine shrugged, almost apologetically. "We locked him in the privy. We sort of had to. I guess I'd better see if he's calmed down yet."

"I suspect," the Bard said, "that he's going to thank us. In the long run." Both his grin and his agitation were growing now. He was on his feet, his fingertips on the warm wood of the table, his faith and hope rising and his breathing tight. "Do we not trust in the wisdom of The Wanderer to defend itself? It seems Phylos cannot have us – not yet."

As if in agreement, the building shook harder, the floor lurching and making them grab for upright beams and table edges.

Silfe stumbled, but she reached the doorway and loosed the huge wings of the bretir past Sera and out into the last of the light. For a moment, it was a shadow, rising into the air, and then it turned south and faded from sight.

Bretir were enormously swift. For a long moment, Roderick watched where it had gone.

The world's fear comes!

Sera said, "The force will not reach us in time. We are free. But we should not return here without an army."

The Bard chuckled. "I'm not sure I can muster such a thing – but think of this. If Ecko was right, and all of this is just a pattern, endlessly repeating itself, then this building is what changes that pattern, what adds the thrill of the random to an otherwise predictable future. If there is a pattern, then we live on its outside. We are The Wanderer, and Rhan was right – they cannot touch us."

Karine said, "What in the world are you talking about? You damned crazed prophet."

"They are coming to try." Sera's hands were clenched in anticipation of a second fight. "If we are going to move –"

The tavern twisted, spun, and winked out of existence.

30: MEGALOMANIAC FHAVEON, THE MONUMENT

Somehow, the location of The Wanderer wasn't even a surprise.

Like some surreal and hastily erected film set, the tavern had plonked itself slap-bang in the Monument's centre. The great grey stones, now lightless, were tumbled about its outer walls. Its doors were open, its windows shining with warmth and light and welcome – it looked both wondrous and shallow, like a tourist attraction.

Seeing it, Ecko knew he was floundering, that this reality was twisting round him. After the glory of the Sical, its temptation and validation, after the superboosting of his adrenaline, he felt as if it was wrong – as if, should he just lean forwards and push, the whole damned lot would go over like some sun-cracked billboard, the grass and sky with it.

And he would be home.

So I won, already. Rescued the girl. Toasted the bad guy. Blew the shit outta the base. Can I go now?

In the foregarden, Roderick the Bard was standing with his hair wet and his arms folded across his chest. Something about him had changed, some touch of steel in his jaw, some cold light in his amethyst eyes.

"Ecko!" As they walked down the bank towards the building, he came to meet them, his expression lit with a fierce, flaring hope. For a moment, Ecko thought he was going to be embraced and backed the fuck up, hands spread wide. The sign creaked, predictably, over his head.

Way too surreal.

He blinked and had to make an effort to speak.

"Don't even think it."

But the Bard was laughing. He had spread his hands wide and he was laughing at the very sky, at the stones, the batshit moons. He laughed as though nothing could ever threaten him again.

He was a barking loony.

"And here we are," Roderick said, "in the very Monument itself, rescued in the nick of time. And here, we meet again, on the far side of tragedy, and with the world changed beyond recognition. I don't know what wonder has occurred to bring us here, but I trust in The Wanderer and I'm glad we're all safe. Come in, be welcome." He nodded at the others, gave Triqueta a momentary, slightly confused second glance. "You're weary, injured –"

"Nice timing," Ecko said. Looking up at the windows, the roof where he'd sat as the tavern first moved, he couldn't wrap his head round it. His head was too full of the Sical, of Maugrim, of home. He heard himself say, "How's it going?"

"What's the phrase you use? It's all 'gone to hell in a hardcart'." The Bard was still laughing. He looked about them at the surrounding stones. One of them had actually tumbled through the garden wall, a visual distortion that was making Ecko's sense of disorientation worse.

"Yet we're fortunate, in many ways," Roderick said. "We live, and we're still free."

"Free." Ecko snorted. "That'll be the day."

"I've missed you too."

"I'm touched."

As the Bard gestured them inside, Ecko ducked through the door and his skin betrayed him. As if his outer self, at least, acknowledged the tavern's existence, it was shifting, changing – splotching from the shadows of the Monument to the rich browns of the building's greeting and comfort.

He found a table, crouched there at the room's centre. Warily, he eyed the walls, the artefacts, the weapons, the shields. It looked fake, like it would scorch and burn through any second, like the whole thing would dissolve into smoking, charred holes.

"Well!" Karine was behind the bar, arms folded beneath her breasts and a look of mock disapproval on her face. "And what time do you call this?"

"Dinner time," Ecko told her, reflexively. He managed a grin.

She tutted. "Get your feet off the table."

The others were coming further into the building, looking around them as though they, too, could not believe they were here.

"We're back," Triqueta said. "We're really back. We've walked the halls of the Rhez itself, but we're here. For love of every *God*, someone get me an ale."

"Make that two." Chuckling, Redlock unslung his pack, dropped it, looked for a chair. He carefully felt the ruin of his nose. Then, with a deep, determined breath, he crunched it back into place, swore. Blinked water from his eyes.

Behind them, Amethea had fallen onto the bench under the window. She sat with her head in her hands, unmoving.

The very last of the sun blazed silver from her hair.

"Ecko, Triqueta," Roderick said. "I cannot express how much your return means to me – to all of us." Karine snorted, grinned. "I understand you have many tales and I am... more than eager to listen – but I fear you are weary beyond endurance. I will aim to be patient." He glanced up as Kale emerged from the kitchen with a steaming leather jug and a handful of mugs. When the Bard turned back, his expression was all mischief.

"If I can. There is so much I must tell you also. The world has changed around us. Radically so."

"Changed?" The word was thrown like a stone. Amethea looked at him, her pale face in shadow, her navy eyes dark as the sky. "The Monument is fallen. The Powerflux is awake. Maugrim may be dead, but..." As Kale silently poured her a mug of herbal, she wrapped her hands around it as though it were the most precious thing in the world. "We've won a fight – but that's all. This is only the beginning."

"We've won more than you know," Roderick said. "If Roviarath still stands, then, I think, at least half of the plan has failed."

Amethea said, aghast, *"Half?"*

His smile was oddly ironic, "As you say, this is only the beginni–"

Without warning, the night was shattered by a distant bellow of thunder.

The taproom gaped and then scrabbled, going for weapons and windows, calling for answers. The noise was loud, the sudden roar of something gunned to pain and fury. It was abrupt, and harsh, and close. It dropped a note, another.

The mica in the windows shook.

"It's the Sical," Amethea said softly. Her herbal tankard slid through her fingers to bounce from the floor, liquid splashing a great, dark stain in the sawdust. Her face haunted, she'd turned to the window behind her. "We can't let this happen, we can't!"

Roderick mouthed, *Sical*, confused.

Triqueta had sprung to the bench by Amethea, in her hand a short, terhnwood blade she'd swiped from the wall. Her face was sharp, eager. Redlock rose to his feet with his brown eyes blazing. He drew his axes, then dissolved into coughing, blood staining the back of his hand.

But Ecko was grinning. "For chrissakes, that's not the fucking Sical."

Suddenly, the tavern was real, solid – snapped into focus by the incoming sound. Ecko was at the door, his heart pounding, pounding. There was a certain inevitable symmetry to this – the feeling, again, of the pattern repeating itself. This was *right*, somehow, it was the final realisation.

Faster than a thought, he grabbed the handles and threw both doors fully open.

"Sical, my ass!" he said.

The noise grew worse. In the rippling moonlight, on a dead straight heading, was a single, glaring, white eye – screaming towards them out of smoke-scented dark grass.

"What the rhez...?" Redlock stared like an idiot, then hands tightened round his axe shafts. "This time, you bastard. This time you're not coming back."

"Fuck me." Ecko was almost laughing. "The ratfuck son of a bitch's got a Thundergod!"

"You know that creature?" Redlock watched it closely.

"You'd better fucking believe it." Ecko grinned at the oncoming cyclopean beast, the red lights in his eyes flashing. "Jesus Harry Christ," he muttered to himself. "Don't bad guys *ever* die when you kill 'em?" He moved to stand in the doorway, arms folded, his cloak hem billowing in the dawn breeze.

Sera came to stand beside him, his expression cold and calm.

Redlock, sniffing like a cokehead, was on his other shoulder.

Before them, the bike was closing at impossible speed, the sound ringing from the stones. Maugrim's eager stance was challenging the tavern wall to a game of chicken.

Roderick had joined them, Triqueta. Karine's hand closed around her cosh. Kale had retreated to the kitchen, his worn face tense. None of them moved.

As it screamed past the last fallen sarsen and into the garden, the bike turned sideways, fell and skidded to a halt, throwing out a wall of dirt and soil. The awful noise cut out, and Maugrim's voice, shouting something, rang in Ecko's ears. The greaser scrambled to his feet, didn't bother to pick the bike up. It lay there like a corpse, rear wheel idly turning, tyre packed with the dirt of the Varchinde.

Maugrim stepped over it, grinning. His t-shirt and cut-down were soaked in blood and oil and sweat, there was a livid bruise around his throat.

"Hello there, Rick," he said. "Good to see you." He spread his hands, weaponless, surrendering. "It's a fair cop, guv. You got me. I'm handing myself in."

"So," Ecko said, his voice a chainsaw rasp. "Look what the cat dragged in."

They'd sat the smirking Maugrim at the table's end, the rocklight glimmering on his dirt-stained skin. The faint scent of smoke lingered in the air.

Redlock watched him closely, as if the axeman was itching to finish what he'd started.

"The Ecko." Maugrim was carefully casual, leaning back, half his face in shadow, his hair a halo of unholy illumination. "The one and only. Bit lost aren't you? Last anyone heard, the Ecko had sold out and joined Lugan's strike team – pitting themselves in a doomed war against the might of Pilgrim Products Inc. Guess you weren't as tough as you thought."

"You know Lugan?" Ecko said. "Oh chrissakes, who the hell'm I kidding? You're my end-of-level nasty – of course you fucking know Lugan."

"Everyone knows Lugan." Maugrim grinned. "Where d'you think I got the bike?"

Round them, Karine was bustling, herbal mugs and plates of food. Sera watched the door.

"Shame you didn't bring him with you – he probably *is* as hard as he thinks he is." He picked up the herbal mug, eyed it warily. "You, Ecko, you messed up. You *died*."

Died?

Landed on the tarmac like a lump of...

"Yeah, right." Ecko was tense, adrenals flickering. He was aware of Amethea's bruised stare, Redlock's pacing agitation. "I didn't fucking die." The 'bot, the screaming London weather, falling. "Eliza put me here to Save the World."

Even as he said it, it sounded ridiculous.

"Eliza!" The name was a guffaw. "They'd waste that sort of expense on you? I'm in the profession, you might say. And I know your profile, Gabriel – you're a screw-up, a screaming pyrophile, a madman. Untreatable." He was still laughing. "And now a megalomaniac. Save the World, my left nut."

I know your profile, Gabriel. Ecko found that he was crouched on his seat, trembling. *Gabriel.* He spat, "My profile?"

"Steady, my friend," Roderick said quietly. "I know his trickeries of old – he baits you."

Amethea's voice was soft. "Don't trust him."

"Your profile." Maugrim had lost his laughter, his voice was cold. "This isn't some psychoprogram, you little freak, your own personal Virtual *Rorschach*." The word was spat. "Who the hell would care about you *that* much?"

I am the pattern, the pattern spreads from me.

Megalomaniac.

His voice as clear as blind faith, Roderick said, "We do. He came here to help us."

"I'm the one helping you, you bloody lunatic." Maugrim was on his feet. "You know this, Rick – you explained it to me! You're stagnant, no progress – your people have just let everything go, forgotten their lore and culture, forgotten it all. Like Pilgrim – it's all apathy! Terhnwood and trade and tedium. Passionless. You know what I mean – we should tear it down, kick over the anthill. Progress has to happen or we'll all fucking *rot*."

Triqueta muttered, "You call that progress?"

"Of course I do!" Maugrim jabbed a ringed finger at her. "This is a fantasy, right? Sword'n'saucery, good'n'evil, law'n'chaos – Ecko, you know this shit as well as I do. And fantasy worlds have to have the Bad Guy, the Necromancer, the Lord of Dark – why? Because without him – or her – paradise'd be pointless. Unchallenged, unremarked. How can you get achievement with no struggle, satisfaction with no effort? How do you value anything when it's just handed to you?"

How can you value anything…?

Ecko was caught. His own beliefs, distorted, slung back at him like a handful of toxic mud.

"This ends now." Redlock muttered darkly. The axeman, at least, was clear of purpose. "All of it."

"It'll never end, warrior. While your terhnwood grows, while your trade cycles, you'll disappear so far up your own arseholes you'll lose sight of everything else. In the end, you'll whine about the small shit because it's all you'll have left."

Roderick said, "Wait a minute – wait. You said, 'While your terhnwood grows…' What's going to happen to it? Phylos…?" His voice faded into horror, anticipation and realisation. "What is Phylos going to do?"

Maugrim laughed, threw his head back and guffawed at the ceiling. "You're not as bloody green as you're cabbage-looking, are you, Rick?"

"By the Gods." The Bard was out of his seat. "I'll carve the damned answer out of your skin if I have to! What is Phylos going to *do*?"

Maugrim stretched, grinned like a challenge.

But Ecko was no longer paying attention. In Maugrim's zeal, he'd heard The Boss's philosophy, Lugan's battle against Pilgrim, the death of the woman he'd burned on the shit-hole bed.

Take away the big shit – it'll be all you've got left.

As Maugrim faced the Bard, Ecko's breathing was tightening, his boosting half kicked. He was poised on the precipice of its speed, its certainty… He wanted to embrace it, it would surge beyond doubt, beyond conscience… but he dared not let it go. The Sical's might may scream in his veins, but its master was here – here, from his own world, from his own *head*.

This isn't some psychoprogram, you little freak, your personal Virtual Rorschach.

What if… *Chrissakes!* His own doubts, his flickers of emotion and compassion. *What if this* was *real?* He couldn't wrap his brain round the possibility. *What if there* was *no program – what if…* Panic was closing his throat. The walls of the tavern were dark, closed-in. There were weapons everywhere he looked.

"We've got every right to carve your answer from you." Amethea's voice was clear, cold. "You've committed torture, rape, murder, corruption – you've rained fire from the sky, set your creatures on Roviarath and that – thing – would've torn the Varchinde asunder." She was as calm as still water. "I'll wield the damned blade myself."

"Little priestess, Amethea." His voice was almost affectionate. "Your crimes are as bad as mine – and you know it."

"No more, Maugrim." She stood up. "No more head games, no more trickery, no more coercion. No more blood. Feren was my friend, my responsibility, his courage puts all of us to shame. I'll pay whatever dues I have to – but you must answer for everything you've done. And not just to me."

"Nice speech," Maugrim told her. He stretched further back in his chair, grinning. He fumbled for something in the pocket of his cut-down.

Amethea stared at him, daring him to speak again. He twisted a smile at her.

"Feren's memory isn't lost." Redlock leaned in and said softly, "You say you've walked the very Halls of the Rhez. Can you torture him, healer? In vengeance? In cold blood?"

"I've never taken a life," Amethea said. "The stallion asked me…" She broke off. "I've never taken a life."

Road hardened, blood covered, the axeman said, "Keep it that way."

Roderick silently clapped his shoulder.

"The stallion was loco, anyhow," Triqueta said, nudging her elbow. "Didn't last too long."

Maugrim chuckled. "Poor creature, my heart breaks for it." He was wrapping something in his hand. "Losing a pet can be heartbreaking... though you can always go down the store for another one. The herd goes on, little lady. It was my gift – not my creation. Wouldn't fit through the tunnels, y'know?"

He stretched further still, blazing with confidence, arms behind his head.

"You still haven't told us where they came from." Triq eyed Maugrim's lazy pose with contempt. "Sitting there all damned smug – we've got you by your short and curlies, sunshine, and you're going to spill it. All of it. Or I'm going to show you what a woman can really do."

Maugrim's gaze ambled all over Triq's lithe body. He smirked.

"No offence, sweetheart – you're a bit long in the tooth for me."

She spluttered. "You – !"

"Don't bother," Amethea told her. "He's just prodding you, making you react. I think he finds it amusing."

"Well, I'm going to find him amusing in a minute." Triq crossed her arms, glared. "Who made the monsters?"

Roderick said, "What is Phylos planning?"

Maugrim laughed outright at them.

Lost by the whirl of interrogation round him, Ecko was only half listening to the exchange. His mind was stumbling, reaching, reeling, questioning, spinning like a centrifuge round one word: *real*.

It couldn't be, it *couldn't* be – like a true believer who'd lost his faith, he was searching for meaning in a sudden vacuum, the vacuum in which Eliza and her program had lived. He was responsible for his own choices, had been all along: he wasn't being manipulated or tricked, wasn't following a pattern...

But –

This had *so* been done to him! He'd jumped, out into the freezing wind from Grey's rooftop, out into Eliza's program and the fight against the corruption of his mind.

Or had he jumped into the certainty of his own death?

He couldn't breathe, couldn't think. The explanations were the same, inside and outside reflections of one another. This was fucking insane!

Pain in his fingertips told him he had Lugan's lighter in his hand. *This is the Bike Lodge, mate...*

Was he dreaming? Was he dead? Was he plugged into a shit-hole console after all? Up until now, he'd been playing some elaborate game – suddenly, he was dealing with the enormity of the impossible.

Real.

Maugrim was speaking again, his voice soft, insidious.

"You people, you're all suffering – and I was told how to help you."

He sat forward, and there was a chain in his hand, a flickering multicoloured light that danced back and forth.

"You should trust me, place your faith in me. I listen, I heed your pain and I heal."

The chain swung gently.

"You misunderstand, don't you? Yes, you know you do. The fire touches you – all of you. You, warrior, hate drives you, it burns in you and it's made you strong. You, Amethea, you crave love, the love of the family you never had – and you'll take that love, no matter how it's offered. You, lady of the Banned, you're all about desire – instant gratification, flesh, comfort, wealth. Karine, Sera, you're outcasts that seek only family. And you, Bard with no memory, you poor deluded fool. You have such might – and you won't use it; such strength – and you have no idea what it is. You're a creature of fear, hiding behind the hoarding of knowledge so you don't have to act. Rhan is gone – your greatest ally. You'll never know how you failed him."

Back and forth, enticing, compelling.

"There is love and forgiveness in Vahl's heart – he'll welcome you, all of you, and you can be free from the pain. You can belong.

"All you have to do is trust me."

Triqueta said, voice low, "We trust you. What can we do?"

"And Ecko, Tam, lost and alone, striving for understanding. Lugan carries loyalty like a flag, he'd never abandon you, you know that. This has to be real, what else makes sense? Ecko, little daemon, Vahl Zaxaar knows you above all, he has a special place for you – you're the darkness in which his fire burns brightest. It's a place that'll make all things make sense.

"Just trust me. I know you, all of you. And I can make you whole."

Flickering, dancing light. Forgiveness and warmth radiated back from the walls as though Maugrim had tapped into the tavern's lenslike focus, its welcome and sense of home. They stretched their hands to it, needing it like a warm bed on a cold night.

The table was still, captivated. Maugrim could do anything he wanted with them.

Except Kale.

In the freeze-frame, in the centre of the tableau, the cook came out of his seat, hands on the table. His voice was a concentrated husk of withheld fury as he said, "And what about me?" His grin was widening as though his mouth were full of knives. "What welcome do you have for me?"

The swing of the light paused.

Kale's hands clenched on the tabletop. With a splintering of wood, there were claws embedded in its surface, dragging savage chunks out of its solidity. He was trembling, crouching, hair rippling across his skin – slowly, so slowly.

Maugrim stared. "You…" he said. "You're new here. I don't know you…"

"You will."

And the beast was over the table in a scatter of mugs, a scrabble of talons, a bubbling snarl of pure hate. Burning, asymmetrical green eyes fixed on the light; claws ripped it from Maugrim's gasp. Startled, the Elementalist held his hands up to shield his face and his chair went over backwards, crashing to the floor. In a moment, the beast pounced after him, lashing tail, dripping teeth, slavering death.

Roderick shouted, "Kale, *no!*"

Around him, the others were shaking themselves to consciousness, questions, shock. *What had he done to them?*

Sera bellowed, "Redlock! He fears white-metal!"

Snarling and struggling came from under the table. Maugrim was swearing.

"Get your bloody animal off me!"

"Don't hurt him!" Karine cried. "Not if you can help it!"

In the midst of the commotion, Ecko hadn't moved.

Redlock skidded round the table's end, grabbed the beast by the scruff and dragged it back from worrying at Maugrim's bloodied throat. As it growled and thrashed, tail sending scattered mugs in all directions, he held one axe right under its nose.

"Kale. I don't want to hurt you. Back off."

The beast turned to him and snarled.

"Back off!" He thumped its nose with the back of the axe. It slashed randomly at him, rear claws raking the floor. "Now!"

"Kale." The Bard's voice was steady, strong. "You have never hurt a guest. Please – not even this one. His blood is not worth your soul."

"Now!"

With a shudder that seemed to wrench flesh from bone, the beast was gone.

And Kale the cook was falling back, blood across his mouth and chin, pushing the axe from his face. His was white, shaking violently.

"I'm okay, I'm okay." He wiped his face, looked at his hands, grimaced. "Sorry about that... I guess he annoyed me..."

"No shit." Redlock hadn't put the axe away. "You calm now?"

"Yes, I..." Still wiping, spitting, he scrambled backwards from where Maugrim lay, blood soaking his chest. "Yes. Yes." He started to scratch like a man infected.

Karine was by him. "It's all right, it's all right. It's over."

"It is indeed." In an unconscious parody, Roderick placed one foot on Maugrim's chest. He said bleakly, "Tell me about Phylos."

Ecko muttered, "This isn't real. It can't be."

Maugrim spat blood, blood stained his teeth and ran from his throat in rivulets, soaking the sawdust, staining the floor.

Roderick's voice was cold steel. "Tell me, Ralph, or I shall throw you in the midden and leave you to die."

"You pick a fine time to find your balls, Rick." Maugrim laughed bloody bubbles.

Ecko said, "This isn't fucking real."

The Bard's voice slashed back from the walls. *"Tell me about Phylos!"*

"I don't know, guv. And I wouldn't tell you if I did."

"Enough head games. Tell me!"

Head games.

The phrase crystallised Ecko's fury like the shine of the Sical itself.

Head games.

The final trick: the final test.

Profile.

This fucker was Eliza made manifest: *Maugrim* was his in-situ shrink. Rummaging around in Ecko's head, building lock-ups like familiarity, loosing fire-beasties that touched him to the very soul... playing hypno-the-rapist with a fucking hexidecimal pocket watch...

Head games. All of it. Fucking head games.

In the echoes of Roderick's anger, Ecko felt the relief of the fiction closing back in about him – and this time, he took refuge in it. He needed it and it made sense to him.

He'd started in a teleporting tavern, for chrissakes. He'd gone down a dungeon and splatted a Big McNasty. He was a bit short on the treasure front, but he had saved the girl. Of *course* it was a fucking program – it had to be – who the hell did this asshole think he was kidding?

Yeah, I got this now.

He rounded on Maugrim, on the Bard. "All right, fuckwit, that's it. You've seen my profile? You so know I don't like having people fuck with my *head*." He stood to his full height, looked down at the still-defiant Maugrim with his head cocked sideways, his teeth bared. "Nice try with the pocket watch routine."

Around him, the others were tense, watching him.

"You know what? I *am* insane. I'm a pyrophile and a madman and a fucking megalomaniac. And Eliza designed a whole Virtual Rorschach just for me. And you? Are just a figment of her code, of my imagination. And you know what that means?"

Maugrim was laughing at him.

"You came back to fuck us up – hand us over. You filthy bag of shit."

Ecko jumped at him, adrenals kicking, faster than the taproom could react. He was on the floor, his hands were wrapped in the front of Maugrim's cut down, the smooth slide of long-oiled denim under his fingers.

"That means I don't have a conscience." His grin was unholy. "It means I can do anything the fuck I want to you. It means I can peel off your skin an inch at a time – you wanna know what that feels like? It means I can cover you in burns, let them heal, and then burn you all over again. It means I can melt your flesh into a blistered puddle on the floor. It means –"

"Ecko." The Bard's eyebrows were almost comical. "Please."

"It means you're fucked. That's what it means." His grin was jaunty. "Now, I think the man had a question?"

Maugrim was trying to back away from Ecko's grip. His defiance was fading, there was fear growing in his gaze, his expression.

He said, "You wouldn't dare. I'm not afraid of you!"

"That," Roderick commented, "may be a mistake."

Maugrim squirmed, tried to get away from the Bard's foot, Ecko's fists. He was shouting now, shouting up at the ring of faces that surrounded him.

"I'm telling you nothing! Nothing, you hear me! I was told that the world was mine – that I could save it, that all I had to do –"

His speech cut suddenly dead. He gagged, his eyes bulging, his hands flailing. His body jacked, his feet hammered the floor, drumming a tattoo that could only mean one thing.

Ecko said, "Well, shit."

He sat back. The Bard moved his foot.

On the floor of the tavern, Maugrim was frothing like a rabies victim, foaming at his mouth, blood leaking from his ears. His eyes were filled with darkness, his body jerking manically from side to side. A final, thin scream came from his throat.

Ecko stood up, wiped his hands on his cloak.

Karine said, pointedly, "The mop's in the kitchen."

And Roderick swore with more viciousness than Ecko had ever heard.

* * *

In the faint, pale glimmer of the pre-dawn, a tail of smoke rose from The Wanderer's chimney.

And a corpse, foam flecked and bloodied, lay on a fallen stone altar.

From their collective refuge on the henge's bank, they could see the glow of The Wanderer and, beside it, the rock upon which Maugrim had been laid. Watching him to ensure that he didn't jump back to life, or rise as a beastie, or anything else, Ecko was mentally totalling his points on the sanity scoreboard – wondering what Collator would have to say for itself.

Success of scenario: 53.78%. Could do better.

But hell, he was still Ecko. Whatever Eliza had wanted to do to his personality, his code of ethics, what*ever*-the-fuck her brief had been... he'd beaten it. He was himself, unchanged.

Wasn't he?

For a moment, he saw Pareus, burning. He saw the warm windows of The Wanderer, and the light of the love of its staff. Redlock's courage and Triqueta's vibrant life. Kale's pain and his fight for his soul.

I'm s'posed to think this shit is real?

I'm supposed to think it's not?

It means I don't have a conscience. It means I can do anything I want...

In the moonlight, he could see Amethea's face, beside him on the bank. He had no idea what she'd been through, but she too, had bravery he couldn't even find words for.

And somewhere in the back of his head he knew that they had touched him. All of them.

No matter how he tried to deny it.

He wondered if that meant that Eliza was winning.

Then a tremor in the ground made him start.

He shifted, glanced at Redlock beside him on the bank. The

axeman was frowning, scrabbling to his feet, flicking weapons into hands – looking for the threat. Amethea stared round her, wild-eyed.

Triqueta said, "There! Oh my Gods!"

Below them, as Maugrim's seeping blood finally touched the soil, the stones of the Monument were shifting, settling. On his feet now, Ecko spun his telescopics. He could see the ground was slipping, concave, crumbling... Slowly, the great grey stones were sinking, like flooded barges drowning in the soil.

And so was the tavern.

"Roderick! Shit, Roderick!"

From far below them, there was a distant, ominous rumble. The ground shook. They could only watch as the stone bearing Maugrim's corpse upended like the fucking *Titanic* and was gone, the soil round it falling away. It was sliding into nothing, spilling the body and tumbling free into capacitor-stone and the ruined cathedral, far, far below.

From where it fell, cracks grew through the ground, reached like hands for the walls of The Wanderer. Another stone hung over the limit, teetered, and was gone.

For a second, Ecko was poised to race down the bank, but Redlock's hand on his arm held him. Aghast, they could only watch.

Triq said, hushed, "Did we just do that?"

The tavern garden was hazy, slued. It twisted sideways in the soft grey light, as if to follow some invisible magnetism in the fallen stones. It shook, the stone embedded in the front wall sank without trace, a black maw remaining to suck at the tavern's life.

He could see – just – Roderick throwing open the door, the Bard was shouting but his voice was snatched away by the brain-fucking, plughole twist of The Wanderer's movement. Kale was in the garden itself, and Sera and Karine stared out of the windows.

"What in the name of the Gods?" Amethea had her hands over her mouth.

With a scrabble, they were all on their feet, grabbing each other and staring.

"The whole world's gone loco," Redlock said.

With a rumble, the entire Monument gave way, grass and soil and stones plummeting gracefully into a huge, yawning darkness.

And The Wanderer was gone, white faces and screaming and horror, downwards into the dark.

"Fuck," Ecko said.

EPILOGUE LUGAN'S OFFICE, LONDON

Her name was Tarquinne Magdalene Gabriel. Her friends called her "Maggie", her employees called her Ma'am. Pilgrim had called her a miracle.

Like her brother, she was extremely bright, afraid of very little and strongly individualistic – unlike her brother, she was worth in excess of three hundred million eurobucks.

She was twenty-eight years of age and one of the greatest financial minds of her generation.

So they said, anyhow.

Lugan could see Ecko in the woman that paced, agitated, across the stained ferrocrete floor of his office – hints of his restlessness, his face shape, his mannerisms and speech. Ms Gabriel was not beautiful – she was a little too thin, a little too chill. But her skin was like porcelain, her hair flawless and her overlarge brown eyes hinted at a familiar fanaticism. She had poise, she was difficult to ignore.

And she was already annoying the shit out of him.

Ms Hotshot Gabriel eyed the grubby glass of the dividing wall, and the workshop beyond, with disdain.

"Beer?" Lugan asked her, not bothering to mask his

sarcasm. "Cuppa tea?"

The tan coat she wore was real leather, kevlar reinforced. He had bikes worth less.

"I want my brother, Mr Eastermann." She paused in front of the crouching, glowering desk, arms folded.

"An' I've told ya, I dunno where 'e is." Lugan leaned right back in his chair. He took a drag on his dog-end, squinting at her through the smoke. "Don't let the door 'it you in the arse on the way out."

Tarquinne leaned one soft and delicate hand on the desktop and smiled. "Tam vanished, Mr Eastermann. He was working for you. You either know where he is – or you need to find him. Kindly don't try and intimidate me."

He pushed the chair onto its back legs. It creaked.

"He's the Ecko, vanishin' is what 'e does best." Smoke curled free with the words. "This isn't your fuckin' boardroom, luv, and I get cranky takin' *orders*. Whether you're 'is sister or you ain't – you can get the fuck out my face."

Close by, bike engines coughed into life, slammed down the gears as they roared away. The blue light of a hoverdrone shone briefly through the window then was gone.

Tarquinne pulled a colour-washed titanium needle from an inside pocket.

"One hundred thousand eurodollars, Mr Eastermann. Half now, half when I have my brother."

Lugan snorted. "Fuckin' suit. You're lucky I don't break both your –"

"I need you to do a job for me," Tarquinne said. "And I ask you to bear something in mind. If you don't find my brother, Mr Eastermann, and someone else does, I'll hold you responsible for anything that... may fall into the wrong hands."

It was not even a threat – the cocky little bitch was completely serious. He drew a last, hard, drag on the dog-end, then pinched it out between thumb and forefinger.

With a deft snap, she clicked the needle onto the desk.

"Like all men, you have a price – name it and it's –" she glanced around her, pointedly "– yours."

"Six eurobucks and a pint." He dropped the dog-end in the pocket of his cut-down, blew smoke in her face.

She smiled, blinked. "Everyone has a price, Mr Eastermann. I want my brother. You could move to new premises, perhaps – I fear I've let you have the bargaining advantage over me." Her smile grew winsome, revealing a diamond in one of her teeth. "Whatever you'd like."

"How about the 'mug' tattoo removed from my forehead?" Slamming the chair back onto all fours, he resisted the urge to stand up – he was itching to slap the smirk off this smug little bint's face. "This is bullshit – and you're runnin' outta welcome."

"This is idiocy – and I'm running out of patience." Her smile was unchanged. "I want my *brother.*"

"And I want 'Arley Davidson to make bicycles. Life's tough."

Outside the rain-spattered window, the hoverdrone had returned.

"He ran on Grey's base –"

"You're stalkin' my *cell*, now?" Lugan enjoyed a sudden flash-vision of grabbing this little rodent by the throat and shaking her 'til her perfect teeth rattled. "You *really* don't want to be doin' that."

"Oh, believe me, I'm only stalking my own." She laughed at his anger, a cold, tinkling sound. "I keep a close eye on Tam. After all, if you'd invested five million in cybernetics for a top-end product, would you want to lose it?"

Product.

Realisation hit him like a scaff bar round the back of the head.

"He's your personal hitman." He leaned back, whistled through his teeth. "Jesus fucking Christ on a fucking motor scooter – you paid that demented Tech…"

Tarquinne laughed again. "What? You think his 'Mom'

changed him for free? Out of altruism? To break the frontiers of cybernetic science?" She flicked the needle with a perfectly polished nail and it rolled across the desk. "Two hundred thousand."

Lugan snorted.

"Five."

"Shove it, sister."

"With his hatred of Pilgrim's control, there's no limit to what Tam is capable of. I need him *back*."

His hatred of Pilgrim's control...

"Holy fucking shit on a stick. You planted him in my fucking *team*." A second smack of scaff pipe – Fawkes' night, last year. He'd walked into it like a drunk into a fucking brick wall. "To take out your boss, to take out Grey. Because you wanna play suit-war." Now, the twat he needed to shake was himself.

She raised her eyebrows at him, amused.

"It's quite simple, really, when you look at it." With a coquettish, artificial smirk, she perched her well-shaped rear on the edge of the desk. "We could be allies."

Really annoyed now, Lugan emptied dog-ends out of his pocket and began to shred them, methodical and savage, reclaiming the baccy.

"No offence, luv, I'd sooner shag my dog." A fresh paper, a new smoke. He lit it, pulled the tar-filled gunk deep into his lungs, considering. "If you take over Pilgrim, what're you gonna do?"

"Get me Tam, and we'll talk."

"If you want him, you'll talk now."

She gave a short, controlled sigh.

"Very well. Simple time-motion analysis states Grey's ultra-passive workforce is inefficient." A second needle joined the first. "Quiescence doesn't make for good employees – or good profits. New ideas are unforthcoming, everybody suffers. It's all here."

"What fuckin' genius told you that?" He let the smoke out in a cough of dark humour.

Tarquinne chuckled. "I'll put you in touch with the Tech – she'll help you locate him." She held out both needles. "I asked you to name your price."

This time, Lugan took them. "You said five 'undred thousand. 'Alf a million eurobucks – in advance."

"One hundred thousand now, the rest if you're successful. And you sign a contract stating you'll not take arms against Pilgrim again."

"Two 'undred now, the rest whether we're successful or not. No contract."

Tarquinne nodded, almost approving. "Two hundred and fifty thousand in advance. A quarter of a million eurodollars, Lugan – and the same at the conclusion. You sign the contract."

"I'm not signing shit."

"You're throwing away a great deal of money."

"An' you're here for a reason. Why don't you ask the Tech yourself? Why come 'ere and pay me to do something you can do yourself? You wanna keep your 'ands clean. Dontcha?" He grinned through his beard. "You need us to do this for you."

"Very well then." Tarquinne extended a ladylike hand and smiled, revealing the diamond. "I see your reputation is richly –"

The glass wall shattered.

A massive screaming implosion of flying crystal pebbles, a detonation of a million pulverised shards.

His brain screaming betrayal, Lugan was behind the desk, hand tearing the gaffer from the sawn-off that lived beneath.

He could hear Tarquinne shrilling orders – wherever her back up lurked, it was close.

Jam her signal, for fuck's sake. He was snapping orders of his own, orders at Fuller in the security office. *Jam her – !*

Done. Collator says... fuck!

Lugan had never heard Fuller swear. *Get me a grid on the*

bastards! As the glass scattered across the desktop, the floor, he snapped home the shotgun's nerve contact, felt the weapon in his hand – in his head.

Fucking bitch. He'd string her up by her...

He heard her swear, a gasp of utter disbelief.

"Holy shit." Suddenly, her poise had gone, her Chicago accent was fully deployed – her shock was genuine. "What the *hell*...?"

Where they at, for fuck's sake? How many? Where the fuck are Strafe and Heels?

Luge... we're not under attack. Fuller sounded bloodless, shocked to the soles of his journo loafers. *Take a look. Collator's having a bloody meltdown!*

Sawn-off in hand, Lugan eased a look over the desktop.

Tarquinne was staring, stock-still, through the shattered remnants of the glass wall.

At a brick-walled, tile-roofed impossibility, at some sort of holographic piss-take – at the arse-back-end of some fucking *building* that had beamed the fuck in where his workshop should be.

"What the fuck," Lugan asked, "is that?"

ACKNOWLEDGEMENTS

For my Norwich Vike Wrecking Crew, my Sigismund Sisters and my Brothers-in-Arms. For Andrew, who first coined the phrase "Virtual Rorschach", and for Liam, for forging a fractal from my name.

For Cath at Titan, whose patience is both boundless and remarkable, and for my agent Sally Harding, crusader extraordinaire.

And, always, for my son Isaac, with no words adequate.

ABOUT THE AUTHOR

DANIE WARE is the publicist and event organiser for cult entertainment retailer Forbidden Planet. She has worked closely with a wide-range of genre authors and has been immersed in the science-fiction and fantasy community for the past decade. An early adopter of blogging, social media and a familiar face at conventions, she appears on panels as an expert on genre marketing and retailing.

WWW.DANIEWARE.COM

ECKO BURNING
DANIE WARE

Ruthless and ambitious, Lord Phylos has control
of Fhaveon city, and is using her forces to bring the
grasslands under his command. His last opponent is
an elderly scribe who's lost his best friend and wants
only to do the right thing.

Seeking weapons, Ecko and his companions follow a
trail of myth and rumour to a ruined city where both
nightmare and shocking truth lie in wait.

Back in London, the Bard is offered the opportunity
to realise everything he has ever wanted – if he will
give up his soul.

When all of these things come together, the world
will change beyond recognition.